AMAZON VERSION ONLY

Ebook/Print OG COVERS: 100covers.com
Alt paperback Covers: Pretty in Ink Creations
Editing, Proofing, backgrounds, & Formatting: Dirty Sexy Words/ Storm shield Editing/Little Tailfeather Publishing
Cassandra's logos: Pretty in Ink Creations/Artlogo
Goosebusters Alpha team: Kat Silver, Becky Ross, Erica Taryn
Arc / Street Teams: Cassandra's claws
Sensitivity Readers: Brit Mason, Gail Jericho
Translation Consultant: Mo Jacobs
Promotional Team: Literary Inspired
Legal Services: Joshua Farley, esq.
Images/Fonts/Maps: Depositphotos, Shutterstock, Canva, Inkarnate, & Photoshop

No GenAI was used within this book. All errors and greatness are by an ADHD muppet.

Little Tailfeather Publishing

Signature Page

CASSANDRA FEATHERSTONE

RETURN TO THE
HOLLOW

M.P.P.

Content Information

This is a *paranormal whychoose romance with poly elements*—our FMC, Jolene, will not have to choose between love interests.

There are many situations included that are intended for mature audiences (18+).

In this book, there may be instances/references (be they small or lengthy) that could trigger some individuals such as:

- liberal use of appropriate consent
- the fucking Fae
- group scenes
- MMF, MM, MFM, MF, MFMMM, and more
- poison
- assassination attempts
- alphahole/possessive MMCs
- cinnamon roll MMCs
- bargains made by asshole Fae
- slightly unhinged chaotic MMC
- unhealthy coping mechanisms
- spoiled, selfish gods, goddesses, and royalty
- extremely aggressive boundaries

- age gap (from 10 yrs to immeasurable)
- weird Fae drugs and tricks
- BDSM
- raw sex
- shifted sex
- traumatic childhood
- Alcohol use and abuse
- threats of bodily harm
- death
- body modifications
- fancy genitalia
- mate knots/barbs
- the goddamn Fates meddling
- bullying (in person and on social media)
- PTSD
- blood
- emotional abuse from outside poly group
- body dysmorphia
- adult language
- pop culture references
- literary references
- emotional manipulation
- power play
- adorable nicknames
- physical intimidation
- emotionally abusive/manipulative parents (MMCs)
- voyeurism
- rough sex
- wings/tails/horns/magic in sex
- masturbation play
- markings/tattoos
- Easter egg character cameos from other series in the universe
- lawyers (ugh, but Jackson is a doll)
- family dysfunction
- super awesome BFF and her poly group
- animal companions

- absolute disrespect for shitty parents
- brief mentions of non-body positive dieting culture
- brief mentions of parental death
- very liberal re-imagining of history
- ancient secret society who only cares about bigger picture
- official corruption
- name calling
- occasional misogyny
- exhibitionism
- hand necklaces
- adult bullying
- magical kinks
- impact play
- elitism
- bribery
- corpses
- fat shaming (not by MCs)
- drama
- physical threats to FMC and others
- species-ism

No sexual practices in this book should be taken as safe or appropriate for real life application.

Content information is important and I don't ever want to harm a reader with inaccurate information.

Stalk Cassandra Featherstone in the Dark Corners of the Web

Join my Facebook group and follow me everywhere!

Want More?

Sign up for my bi-weekly manifesto for a free series sampler:

*Join my Ream as a **FREE** follower or exclusive subscriber to get access to cover reveals, WIPs, Serial Stories, and personal chats from me!*

CASSANDRA FEATHERSTONE

Author Ramblings

Readers,

I was _blown away_ by your love for my newest FMC, Jolene!

If you are just picking this up, I **highly** recommend reading the prequel, _Road to the Hollow_, first. It actually introduces the players and world—you may feel a little lost without doing so.

There are Easter eggs in this book for those of you who have read _Codename_, but the references will _not_ keep you from enjoying this book if you miss them.

Jolene's world is expanding—from animals to new men to old enemies to new jobs—you're going to love what you learn in this book.

I worked very hard to ensure parts of this book were both sexy and safe because I feel a responsibility as an author and creator to ensure I am not harming others. If I write something that is not immediately identifiable as dangerous, I will make certain to note it is an inaccurate representation of something and should not be taken as a 'try me at home' situation.

Many authors believe they can write whatever and insisting that people give appropriate disclaimers is unnecessary, but as a two decade long member of the kink community, I cannot be party to that type of reckless, disrespectful behavior. I am unconcerned with being called a gatekeeper when I want to make certain a reader at home doesn't emulate a throat hold that could kill them or a situation in one of my books is not written well over the line of sexy into abusive.

Experience combined with research is always a good beginning, but admitting what you don't know is even better. I do the best I can to cross check information and sources for my books, both PNR and contemporary. I will consult real life experts, if necessary. If I mess something up factually, I don't want it to be because I didn't put in the effort.

Romance novels are sexy because they are women's fantasy—not because they pretend lube doesn't exist and belts won't bruise your brachial nerves. You can write kink and BDSM play both hot and safely and I hope I've done that here.

Thank you to everyone who has read and recommended on Facebook, TikTok, Instagram, and even Goodreads. Your help makes this indie muppet get closer to her dream of being a full time writer.

I also want to thank my PA, street team/arc teams, author colleagues and friends, alphas, and everyone who helps me every day. You're all rockstars!

All y'all make this a community and it makes our genre strong. Much like our children (furry, leaved, or human), we love you with all of our hearts and occasionally, want to strangle you.

(I've got jokes, people. Laugh along with your favorite Muppet.)

Enjoy the first step in Jolene's journey to find out who and what she is, why she got denied her dream job, and what she *really* wants out of life.

Blood and guts,

Cass

Reader's Note

A few things you should know…

Given Jolene's past and the mysteries of the Hollow, there is a decent amount of foreign dialogue. I have made the *translations clickable end of chapter notes* to help.

This is multi-book series, so *everything will not be revealed in book one*. I promise it will all tie up with a HEA; don't worry!

There are some words that are slang, jargon, or foreign that may seem to be spelled wrong—*please use my form at the beginning of the book rather than report to Amazon* if you think something is wrong. It may not be and I want to make sure it doesn't get taken down so everyone can read!

Characters who live in this universe (but not this series) make cameos. *If you haven't read their books, it won't keep you from enjoying this one.*

If you see this book *anywhere besides authorized retailers or my website (in ebook format)*, please reach out to me via social media. Pirating kills my ability to write full time and I am so grateful for your help.

A Note To My Loving Family Members and Their Friends...

THANK YOU FOR SUPPORTING ME BY BUYING THIS BOOK!

UNLESS YOU CAN DEAL WITH GROUP SEX, BDSM, FOUL LANGUAGE, DICK PIERCINGS, AND MORE... YOU SHOULD TRY A COZY MYSTERY WITH RECIPES IN THE BACK.

I'M NOT EXPLAINING TO AUNT SO-AND-SO WHAT A REVERSE COWGIRL OR JACOB'S LADDER IS, AND I LOVE COOKIES.

IT'LL BE MORE PRODUCTIVE FOR ALL OF US.

CAVEAT: IF YOU CHOOSE TO KEEP READING, KNOW THAT AT NO TIME WILL I EXPLAIN TERMS, POSITIONS, THEMES, TROPES, OR ANY OTHER PART OF THIS NOVEL AT FAMILY EVENTS, IN GROUP CHATS, OR ON SOCIAL MEDIA.

DON'T ASK.

Return to the Hollow Playlist

CHAPTER TITLE SONGS

Return to the Hollow Chapter Playlist

BONUS PLAYLIST

Julia's Kick Ass Playlist

*SOUTHERN WOMEN BLESS HEARTS...
BUT THEY TAKE NAMES, TOO, SUGAR.*

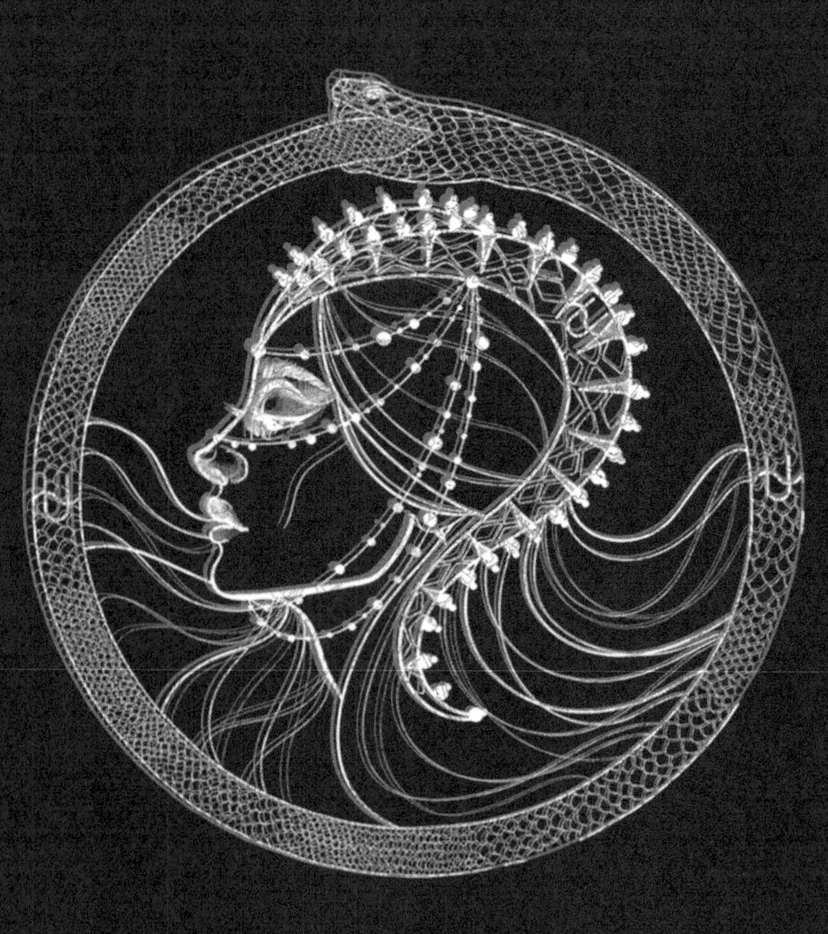

Wait!

A final reminder before you read...

My series typically have prequels, gap novellas/novels, and bonus material that are integral to your having a satisfying reading experience.

If you have not read the other pieces in this series, you may feel as though you have missed critical details, developments, plot points, and other information. This will cause the book to appear to have continuity gaps that it does not have.

If you have not read the bonus material for this series, it is available online here, in audio versions (if applicable), and in print special editions (if applicable).

I highly recommend consulting the bonus page prior to reading this new title so you're up to speed on all the things going on in this world.

Happy reading!

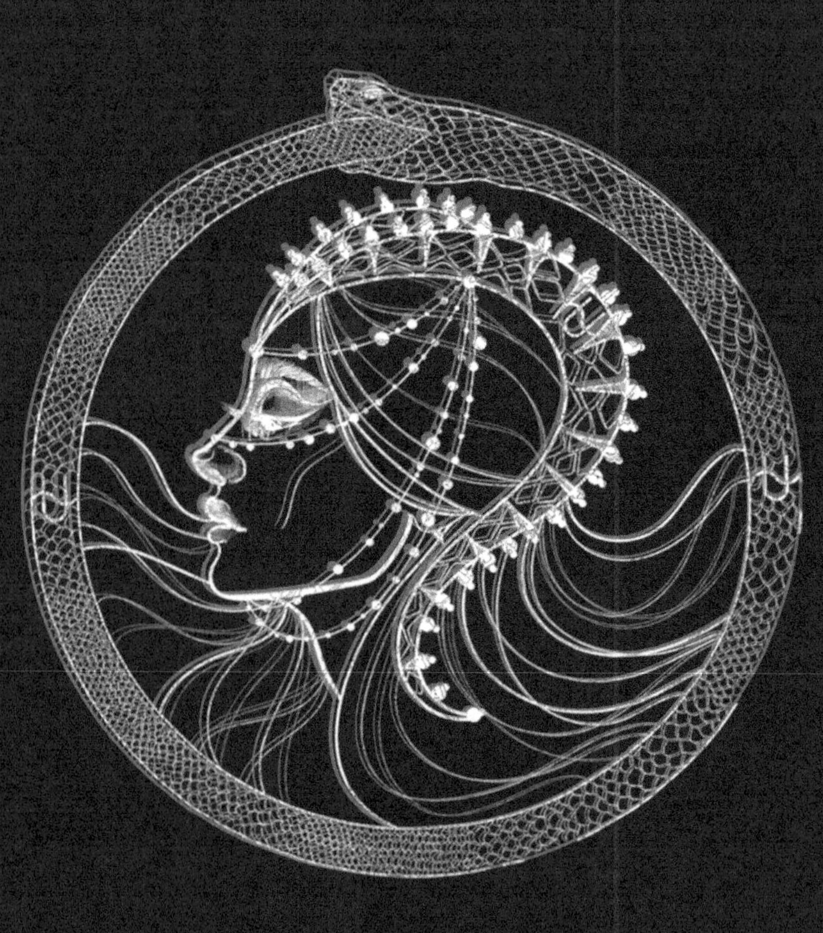

"Aye, Peanut. I s'pose the cute bum on the right is tellin' ye true. Y'don't have 'nough participants to make an orgy. I'm sure I can help y'fix that soon 'nough."

I blink in confusion as the boys decide to join the land of the living, sitting up with matching smirks.

"You know, sugarplum, an audience is a novelty but your friend needs to give us some privacy to get dressed."

"Unless you'd prefer we—"

"NO!" I cover my mouth when the vehement response to Presley's snark pops out. "I mean, uh… Seer, go down to the kitchen. We'll dress and I'll… make breakfast."

Her tinkling laugh echoes off the walls as she eyes me, not believing my fumbling cover for a second. "Fair play. I'll leg it downstairs and we'll chat once you're settled."

Once she's out the door, I groan, burying my face in my hands as the guys roll off the bed. I don't have a clue why Saoirse is here, or how she ferreted her way into my house—this is a disaster. How am I supposed to deal with the two hot guys I boned—who did *not* hot foot it as soon as possible—and interrogate her?

My life continues to be one colossal joke on a cosmic scale, I swear to Hecate.

"Sugarplum, why do you have men's clothes in your closet?"

I look over at Wolfie, a fond smile coming to my lips unbidden when I see him peeping out of the closet with a handful of jogging pants. "They were my dad's. I cleaned this room, but something told me to leave a few items."

Presley strolls out of the bathroom, picking up his glasses from the nightstand. "That's just our good luck for the day, eh, Lucy?"

Wolfie grins and tosses him a pair, nodding. "Sure is, Prez." His head tilts as he studies me, still wrapped in the sheets. "Did you get shy with us overnight?"

Us? Jesus, am I a part of an 'us' now? What in the fiddling fuck have I stumbled into?

I give him a smile, shaking my head as I rise. It won't do to hurt his feelings by looking terrified about whatever all this means. Presley's already studying me like a hawk—which is fitting, I guess—and I don't think I can explain what's going through my mind now. "Not at all, puppy eyes. I was waiting until you two got settled."

The look on his face is one of relief, but the other half of our triangle doesn't seem convinced. Presley walks over, cups my face, and looks into my eyes. "Nothing has to be decided today. We have plenty of time to figure it all out, magpie."

I nod, a small smile curling my lips. Leaning in, I peck a light kiss on his lips before walking over to give one to Wolfie. His bright smile lights up the room, and I chuckle as I pad into the room with an extra sway in my hips. Dr. McNuggies is right; I don't have to decide right now, and I'll be damned if I let anyone judge me while we explore our little menage.

Once I've pulled on a comfy tank and leggings, I join them, arching at a brow at their whispers. "Something I should know about, boys?"

"Only that I think Lucy should bring a few things for the dude side of your closet, just in case. And maybe a few toiletries," Presley says, his handsome grin spreading at my expression.

"Sugarplum, you look like a ghost. We should get downstairs and get you fed. Your friend may have gotten eaten by your companions by now."

My eyes narrow as Wolfie changes the subject, knowing the discussion is closed in their minds. I'm going to get mysterious deliveries next week; I'm certain of it. "Uh-huh. Well, Seer can manage herself… trust me. But I am hungry, so I'll let your little secrets slide for now."

They each take one of my hands and lead me out of the bedroom, chattering away about waffles versus pancakes.

I'm like the Pied Piper of Cock this week. It's astounding.

Gunpowder and Lead

"**S**ugarplum?"

I raise a brow at Wolfie before glaring at Seer when she cracks up in her seat. She's never seen me keep a bedmate more than the time to hit the sheets, so the boys scarfing down to breakfast with us at the counter is more than unusual. They have no intention of buggering off soon, and the nicknames are making her lose her mind. Neither of my Steamy Dreamy Panini members seems to notice her mirth.

"Yes, Wolfie?" His bright grin makes my insides melt and I feel bad for letting my friend's amusement color my attitude towards him. Neither of them has been anything but adorably saucy throughout the meal, and my self-conscious idiocy doesn't mean that I can be a twat to them.

"Prez and I have been thinking since you talked about that night you felt like someone was watching your house." The vet hesitates, looking at his cohort for help.

Uh-oh. I sense a ganging up about to happen, and it's not the yummy one involving my giant bed.

Presley sighs, pushing the skater cut out of his eyes. "What Lucy is failing to communicate is we're worried your house is on the edge of the populated part of town. We don't think getting a Ring camera is enough, even with your companions."

Saoirse frowns at them, her brows furrowing. "Y'said there hasn't been actual crime in donkey's years before. Why the feck should she be worried? Don't ye have peelers here?"

I chuckle as they glance at each other in confusion. "Yes, we have a small police force, Seer. They're useless—or they used to be."

Wolfie shrugs. "Detective Santos is new. He transferred into the Hollow from the city a month ago. He spends a lot of time being run around by the founding families."

Translation: this new guy is owned by the rich folks in town and I will not get a lick of help if I have someone stalking me.

"That's shite!"

Presley nods, sipping his herbal tea. He insisted on going through the cabinets until he could make a 'proper' tea, which endeared him to Seer. Wolfie is downing coffee and eyeing my energy drink. These guys don't know me well enough yet to realize how fast I metabolize caffeine, so I don't blame him.

"It is, Saoirse. And I worry about magpie being here with no one close enough to arrive."

Wolfie clears his throat. "What if the person *does* break in? If the animals get immobilized, she'd be at their mercy."

Saoirse blinks, then lets out a booming laugh that echoes off the kitchen marble. She laughs so hard that tears stream down her face, and the boys give me quizzical looks as she clutches her sides. My lips quirk, waiting for her to expound. I've never been one to brag.

"Aye, Peanut. Is your stash in bits or have ye set it up like usual?"

I shake my head. "I want to clean out the basement and set it up there. I haven't gotten that far yet."

"Grand. Normal cabinet in the drawing, then?"

Nodding, I press my lips together to keep from smiling as I clear the dishes. The boys help me get everything into the dishwasher and they wipe the counter down while my friend disappears. When she returns, she's carrying a large bag on her shoulder.

"C'mere to me, boys. I need you to gather those soda cartons and take them out to the back fence. Put one can on each pole and don't open them. It won't make a bloody difference."

"Seer, that's wasteful!"

"I'll buy you new ones when we go out to get the messages, Peanut. I've a mind for you to show them the Peanut I remember from our travels. I'll bet they don't even realize why you moved back to this Carson McCullers fever dream."

Dr. McNuggies—sweet baby Jesus, I need to think of a better nickname for him—arches a brow at me, and little Wolfie walks over to pick up the two twelve packs of pop. I sigh, waving my hand at them to show they should do as she instructed. When they head out the back door, followed by Jekyll and Hyde, I turn to my friend.

"*Seer!*"

Her grin is evil. "What, Peanut?"

"I came back semi-undercover! I have to show them what I can do because you opened your big mouth."

"Well, yer men there were gettin' worried about ye, and they need to learn who they're cozyin' up to. Give it a lash and see what happens. If they're keepers, they'll think it's grand."

Rolling my eyes at her, I stomp my foot. "I wasn't planning to hide my skills as much as not scare them away on day one, Seer."

Cackling, she shrugs. "Looks like you're goin' through door number two, Peanut."

"Ugh!" I growl at her. "Go out there and check on them while I find a hair tie. I can't do this with hair in my face."

A mock salute is her answer, and I make a face at her back as she skips out the backdoor like a drunken fairy. If I didn't love that girl like my sister, I'd wring her Irish neck. I walk over to my messenger bag, pulling out a scrunchie and my sunglasses. I won't be able to wear them during the demo, but I'll be able to scope out the landscape. That will help in the bright morning sunlight.

I walk outside, looking at the boys, cats, and my friend setting up the cans on the fence. It's about a thousand feet from the porch and that's not a hard ask at all. I could be a lot more impressive if Seer made me show off. Our three-month stay in Belfast was a whirlwind of jobs, but we shacked up with every eejit with a bad boy past—hence the training that would one day mean I'd ace parts of Quantico's courses with my eyes closed. I may have grown up in the country, but there's always been an odd lack of the 'good old boy' gun fueled orgy that the South has become in the Hollow.

The boys of Belfast made it their mission to teach me the trade. I was shitty for a long time. It took hours and hours of practice in various locations, conditions, and situations before I found my center. The first time I hit a target, I did a booty dance of joy and they laughed until they cried. Americans who don't know a fucking thing about guns are a novelty, I guess.

Euryale swoops down, perching on the smoker. I tilt my head, looking at the bird. I don't have a clue whether this will scare the shit out of it or not.

"Okay, my dude. I'm going to do this because Seer made a big deal and there's gonna be a lot of loud noise and some muzzle flash. Don't lose your shit on me, okay? I won't aim at you. I promise."

The giant bird lets out a screech that I take as an assent, and I pull a side table over from the patio set. I take less than a minute to unpack the bag Seer left for me, assembling the pieces without even thinking about it. The boys taught me that as well, stating I needed to learn the damned thing like I know putting on my shoes.

It could be the difference between living and dying. I asked what war they were drafting me into, and they shrugged. Two women traveling alone should be able to defend themselves, was the only answer I got.

As if Seer and I were going to need to use a goddamned Macmillan Tac 50-A1-R2 while gadding about Europe and Asia. I mean, customs alone would be a nightmare. I had to have this baby and the.50 BMG cartridges shipped home on a private plane by a friend with high security clearance.

I check the bipod for stability, ensuring that my roost will be sufficient. Loading the ammo, I frown at the ground. Too hard, and it will be distracting. I walk over to a chair and pull a cushion off, settling it in front of my makeshift stand. That should do it.

Once I'm settled, I position myself in front of the Schmidt and Bender scope, slowing my breathing as I study the cans. Seer ushered the guys and the cats away from my field of fire once they finished. She's seen me do this a bazillion times, and she knows not to have collateral downrange. A shift in wind could cause a tragedy. The docs are peering at me from under their hands, looking confused. The scope is powerful enough that I can see the wrinkles of worry at the corners of Wolfie's eyes.

With a final breath, I let go of everything around me, only seeing the rifle and my targets. Nothing around me registers as I slip into the singular focus of the task I'm about to complete. There are no mysteries, no companions, no asshat Edgar... only 24 cans and 24 bullets. I lick a finger and raise it, considering the light breeze for directionality. Recalculating in my mind for shear, I continue breathing, my heart rate slowing as I go into the trance that true long shots slip into when they're in the zone.

When I'm ready, my finger squeezes the trigger without a thought, rapidly adjusting one after another until I've fired 24 times. I'm still for a moment after, my mind calm and focused. Then I hear a loud whooping down range, followed by two '*mows*' and a holler that is likely Seer. I stand, clicking the safety on before I walk towards the sound.

I'm still zombified—it takes time to get out of that headspace and be a normal human again.

Walking up to the group, I see Presley kicking the cans on the ground, the rattle of shells clanking against aluminum. His head turns as I approach, and I can see he's impressed. I didn't miss a single can, and the holes are dead center. The time I spent obsessing over improving my skills is terrifying and I've been doing it for years.

"Sugarplum! Where in the name of Paula Deen did you learn to do *that?*"

Saoirse clutches her guts as she laughs, waving her hand at me to tell the story. I sigh, giving McBaby Vet a small grin. "Seer and I spent three months on a project in Ireland for a client we can't discuss. We stayed in Dublin and Belfast—they're only two hours apart on the M1. Being the butterflies we were, we made... friends in Belfast. These friends decided I should learn how to defend myself sniper-style. I never got why, because starting with a handgun would have been a *lot* easier, but we didn't argue. I've been sharpening my skills ever since."

Presley arches a brow, looking as if he's filing that information away for later. He doesn't vocalize his thoughts, though. Instead, he winks. "Well, magpie, I suppose if you need to take a target from a distance, you're covered, but what if it's close combat?"

"Bloody hell, Peanut. Tell the boys you spent the last couple years training for the F.B.I. interview an' be done with it! I've seen ye gut a back-alley pox when he tried actin' the maggot. Ye can protect yer own arse."

Both sets of eyes widen, and I frown.

Is this the secret that ruins my Dreamy Steamy melt?

"That puts my heart at ease, sugarplum. I worried that livin' this far off the town was going to be dangerous for you. I've never heard of people sensing they're being watched like you described—not here in the Hollow, at least."

Dr. McNuggies nods his agreement, and I let out a long sigh of relief. I don't understand why I was worried that two guys I met this week would abandon me over my badass side, but I can't describe the weight their acceptance took off my shoulders. I try to pin down the source of that disquiet inside, but all I find is my psyche re-adjusting to post-shot brain functions.

"I'll still set up a system. I'd like to catch the asshole in question snooping about and have a friendly conversation about why the hell he or she is trying to give me a coronary. Maybe I'll let Euryale do the restraints. Looks like my eagle friend could hold on tight."

"And break the bones, but who's worried?" Presley winks, walking over to press a kiss to my temple.

I flush as Wolfie follows, tucking me against his side. "Sugarplum, I think we should leave this as a warning for the moment. We'll go in and put your big ass gun in its place, and then Prez and I will go home to give you two time to catch up."

Saoirse claps her hands with glee, but something in my chest aches a bit. Not wanting to sound like a clingy weirdo, I nod. "She can help me with the basement. It would be better if I can move the weapon storage to a more appropriate place. The living room is *not* my preferred location."

"Right," Presley says, taking my hand to tug us along. "We'll come back after we do our stuff and the four of us can have dinner at Bottles 'N Cans tonight."

I frown, tilting my head. "Not to sound dumb, Dr. McSteamy, but Bottles 'N Cans is a liquor store. Are we eating beer nuts as a meal?"

Wolfie grins, his sky-blue eyes dancing. "Oooh, Prez, she doesn't *know*. This is gonna be *great*."

Seer crosses her arms over her chest, giving them both a reproachful stare. "Oi, boys. S'not nice to tease Peanut. Even if she has the best bloody pouts on the planet."

My eyes narrow at my bestie, and then at my lovers. "Listen up, you eejits. I'll not have you tag-teaming against me; got it?"

The boys laugh, and Seer bobs her brows.

This does *not* bode well.

WIPING THE SWEAT OFF OF MY BROW, I GRIN AT THE WORK Seer AND I completed.

Together, we cleared the basement of junk, creating a pile in one corner that is headed for Gene's donation bins. Next to it are bins full of things I want to go through later to see if there are clues to my current predicament or to my parents' secret shit. I didn't tell her why those things got segregated because I'm not ready to share all my findings with her just yet. I trust her with my life, but I also don't want to bring her into something dangerous.

I prepped the other half of the sizable area for the safety cabinet I ordered online. I use multiple sources to find the equipment to store my weapons and, for the moment, everything was organized by type and locked up while I wait for the delivery.

I'm not a crazy weapons person, but I did train for a career that required proficiency, and during that time, I picked up my personal armory. Serious people never want to use other people's gear because it's not made to fit your quirks and body type. I have specialty items that are custom made for my size and strength.

That's common sense, and despite moving to a safe area, I'm not getting rid of my babies.

"*Mow!*"

I peek at the stairs, chuckling under my breath. "We are close to dinnertime."

"Mrrrp?"

"Aye, lad and lassie. We're comin'. Keep yer britches up!" Seer grouses as she lugs one more lockbox to the pile. "I suppose we have to feed them, an' then we'll go get to the nines."

Wrinkling my nose, I nod, waiting for her to join me before I flick off the lights. I follow her up the stairs, muttering, "*I suppose so.*"

Her tinkling laugh mocks me as she heads for the kitchen. "Don't sound so overjoyed, Peanut. I might not think ye like your little tea biscuits."

O

"Seeeeeeer!" I whine, tilting my head back into her hands as she continues to rat my hair in a way that feels like I'm being scalped. "Is all of this really necessary?" Another yank is my answer and I frown at the mirror like a petulant child.

"Wind yer neck in, Peanut. I haven't gotten to do this in a dog's age."

I sigh, knowing she's right. If we're going out on the town on Saturday night in the Hollow, I gotta seem like I tried with my appearance. People will be watching. I don't know what the hell secret this stupid liquor store holds, but the way the boys lit tells me it's a big deal. My eyes drift back up, watching my BFF tease my curled hair into a half-updo. She's giving it volume commensurate with a small Southern town, I suppose, even if I don't look a goddamned thing like myself.

"Do we have to beat my face, too?" Seer gives me a face that is dripping with sarcasm. Guess that's a 'yes'.

To her credit, she's primped and ready to rock. My cosmopolitan friend is going to raise over one brow in her tiny satin shorts with dragons embroidered on them, a cropped purple corset, and ankle length black mesh duster. She's paired it with thick soled, heavily buckled rave boots in bright iridescent patent leather that have fairy wings on the back, rainbow eyeshadow, winged liner, and her fiery hair is teased into a fat Viking braid with the sides in smaller braids that connect to it.

She looks fierce and otherworldly, which is sure to draw attention.

"Stop being self-conscious." She raps me on the head with her brush, grinning at me in the mirror. "I've had as much trauma in my past about being a two-by-four with limbs as you have with being a curvy goddess."

Chuckling, I twist my lips. "You got me. This place brings it all back. I mean, somehow I've found sexy ass men who want me, and I still worry about what all the busybodies and mean girls will say."

Saoirse walks in front of me, leaning against the sink as she works on my eyes. "Memories are blessings and curses, Peanut. We have a helluva lot of good ones, but without the bad, you can't appreciate the best stuff. Our past shapes our present and future, and everything you've done until now led you to this moment."

"Aren't you a fuckin' fortune cookie tonight? I shouldn't have let you do a bourbon tasting flight before we ate. Saoirse the Wise *always* comes out when you drink brown booze."

"Too bloody right. Now, while I finish this, tell me: playsuit or dress?"

I frown at her. "I didn't buy 'going out' clothes for home yet. I have very European stuff, which may work for you, but it's the wrong impression for the Hollow if I want these people to accept me. I also have day-to-day grubby stuff, workout clothes, and a bunch of work-ish clothes I bought for school. That's it."

"Aren't ye lucky yer personal seamstress blew into town, then? I brought a thing or ten. Now, playsuit or dress?"

My eyes widen with fear. Seer knows every inch of me, and whatever she created will be amazing, but I hate to imagine what she thinks is appropriate for a town like mine. "Um…" I fish for an answer, trying to work out what I should do. "Well, playsuits are bathroom unfriendly. So, how about the dress?"

Her smile widens into a beam, and my chest tightens. This is going to be a disaster. "Grand, Peanut." She goes back to my face, humming under her breath as she picks up another palette. "I'll just adjust this color and we'll be ready soon."

Oh, goody.

Pulling up to Main Street, I peer over at Seer. She's goggling at the business names as she holds Jekyll and Hyde on her lap. The terror twins turn to me as I slide into a parking space. I can't help but laugh as I shake my head. While I got my clothes on, Seer accepted my Amazon delivery and my companions are now wearing cat sunglasses and spiked collars. They seem to like them, though, so I guess I can't complain.

I've officially become a crazy cat woman.

A loud honk followed by a screech and thump on the roof of my car jars me out of my thoughts. Speaking of crazy, there's my other stalker making its presence known. "Watch the *Paint, Eury!*"

Seer laughs, squeezing the cats in her lap as they squirm. They can't wait to be free, and the eagle flying behind us must irk them. "Aye, Peanut. Your bloody menagerie is feckin' impatient."

"They are," I grumble. "Hopefully, the boys are less troublesome." I grab my messenger bag, whistle for Jekyll and Hyde, and climb out of the Impala. It's night, so I don't have my glasses on, but the small-town twinkles in the moonlight like a Hallmark special.

"Or not, because I could get behind a bloody rager. It's been forever since—"

"We *do not* talk about Thailand in front of the guys or in public, Saoirse Viola O'Flanagan!"

Pouting, she strides ahead of me, tossing her thick braid over her shoulder. "You aren't a genteel petal, Peanut; don't let this place make ye pull a beamer."

I whisper to the cat on either side of me, "I think after banging three dudes in the first week I'm back, I have nothing left to worry about. What do you think?"

"*Mow!*" they reply, looking like punk rock kitties in the cat aviators they won't allow anyone to remove.

"Agreed," I murmur as we approach the door. Euryale swoops down, hovering behind Jekyll and Hyde as we wait for what appears to be a bouncer at the door to check Seer's passport.

What the fuck is a liquor store doing with a bouncer at the door?

The beefy dude takes one glimpse of Seer, then me, and then the animals following me. Grunting, he arches his brow. "Not from around here, huh?"

I squint at him, trying to figure out why something about him is making my skin tight. "I just moved back. She's an old friend from out of town. Are quizzes part of your job?"

Blinking at me for a moment, the guy pauses, then lets out a booming laugh that rattles the windows next to us. "*Jolene Whitley!*"

"Oi! Not chopped soddin' liver," Seer grumbles, cocking out her hip. "Part of the Peanut entourage, that's me."

"I-I'm sorry. I don't remember you," I confess, giving the beaming bear of a man a sheepish smile.

"Well, *of course not*! I hadn't grown into my skin yet!" He laughs again, turning to holler behind him. "*Boone!* Jolene's here!"

My eyes widen at Seer. "Oh, no. Oh, no. No, no no…"

Cackling, she pats Jekyll and Hyde on their heads to l reassure them. "Stop making sounds like a bloody Tikky Tok. Just because you haven't ironed out your differences doesn't mean he's going to make a—" My friend stops talking—a minor miracle—when Edgar arrives to stand behind mystery mountain man. Her voice is a wisp of air as she mutters, "Holy feckin' dildo gnomes."

Turning bright red, I put my hands on my hips. "Teddy, I don't know who this monster is, but I'm supposed to meet people inside. Can you get him to let me buy a vowel so I can go in?"

His perfect teeth shine as he grins, the fresh stubble on his chin enticing as hell. "Well, Tilly, I don't know about that. You've been avoiding me. Can't say as I'm inclined to do you a favor."

Euryale saves the day by swooping past, beelining for the boys since they're the only people it knows. I smirk, tilting my head. "Pretty soon you'll be obsolete, Teddy. Is that… *familiar?*"

The giant guffaws again, slapping my childhood—and current—nemesis on the back. "She's a *fiery* one now. You're right, Boone—she grew up and got saucy."

Looking bored, I study my nails. I realize the only way to deal with dick waving like this is to pretend that I'm not affected in the slightest. Men are the same whether they're dictators, CEOs, bouncers, or hobos—they just want to swing their dicks around and have a woman coo. Not this girl, no matter how fucking hot Teddy looks or how built like a brick shithouse this dude is.

When I decide I've waited long enough to make them uncomfortable, I tilt my head and give them a disinterested expression. "Since you boys had your fun, does anyone want to tell me who the goat fucking hell he is?"

"Tilly, I'm surprised you don't recognize Benjy. He owns this little slice of Heaven that we call the Speakeasy."

Seer cocks a brow at me as I goggle at the gargantuan in front of me. Despite being on the football team and one of the elite, Benjy was the scrawniest little asshole in our class. He was the kicker—of course —and no amount of training they did when we were in school seemed to put any weight on him. He's now one of the biggest dudes I've ever seen.

"I'm gonna assume the steroids were kind?" I ask, giving them both a smirk.

Teddy barks a laugh and Benjy snorts. Before they can respond, though, my darling doc club sandwich approaches. Euryale perches on Dr. McNuggies' shoulder, and I worry that its weight is more than he can manage. He seems not to care, and little Wolfie is vibrating with excitement as he walks up behind him. I beam at them, grateful for the rescue from the terror twins.

Danny Boy

"Well, look at ye, ya jammy hoor!"

Startling awake, I sit straight up, clutching the purple satin sheet to my chest. I glance around for the early morning intruder warily. My free hand pushes my mass of tangled raven waves out of my eyes so I can see. Where the hell are my animal protectors? Who the *fuck* is in my bedroom yelling at in me in Irish—

"*Seer!*" I shout, my face breaking into a broad grin when it occurs to me who it is.

"Don't eat the head off me for not calling ahead, Peanut," she begins, her lips quirking into a mischievous smirk. "Seein' as I've walked in on your orgy an' all."

"Not an orgy."

The muffled sound makes my eyes widen, and I peer across my Alaskan king in surprise. In a tangle of limbs and sheets on either side of me, my doctor panini. My gaze shoots back to Seer, a deep red flush spreading over my skin. Despite the many wild times the two of us survived as we globetrotted for years, being caught like this makes me flush.

"Sugarplum!" Wolfie grabs me by the waist, lifting me to swing me around. "Look at you all fancy-like."

"Yer welcome, puppy. She was a pisser about makin' her a flah, but I knew you lads would appreciate my sacrifice." Seer winks at Presley and he winks back.

What did I tell them about ganging up on me? Assholes—I'm surrounded by assholes.

Switching my attention back to the one person who isn't being a pain in my ass, I smile down at Hottie McBaby Vet. "Put me down so I can hug you." His face lights up and he lets me slide down his frame until I'm eye to eye. I peck a soft kiss on his lips and give him a quick hug as a reward. "I see why you two were so excited to show me this place—or I would be if someone would *let me in.*"

Wolfie glares at Edgar and Benjy, and Presley arches his brow. The other two stare back, and I sigh. Men are a serious pain in my ass in this town, and not enjoyably. Jekyll bounds past Seer with Hyde in tow and hisses at Benjy. Hyde yowls her disapproval next, and Euryale honks loud enough to make Presley wince.

"My companions humbly request you jackasses allow us entrance before they get pissed," I say, bending my legs as I do a sarcastic curtsey.

You can abso-fucking-lutely do a sarcastic curtsy.

I know because a duchess taught me. It's effective for a polite 'get bent' in monarchy-based countries, but also works in sultanates and a few democracies.

Edgar's eyes narrow at the familiarity I have with my new guys, and he lets out a piercing whistle. Two enormous black beasts come flying out of the bar area, teeth bared and snarling. Something inside takes notice and my skin heats. Standing taller, I slide past all the men, eyeing the oversized Dobermans as they approach. They stare at me as they skid to a stop, their heads tilting in confusion.

I feel Jekyll, Hyde, and Euryale flank me. The air in this place is stifling, and even though I'm only wearing a tiny lavender lace dress, sweat trickles down the center of my back. Blinking my itchy eyes, I wonder if I'm having an allergic reaction. I've never had any before, but who the fuck knows what kind of shit this town is hiding. Tapping the toes of my white platform heels on the ground, I continue to stare at Teddy's dogs until they back down. First one and then the other sit on the ground, ears and snouts at attention.

"Good dogs," I murmur. My head gets weird, and I glance around, trying to take in the place's décor, but my vision is blurry. I can sense what's going to happen, and I croak, "Boys... a little help..."

Then everything goes black... again.

Love Her Madly

Edgar

She's got to stop fucking doing that, especially in public.

If she doesn't quit blacking out, there will be many questions asked—ones she's not ready to answer—and none of us will be able to help her.

Not that she seems inclined to *let* me help. I can't get a moment alone with the woman of the hour, which means I've yet to explain why I made myself scarce after our tryst. Although, from the looks of it, Tilly's formed a merry band of companions and acolytes since we last spoke.

That complicates things.

Both doctors are inductees, but the wild woman is unknown. I'll get Doyle to use his contacts in ICE to find out who this chick is and why she's here. Tilly's yet to awaken, and until she does, the situation is far too sensitive for a random girl to be hanging about.

Her awakening is no longer an 'if' as the council believed, but a 'when'. Despite our lack of knowledge about her true lineage, I realize that she's going to. I can feel it in my bones, and I sure as fuck felt it when we screwed. This woman is no mere human, and why in Satan's name her awakening hasn't happened yet, I don't know.

She's also goddamned *made* for me, and it's hard not to take her over my shoulder and smack that round ass when she gives me sass.

Growling under my breath, I watch as the docs flutter over her. Her weird friend is trying to calm her eagle and the cats because they seem to object to Kali and Hecate standing nearby. I take pity on the Irish girl, whistling low so my hounds will observe from further away. The girl looks at me, squinting her eyes, and it's like a light goes off in her head. Her grin returns and she dips her head at me.

What an odd woman.

Sauntering over to the bar, I jerk my chin at the bartender, and he scurries over. I don't tell him what I want to drink—I'm here often enough—but I ask for a cold cloth from the kitchen. He asks me about the line on the Polecats, and I give him enough information to entice, but not be helpful.

If he wants to know actual info, there's an Internet full of it, and that doesn't belong to the man taking the bets.

When Henry returns with my Blanton's and the cool compress, I walk over to the group of people wringing their hands in front of the prone woman. Sighing, I stare at the girl first. "She's done this in front of you before, right? She did it in school, too."

Presley and Wolfgang both appear puzzled, but then shoot one another with a glance that says they're hiding something. Her redheaded friend nods at me, and finally, they give in and do the same.

"It's never lasted for more than a couple of days, but that was a long time ago. Anyone else have more up-to-date information?"

"Couple of hours," Wolfgang offers.

"Aye. Never more than a few hours," the friend agrees. "Maybe we should take those bloody sofas and let her lie down. Seems like you gents could use a chat."

Arching my brow at her, I nod. "Agreed. I'll carry her over if you three will oversee the menagerie."

Wolfgang glares at me, crossing his arms over his chest. "Who died and made you the sugarplum whisperer, Edgar Boone? Last I heard, you were a *ghost*."

As the doctor digs his heels in, I blink, surprised. I wouldn't say that I'm the most powerful guy in town, but I'm damned near the top of the food chain. I'd think his outburst was a fluke, but the normally tranquil birdman joins him, and the Irish car bomb gives me a smirk. Whatever power Tilly has, one thing she has in spades is the power to pass on her big dick energy to those around her.

"Fine, fine. You two can settle her in, *and* deal with her animals. I'll get Henry to rustle us up food and drinks. Benjy will get Amelia to throw a net over where we're sitting so we can have a private conversation. Good enough?"

The redhead squints at me as she tilts her head. "*Diatírisi, prostasía, yperáspisi… o kýklos den teleiónei*[1]."

Son of a hog wrangling shine swiller. I should've known. Of course, she has one. They're always watching, but not this closely. My eyes narrow as I reply, "*I epivíosi enós eínai aioniótita gia ólous*[2], sugar."

"If we're all done showing our cards before we find a table, may I suggest we retire to a less public space? Seems like there's going to be a lot of dick swinging, and y'all remember how 'Nelia hates public spectacles. Nothing gets by that woman," Presley counters, picking up my drugar like she weighs next to nothing.

Nodding, I whistle for Kali and Hecate, noting the looks they give the prone woman slung over the doc's shoulder. Their reaction to her was unusual and suspicious at worst. Paired with her black out act, I have ideas, but this squad of misfits Tilly has gathered might help me put some pieces together.

If I can get them to shut the fuck up and do what I tell them.

"THEN WE AGREE? NONE OF US HAVE A CLUE WHAT SHE IS, AND NO one's *cheiristís*[3] knows?"

"I don't even think Nelia knows," Wolfgang murmurs. "If they knew, they wouldn't have assigned a personal Guardian to keep tabs."

Saoirse—that's her name—nods. "I've been mates with Peanut since they assigned me. She consulted in Europe and Asia for yonks before she got a wild hair. Moved home and started training for the peelers before I could bat a lash. Wish I knew what shitehawk let that go on for yonks without stalling the ball before it hurt her."

Presley snickers. "I don't envy the person in Richmond if you ever find out who it was, O'Malley."

"The biggest problem is that we all know, and she doesn't," Wolfgang murmurs. "Whatever happened when she was young that stopped her awakening shadows her memories and perception, according to Saoirse. When Sugarplum finds out we've all lied to her, she'll be furious."

"Aye," Saoirse nods. "I don't have a baldy notion of when we'll get clearance to spill the beans, but she'll eat the heads off us."

Looking at the raven-haired woman still out cold on the couch, I frown. I like her fire, to be sure, but I don't want to be her enemy. No one does, and not one of us has the pull to fix this problem. She's come back to the beast's belly, and the people she's connected with are bound by more than honor to keep her in the dark.

"This fucking sucks," I mutter, reaching for my glass and tossing it back. "And it's dangerous. Not having any information puts the entire town at risk of exposure. Why did they let her return?"

The tinkling laugh of the Irish lass echoes off the walls. "The only way to stop this was to act the maggot with Fate, *moiraíos sýntrofos*[4]. Sounds like fair play to you?"

Wolfgang shakes his head. "Absolutely not. No one should live their life tied up like breed stock. Certainly not sugarplum—there's a well of passion screaming to be let loose."

A grin twists my lips, and I raise my glass to his, clinking them together. "Indeed. What are our next steps, then? We can't report this conversation, and until the fog lifts, we can't let anyone trigger events that could get her recalled."

"Look at you, the disappearin' man thinkin' he can order us all around," Saoirse snorts. "I'll work on getting meself reassigned. The doctors over there will help manage my girl and the companions. Since you're an eejit, you get to figure out how to get her to forgive your thick arse."

The other two snicker, and one cat chimes in with a "Mow!" followed by a honk from that enormous fucking bird.

Just fucking great. Now I'm being taunted by her entourage and her animals.

I thought this week couldn't get any worse.

"Fine. We agree. Now," I look at the bespectacled doctor with a smirk. "Do whatever it is you do and wake the lady up. It's time you show what *you've* been hiding, good Doctor."

Presley glares at me and nods. "As you wish, Your Honor."

My lips curve. *That's more like it.*

---

1. Conservation, protection, défense…the circle does not end.
2. To survive, we must protect the young.
3. Handler
4. Fated companion

Spy

The assholes I'm fucking and my best friend won't tell me what happened after my close encounter with the canine kind last night. I'm pretty pissed, to be honest, and I sent them all packing.

When I woke up, I was at home in my bed, surrounded by warm bodies. I was a little surprised—to say the *goddamned least*—to find all *three* dickwhistles smothering me in body heat. My ass got pressed against the mountain of asshat I call Teddy, while Dr. Mc Nuggies tucked himself into my other side, and little Wolfie was lying with his head on my thigh. His body was curled between Presley and me, so close that I could feel his pulse.

If I'm honest with myself, I was so fucking comfortable that I almost let go of my fury to sample the dessert cart. But my stubborn pride reared its head, and I couldn't allow them to decide for me without being conscious. I don't mind them bringing me home if I was in full black out mode, but I sure as fuck mind everyone being cuddled up like we're one big happy family in my enormous bed.

I'm a wee bit surprised Teddy consented to the tangle of limbs. I bet that was a hell of an argument; I'm salty that I missed it. Seer is another story. She *absolutely* gave her blessing to that nonsense because she always thinks she knows what's good for me, even when I'm being recalcitrant. So, I opened my eyes, blasted them all loudly enough that the menagerie of animals came running, and kicked them out of my house until I cooled down.

Biting off my nose to spite my face is a specialty of mine, and I'll have you know that it's my favorite flaw.

I watch the forums on my laptop, hopping from window to window. My latest stroke of genius regarding the mysterious codes, symbols, and boxes involves impersonating a conspiracy theorist online. I've created a complete persona, backstopped with enough information to satisfy a deep-web level check just in case one of these nuts has enough skills to out me.

My experience as a high-level fixer didn't make me a hacker, per se, but I've got the chops to pass most checks unless someone is a multi-level encryption, VPN busting bad ass. If they're that good, nothing I could have done with consumer equipment would have saved me, anyway.

As the screens move, I look at the back window. Being the complete motherfucker he is, Teddy left his two monsters here with Jekyll and Hyde while he went into town to 'take care of some business'. I protested, but the insistent 'mows' and 'honks' from my own companions broke my resolve. They're all chasing Euryale around the yard as she dips and dives from the air like a living frisbee.

Damn him for endearing his companions to mine so that now I'll feel guilty for punting his ass to the curb. He *still* hasn't apologized for leaving high and dry the other day, and I feel he's not going to. What the hell do I do with that? He's the one who gave me the metaphorical one-finger salute after screwing me into the baseboards; why should I be the one to bridge the gap by letting it go?

I don't know what chicks he's used to dating, but I'm not a simpering Southern belle looking to marry into a founding family. I don't give a fuck if he's rich, connected, or a step up the social ladder. If he wants to join my puppy pile, he better goddamned figure out his shit. I don't have time for childish bullshit, and I am *not* wanting for dick at this point.

Even if it was a pretty goddamned magnificent one.

A chime dings, and I look around, making certain that no one is around as I pick up my black cat-eyed glasses. DOS screens bother the hell out of my eyes, and the special lenses in these are more for helping my sensitivity than for sharpening my vision. They're another gift from my old MI-6 friend—he gets himself into a lot of clearance risking scrapes—and I hate people seeing me when I wear them.

I look fabulous. The appearance throws me back to the chunky nerd from high school, pre-weight loss and LASIK, though. I prefer to keep the illusion of the current Jolene in the heads of my friends and lovers for at least a while. Seer's never even seen me wear them, and that's been a rough road to hoe, because I need them for activities like this. I've chosen migraines over my vanity several times in the past.

YOUCANTHANDLETHETRUTH1969 is indicating that they have seen the symbol before. *Interesting.*

Tapping my lips, I run a quick reverse IP search, back tracing as it pings across the globe like a rabbit. When the trace stops at another IP in Florida, I groan. This means it's likely a tin foil hat jackass that believes a mythical letter has predictions about the government. I feed information from that location and IP into the system I got granted illegal backdoor access to by yet another friend in the intelligence community. I get a name and address. Following that lead to the normal internet, I run smack into a Facebook page *full* of crazy.

Definitely not credible. Someone who has knowledge of something buried this deeply is likely to have no public internet presence at all. I thank the nut job, promising to check out the website he's now hawking and move on. The windows are scanning comments for replies to my queries across multiple TOR and dark web servers, so it might take a bit to find real info.

My strategy was simple, you see.

I'll invade their common spaces, gain their trust, and when they least expect it, I'll plant a bunch of posts to draw attention to myself. What I'm hoping is that someone connected with the secrets has their own plants and I can follow the breadcrumbs back to whoever the hell is in charge. The hard part is getting these wack-a-doos to believe that I'm one of them.

I used a similar campaign of disinformation in Thailand that worked so well that Seer and I barely escaped the wrath of the government. That's what I get for trusting some tin pot general to cover my ass when I'm faking shit for him. Men are straight up garbage no matter what language they speak.

Speaking of women, I wonder where Seer went. I was so angry when I gave them all the heave-ho this morning; I didn't even ask where she planned on spending time while I stewed. I pick up my phone, shooting her a text to check in. I love my BFF more than milkshakes, but the thought of her unaccompanied, wandering around the Hollow in overalls, Docs, and a rainbow crop top does not give me confidence that she'll stay under the radar. In fact, I'm a wee bit surprised I haven't gotten a call from the police asking me to pick her up.

Cheeky Monkey: aye, lass. I'm right as rain. Found a few things to occupy meself while ye have your ruction. Don't worry; I won't end up in the clinker.

I frown at her reply. Something about the way she avoided telling me where she was spiked my intuition. Typing my response, I shrug off the concern, deciding that she's a grown ass adult and if she ends up pissing someone off, it's not like she's going to stay here forever. She'll pick up a contract soon and be on her way. That's what Seer does best, and it's why she's so sought after.

Another text buzzes my phone and I look down at the window that pops up, my expression turning to one of annoyance. Who in the *hell* unlocked my phone and started a group chat? I *hate* group chats with a fiery passion, and I would have never consented to being thrown into one, especially not with…

Bully Asshole: Is that an appropriate contact name for me, drugar?

Doctor Asshole: Mine's no better. Quit complaining, your royal judgy-ness.

Bully Asshole: You think you're so funny, Hamilton. I'll remember that next time you want info on a game.

Sugarplum: Wolfie, you changed my name in my *phone*!

Cute Asshole: I sure did, sugarplum. Since I was the one to figure out how to unlock, I got the honors. These idiots would have been playing with it all day.

Doctor Asshole: Watch it, Lucy.

Bully Asshole: Oh, this is rich. Now the bird man thinks he's in charge.

Sugarplum: I have news for you, jackholes. None of you are. I am. I'm going to tan the hide off whoever thought including me in a testosterone laden bullshit session was a clever idea. I have shit to do!

Bully Asshole: Well, now, drugar, we all do. We wanted to make sure everything was okay. Are Kali and Hecate behaving?

Sugarplum: They have much better manners than their human, if that's what you're asking.

I'm about to peace out of this nonsense when I hear a loud howl, followed by a screech, and then two yowls. Of course, the minute he asks about the animals, a goddamned ruckus starts out in the yard. Dropping the phone, I slide off my stool and run out the back door to figure out what in the name of bourbon barrels is going on. I look around, not seeing the menagerie close to the patio like they were when I checked earlier.

Reaching under the cover of the grill, I type in a short code on the box mounted under the bottom of the wheelbase. The Sig pops out just as intended, and I click the safety off as I creep along the fence line. Seer and I just hid the weapons in their fast deploy fixtures yesterday while we were setting up the basement, and on the patio was her idea. I could kiss her for that now as I move through the tree line, trying not to rustle branches and sticks as I search for companions.

I find them at the edge of my property, staring at a copse of trees beyond it like they're shooting lasers with their eyes. None of the animals are moving, just glaring into the distance, and I frown as I lower the .45. "What in the bug-fuckering *shit* are you guys making so much *noise* about?"

Jekyll looks up at me, his kitty face indignant. "*Mow!*"

Kali and Hecate let out a bone chilling howl of agreement, and I look up as Euryale swoops down to sit on the fence. The eagles' feathers ruffle, and it moves around on the wood, shifting in irritation.

"No one wants to share. Not a clue for ol' Jolene who just ran out here with a hand cannon to defend your honor?" Hyde pushes closer to me, rubbing against my legs in a serpentine pattern. It seems like normal cat behavior, but when in the hell have these two ever done anything normal? "I take it Timmy is *not* in the well? Something out here spooked you all?"

They all look at me with furry and feathered concern, and I sigh. Damnit, animals don't talk, and I have no idea what has a group like this losing the goddamned plot.

"Okay, guys. We're going inside, and you're going to eat. By the time the rest of the circus makes its way back to camp, I'll figure out what has you so freaked out." I look out over the horizon where they were staring and murmur, "And I'm going to call Jackson about that goddamned security system. It can't wait a week after all."

High School

Hugo

As always, they set the conference room to a brisk negative forty degrees. I watch Maryellen fuss over the preparations. I'm always early, and I'm always prepared, which is a stark contrast to the bulk of the teachers who work at Whistler's Hollow Finishing School.

Many of them have taught here under over three headmasters, and though they don't look their age in the slightest, they've long since given up the illusion of having control over their curriculum or classrooms. Bobbi Jo is the most progressive one they've had yet, but the lifers have lost their zeal for innovation.

Make no mistake—the students receive a high-quality education, and the school is nationally ranked in every category. However, the influence of the Council and the founding families is far-reaching. It makes teaching a challenge, one the folks here are no longer willing to face. So, they show up late, rarely have their work done on time, and don't seem inclined to intervene when the elite kids decide which targets they'll spend the rest of their time here torturing.

I seldom intervene, but for differing reasons than fear of powerful society mavens. My lack of empathy stems from knowing what the price of intervention could be, and they have taught me since birth that I am not to interfere as the wheel spins. I didn't grow up here, and the minuscule amount of information I may impart to the citizens regarding my life prior to being assigned to the Hollow hampers my influence.

Those directives come from a much higher authority than the Council or the others. They may control the supes here and the Society has global control, but for beings like Doyle and I, a more powerful authority dictates our actions within their framework. Those we are pledged to would not be happy if we allowed our loyalties to come into question.

"Good morning, Hugo!"

The sunshine filled voice of our headmaster pulls me out of my reverie, and I give her an amiable smile. She is a pleasant woman, if simple, and I hate that she's being manipulated the way she is. "Good morning, Bobbi Jo. Did you have an enjoyable weekend?"

Her bright smile and loud clothing are a bit much, but she brought doughnuts from *Close Encounters of the Baked Kind*, so we'll have to forgive her.

Jillian Marie Remington might be an absolute bitch, but the woman inherited the family recipe vault, and her roots go all the way back to New Orleans during Lafayette's days. Her fusion of European and down-home country techniques makes the shop famous enough to draw tourists in the season, and anything her staff produces is enough to make up for Bobbi Jo's boundless cheer.

"I did! I worked in the garden, got some reading in, and just loafed like a lazy polecat!"

I give her a nod, as if that sounds interesting and amazing, and she beams. Our boss is easy to please at all between her general daffiness and the effects of the ritual. "I had meetings out of town, I'm afraid. All work and no play makes Hugo a dull boy."

Her baffled expression is comical, but she also nods. "Indeed. Well, grab some grub, and have a seat. You know they'll all trickle in soon enough. And we all know who the last man seated will be."

Of course, we do. 'Coach' Edgar will bustle in ten minutes late, dressed like a model for Underarmor, and claim he had to 'rearrange' his bench schedule for this. No one believes him, of course, because the amount of actual 'judge' work he has to do is so minimal that it's laughable. There's little to no crime in the Hollow, outside of kiddy shit, and most they take large disputes to the Council for resolution. The title is almost honorary at this point— Edgar spends most of his time with the football team or running his multi-state sports book.

Isn't that ironic?

"Jolene! You're here!"

My head whips around as Bobbi Jo crows her delight at the woman entering the conference room. I only met her briefly this week, and duty called. She intrigued the hell out of me, and I still haven't puzzled out why I reacted to her presence for that brief conversation.

Bobbi Jo must have already let her know that the dress code here is informal. She styled her raven hair into an intricate poofy braid, and I doubt she did that to herself. More interestingly, she's dressed in a pair of strategically ripped, paint splattered jeans and an oversized man's shirt tied in a knot at her waist. A pair of knee-high Doc Martens grace her legs, emphasizing her thick thighs and round hips.

Our eyes meet as I finish my perusal of the girl who is so different from the primped, plastic enhanced women that populate this town. The startling emerald color seems to flash with a rainbow of color for a moment so brief that I almost don't catch it. Sucking in a breath, I frown. This woman is unidentified, and the glimpse of a color change such as that doesn't jibe with any possibility I'm familiar with. I'm also concerned about it occurring when we looked at one another, but then left as soon as we broke eye contact.

Jolene Athena Whitley is an enigma wrapped in a riddle covered in delicious-looking powdered sugar.

Or at least she is now. She's chowing down on coffee and doughnuts like there's no tomorrow. My lips curve up as I watch her eat with more gusto than any woman her age in this town and half the ones older than her. She's so comfortable in her skin I wonder about the reports that say she had a rough childhood here.

She seems to have adjusted well, if you ask me.

"Bobbi Jo!"

Again, I'm startled as the Judge himself enters five whole minutes before the meeting will begin. Edgar Olivier Boone III strolls in like a jolly fat man distributing presents, planting himself in the chair next to Jolene as if it was reserved for him. She gives him an eye roll, and it makes me chuckle. Whatever is going on between those two should be *remarkably* interesting. I'm sure I'll have the pleasure of knowing now that seeing them will trigger the effects. He whispers in her ear, and she swats his shoulder none-too-gently.

I will enjoy the *hell* out of this meeting. That is becoming apparent.

Walking over to the pastries, I grab one and pour myself a cup of coffee. I'd prefer it black, but Maryellen makes coffee that tastes like eagle piss. I drop a random assortment of flavored creamers and sugar into the cup, mixing it to make my personal addiction drinkable. Edgar is still aggravating Jolene, and it occurs to me. I don't think I've seen that jackass in a mood this good for a long time. He's tolerable with her beside him.

Once I have my goodies, I maneuver to my usual seat on the other side of the table near the front. Bobbi Jo needs help with tech during the meetings, and no one else is inclined to stop her flustered babbling when it happens. The muffled snickers and eye rolls make me irritated, so I try to sit close enough to help when needed. Some of the staff are no better than the students with bullying, that's for sure.

When the clock on the wall hits 8:30 am, a large group of teachers rush in. They've all been in the lounge gossiping and griping about having to come, and the late arrivals are all moronic power plays. Bobbi Jo is not the typical choice for headmaster, and though she's one hundred percent behind the staff, they treat her like crap because she doesn't fit their idea of the head for the illustrious Whistler's Hollow Finishing School.

The bloody Council *chose* her, so I can't figure out what in the fuck their problem is. She's done nothing but make their lives easier, but I guess that's small Southern town politics for you.

As my colleagues find their seats, I see the looks they give our new art teacher. Some are speculative, some are envious, some are outright hostile… I understand curiosity and even the jealousy wafting off the younger female teachers at Edgar's obvious familiarity with Jolene. He's a catch by local standards—hell, by any standards given his fortune—but he doesn't fish from the same pond. Every single woman in the room is sizing the returned beauty up to figure out how to tear her down, that I guarantee.

"Okay everyone! Settle!"

The noise level doesn't change a bit, and I sigh. Every. Damned. Time. I open my mouth to yell at them when I'm shocked to see Edgar stand. What's he playing at? He's the worst of the bunch.

"Now, folks. Bobbi Jo is trying to start the meeting. In the interest of efficiency, let's all give her the floor so we can get on with our days. Some of y'all have classrooms to explore, and lesson plans to submit."

I'll be a son of a bitch. You could hear a pin drop as the room goes silent and our fearless leader beams like he handed her an Oscar.

"Thank you, Edgar, darling. I appreciate your help," Bobbi Jo simpers.

She never thanks me, and I've had to shout like a referee in the past. Humph.

"Today marks the sixth 'first day back' meeting I've led, and I couldn't be prouder to be the head of this amazing team. We have a new member joining us this year, though many of you may recognize her from her days at our schools when she was growing up. Jolene Athena Whitley, welcome back to Whistler's Hollow Finishing School!"

Bobbi Jo claps like a maniac, Jolene turns a delectable shade of pink, and Edgar smirks as he claps along. I join the applause, and the rest of the staff does as well. It's interesting watching the reactions of the others now that they have an identity to attach their emotions to. Some of the initial assessments change, and I can see a few of the jealous ones' eyes glitter with intent. Looks like Jolene's tenure at this school may have been rougher than I realized, and her position at the school may not be any better.

"Jolene, of course you know Edgar. He's the football coach, but he teaches advanced personal training classes to select athletes at the school as an elective." Bobbi Jo turns to me and points. "Hugo is our one-man history department—his classes rotate so he can fill all the needs for the subject.

The ladies in the corner there represent the Science and English departments, and Marcel looks grumpy, but he teaches French, English, and Greek studies. The Math department is at a conference until Wednesday, and the other arts teachers are finishing up a summer camp at one of the Cantwell's event spaces until Friday. You met Maryellen and—"

"Excuse me, Bobbi Jo? Do you think we could move it along for those of us who have actual lives to lead?"

The tone of voice that comes out of the woman I thought was a sweet heiress of the Atwater fortune is a shock to me. I went on several dates with Dolly when I first moved to the Hollow, but we just didn't click. She was never anything but kind to me, though, and I honestly did not know this kind of person lurked inside of her. A smirk that carries more malice than I can fathom mars even the doll-like perfection of her blue eyes and cupid bow lips.

What in the hell has been going on in this town since Jolene arrived?

"Um, well… yes. Yes, Virginia, there is an agenda!" Bobbi Jo jokes to a silent staff. "Hugo, if you could fire up the smart board for me, we'll get into the objectives for today."

I nod, looking over at the star of the hour. She's chewing her lip hard, eyes on the table in front of her as Edgar whispers something into her hair. Her head shakes, and she shoos him away, picking up a pen to doodle in her open notebook. Sighing, I turn to the laptop and start plugging in the mess that Bobbi Jo's made of her presentation into the viewer.

Looks like battle lines have been drawn at WHFS, and the students aren't even in session yet.

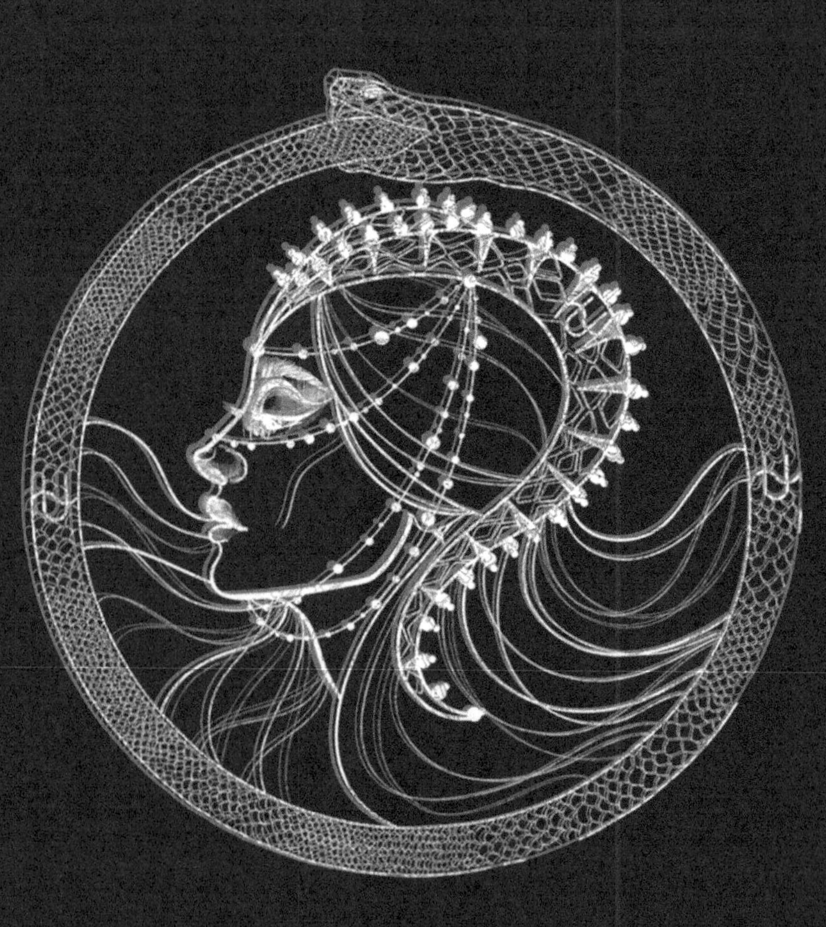

I'm Not Pretty

Jolene

After that clusterfuck meeting, I got the hell out of the building before any other founding family witches could track me down. Bobbi Jo made sure I had alarm codes and keys, which meant I could come back later when the dust settles. I collected Jekyll and Hyde from the playground, gave Kali and Hecate a pat, and jumped into the Impala so fast you'd think an assassin was on my tail.

My cats are hanging their heads out the window and letting out a loud *'mow!'* when Eury swoops too close to the roof. They seem to have done okay in the companion play area where I left them… I'd like to imagine that Teddy's dogs introduced them to the odd assortment of winged, furred, and scaled animals the staff left there while we attended the staff training. It gave me pause, though, because I don't remember this many exotic animals hanging about the Hollow in public when I was growing up here. I don't know whether this is a recent development or my wonky memory is playing tricks on me.

Either way, it's common now, so much so that the school has a mini-daycare area to keep the animals from disrupting.

My phone buzzes on the seat and I turn on the text-to-voice feature, so it comes out of the speakers. Safety first and all the jazz, right?

The electronic voice announces that there are incoming text messages and I brace myself. I left telling no one where I was going because I'm a grown assed woman and I don't have to check in with anyone. That should go over well.

Message from Bully Asshole: Where are you, drugar?
Message from Cute Asshole: She doesn't have to clock her movements with you, Boone.
Message from Doctor Asshole: Lucy's right. Back off, Coach.

For the love of leather chaps, these men are going to be the death of me. What possessed me to come home to solve a mystery and instead get trapped between three dudes who are now obsessed with me?

Oh, yeah—dick, that's what possessed me. That one's all on me. More pleasantly so when their stupid mouths are occupied.

"Send reply: Little Wolfie's right. I don't have to tell anyone where I'm going and I don't have a curfew, DAD." I grin to myself, satisfied with my retort, until I hear the telltale sound of a ding.

Message from Bully Asshole: You're welcome to call me Daddy any time you want, sugar.
Message from Cute Asshole: Don't be gross. Sugarplum? I'll smack him in the back of the head later.
Message from Doctor Asshole: I'm going to need front row seats to *that* show.

Jesus Christ and his merry band of groupies. I cannot with these guys.

"*Send reply:* Number one, in your dreams, Teddy. Number two, I'm headed to the farm to go riding. I'm going to work on the classroom stuff when the harpies have exited the building. A little warning might have been *nice*, Teddy!"

Before they can answer, the sound of Lucky the Leprechaun announces Saoirse's incoming text. I set that a few years ago when we were drunk off our tits in Dubai and I've never changed it. Maybe if those idiots behave, I'll set special tones for them, but to be honest, Seer's the only person who stayed in my life long enough to have personalized ringtones.

Message from Cheeky Monkey: I'm havin' a grand time at the house, Peanut! The feckin' security guys are settin' up yer cams and sensors and shite how you diagrammed them. They may be a wee bit annoyed with me watching them work, but a lass has got to eat, right?

I hope the team Jackson sent isn't busy getting their dicks sucked by my BFF instead of installing my goddamned security system. If there's a sensor out of place, I'm making Seer pay for the return visit. However, leaving her there instead of terrorizing the locals on her own or cackling during the staff meeting seemed like the better choice.

Message from Bully Asshole: Kali and Hecate are pouting because you left them behind. Come to think of it, *I'm* pouting. Just so you know.

I growl in frustration, and Jekyll pops his head in to glare at my phone like it offended him. Chuckling, I used my free hand to ruffle his fur. "I know, buddy. He's still got splainin' to do before his antics are cute again."

"*Mow!*"

Message from Cute Asshole: Sugarplum, ignore him. The pregnant mares are getting a check-up. I'll get finished in about a half hour. I can take Puck out for a spin and find you.

Wolfie's horse is named Puck?

That sounds about as fitting as one can get without hitting a nail on the head. I smile despite myself because I'm developing a major soft spot for the easygoing vet. I intended to work out my frustration with the bitch squad by riding alone and moping, but I can't seem to tell him no.

"*Send reply:* Sure, McDreamy. I'll see you then. For the rest of you, I'm putting my texts on 'do not disturb' for a while. I need some time."

I don't wait for their responses; I click the slider to mute the chat group and close the window. Sighing, I turn on my Spotify and hit my bad ass bitch mix, grinning as Joan Jett blasts through the speakers. It's not an inappropriate song at the moment. And I enjoy the thought of rolling up to the employee lot like a rock and roll princess in a muscle car. Especially if that dimwit is working in the office again.

Flashing my badge as I roll up to the gate to the employee entrance, I zoom past the guard from last week with a cheeky grin. He'll never forget me now that I saved his ass from the devil woman, I'm sure. It's always a good plan to make friends with people in low-level positions because you never know when they're going to be the exact person you need later. Plus, everyone ignores guards and grooms and maids and shit. It's bullshit.

My car slides into the spot marked with a shiny fresh sign with my name on it and I chuckle at the old-world style power play it represents. This is Jamie's way of ensuring that chick knows every time she pulls into the lot that her space—next to mine—says administrative assistant and mine has my name on it. That should help keep her in line if I have to breeze by the office at any point.

Jekyll and Hyde hop out of the car, giving me happy cat smiles that are hysterical with the aviators. Euryale glides down, landing on the roof of the car, looking at me as if waiting for instructions. I walk to the trunk, pulling out a bag with clean riding gear and slinging it over my shoulder. Once I shut it, I look at my companions.

"Okay, guys. I'm going for a ride. I need to work out my frustration, and you're free to roam, according to Jamie. *Stay away* from the office and that bitch Agatha. Euryale, you can swoop and soar, but stay high enough that you don't spook anyone."

The trio of animals honk or meow their acceptance and I leave them to wander as I make my way to the employee restrooms. I find a cushy staff locker room and claim a locker to store my precious bag and clothes in. The directions for the electronic locks are easy enough to follow—which means they'd be even easier to hack into—and I shove my things in after I strip down. Pulling on my socks, then my breeches, I chuckle as I remember the last time I came here to ride.

My underwear isn't as ugly this time, but they should suffice for a quick jaunt.

Once I get my boots on, I tuck my phone into the side pocket, grab my gloves, and head for the stables.

It's time to fly.

As the scenery goes by, I beam. Riding is one of the few things that can calm my mind when I get trapped in the black hole of the past. The women giggling in the background of that meeting in that building brought back every terrible memory, and I'm having trouble disassociating from the girl I used to be and the woman I am now. It doesn't matter that I've travelled the world, dined with princes, or even that I fucked the great and powerful Edgar Olivier Boone III.

I'm a lonely, chubby girl with distant parents and a yearning to be accepted.

High school is absolute bullshit, and anyone who tells you differently is living in a dream world. Regardless of what automatic bonus they had to make them popular—talent, looks, money, fame—they started the race in the middle of the track. The rest of us had to pant our way through the whole route. I didn't expect to have to do it again at work, but it's obvious I will.

I have to learn to compartmentalize my childhood trauma and channel the bad bitch I've become.

The palomino I'm riding whinnies like it agrees, and I chuckle. If I don't figure this out, I'm going to lose my mind and start talking to every animal I encounter. That habit won't endear me to my colleagues, so I gotta get my head on straight.

Damn. I wish I'd brought my headphones, but that's a dangerous proposition on a horse I don't know very well. I'll get comfortable enough with the horses here to ride while listening, but safety first and all. Flicking the reins, I change the speed of our trot to a canter, and the pretty girl beneath me takes the head. I relish the wind in my hair and the rush of a full run, my hips rolling with the movement.

The sound of hooves thunders behind us, and I chuckle. Wolfie told me he'd find me, and though I've been out here moping for an hour, he didn't disappoint. My lips curve and I lean down to the horse, whispering, "Let's make him chase us, Arabella."

With another flick and a press of my calves, I encourage the palo into a faster gallop, leaning down to cut through the wind as we race into the horizon. The beat of the hooves behind me picks up, and it occurs to me there are over four. In fact, it sounds more like eight.

Why does Wolfie have an extra horse with him?

Tugging on the reins, I urge the palomino to slow down until she comes to a halt. The thumps behind me also come to a stop as I slide from my saddle and turn to look. My jaw drops, and I'm stunned into silence as I take in the sight of my baby vet and the horse he brought with him. I can't decide which one is more gorgeous, so I continue to stare like a hooked trout until my brain resumes functioning.

Wolfie is sitting on a beautiful chestnut Andalusian, shirtless, his smile bright and his skin glistening in the early afternoon sun. He's holding the reins of a golden Akhal-Teke that looks like Rumpelstiltskin, himself spun its coat out of straw. I've never seen one in person, though I know how rare they are, and I can't believe there's one on Jamie's farm. Given the expense and lineage of that breed, they are owned by sheikhs and princes.

"Where in the ass-reaming *fuck* did you find that horse?" I practically shout. All three animals flinch, and I regret my shrill tone. "Sorry."

His laugh is rich, the tanned skin of his face standing out against the whiteness of his perfect teeth. "Oh, sugarplum. You never mince words, do you?"

I roll my eyes and put my hands on my hips. "Are you gonna tell me where the Midas touch horse came from or sit there looking like a Greek god while you laugh at me?"

"I'm pretty sure I can do both, love." Little Wolfie slides from his saddle, hitting the ground in a lithe motion that I could never imitate. "This is Mehdi, and she belongs to Jamie's new friend from overseas. She arrived today without a word of warning, and he decided you were the only one he wanted to work with."

Being the only trainer for a pureblood of this caliber is terrifying, especially since she doesn't belong to the person who assigned me the task. I'm good with horses, but I'm not a professional trainer. Only people with years of experience should break in a horse this valuable. She could be a contender for the Crown in a few years, and formative training is a large part of that viability.

"No. No, no, no, no. Not in a million years, Wolfie. I won't be responsible for some rich douche's new toy being improperly trained and costing him Derby prospects." My nose wrinkles as I approach the stunning mare, tracing my fingertips over her luminous coat. I can't even do her justice with a description because in the sunlight, she looks like she belongs to Apollo himself.

"Sugarplum, I don't think it was a request. Jamie told everyone that outside of grooming and checkups with me, this horse was off-limits. The trainers are fit to be tied—you can't say no. It'll only make it worse."

Mehdi nickers, shaking her head as if agreeing. My eyes narrow and I step closer, looking at her. She tilts her head and jerks it back as if indicating that I should shut up and climb on. Indecision wars within me—I've had a rough day, and this is an astronomically expensive horse that I've never ridden before and she seems to want me to hop on bareback.

However, no one's ever accused me of being a coward, and I won't let this be the first time.

Steeling my spine, I grab a hold of her mane and swing myself up onto her back with my right leg. She's taller than the palo by several hands, and if I hadn't gotten a start, I might not have made it. Mehdi lets out a loud whinny, and I hold on as she rears back. She's not trying to toss me, but she's fucking excited, and before I can get my bearings, she takes off like a shot.

Scenery flies by as I grasp the reins and her mane, gripping her back with my thighs so tightly that I'm certain I'll be sore as hell later. The excited horse gallops across the fields like she's racing in her own personal stakes, taking the unfamiliar terrain in stride without batting a lash. I hear Wolfie behind me on Puck, whistling and calling out to her to see if he can get her attention, but it's to no avail. Now that she has her head, my girl is determined to show what she can do.

I'll say one thing: this son of a bitching horse is going to earn roses when she's ready.

That time isn't now, though, and we're headed for the fence line at an alarming speed. I need to figure something out, or we're both going to get injured. I rack my brain, trying to access the part of my memory that's storing the six weeks Seer and I spent in Dubai. We met our fair share of horse loving princes in the casinos, and if I can just… ah-ha!

"*Khalas!*" I cry, giving the reins a tug hard enough to get the attention of the speeding equine.

Mehdi's ears flick, and she slows, dropping to a canter, and then a trot before she comes to a halt mere inches from the inner fences. I blink, sucking in a breath as I look behind me to see Hottie McBabyVet thunder up beside me with wide eyes. I run my hand over the silky mane of the hot-blooded beauty I'm riding to reassure her and slide off. My legs are like jelly, and my hands are shaking with adrenaline as I stumble over to Wolfie with a huge grin on my face.

"Did you *see* that? Holy cock-sucking donkey balls, that was amazing!"

He frowns, catching me as my knees crumple, and shooing the horses away so we have room to move. "Sugarplum, we are going to chat about your daredevil ways. You scared the bejesus out of me! I had to leave Arabella to chase you."

Beaming at him, I feel the air around us shift, and the electricity shoots through my veins, twisting with the high from the breakneck ride. I press my body to his, eyes dancing with mischief as I toss my glasses aside. "Time for that later, little Wolfie."

His brow arches and he chuckles. "Sugarplum, you can barely stand."

"We don't need to stand, darling," I reply, giving his chest a little push.

That's all it takes for him to topple us to the ground, his back hitting the bluegrass with a thump as he brings me with him. I tug the shirt off, discarding it as recklessly as I did my sunglasses, and he peels my sports bra off while my arms are up.

"No binding this time?" he smirks. "I think you lured me out here with plans."

"I sure as fuck did."

Rolling us over, his hands help me wriggle the tight breeches down while I work the buttons of his jeans. He gets distracted by the jeweled cages on my nipples as they sparkle in the light, and I growl in frustration. I grab his hair and pull his head up, shaking my head. His soft snort makes my lips curl up, and he shucks the jeans like a pro.

"Better, sugarplum?"

"Not yet," I mutter, wrapping my fist around his cock and stroking. The smooth steel on his shaft slides over my palm, and he groans. "Once you fuck me, I'm sure it will be."

His lips capture mine, and I let go, allowing him to lift my thighs off the ground. Long fingers grasp my screaming muscles, parting my legs so he can line up with my dripping pussy. When he raises his head, I raise an eyebrow, and he grins at me, placing my ankles on his shoulder.

"Can't have you doin' too much work after that ride, love. You won't be able to walk."

I open my mouth to sass back, but he drives his dick into me so hard that it feels like he's going to split me in two. A throaty moan of pleasure escapes instead of bratty sarcasm, and he takes that as his cue to start a punishing rhythm that knocks the breath out of my lungs. His hips crash into me as he does what I asked… fucks the living shit out of me.

Flinging my arms over my head, I close my eyes, letting the sensations course through me as he holds me in place. He doesn't have control—I do—but I'm enjoying every second of his hard cock spearing me into the soft ground of the field. His hand shifts, one holding on and the other snaking around to find my clit, pinching it every time he buries himself to the hilt.

A shimmering sensation floats over my skin, and the whisper of softness makes every inch of me tingle. My toes curl, my fingers dig into the dirt, and my wail echoes over the quiet field when I come, squeezing him inside as I'm never letting go. His hips stutter as his orgasm rockets through him on the tail of mine, and something feels like it clicks into place.

My eyes open as I pant, my gaze finding his through the haze of my climax, and I could swear his blue eyes are swirling with color. I lift a trembling hand to his face, giving him the closest thing to a smile that I can as I return to reality.

"You, my little wolf, are mine, you know," I rasp. "I don't know how you worked your way in, but I don't think I can ever let you go."

The smile on his face is as bright as the golden horse I rode here as he leans in and whispers in my ear, "I don't think we ever had a choice, sugarplum."

Amen to that.

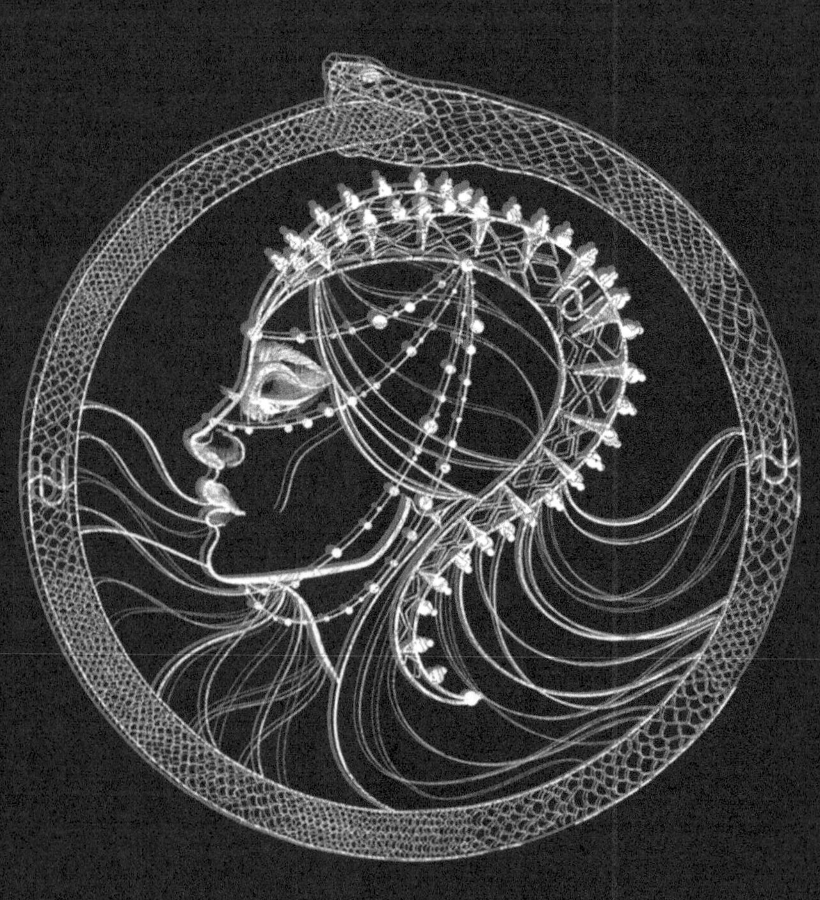

Lovely

The lovely Miss Whitley comes striding up the steps of the school with her animals in tow like she's storming the beaches of Normandy. Of course, that's the imagery I teach in my class, so I watch her. I know she hot-footed it out of here like her ass was on fire this morning, but I think something about the behavior of those harpies in the English department triggered her. She let Boone drag her out, but she was still as a board and had all the emotion of a robot as she pretended to joke with him.

I assembled her history here in the file on my desk, but I'm more inclined to figure it out myself. They did not tie my assignment here to her—no one even knew she was coming until the team in Richmond contacted their handler. Now that she's here, though, they bound all of us to monitor events as they unfold. Mystery surrounds Jolene Athena Whitley, and even the people who *should* know aren't certain what will happen.

Even people like me, and that's saying something.

Frowning as I watch her take her companions to the play area and give them what looks like a stern talking to, I contemplate what it might mean that I can't seem to get a good read on this woman. Is it an intervention? Is it a path that cannot diverge? Does it involve me somehow? That explains a complete lack of information where there is always information and shadowing.

Jolene seems to pick up a crowd, both companions and followers, which is also puzzling. Many of us have multiple companions and some have many mates, but she's walking through the town like a magnet for trouble. When combined with all the question marks surrounding her, it doesn't bode well.

I will have to ask when I get home. Perhaps my source can enlighten me further…

MY CLASSROOM IS NEARLY READY. I HAVE A FEW THINGS TO HUNT FOR online, but barring those, I think I'm ready for the brats and bullies to come back. I hate to sound rude, but as much as I love teaching, the students at WHFS try my extensive patience.

Many of them have little to no interest in world history or even US history—they know their family name and money guarantee them a spot at State U even if their grades are subpar. Some of them know their legacy before they are supposed to, and those elite few are determined to stomp the life out of the ones who are less fortunate. I don't allow poor behavior in my classroom, but my calling hampers my ability to prevent bad things from happening. I can only stand by, observing, and let the chips fall where they may.

It's the most infuriating part of my heritage and it makes teaching teens a nightmare.

Sighing, I sling my backpack on, flicking off the lights as I head into the dusky hallway. A few lights are on because the cleaning crew knows that a handful of teachers are in the building. As I start towards the back stairs to make my trek up to the main exit, I hear music and the absolute worst karaoke someone has ever forced me to listen to in my life.

It's like someone is strangling a cat.

Curiosity gets the best of me, and I walk down to the end of the corridor, taking the right turn towards the art wing. When I get closer, a grin teases my lips because I know who it is. Miss Jolene Athena Whitley—the misfit puzzle piece—is singing along with a playlist and she's a fucking awful singer. Like truly horrific, in fact, and so off-key that I wouldn't recognize the song if she weren't screeching the lyrics like a drunken sorority chick.

I round the corner and peek into the outer classroom, noting that she set every station up with a note folded in a tent in their work area. The sound is coming from the back of the room, where the door to the equipment area is hanging open. Creeping quietly, I move towards the racket. I don't know if I ever met a woman unconcerned with people seeing her look ridiculous.

That has to be it, right? There's no way that she thinks she's a good singer. Anyone with ears would tell her she's not.

The sight that greets me as I stand in the doorway is hysterical. Our new art teacher is caterwauling to the tune of some long forgotten nineties girl group, covered in paint from head to toe, and dancing with her cats. She also covered the cats in paint, and it looks like the giant bird is watching them like a sentry. It lets out a screech when its eyes fall on me, and the cats turn, their bodies going rigid as they let out a non-threatening snarl.

"Oh!"

Chuckling, I hold my hands up. "I come in peace. I was leaving, and I heard... unusual sounds coming from here, so I came to check it out."

"You're... Hugo, right?" she asks, pushing strands of paint-covered hair out of her face.

I can't help but smile like an idiot as she pulls a scrunchie off her wrist and piles the mess of hair on top of her head as she looks at me. This girl is a walking, talking bundle of chaos, and it's so damned cute that I don't even know how to respond. "Yes. I teach history."

What the fuck was that? 'I teach history'? That's as bad as 'I carried a watermelon.' for dumbass responses. I'm glad I didn't say it out loud, because my love of late 20th century rom-coms is a little embarrassing when not in the right crowd. I have no idea if Jolene IS the right crowd, so I shove my hands in my pockets.

"Yes, that's one of the few things I learned at the meeting this morning," she says as she grabs a pack of baby wipes off of the counter. Her small grin makes my chest lift, and I watch her wipe down the two servals gently. "We came back to set up, but I let them try pawpainting and, well... we got carried away."

Nodding as if I understand how what she described turned into an orgy of paint, dancing birds, and cats, I reply, "I can see that. Do you need help? If your eagle got any on—her, his, its—feathers, you'll have to call Presley."

Her laugh is like a fucking fairy, I swear to hell. "I haven't asked Euryale about gender. It's rude. Little Wolfie told me that Hyde is a girl. I suppose I should have McSteamy or McDreamy check, though. I wouldn't want to be offensive about their pronouns."

This girl. I mean… where the hell did she drop out of the sky from?

Historical and literary pet names aside, she cares about misgendering animals when half the population can't wrap their heads around it with humans. I don't even know how to describe how goddamned perfect she is. "That wouldn't do at all. I take it you're friendly with our town medical team, then?"

The look on her face flashes from fondness to heat to confusion to possessiveness within seconds, and I know Boone isn't the only one to get his claws into our mysterious new colleague. "I am. We're..." She struggles for a word, scrunching her paint covered up, and shrugs. "... well, we're definitely fucking. I don't know what else, to be honest. I'm hopeless with this shit."

I blink, and she covers her mouth, looking aghast. Her natural candidness is going to shock the shit out of many people, but I don't want her to think I'm judging her. In fact, it makes me even more intrigued. "Don't worry...you won't offend me. I'm a fantastic secret keeper."

A pout forms on her lips and her brows furrow. "It's not a secret. I'm not ashamed of being who I am or who I'm with. If the fuddy duddies in this town don't like it, they can suck a giraffe dick. They're *mine*."

Her eyes flash with alternating colors for the briefest second and the surrounding air thickens, then goes back to normal within a nano-second. Athena, mother of wisdom, this girl has no *idea*. She's not human, but she hasn't emerged, and she must not know about… any of us. Not the town, not the people—nothing. This is so very danger-ous, but I can't seem to make my mouth say 'goodbye' or my feet walk away.

Instead, I offer a half-hearted platitude, knowing that I'm going to get home and do some serious consulting to try to uncloud my connection. "I'm sure they appreciate that. And you're right—no one should dictate who you love or how you love them."

Her skin goes deathly pale, and she turns on her heel to walk over to the counter, scrubbing it with a brush. "I said nothing about love. It was nice talking to you, but I have a big mess to clean up. I'm sure I'll see you again before school starts next Monday."

Well, fuck. Open mouth, insert foot, Hugo. Smooth.

"Um, yeah. Well, come find me if you're here during the day and you need help. I'll, uh, be around." I try to smile, but her back is still to me, so I beat a hasty retreat through the classroom. I've upset her, and I'm not sure how.

Maybe *astéri mou*[1] will be in a better mood tomorrow, and I'll try again. At least then I might have enough information to figure out what her arrival means for everyone, and why she's unemerged so late in life.

I'm going to help her, even if it goes against my oaths.

This girl is too special to let go of.

---

1. My star

Trouble

"What the bloody hell do you mean 'that's not the plan'? I think it's perfectly feckin' clear your plans haven't been working so far!"

Glaring at the phone in my palm, I try to take a few calming breaths, like Peanut's taught me. My Irish temper gets the best of me, and I've had my fill of the blessed Council and the higher-ups, leaving everything up to fate. My girl hasn't emerged yet—it's true—but it's becoming clear that she will soon enough. She's definitely one of the 'lost' ones, which is why they assigned her a Guardian.

That would be me, though I haven't been her Guardian for her entire life, as most are.

"We have been made aware she is not the only lost one to emerge. There is another, and there may be more. The leaders are both excited and concerned. We've never had this happen so late in life— typically the lost emerge later than usual and we find them as we did the vet you've spoken of. When it happens, we can have their Guardians notified and get them inducted. This is unprecedented, Guardian 1989."

The disembodied voice bit always gives me the giggles, and I canna wait to share this James Bond shite with Peanut when she gets inducted. Being a Guardian without a charge for most of my life was bollocks—all I could do was train for the day I got tapped. The day it happened, I was on tour with a famous rock band, working their stage costumes and I had to drop off to locate my new bestie.

Lucky for me, my charge was feckin' amazing, and I didn't have to hide in the shadows. Some Guardians get right arseholes, and if they didn't grow up together, they spend their time lurking like a stalker.

"Look, ye ruddy control freak. There's more at stake than some grand plan. They tied myself and a few other inductees to her, and the longer we keep this secret, the more likely it is she'll cut us all out and go on the bloody run," I growl, my frustration making my tone sharp.

"Your personal needs are not our concern, 1989. The other lost to us by an...ally, of sorts, brought one to us. This organization is completing research of the utmost importance to us now that we are aware they have a sample of this individual. We rarely engage with this sort of group, but they have proximity and unparalleled access to the lost one. Their research may hold the key to the mystery we've been trying to solve for hundreds of years. We may save everyone if they are successful."

This whole situation is minus craic, and I'm about to lose my marbles. They're worried about some greater good for all of us, and I'm worried about my friend. She may have had Bane as her Guardian as a child, but once I got assigned, she became mine.

Speaking of which…

"Where the bloody feck is Bane? I haven't seen hide nor hair of the bitch, and Peanut hasn't mentioned her being at the school. When is she coming back?"

A sigh echoes over the line, and I'm sure I'm trying their patience. I never know if I'm talking to one handler, a room full of cheeky bastards, or a sodding goddess in a temple. I do know I always get this reaction because I'm not the type to take orders and hup-to. I ask questions and demand answers—which have kept both of us alive, thank you very much.

"Agent 1989, you notice more than most. Agent 302 is meeting with Agent 1985 about the lost one she has reconnected with. 302 is attempting to keep 1985 from doing what you do—going off half-cocked and ruining our ability to monitor without involvement. Since 1985's charge was not only reported by our ally, but through seeking 1985 in her home, we must tread carefully. The lost one that is now found is extremely powerful, and connected across the globe, both through the human world and the supernatural. Negotiations are beyond delicate."

Frowning, I try to remember which Guardian is 1985. We get together once a year to bitch about our charges, the handlers, and the world on the whole. But I can't seem to remember ever meeting 1985. She must not attend, and for that to be true, they shamed her for losing track of her charge. I hope she's able to reclaim her heritage and help rather than stay on the outside. It's freezing in our world without connections to the larger society.

"If you could let me know when other Guardians are passing through this place, I'd be chuffed, mate. I need to know who's safe and who's not, because we have some issues here. I'm handling it with the help of the other agents, but I'm also distracted. I have to secure a place of my own so I can set up all the things I need for the assignment."

I know they won't, but it never hurts to ask. At least then I know if it's a rogue shifter, a threat, or another of my kind slinking around Peanut's house at night.

"Find Cantwell and Boone. Arrange what you need through them. Agent 302 will return in a week, and it will please you to know that Agent 1998 and her..." The pause is deafening as the idiot on the phone flounders. "... associates will join you in your abode. Expense the construction, labor, and supplies, but get it done before they arrive. Have Boon throw his weight around if need be. I want every Guardian in that town on high alert."

I sigh, rubbing my temples. They took my concern about the night wanderer and determined it's a threat to everyone in town. It doesn't matter that three-quarters are inductees, retired agents, retired Guardians or even active agents and Guardians. All the big wigs heard is there is danger lurking and we must protect Project Chimera.

Politics can suck donkey balls, that's for bloody sure.

"I'll do as suggested, but I am concerned that we don't know enough about the threat to flood this town with foreigners and new people. It's a wee bit backwards here, and I'm drawing enough attention. Agent 1998 and her crew will stand out like a virgin in a strip club," I chuckle, my lips curving. I don't mind Agent 1998; in fact, I dig her.

We had a few wild times before I got assigned to Peanut, and her charge was the hottie vet. Once he got inducted, she became a free-lancer, helping other Guardians when needed and traveling the world with her two lovers. That was the bit that gave my echoing voice pause, and most of our species have multiple mates or spouses makes it even funnier. Why such a struggle to talk about something so mundane? Guardians are polyamorous by nature and necessity, given our lives of travel and vigilance.

Do the weirdos who run all of this stick with one mate or lover? How odd and old school.

"We have decided that you will cloak yourself in a more normal speech pattern, and not seem like an outsider to the people who live in Project Chimera's headquarters. We will instruct Agent 1998 and her...associates...to blend in more thoroughly when they arrive. Get to work, 1989. We must confer with the elders and with the colleagues who are running their own experiment with one of our subjects. It would be tragic if they somehow destroyed hundreds of years of work to achieve a short-sighted goal related to money."

"Let me get this straight... You feckers think that if I talk without an accent and get a house, we'll be able to hide four new people that look like we do in a small, Southern town in America. How out of touch *are* you people? Do any of you ever leave the Conclave at all?"

If we were talking about Europe or Asia, this wouldn't be an issue. Hell, if we were talking about New York or L.A., no one would even notice us. But here, in the land of Vineyard bloody Vines and Lilly puking Pulitzer, we do *not* blend in. They did not train us to blend into places like this.

Lost ones gravitate towards large cities with diverse populations— we're not sure why, but given that the areas where the Society's various projects are located are rural, it makes sense. A need to escape the grasp of the small and embrace being lost in the new is appealing to those who don't feel as though they belong.

"Figure it out, O'Flanagan! We select Guardians from the strongest bloodlines, and are raised with immeasurable skills. You do not need us to give you instructions. Your obstinance is tiring. We expect a report by the end of the week."

The line goes dead and I drop my head. It sucks great yak balls, but the great git on the phone is correct. Chance did not choose this life for me. I've earned it every day since I was wee, and I can figure this out. I have a little time before Julia and her men arrive, so I should find that idiot Boone and get started. He can't ignore a direct order, either, and he'll have to help me bend the rules to find a fucking supe team that can construct, detail, and then hide a massive building project in a town full of nosey Southerners.

Guess I'll have to be a miracle worker, huh?

"Look, leprechaun. I don't have the time to—"

"This was *not* a request, Boone. They said 'get Cantwell and Boone to sort it out'. Here I am, and here you are, so sort it out!" I screech, rolling my eyes into the back of my head.

I don't have the foggiest how this bastard is going to get Peanut to forgive him. He might have had a good reason for hot footing it after they had their moment, but his bloody alpha tendencies were going to be the death of him. Edgar can't keep his own mouth shut long enough to keep his size thirteen feet out of it. If I know our girl—and I sodding do—she's going to make him squirm for a dog's age until she even lets him attempt to explain himself.

"Fine. I'll go to Jamie and get the deed settled. He can finagle Nelia with some excuse. I'll even call the bitchy elves for you, but you're dealing with the pointy-eared little shits. I don't have the patience or self-control not to eat the damned things when they mouth off," he growls.

Rolling my eyes, I sigh. I cannot imagine Peanut dealing with one of him, much less him and the other two in tandem. How is she going to wrangle that much dick and attitude without losing her bloody brain cells? The testosterone is drowning me and we're only on the feckin' phone. "Thank you, Edgar. I will mention to Peanut how helpful you were."

"Fuck off, O'Flanagan. I don't need your help with my drugar. She'll see reason soon enough."

"Edgar, you might as well buy stock in tissues if that's going to be how you handle her. Jolene Athena Whitley will *never* let you tell her what to do. She's like a bolt of lightning on a spring day—she goes where she wants and shocks the shit out of you when she gets there. But good luck with your grumpy asshole schtick."

The line goes click on my end this time, and I giggle at myself. I'm not wrong, and even if the good docs get it, this professional moron does not. I cannot *wait* to watch Peanut put him in his place.

It's going to be grand.

Talk of the Town

Jolene

This morning was a flurry of activity. A house full of animals, people, and food smells filled my senses from when I woke to when I walked out the door. Wolfie and Presley got up and made waffles with an embarrassing amount of fixings. Saoirse flitted about the kitchen like a Disney fairy. We all had to be at important events, so the fashion show before we left killed me.

My first parents' night at WHFS is tonight, and I've been working on my syllabus and displays all week. Presley has a presentation at the lower school; being the town doctor, he's in charge of vaccination drives and physicals for sports. Wolfie is even more nervous than me. The sheikh arrived, and he's meeting with Jamie and my baby vet about the training and care plan for Mehdi. I tried to talk him through some of the cultural aspects, but he's been on pins and needles. Seer chuckled at him and gave me a big wink before she took off on whatever adventure she's got scheduled.

I haven't had this many people around in a long time, much less occupying my home as if they've moved in. It's both cozy and weird at the same time. In Richmond, I was almost a hermit. I learned to keep myself busy with training and studying; here, I'm spending an equal amount of time working and socializing with the crew filling my house.

"*Mow!*"

Turning my head, I look over at Jekyll with a grin. The animals are the biggest change, and the one I'm having the least trouble accepting. Hyde adds her own yowl to her companions before sticking her head out the window again. I know Eury is flying above us, following with her sharp eyes, watching the landscape for threats. I'm not sure that I agree with the guys' OR my animals' overprotective stances, but rather than hurt any feelings, I've allowed them to fuss over me a little.

See? Even I can bend when I choose—I'm not a complete brat.

The facade of the municipal building comes into view, and I whip into a parking space near the front, humming under my breath. The purpose of this trip is to register Eurayle as a companion animal, but I have a hidden aim as well. My plan is to wander down to the public records section and take a peep at the history of the town. I want to figure out what that 'hostile takeover' nonsense Hazel spouted was. I have a feeling that it's tied to whatever the hell my parents were into. Nothing in this town happens without the Town Council hearing about it, so I figure it's got to be in the records somewhere.

I stride towards the front of the building, nodding at Eurayle when she finds a suitable perch on a bench outside. They can license her— or whatever—without cramming an enormous bird into an office building, I think. Jekyll and Hyde continue following me, and I chuckle under my breath. Neither of them let me out of their sight unless the guys are in my room, and even then it's reluctantly. Wolfie has the best luck with getting them to trot off without a lot of glares. I don't know why, but Prez always gives them a wide berth.

It's weird, but what the hell about this town, the past week, or my current life isn't?

The first set of steps is flat, but the second is older. The building is antebellum architecture—brick with a tall, domed clock tower. They've added onto it, but someone took great pains to match as much of the original structure as possible. The ornate wooden doors at the entrance look beautiful, but I can't help thinking that Whistler's Hollow always feels like it's frozen in time.

Even in smaller cities across America, they have retrofitted city buildings to include emergency doors that lock and surveillance systems. The fear of mass shooters is real in our country—from the farm to the big metropolis—but our town looks much like I'd imagine it did sixty years ago. If it weren't for the 'hip' new business names, I'd wonder if we lived in a Norman Rockwell painting.

Cold air rushes out as I push the heavy oak open, and I stride into the building with the air of someone that knows what she's doing. I don't, but fuck if I'm going to give the gossips here a chance to call me weak. Jekyll and Hyde tippity-tap across the marble floors as we step up to the huge maple desk. Aldous Basil Longworth sits on what has to be a special order desk chair that would make a Wall Street coke fiend weep with jealousy. His smug smile as he looks me over from head to toe makes the servals tense beside me and I try to send some sort of quiet... vibe… that lets them know to behave around this vulture.

"Aldous. It's lovely to see you again," I say as I widen my eyes and broaden my smile into the affect of a polite socialite. "How are Ophelia and her children?"

The little shit leans back in his enormous chair, folding his hands over his stomach in a mockery of a power pose. "Why, Jolene Whitley, I'm pleased as punch to see our newest citizen. Ophelia and the heirs are superb—in fact, I daresay they will be on top of their classes yet again this year. What brings you to my neck of the woods?"

I roll my eyes inwardly. School hasn't started, so his rant about their academic prowess is wasted. Also, I went to school with both Ophelia and Jackson—neither of them were candidates for a *Mensa* membership. However, I smile again, nodding as if I agree. "Excellent news, Aldous. I look forward to meeting them. As for why I'm here, I need to register a third companion. My harpy eagle, Eurayle, showed up at the end of last week, and I've been remiss in getting the paperwork done. I apologize for my tardiness while I prepared for students."

His eyes narrow, and he taps his fingers in annoyance. Aldous didn't know that a third companion chose me, and hell if I know why that's vexing him, but he's got sand fleas up his ass about it. Sitting up in his chair, he reaches for a folder, pulling out a piece of paper and sliding it over the polished surface. "This is your application. Since the Mayor rushed your last one as a personal favor, you won't be familiar with it. You will need young Dr. Fletcher to sign off on the health of your companion. He's in demand, so it might take you a bit to get an appointment."

"I don't think I'll have a problem," I murmur as my lips curve into a smug smile. His gaze narrows as if he is studying me, and I switch back to the Southern ingenue expression to divert suspicion.

"Rumor has it the uncatchable Judge Boone has been following you around, Miss Whitley. I'm sure he wouldn't appreciate hearing unseemly gossip about you and the town vet. Perhaps you should be more cautious about how you react to suggestions," he snarks, a cruel smile gracing his features. His eyes are full of promises about just how that rumor would get started.

This little hobgoblin has *no idea* who he's messing with. I've tried to play their game while I began my investigations, but I refuse to let the snotty elites rule my personal life. Who I spend time with—in or out of the bedroom—is no one's business but my own.

I bat my lashes, tilting my head as if considering. "Well, he seemed a bit put out that he had to take the middle, but he didn't get along poorly with them. Thank you for the advice, Aldous! I should take a survey of my men and ensure they feel they're getting equal attention." His eyes widen until I think they might pop out of his head, and he swallows. It looks like he's going to reply, but nothing comes out as his mouth works.

Never one to look a gift horse in the mouth, I stare back at him as I wait. Jekyll and Hyde sense my impatience, and they jump up, putting paws on the desk as they snarl. When Aldous still doesn't speak, I hold back a sigh of irritation and ask him the questions I need answered before I go. "I'm so glad we caught up! If you could point me to the town archives, I have a few things to check about property lines, and I'll be on my way."

A shaky hand points towards the stairs on the east end of the building, and I nod. Whistling as I walk away, I listen for the telltale tapping of my cats' claws as they follow me. I can't have them staying to menace Aldous, even if it would amuse me. I painted a giant target on my back to spite an odious boil, and I'm going to have enough to worry about without adding a second person claiming my cats attacked them, especially since I sort of want to let them.

Being a functional adult is bullshit, and I hate it.

Our trio takes the stairs to the creepy-looking basement, and I cross my fingers, hoping I can find some of the information I need in old dusty records and stacks. If not, I don't know where to look next. My contacts online seemed to think that one of the best places to start is to sift through minutes from Town Council meetings. I'm not sure why they think reading through people complaining about non-themed holiday decorations or dog poop issues will reveal anything, but I'm willing to give it a go. I can't imagine a 'big secret' being discussed in public forums.

Who the hell am I to judge? I'm hiding valuable clues in linens in the bathroom; I'm not the international super spy type.

I find the room marked 'Records' and open it, letting Jekyll and Hyde precede me. They bolt into the rows of shelves as if looking for hidden stalkers, and I chuckle. My crew needs to calm down. It's unlikely that an assassin is hiding amongst the files and papers in this musty municipal building. However, just to be safe, I leave the door cracked before I drop into a chair at an oak table. Pulling my laptop out of my bag, I set up a space to take notes and file snippets away until I can print and assemble it on the board I'm keeping in the basement.

Yeah, I have a crazy, tin foil hat board with strings and post-it in my gun room. I've become a closet conspiracy theorist. Luckily, the guys don't go down there and Seer doesn't bother, either. I can escape to my basement of secrets whenever they're all off on whatever adventures they have without me.

Once I'm set, I get up and walk to the rows, noting they're organized by year and month, going back at least a hundred years. This must be the bulk of the town records—I can only assume the older stuff is stored somewhere less accessible. Documents prior to the 1900s would be valuable and delicate, and I suppose you'd have to request to view them. I hum under my breath, deciding that I should start about fifty years ago because it would be around the time my parents were born. I know that my father's family tree begins in the Hollow and my mother met him in college at State.

I should be able to trace the changes in the town makeup by reading through the documents month by month until I hit the jackpot.

"*Mow!*"

"Yeah, Hyde. We're in for a *looooong* afternoon, lady. Settle in. We have research to do."

I Knew You Were Trouble When You Walked In

Doyle

That big arsed bird has been perched on the bench for four hours. Word is it belongs to the new lass in town. It's watching the street like it's guarding the doorway—I don't blame the bloody thing. I haven't once heard jaws flap about any one person in town like they are about her since I got assigned here. Sure, there were wee scandals and outrages befitting a town of rich supes living amongst humans, but nothing on the scale of Jolene Athena Whitley's arrival has generated.

It's ironic she's named the way she is. Can't say I'm surprised someone has a rich sense of humor at the expense of the clueless. The relatives amuse themselves with shit like this all the time. It's what living for millennia does to your mind—boredom is a constant battle. I'm sure dear auntie had herself a great big guffaw when the prof or one of his ilk told her.

Taking a drag, I look down the street and chuckle as I exhale. The names of the stores get me every time, and I can't believe I managed that. Fine, I indulge in a bit of mischief to quell the monotony as well. Sue me—or don't, because the last person who needs to be on a stand is me. His Honorable Dickweed would lose the sodding plot if he had to listen to one of these rubes try to elicit truthful testimony out of me. Actually, it might be fun. I may commit some sort of crime just to see what happens.

Sounds craic to 90, and I'm always game for that.

"Doyle, why are you standing out here drawing attention to the building like a fucking gargoyle on fire?"

I sigh, rolling my eyes as I face the dishonorable judge himself. "What are *you* doing here instead of meting out justice with Vlad and Randall? What do my taxes *pay for?*"

Edgar snorts, shaking his head. "You work for us, idiot. You don't pay taxes. Hell, very few people in this town do outside of tributes and the humans. Answer my question."

"I'm having a fag, Boone. Even in the South you can't do that inside city buildings anymore," I shrug, my eyes cutting to the bird again. I've heard some members are involved with the pretty lass with eyes the color of the rolling hills of Tara, and I'm curious. I only saw her once, and that's all it took to know that she's bloody enchanting.

"Look, Haggerty. I can tell you're up to something, and if I find out you're meddling where you don't belong, I'll inform the Town Council. Don't think I won't go higher if I need to, either." His eyes narrow as he follows my gaze, and something changes in his posture. "And leave Jolene Whitley alone—she's mine."

I put my hand on my chest, batting my lashes as I taunt the testosterone filled git. "Edgar, I'd swear you were sweet on the lassie. Must sting like a bee that rumors have the doctoral duo warming her bed most nights. Did you not measure up?"

His growl startles me, and before I know it, the air is filled with a fog that threatens to take over my senses, and large feathered appendages smash into my head. Motherfucker hit me on both sides, eh? We'll see about that. The pheromones continue to choke the air, but I close my eyes and let it run through me. It'd be a waste of a good power boost not to. One of his wings hits me again, and I snap.

"You're out of your league, Boone!" I snarl back. I won't use both sides—it would only end in disaster for all of us. I haven't used the gifts from my mother's side for hundreds of years. However, my father's side is much less destructive. Feeling the energy coast over my skin, I look at him in the eyes despite his glittering half-shifted form. My voice is smooth and low like warm honey being poured as I murmur, "You don't want to do this, mate. The fog can't charm me, and this will draw more attention than my smoking outside of the club. Shift back, and we'll go have a drink at Benjy's."

Blinking, he tilts his head, not replying with more than a hiss of breath. I keep muttering the same instructions over and over, tracing a circle in the air as I do so. After a few minutes, the feathers fade, and I sense the mist in the air pulling back. My eyes glow as I check out the deserted street, hoping that either we got lucky and no one saw, or his powers drove them inside for more... pleasurable activities.

"Haggerty, I'm going to wring your fucking neck," he groans, shaking his head and running a hand through his hair. Before I can reply, he whistles loudly and his two giant beast dogs come flying out of the building like the hounds they are. "Leave Jolene alone and shut your mouth about her bedmates. She can have whatever she wants, and it's none of your goddamn business."

"Mmmmm. Methinks the uncatchable Judge Boone has met his match," I say, grinning. "And she must be a *very* special supe indeed to convince one of *your* kind to accept this situation. Color me intrigued."

Sighing, he shakes his head. "I mean it, Doyle. She doesn't *know*. Not any of it—even what she is. Hell, the snakes don't know. So leave it alone until we figure out why a lost one came back without being awakened first."

"Mate, I'm known for my... discretion. I won't let it slip, but I'm hurt that no one's asked me to unlock the secrets. It's one of my fundamental skills, as you well know," I wink at saucily, and he rolls his eyes at me. Taunting Edgar Olivier Boone III has been a substantial source of amusement for me since I arrived, and I doubt that will ever change. The git has a sense of humor, but he acts like he has a great stick shoved up his arse all the time.

"We could have had Prez work his mojo as well, but the Council says the directive is to allow things to progress naturally. They have their hands full with several lost ones emerging across the globe, and they're more focused on the ones they don't have eyes on. Tilly is among our kind, and they've even sent her a Guardian. Speaking of which…" He looks at his Apple watch and runs a hand through his hair in aggravation. "I have to meet her and Cantwell at a site. We've been ordered to get her and an incoming team of Guardians settled in very short order."

My eyes flash as I process that information. An individual Guardian *and* a team? What do the snakes think she's capable of? Boone is texting something, and I let my power slip to see if I can get a better read on him. It's easier for me to get into another member's mind if I do it when they aren't paying attention. He ignores me in favor of his phone, and a smile curls my lips. This is my opening.

~This woman pisses me off. The Council put me in charge of her accommodations, and I don't know why. I'm not a real estate agent; I'm a bookie and a judge. Cantwell runs a horse farm. Why the fuck are we the contacts and why the hell is there another team coming? Who are these special Guardians? Why is Saoirse hiding their identity? I won't let them hurt my drugar—even if it means losing my spot. The docs will agree. I need to talk to them after my meeting at the site. Yes, that's the plan. After I get rid of this annoying flea, I'll contact them. ~

Huh. A flea, am I? His Honor just earned himself about a thousand hours of juvenile delinquent pranks gone wrong, I think. Maybe I'll even tap his beloved football idiots. That should teach him some respect.

I shake my head, considering the other information I pilfered while he worried about someone sending him messages via electronics. He's worried that our local or global leaders have plans for the lovely Miss Whitley that are less than earnest. And that word he used... I've been around long enough to pick up a few languages and I know what he means. I wonder if the others know? Hell, I wonder if *she* knows. I doubt, given the speech the surly jock gave me moments ago.

Another interesting development. I love secrets.

"Boone, if you're done ranting at me, I have things to do. You know where to find me if you'd like your ass handed to you again." I give him a little wave as I saunter up the street towards the city building. His glare burns into my back and I laugh to myself, satisfied with the chaos I may have sown by taunting him. Alpha supes like Edgar are delightful to toy with—the dumber ones are easy to manipulate and the smart ones present just enough of a challenge to make this backwater town less grating.

When I reach the stairs, the giant eagle gives me a dirty look, using its sharp predator gaze to let me know it doesn't like me. That's too bad, but I suspect it's fond of Dr. Birdman and the little vet. Companion animals are attuned to their supes, so much so that many learn to summon them without words or sound. I've never had one choose me and it's always puzzled me. I figured it's because of my father's influence. Deceit isn't an emotion companions prefer to spread, I suppose.

"Doyle!"

I look up the stairs, arching a brow as our illustrious Mayor and her menacing lion approach. This is unexpected—Nelia works late into the evening. Tilting my head, I give her my most charming smile. "Afternoon, 'Nelia. What can I do for you on this balmy day?"

Her eye roll makes me grin wider, and Zareb shakes his mane. "Doyle Aloysius Haggerty. Do not use your... skills... on me, young man. There is an urgent meeting in the city that I must attend. I need you to lock up the office after Jolene leaves the archives. I sent Aldous and the others home before I left, but she's busy researching. Parents' Night is tonight, so she shouldn't be much longer. Just amuse yourself until she leaves, please."

Ah! What a fabulous opportunity to right our poor introduction last week. I'll head up and poke my head to say he—

"Do *not* disturb her, Doyle. Miss Whitley has much to learn about our town now that she's home, and I wouldn't want anyone to prevent her from grasping our history."

If those instructions were from anyone in Whistler's Hollow other than Mayor Cornelia Sykes, I would ignore them. However, even without Zareb, I know I don't want to cross her. So I nod. "Yes, ma'am. I understand the situation."

"Good. I'll be gone for a few days, and when I return, I hope to find Jolene settled in at school and her studio. We have made our guest welcome and I expect that Judge Boone and Mr. Cantwell will have achieved their tasks. I will appreciate anything you can do to speed that process along. I will make sure the Council informs your family."

The statuesque woman and the surly lion head for the parking lot, striding as though they own this place. They don't, but they hold the highest seats of power available here, and even I know I have to respect their wishes. Unfortunately, that means I have to assist that dickwaffle Boone and whatever cronies he's gathered for his project.

Fuck me raw, I hate small towns.

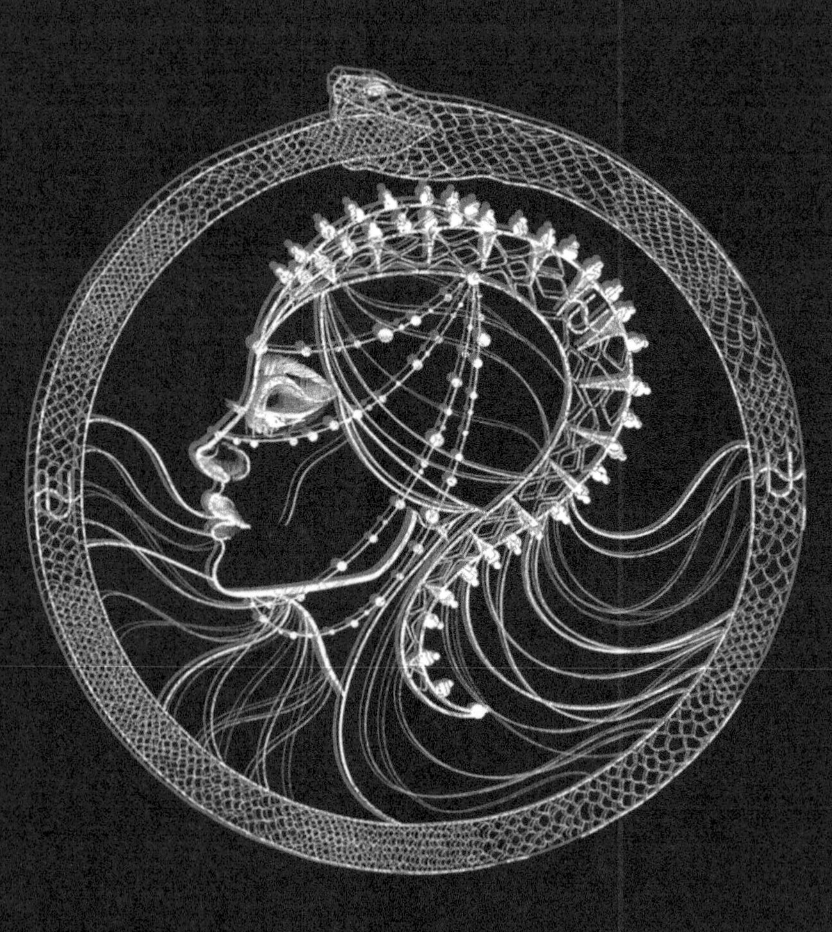

Mean Girls

Jolene

"We have to hurry!" I mutter to Jekyll and Hyde. They're prancing around the backyard as they chase Euryale. I know they'll get upset if I have to leave them, but I got home from my deep dive into town history later and it was dirtier than I expected. Neither Seer nor the boys were home yet, so I sent the animals outside with dinner while I hopped in the shower.

I picked out a decent outfit on my own—which is a miracle precipitated by Seer filling my closet—and apply a little makeup to appease the society mavens in town. I tossed my hair into a messy bun with loose curls because I'm hopeless with fancy hair shit and donned my favorite combos. If I have to wear a frilly dress, I'm at least going to come home able to feel my feet.

"Mrrp?" Hyde says, wandering up with wide eyes.

Of course, she's the first one to respond. She's the best behaved out of the three, and if I'd ever wondered if I have the patience for children, two guys and three pets tell me that's not the path for me. "Jekyll! Eury! I'm headed to the car and if you don't move your asses, I'm leaving you!"

Turning on my heel, I walk through the kitchen, picking up my messenger bag and a water bottle. My evening meds are in the front pocket, so I should be able to sneak them in after the first wave of parents. I can't forget; I learned a long time ago that my health quirks get worse when I do.

After an embarrassing incident in Prague, Seer programmed reminders in my phone that ping both it and the fancy Apple watch she bought me for Christmas last year. It helps if I'm at events like this where I get distracted by interacting with large groups of people and lose all track of space and time. As much as I enjoy being at home and comfy, I always feel refreshed and rejuvenated when I get home from a big party or outing.

I'm a study in contradictions, and no one has ever explained all the odd facets of my behavior.

As I open the door of the Impala, Jekyll and my winged guard zip up, and I grin. "Didn't want to be left to wait for the boys, eh?"

"Mow!" Jekyll agrees, as he jumps through the open window on the passenger side. Hyde follows, and Eury hovers above the roof as she waits for me to get settled and gun the engine.

It's time to face the firing squad.

"As I was saying, Sherilynn, the programs for younger children will get registered through my studio. I will host the registration and grand opening next weekend. With the move, the beginning of the school year, and the renovation of the studio space, I could not have the sign-ups available tonight," I explain, trying not to let my frayed nerves show.

"I should've known the Catastrophe wouldn't be able to organize something as ambitious as the Council promised when we voted on your license. It's criminal for you to tie up valuable real estate on the main strip if it's not open for business."

Sherilynn Foster-Grant is one of my former bullies. She's obviously continued that pattern in her adult life. I'm not intimidated by her posturing—Mayor Cornelia inspected my progress last week, so I know she's aware of the status of the gallery/studio.

However, Sherilynn is only one of the six parents with children in the Lower School who showed up at the high school teacher event to make their displeasure known. I'm not shocked there's a coordinated effort to smear my name before I get started; in fact, I'm surprised I have seen none of the boys with them. There's nothing an elite family loves more than lording their connections over anyone they consider beneath them. Lysander, Billy, and Joe should be here expressing righteous fury along with their wives.

After going to the Speakeasy, I think it's possible Benjy has changed. I can't resist twisting the knife a little—Sherilynn has been the nastiest so far. "Sherilynn, if Benjy would like to see the remodeling, I'd be happy to show him the progress. I know it impressed Nelia when she stopped by last week."

Her face contorts in rage, and she goes as red as a beet. The color contrasts with her platinum locks, and for a second, I get lost in imagining a painting of a tomato with a blond wig. Her voice screeches as she glares daggers at me. "*You! I never!*"

I watch her stalk off with the fury of a valkyrie in puzzlement. What in the hell did I say? According to social media, she married Benjy and they have three kids. He runs the bookstore and speakeasy; she runs the bakery.

Did I miss some new rule that I can't mention a spouse to one of these twits?

"They're getting divorced," a low voice murmurs in my ear.

When I turn, I see the handsome history teacher giving me a tiny grin. I don't know how he sneaked up behind me without my noticing, but he must not be dangerous because both of my cats are still planted in the large nest with their tails flicking lazily. I narrow my eyes at Hyde and she maps as if I should understand. Putting my hand over my eyes, I pinch the bridge of my nose and whisper back to Hugo. "How ugly is the divorce?"

"Very," he replies. "He filed at the courthouse yesterday and there was a screaming match in front of Edgar's door."

"Son of a pumpkin eating pole dancer," I grumble. "I'll *never* hear the end of this, and she's never liked me. Any chance you have the scoop on *why* they're splitting?"

Hugo gives me a mysterious smile. "Perhaps, but it's not my story to tell. You know the Hollow better than I—it'll be public news soon enough, I'm sure."

Great. This dude is swathed in riddles every time I meet him. "If you say so. Thanks for the heads up," I reply as I brace myself for the next wave of parents.

A small wave and a wink are my answer as he disappears. There must be a passage or crawl space or some bloody way to get in through there and I'm annoyed as hell that he knows and I don't. I continue muttering under my breath as I shuffle papers around, vexed by men, bitchy rich women, and life.

It's not his fault that no one is monitoring the parents coming into my room despite not having children old enough to attend this school. Every staff member Sherilynn passed in the hallway knew what she was up to, and they did nothing.

That feels familiar, and I rub my hand on my chest. Whistler's Hollow hasn't changed since I was a kid, and I'm disappointed. The secrets I'm hunting here are hidden—especially given the lack of detail in the town records from thirty years ago.

I can only assume that's where the 'takeover' began, and it's not long after I was born. I don't know why my parents never talked to me about our family history or why the Hollow seems to have changed around 1990, but I can feel in my gut that I'm on to something. I may be here quite a while ferreting out the truth, and though I'm much stronger now, I can't imagine re-living my high school years as an adult.

Girls like Sherilynn in my face will lead to terrible things; look at the idiot at Jamie's farm. I couldn't stop myself from putting her in her place, and I won't be able to do that at school or at the gallery. Hopelessness overtakes me and I plop down on the beanbag next to my cats. "What if I can't do it, guys?"

"Can't do it? That's not the Tilly I know."

With an enormous sigh, I turn my head to glare at Edgar. His intrusion on my introspective moment is not only unwanted, but it exacerbates my anxiety. After all, he was part of the crew that damn near destroyed me as a teen. My hands shake a little and I turn back to Jekyll and Hyde, who are ignoring the towering ex-bully as if he's not even in the room.

I scratch Hyde's ears, shrugging as I murmur, "I survived this once and came out stronger, Teddy. I don't know if I can do it again. I've lived a fantastic life since I left this town—jet-setting, meeting Seer, hobnobbing with kings and CEOS—none of them saw the awkward teenager who spent most of her time at home alone with a book. The men and women I was with didn't know about the Catastrophe or how it affected me all the way through college. These people do." I look up at him, my gaze fierce as I meet his eyes. "*You* do."

His head drops, and he spins on his heel, whistling. Hecate and Kali come bounding in, yipping at my cats, and they jump to their feet to meet them. "Companion area. Now," Edgar says sternly. The hounds bob their heads and trot out with my cats in tow.

I gape, my mouth hanging open like a fish on the line. Jekyll and Hyde don't take orders from anyone but me; Wolfie has to cajole them with treats, and they ignore Seer and Prez. What the hell? "How did you *do* that?" I ask as I continue to stare at the doorway. "Do you have magical powers?"

"Not exactly," he replies, his eyes dancing as he gives me a half grin and walks over to the door. I watch him flip the sign on it to 'In Conference' and lock it with a click. "But I know how to give orders and everyone around me falls in line."

My eyes narrow, and I rise to my feet. "Not me, buddy. Since high school, I take orders from no one."

"Well, that's the Tilly I like to see: fiery, giving me shit, and messing up the natural order of everything."

That fucker. He spouted that tripe just to rile me up! "Look, Teddy, about the other night…"

Taking the room in three quick strides, he stands toe to toe with me. His expression is softer than I've ever seen as he cups my cheek and brushes his thumb over my bottom lip. "I didn't know how to handle it. The past… the present… the things you don't know. I still don't."

I swallow hard, unwilling to let all of it go. Whatever is going on with Teddy isn't like the quiet siege of Wolfie and Presley—they slid into my life like they'd always been there.

This is so much more complicated, and if I still don't know how I feel about them, how can I know what I feel about my tormentor becoming my bedmate? It's like there are parts of me straining to be freed, and my mind is fighting their release. I don't understand why everything has reversed since I stepped foot in my hometown, but I can't get a grip on anything.

Teddy leans in, brushing his lips over mine before he speaks again. "My...family...has a long history in this town. There have always been expectations, even when I was little.

Unfortunately for my father, his aspirations for me are not possible, even if I wanted to fulfill them. When I grew up, it hit him like a feed bag to the face. So now... I can be me without reprisal. He doesn't dictate my actions, and neither does my mother."

Frowning, I tilt my head and look at him. "They did before? You were always the bad boy of the elites. You ran a statewide gambling operation, Teddy."

"Run," he grins, his white teeth flashing as he grins. "The Honorable Edgar Olivier Boone III, bookmaker extraordinaire, at your service."

"Are you shitting me, Teddy? You *still* run the state betting...as a *judge?*"

He shrugs, his expression roguish as he pushes his hair out of his eyes. "Who better to keep a multi-state operation that brings in millions of dollars in revenue secret? No one wants to rat it out for fear of the gossip making its way to my courtroom."

I push him away, putting pieces together in my head. "You asshole! Are you the reason my background check failed? Is your... ring... on the F.B.I.'s radar? Do they think I'll lead them to your crime empire?"

One of his large hands grabs my wrists, and before I know it, he has me pinned against the back wall of the studio. His free hand slides up my side to rest on my throat, giving it a little squeeze as he whispers in my ear. "*Drugar*, they don't even know I exist. I'm the Kaiser Soze of the underworld. My connections are much deeper than my little hobby."

He's not keeping me from breathing, but the pressure is doing something else to my body. Every cell screams I should teach him a lesson —that I'm in charge here—but other parts of my mind whisper it's okay to *choose* to let him lead.

Squeezing my eyes shut, I try to focus my mind, but I can't. Too many sensations and thoughts are flooding my senses. It's like when I forget to—fuck. This happens when I forget to take my meds, but at this moment, I don't care. I'll deal with the aches and pains later; future Jolene is going to be sore, anyway.

A low, rumbling growl echoes from his chest when I slide my legs on either side of his to fit our hips together. The hand holding my wrists lets go, and he uses that arm to tug on my thigh until I wrap my legs around his waist. The thumb on my pulse caresses gently, and I give him a lazy, heavy lidded expression. I've acquiesced, and that's as much confirmation of my submission as he's going to get.

After all, he's not really in charge, now is he?

Level Up

"You know, I've half a mind to suggest you wore a dress for a reason," Teddy murmurs. His teeth nibble along my jaw, but the hands moving up my thighs are more demanding.

I don't answer, deciding he can wonder whether I considered liaisons with him or anyone else this evening. Besides, it's amusing to feel the growls vibrate across my skin when I frustrate him, and before I know it, I get what I was looking for. When he lifts his head with eyes full of fire, I smirk. "I could ask the same thing about these easy access athletic pant things you've got on. I mean, one yank and you're on display, Teddy bear."

This time, he snarls. "Watch it, Tilly. If you poke the bear, you'd better be ready to handle the paws."

"I've been ready for five minutes at least. Are we going to fuck or swing our dicks around, Teddy bear?" I shoot back, enjoying his ever tightening grip on my body as I agitate him. He can't decide if he likes the Teddy bear thing or not, and I can't help but continue to push his buttons until he cracks.

"Your mouth is less annoying when it's put to good use," he mutters, diving in to kiss me so thoroughly that I can't breathe. When he lifts his head, he whips us around, walking away from the wall and over to the wide work table nearby. Dropping my ass on it, he smirks back when I yelp. "The landing is the hardest part, right?"

I rear back and punch him in the arm, but that only seems to make him grin wider. The son of a bitch likes a little pain, does he? That's information I'll find handy later, I'm sure. For now, I want him to quit playing around and give me what he's promised. "If I'm not coming in the next five minutes, Edgar Boone, I will find someone else to do your job."

His eyes narrow, and he drops to his knees. "I love a challenge, Tilly. Make sure you're keeping time."

Before I can retort, he yanks the thong clean off me and licks his way up my thighs. The fight's not gone out of me, but I'm distracted. No way in hell I can time anything, and something tells me he's serious. I lift my arm and mutter to my watch, asking Siri to set a timer for five minutes. The bitch isn't getting laid, so she can track Teddy's prowess. A dark chuckle vibrates over me, and the Honorable Judge Boone pushes my thighs apart and dives in like he's starving.

My eyes roll back into my head as he thrusts two fingers inside of me, pumping them as he nibbles and licks along the most sensitive parts of me. I'll give Teddy one thing: he does nothing half-way, and my back arches off the table when he suckles my clit. I can't scream or it'll draw attention, so I focus on biting my lip and rocking into his touch. The noises he's making aren't loud enough for anyone but me to hear, but they're so primal and hot that a fucking nun would beg for more. It's like he's possessed.

Fingertips curl inside of me, and I almost lose control of myself. I dig my nails into the wooden table, arching into his mouth. "Teddy…"

He doesn't stop; instead, he slips a third finger inside of me, pushing me faster and harder towards the inevitable. When the trembles take over my body, I feel my skin heat like before and my chest tighten. The sensation of something breaking free within me slams into my gut, and I raise one of my hands to muffle the moan that I can't hold in. The raven haired fiend is covering me in a blink, yanking my thighs up as he slams into me with a force hard enough to make the table scoot.

"*Drugar*," he murmurs into my ear. His voice is low and dark, like a velvet glove running over my body. "I can feel the heat of your skin; let yourself go. Don't fight it, Tilly."

His hips piston against me and I squeeze his cock like I'm trying to wring every drop of cum from his body. I have no idea what the hell he wants me to let go of, but in this moment I'd turn myself into fucking Elsa if he keeps fucking me like this. I open my eyes and turn my head, meeting his gaze as our bodies move. A languid, drunken haze slips over me as the next orgasm builds, and I must be drunk on dick, because his eyes flash black and then a brilliant red as he looks at me. "Teddy, what in the—oh...."

I don't have time to finish my sentence because my climax smacks into me, and my body lifts off the wood to meet him in a symphony of groans and slapping flesh. My hands come up and bury in his hair as he darts his head in and bites my neck. I've never been a vampire coveter like many girls my age were during the Twilight/Buffy years, but I'll be damned if those teeth don't rocket me into yet another peak. His voice is low as he mutters something unintelligible and foreign sounding, and I have to bite my lower lip hard to keep from screaming as pleasure courses through my veins.

When our bodies come to a stop, his weight blankets me, and I suck in deep breaths. My pulse is racing, and every inch of my skin feels like electricity is dancing over it. Licking my lip, I realize I drew blood, and a soft giggle escapes before I can catch it. Teddy lifts his head, tilting it to the side as he studies me. I wait for him to speak, but he doesn't. He leans in and licks the blood off, a growl of satisfaction rumbling in his chest.

"That's... well, it's kinda hot. I mean, all of this was hot. You're hot. I..." I let my head thunk back against the wood, closing my eyes as embarrassment floods me. Jesus, this town brings out the most awkward fucking parts of me, like it's a goddamned documentary on being a nerd.

Edgar doesn't answer. He licks my cheek and buries his face in my hair.

What in the actual fuck is going on?

He's being super weird and—holy mother of cheese eating Frenchman. We just screwed our brains out...in my classroom. The door is locked, but we're at school. It's fucking Parents' Night, and I'm sprawled over a drawing table with a half naked judge, cum on my thighs, and ripped panties.

A knock on the door pauses my mental freak out, and I clear my throat, trying to gather my remaining wits about me. "Yes?"

The voice on the other side of the door answers in a wry drawl, "I don't know what you've been getting up to in there, sugarplum, but it smells delicious."

"Wolfie?" I squeak. "What are you doing here? You were meeting with the sheikh."

"I did, and he wants to meet with you this weekend. I promised I'd come set it up with you right away, but it seems like I've interrupted a *very* important conference."

I can hear the laughter in his voice, but I can't scold him because Teddy is still weird as fuck. "Um, well, that's true. But... I could use... some help? I think there's a back way in here; earlier Hugo got in without—"

Like magic, the door opens a crack, and McBabyVet slips in, then re-locks the door behind him. His eyes are full of amusement as he looks at us, and I wrinkle my nose. As if I knew I was going to *break* Edgar Boone this evening. How could I have predicted *that?*

"Having trouble with the bully, darlin'?" he asks, his lips curving up as he walks over and tucks a strand of hair behind my ear.

I frown. He's not even the least bit concerned that I'm laying here with Teddy dribbling down my legs in the art room. *Why* isn't he concerned with that? I mean, Presley, I get—they're together already, but Edgar should be an issue, right?

"Relax, sugarplum. Different doesn't equal bad. If you're sweet on this asshole, I'm not upset. As long as he treats you like the queen you are and respects our place in your heart, Prez and I are happy to share." His eyes cut to Teddy, and he chuckles. "Although, I think this instance, you may have... ahem... bitten off more than you can chew, Boone."

"What in the fuck does that mean? And why is he acting so damned odd?" I demand, pushing on the heavy shoulders pinning mine down fruitlessly. "We have to get him off me before anyone else finds out we should *not* be unsupervised!"

Wolfie grins, walking around the table. He picks up the torn thong, whistling, and I glare. The lace gets stuffed in his pocket as he sidles up to Edgar. Laying a hand on his back, he winks at me before leaning down to whisper something in his ear. The body crushing mine stiffens, then lifts off of me, and I can breathe again. Edgar looks down at me with a sheepish smile, and I give them both my best death stare.

"How did you do that? That wasn't even English, and since when does Edgar Boone speak another language? Your father would tar your hide, buster."

His chuckle is dark as he adjusts his clothing and sits up on the table. "I told you, my father doesn't control me anymore."

"It was Aramaic," Wolfie says, his eyes full of mischief. "But I think that's a story for later. Do you keep wipes in here? I'd assume you do, because duh...art."

Wipes?! What in the... oh. Jesus refried Christ in a tortilla.

He's trying to help me get cleaned up before a Sherilynn clone comes banging on the door of... where we've been banging. "Um, yeah. In the back room? By the sink?"

Teddy reaches over and grabs my hand, tugging me to his side. His fingers stroke over the mark he left absently as he murmurs, "I didn't hurt you, did I? I mean, I didn't intend to—"

"No. Absolutely not. In fact, I feel…" I struggle for the words, not knowing how to analyze, much less express, the emotions careening around in my heart and mind at the moment.

"Free?" he asks, his smile hopeful.

"Hm no. Not free, but…like a slight weight has lifted? Like a part of me is lighter?" I look at him, and something flashes behind his eyes. I don't know what it means, but his expression says that he understands. "I have a lot of baggage, I suppose. From here, my parents, my life before I got out of this town. Maybe one piece of it got chucked out of the plane."

"That sounds delightful, sugarplum!" My adorable vet walks up, planting a kiss on my head and then Edgar's, and hands me the pack of wipes. "Might I suggest you get cleaned up while His Honor charms Bobbi Jo into letting you leave a little early? We can pick up the animals, meet Prez at your house, and order takeout. That should relax you."

My lips curve and I look at them pleadingly. "Can I have a milkshake?"

Teddy bursts out laughing and squeezes me against his side. "Tilly, after that performance, I think you can have *two*."

Hot damn. Orgasms, food, and two milkshakes? A girl could get used to this.

Circus

"**I** need lots of bloody booze," Seer mutters, looking at the list in her hand.

Laughing, I follow her around Atwater's as she picks out food and drinks to feed an army. She insisted I come with her to stock the pantry in her shiny new house—the one I didn't know she was buying until this morning.

According to my irreverent friend, she's taken a shine to my 'humble beginnings' and wants to put down roots here. It's a bit sus because Seer hasn't maintained an actual residence of her own for more than the length of her contract the entire time I've known her. She stores most of her belongings at her family estate in Ireland and buys what she needs when she moves.

Not once has she considered purchasing a space of her own.. until now.

However, she convinced Jamie to sell her a tract of land that's down the road from me, and I can't find it in me to question her about it. I missed my friend in Richmond, and the thought of being alone in this town makes me sad. Obviously, I have the boys, but I'll make no female friends here with the Bitch Squad on high alert. I could use an ally I trust that I'm not fucking.

Of course, it won't help my reputation to flit about town with another misfit, but who cares?

I see all the judgmental stares the buddies and genteel Southerners are giving my bestie as we stroll through the store. She's dressed slightly less wacky than normal, but her mere presence demands everyone gawp like they're at a carnival freak show.

Fuck them and their shitty attitudes. Seer is the kindest, most loyal person I've ever known. If they don't want to get to know her because she's more authentic than anyone here, it tells me everything I need to know about *their* worth.

I link my arm with hers, grinning as I reply, "Definitely. Lots of hooch and lots of terrible food, plus milkshake fixins."

Her laugh tinkles like a wind chime and I tug her towards the produce section to grab what we'll need for my biggest vice. As we pick out fruits, she tilts her head and studies me.

"Peanut, I surprised you with my plans, and I'm sorry. I know you don't take rapid change well. I should have told you where I was going when I headed out to arrange all of this. It's a big deal for me —my folks are even sending my stuff from the castle. I want to be with you, and whatever brought you back here doesn't seem like a quick stay."

Blinking, I whisper, "You're having your stuff shipped over? Like, all of it? Even the wardrobe?"

She nods, giving me a shrug. "I am. This is my new base of operations, so to speak. Me ma was feckin' thrilled. You don't know half of it."

"Seer, you said you'd never settle down—that you have wanderlust in your veins."

"Well, I do, Peanut, but we can still travel the world together, even if we have houses like actual adults. It's not illegal, I'm told," Seer teases as she tosses me an orange across the aisle.

As I catch the fruit, my vision blurs, and a wisp of a memory flashes in my mind. I'm small, and I'm in Atwater's—maybe for the first time.

My mother and father are fussing over ripened fruit, and a boy tosses me an orange. I drop it, and my mother scolds me for playing with the store's stock. The boy winks at me, and I turn away, mad that he got me in trouble. He's trouble, and I know it.

"She's not lost, Andrew. They're wrong. They gave us a fake. I told you not to make Xerxes angry at the meeting. He has no patience for your kind."

"Relax, Ellie. Jolene is one of them. She'll grow up stronger than the others and when you train her, you'll rise the ranks just how you planned. Be easy with her. She's just getting to know us."

I suck in a rattling breath as my eyes find focus again. Reality snaps into place and I see Seer pondering over a flat of strawberries none the wiser. When my breathing returns to normal, I steady myself on the cart.

What in unholy fuck was that?

The scene wasn't part of anything I remember from my childhood, and the things my parents were saying made no sense. Who is Xerxes? What did she mean by 'lost'? How could their child be fake? Is this part of the mystery I came to solve or a random synapse misfire?

Shaking my head, I type the description into my phone. I'm keeping all my notes on the Whistler's Hollow puzzles there because I've never been able to trust my memory. I need all the myriad of clues and thoughts somewhere I can access when I'm searching and where I can noodle them.

I need to figure out why parents were talking in riddles, and as if we'd just met. It's the key to something, but I don't know what.

Maybe if I can find out who the hell that boy was, he'll have answers about my younger years—if he's even real.

THERE'S STILL CONSTRUCTION AT SEER'S PLACE, BUT THE SPEED THE crew is working at is inhuman. There's fifty of them and they move like lightning as they flit around, inside and out. None of them gives me a second glance, but they all dip their heads to her respectfully when we pass.

Maybe her parents hired them?

I've only been to her family estate twice, but they have some nebulous connection to royal lineage, and the staff made me feel like I was living in Downton Abbey. I wouldn't put it past her overbearing mother to find a specific company and pay them through the nose to get Seer's first house built in record time. At the rate they are going, it'll be completed by the end of next week.

Seer heads for the kitchen, dropping her bags on the granite counter. "It's grand, innit, Peanut?"

I arch a brow at her. "Yes, but it's built to house an army. Who are you planning on kidnapping to fill these rooms?"

She shrugs and winks. "I may invite some old friends to stay once it's ready. Or... who knows? Maybe I'll build meself a polycule like yours."

"A... a what?" I choke.

"*Please*, Peanut. You've got the three eejits wrapped around your pinky, and I'll bet they aren't the only lads you've had run-ins with. If you keep at it, you'll have an entire group of lovers feeding you grapes within the month."

My eyes widen and I shake my head. "No way. Not a fucking chance. Three dudes and three pets are *more* than enough. I'm already feeling claustrophobic because I'm almost never alone. That stupid prankster is making them all edgy."

As she puts away the groceries, Seer gives me a wry look. "Prankster? I doubt the animals would react this way if they felt you were safe. Men overreact all the time, but animals have good instincts."

"I don't understand why anyone would lurk around my house. I don't have a lot of valuables; hell, I'm not even in the top twenty wealthiest people in the Hollow. They don't want to steal something. I've only just returned, so I haven't made any *new* enemies."

Giggling, she waves a bottle of vodka at me. "Maybe it's your *old* enemies. They can't be happy that you're gobbling up all the eligible bachelors. Are all of your ex-bullies spoken for?"

I frown, pulling my laptop out of my messenger bag. "You know, I haven't delved that deep into the townsfolk yet. Lemme do a cursory check." With that, I plop on the stool by the counter and connect to the hotspot on my phone. "You gotta get your Wi-Fi squared away."

Seer rolls her eyes and continues putting away the rest of the food and drinks we filled our cart with. "Yeah, yeah. Give me time. I've got a mess of plates in the bloody air, you know."

"Mmm," I reply, clicking at the keys as I surf through the dark web sites until I find one that should give me enough background to be useful. I pull up another screen with a list of ex-schoolmates, humming under my breath as I start queries.

"Speaking of animals, how did you get away from your menagerie?"

Blinking, I look up. "Uh, Teddy took them to the park with Kali and Hecate. I'm thinking that idiot doesn't work at all. The Judge thing is just a feint." A beeping noise catches my attention and I watch the crawl of information trickle into each small window. "Sherilynn is getting divorced. No one knows why, but it's recent, and it's going to be ugly. At least, that's what Hugo told me."

"Hugo? And who is *this* valiant young suitor?" she cackles.

"Another teacher, you silly woman. He's not a suitor. In fact, I'm not even sure he likes me. He's incredibly hard to read and super mysterious." Another ping shows me the next name's info and I grin. "Jillian married Billy and has *five* boys. She has to be livid with her uterus."

"Why? Seems like she's had a good run and can shut it down for a bit. This Billy should climb off her for a decade or two," Seer says, bobbing her brows. "Five boys is enough for you Yanks to field a basketball team, you know."

I snort, covering my mouth. I doubt Billy's kids will play basketball; he never grew beyond 5'6" when I knew him. "I guess that's true." I watch the next query finish and curse. Damnit. "Ophelia married Jax and has four kids. They're all old enough to be pains in my ass—some are starting WHFS. That's gonna *suck*."

"Only you would worry about the kids of your childhood bullies. Even if the little shites are clones of their parents, you're in charge, Peanut. Teach them a lesson if need be."

"If only, Seer. The parents have control of that school, I guarantee. I like Bobbi Jo, but I don't get the impression that she's in charge of anything. The staff run roughshod over her, and I'd bet the rest of the town does, too. It's a shame—she seems like she could be a good boss." My friend hands me a rocks glass with a neat bourbon and I laugh. "Well, a shot of bourbon fixes damned near everything."

"Shot of bourbon for you, Jameson for me," she agrees. "Is that all of them?"

My hand flies to my face as the last two results flash on my screen. "No. Reese has two girls starting high school, and Amy Behle—the queen belle herself—has three kids in various stages of schooling. The Universe hates me, Seer; I told you! That woman makes the arctic tundra look warm, and just because she wasn't there last night doesn't mean she won't come after me to amuse herself. Amy Matilda Behle is nightmare material."

Cocking her red brow at me, she shakes her head. "I don't believe someone that small can hurt a woman like you, Peanut. But if you're worried about these bitches, I suggest you circle the wagons with your boys before they take aim there. Women don't fight with fists—more's the pity. They fight by taking away the things you love."

A sharp ache builds in my chest as that statement hits me. Oh, hell no. *Hell no.* Those bitches aren't taking my men. "I mean, they're married, except for Sherilynn. Outside of cheating, which I think would go poorly within town, what can they do?"

Seer's expression is grim. "They could send single friends or family members, Peanut. Never discount the ugly things sisters—familial or organizational—will do for one another."

The look in her eyes makes me want to question how she knows this, but I'm too busy having a mini panic attack of my own. "I've… I've got to go home. Now."

Her harsh snort follows me as I race out the door, headed for my house before I lose my shit in the kitchen.

"Good luck!"

I'll need it. There are serious conversations to be had, and I don't have a fucking clue what to say.

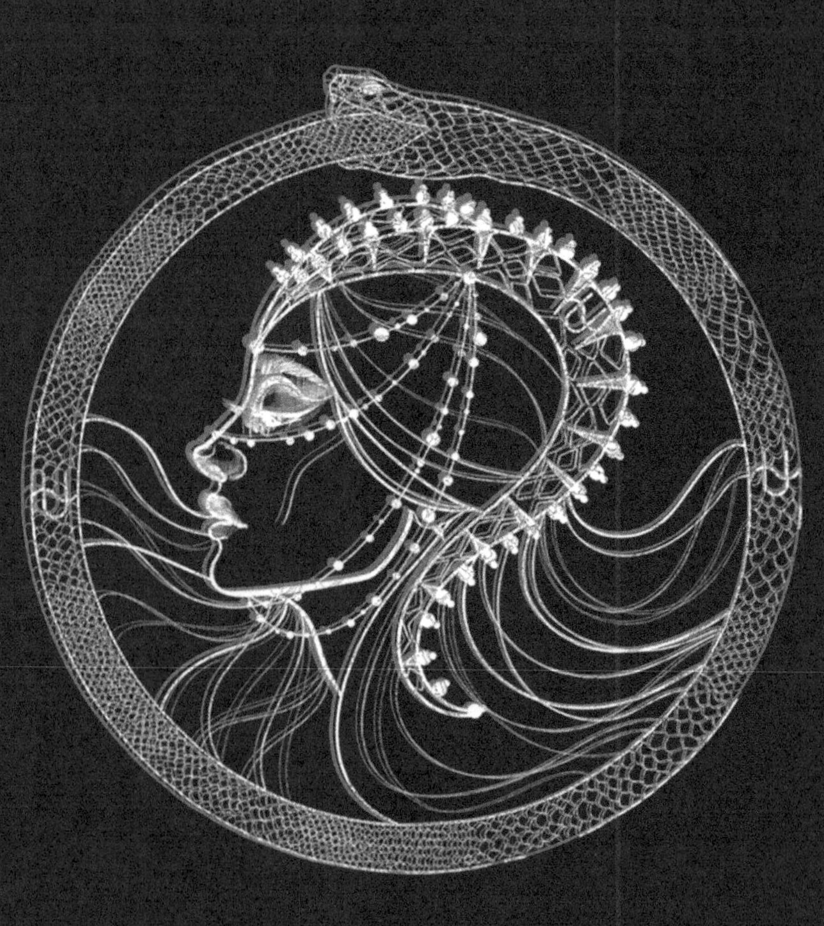

I Choose You

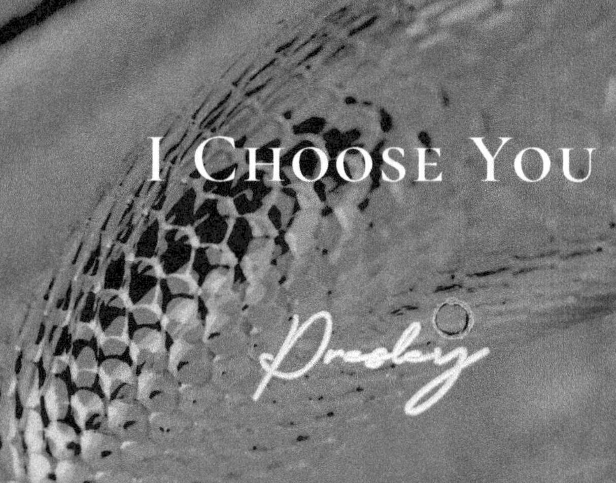

Sliding into the long drive next to the Cobra belonging to Boone, I turn the motor off. I'm not sure why Magpie called a meeting, but Lucy sounded worried. I've been busy with my practice because school is starting next week, so I haven't been around as much as I would prefer. The influx of both normal patients and the special ones has consumed me—being the only doctor in town is rough this time of year.

Spring is much *worse, but the beginning of the school year is a close second.*

I worry about our magpie.

Being a teacher at WFHS is going to put her in the middle of several vicious circles, and I don't want any of them to use a loophole to make her aware of things she doesn't need to know until its time. My power tells me she's getting closer, but the women in this town already have her in their sights because of the past. It's a very thin tightrope to walk, and I hope Lucy and Boone will help me maintain the status quo as long as possible.

The thought of her being hurt bothers me more than I care to admit. Before I got assigned here, I tomcatted around Asia consulting for various communities of supes. I'd just graduated med school at State, and the Society felt I was best positioned to work with young emerging supes there because I attended secondary school in Japan. Traveling around to meet different species and struggling teens appealed to me, so I happily obliged.

I couldn't turn down the assignment if I wanted to, but I've always appreciated that they used my talents for something positive. My kind has a long history of being placed in problematic positions because of our abilities. The suicide rate for my species is much higher than average, and my parents were both casualties of such an arrangement when I was a teenager.

Sighing, I shake my head to clear the threads of pain from my psyche. The past is the past, and dwelling on pain has solved nothing. True healing comes with acceptance of the good and the bad, and my assignment to Whistler's Hollow was specifically to allow me to do so. Not because of my parents, but because of the young shifter I lost in China.

Guardians never get over losing a charge, and I suppose I haven't, either.

I open the car door, swinging my long legs out to roll to my feet. The vintage gullwing Mercedes SL 300 fits me like a glove, and I paid more for it than my first house.

However, in this town, you stick out if you drive a normal car, and the Society wants us to blend in as much as possible. It keeps the illusion of being a cookie cutter rich Southern town when visitors float through for various reasons. We have to set expectations for the young possibles—to be one of us is to present a certain image to the world. It helps us stay hidden and survive.

At least, that's how it is at Project Chimera HQ in America. The enclaves I visited in Asia had vastly different rules, and I assume it's about respecting cultural norms. Whatever it takes to hide in plain sight, that's what the Society aims for.

I walk up to my magpie's door, hoping she doesn't have bad news. Lucy's grown quite fond of her, and I think they may have completed part of the bond. He won't talk about it, and I understand why. He and Boone both had no choice, but they can't run around blabbing about a process Jolene doesn't understand. If it gets out, someone will tell her out of spite and ruin a deeply special thing for them.

Petty jealousy shouldn't be how Magpie finds out that information.

"Prez!" Jolene says, throwing her arms around me as she opens the door before I can knock.

My brows furrow. She's not this effusive normally, and I don't smell alcohol. At least, not fresh booze anyway. Why is she so affectionate? Magpie gestures to the stairs, and turns to climb them, her ponytail bouncing behind her. If I wasn't suspicious before, I am now.

"Not that I'm opposed to going to your nest, magpie, but I'm curious why a meeting with all three of us is being held there?" She stops on the stairs, giving me a blinding smile. Her green eyes dance with a fire I haven't seen before, and her gaze hits me in the chest like a lead weight. My breath catches, and I just stare at her like a virgin in a strip club.

"We have things to discuss, McSteamy. Follow me and you'll see," Jolene smiles again and my heart damn near stops.

What is she doing to me?

Rubbing my chest, I ignore the source of my powers as it awakens. Whatever changes Magpie's gone through, she's not ready for the truth about all of us, and if Reiki takes control, there won't be a choice.

I follow Jolene into the bedroom, my eyes seeking Lucy first. He gives me a surprised look when he feels how close Reiki is to the surface. His nature is less volatile than mine because it's not singular, and he's used to me having precision control. Edgar is pacing frenetically, and I don't know what's up his ass, but he needs to lock that shit down. He's well known for losing control of his powers.

"I asked you to meet me here because we need to set some ground rules," Jolene says. She's twisting her fingers nervously, but her expression is determined. "I've never... well, I've done SOME of this before, but not like this. You'll have to be patient with me."

"Just talk to us, sugarplum. What has you in knots?"

That's Lucy to a tee. He's the antithesis of what everyone assumes his people to be, and I smile as he reaches his hand out to get our woman to settle on the bed next to him. As soon as she sits, it's like all the tension ebbs out, and she clasps his hand.

"I want to define our situation. This is the first time since college that I've even considered having people in my life regularly—I mean, outside of Seer, which isn't the same. That story is long and I'll share it with you later, but it taught me to be guarded. So you three are the first people—male or female—to stay in my life for more than a night in years."

Lucy looks taken aback, but I suspected as much. Our girl has struggled with things that should have been easy, and while it amused me to watch her hide it, this is a big step. Edgar crosses the room, dropping to a knee.

"Tell us what you need, drugar," he murmurs as he looks up at her.

That was unexpected. I almost feel like I should alert the press. The alpha of all alphas just kneeled in front of a woman he bullied out of town fourteen years ago. I'd need pictures to prove this happened if I told anyone. "I agree. We need to know what you want, Jolene."

Her lips curve into a pout as I use her real name. "This is hard for me. It requires trust I'm not sure I'm capable of, and vulnerability I never show. But… I want this," she gestures at us awkwardly, "to work. I want all of you, and I won't settle for less. I don't *know* why, because I haven't wanted anyone to stay around since Trevor. I've been happy taking what I need and moving on. The thought of anyone touching *any* of you has my gut twisted into knots, though."

"Sugarplum, you know what I told you at the farm," Lucy says, squeezing her hand before bringing it to his lips. "I'm yours." I arch a brow, and he chuckles. "And Prez', of course."

Boone nods, taking her other hand in his. "*Drugar*, I told you yesterday how I felt."

"Well, you apologized for leaving me alone to wonder if I was going to end up getting roasted on social media. And you intimated that your bullying had to do with your parents, and you regretted it. But you didn't say what you felt." Her chin lifts and I can feel the air in the room change as she steels herself for disappointment.

If only she knew.

"Tilly, I've always liked you. I wanted to be a part of your life from the minute I first saw you—there were extenuating circumstances. Both of our parents were less than thrilled at our connection. You probably can't remember…" he trails off and I know he's getting close to lines he can't cross yet.

I save him by cutting in. "I played around a lot after college, too. I traveled to Asia extensively for work before I settled here. I understand the appeal of having no ties, no one to hurt you, and nothing to hold you back. However, I knew when I saw you telling a story to a harpy eagle you were terrified of moments before that I couldn't let you get away. I don't know where we're all going, but I'm on board, even if the crew gets bigger."

Lucy and Edgar give me questioning looks, but I ignore them. Something about our magpie tells me she's not finished gathering yet, and I want her to know I won't stand in her way if another potential steps up to the plate. Crossing my arms over my chest, I lean against the wall, waiting for the other two to chime in. If they don't, we're going to have issues later.

"I'm happy to share," Lucy whispers, giving her a shy smile. "I want you to be happy, sugarplum."

"For fuck's sake…" Edgar sighs and rolls his eyes. His hand reaches up, and he runs his fingers over a mark on her neck I didn't see until now. "I'm not threatened by these idiots or anyone else you decide to take a shine to. I know what I want."

I squint at the mark, walking closer with an air of nonchalance that I don't believe. When I see the shape, I glare at the back of the judge's head. Lucy tilts his head, and I shake mine in response.

That son of a bitch.

Edgar Olivier Boone III has been hiding a third, and that's so exceedingly rare that they don't even *teach* agents or Guardians about triplásia. I only recognize it because I've seen him lose control of the other two sides.

This bite mark is something different, and I'm going to call my mentor, Yoshiro, about it. He's retired a hundred years ago, but that's a speck of time for a dragon. He served the Society for five hundred years before he retired, and he trained me when I got assigned to my concierge position.

I've only heard of a *triplásia*[1] a few times. Yoshi said they suspected they had one about twenty years ago, but that can't be Jolene or Edgar. They're too young. Before Project Chimera, it was impossible to know how many and what supes were intermingling because it was beneath us.

It still is, and that's why the Society keeps our enclaves so well disguised.

As odd as it sounds, I wonder if Boone even knows. It would mean he had to be a lost one, not a true Boone heir, and that secret might be one worth killing over. Senator Boone wouldn't want the humans knowing about his son, and he wouldn't want the town knowing Edgar wasn't genetically a Boone. This could get interesting if it leaks.

Best to keep it away from that sneaky bastard Haggerty, then. He and the judge are like oil and water as it is. He'd relish humiliating his self-identified nemesis.

"Magpie, I believe you said you'd done *some* of this before. I'm inclined to believe it's not asking three idiots to be your boyfriends. What did you mean?"

Her cheeks flush, and it's absolutely delightful. Jolene doesn't show her soft side often and today is a smorgasbord of adorable tics. "I said that. But I feel like we have to address the leather elephant in the room or I'd hate myself."

"Leather… elephant?" Edgar chokes.

Huffing, she glares down at him. "Yes. It may not be the greatest metaphor, but you, Teddy, have a domination fetish. Little Wolfie over there likes to be topped, and the good doctor is a switch. I'm not stupid or naïve. If that's going to be part of our lives, then you all need to understand ME, and we will come to an agreement."

My mouth drops open. I sure as fuck didn't expect her to say *that*. "Magpie…"

"Prez, she's right. We have to say the words and you know it."

Jolene nods, smiling at him softly. "I know you said them to me, but are you comfortable with everyone else, or do you have a line?"

Edgar arches a brow, and I shrug. "I'm game, regardless. But I'd need express consent for anything more than typical club play—on either side of the fence."

"Prez, y'all won't be able to handle me." My magpie titters and I grin back at her.

"Why is that, Tilly?"

Huh. Boone added nothing, not even sarcasm. Isn't that interesting?

"I'm a switch as well, but I'm a bit… chaotic. At least, that's what I've been told. I consciously decide when to submit and when to control, and it's pretty unpredictable," she admits, her cheeks getting pinker.

"Sound like a brat to me," Boone grumbles.

He's not wrong.

"Well, it's more like a Power Bottom and a Brat had a baby with a god of mischief," Jolene says, giving me a grin. "We're more trouble than brats and less annoying than powers. But it's easy to figure out where I'm falling, from what I understand."

Lucy stands and tilts his head. "Sugarplum, I'll play however you like. I'm fairly fluid, and I don't have a lot of lines to cross."

Fucking duh, he doesn't. His kind practically invented genderfluid, and he's about as sexually unencumbered as anyone I've ever met.

Even though I know the answer, I know why Jolene wants to hear it out loud. A good Domme always does. "Lucy, do you have concerns about who is where or taking it further than standard club play?"

"Hell, no. But my safe word isn't pineapple."

Magpie bursts out laughing, her eyes dancing with mirth. "Dear Aphrodite, help me with that. Some clubs sounded like a tropical fruit salad with all the 'pineapples' going around. I'll confess mine is 'bubbles'."

"Pumpkin Spice," I add, winking at her.

Lucy wrinkles his nose. "Unicorn. *He* picked it!" His finger shakes at me and I shrug, pleased with my choice, especially now.

"I don't have a safe word, and if any of you think I'm letting you top me, I'd suggest you work out," Edgar growls.

The three of us look at one another and peals of laughter echo in the room. Jolene walks up to him, tiptoeing her fingers up his chest slowly. "Not even for me, Teddy Bear?"

His eyes narrow, and he snarls low. An answering sound comes from Lucy, and I feel a tight knot in my chest.

Jolene looks at each of us for a moment and smirks. "Be patient, boys. I have just the thing. Back in a few."

With that, she sashays out of the room, leaving us to watch her go.

---

1. Triple sided

Closer

Getting through the conversation with the boys was easier than I assumed it would be. They were a lot more accepting of my terms than I expected, and I feel like they deserve a treat. I stride out of the closet in the guest room, the spiked heels of my boots making dents in the soft pile of the carpet. This outfit was part of the stuff I kept in the storage unit in Richmond; I knew I'd never need it there.

However, for tonight? It's perfect.

I tap the tip of the crop on the doorframe, smirking as their attention turns to me. Dropped jaws and shocked expressions follow me as I enter the room with a hip-swinging swagger. This isn't my every day 'sexy time' attire, but I know how to make an impression when the occasion calls for it. Their eyes roam over me, taking in my favorite bondage club gear: a tightly cinched black leather and lace corset with garters attached to wide fishnets, a tiny, crotchless lace thong, and six-inch heels with spikes all over them. The lace is thin enough to showcase my piercings, and we placed every cut of the corset to feature my tattoos.

Saoirse is one of the best seamstresses in the world for a reason, and she always outdid herself with my outfits when we travelled together.

I walk up to Wolfie, giving him a heated smile as I trail the leather over his chest. Turning, I look over my shoulder, swishing the high ponytail as I look at Teddy and Prez. "Say them again, boys," I murmur huskily.

"Unicorn," Wolfie gulps, carefully keeping his hands on his thighs.

"Good boy, little Wolfie," I murmur, leaning down to kiss him. I know my position has achieved its goal when low growls and groans echo from behind me. My back arches more, putting my ass on display for them.

Prez approaches first, looking at me for permission before he sits next to the vet on the bed. I nod, lips curving in pleasure, and he clears his throat. "Pumpkin Spice."

"I'm sooo pleased," I coo, treating him to the same kiss. This time, I wiggle my ass for effect.

Before I can stand, Teddy is behind me, pressed against my curves with the hard plains of his. "Tilly, you look positively edible. If you're inclined to keep pets, I'll allow it."

I laugh throatily, rising and twisting until I'm facing his handsome face. "Teddy, we can't have pets without the right equipment."

He snorts, arching a brow. "Who says I don't?"

Wolfie makes a noise, and I reach behind me, flicking my hand at his clothes. It should be enough instruction if he's truly well trained. I hear the springs creak as both of my doctors stand and clothes fly past us piece by piece. Teddy and I are locked in place, both asserting dominance and neither giving in. I bat my lashes at him, and he growls, grabbing my chin roughly.

"I think Tilly needs a little encouragement, mates. Take the crop and warm her ass for me," Edgar commands. He yanks my mouth to his, kissing my breath away as his other hand slides up my throat to place the enticing pressure on it. Our lips break, and this time he speaks to me, "Before they start, say it for me, *drugar*."

"Bubbles," I whisper, and not a second later, the first strike of the crop hits my right ass cheek. It's firm enough to sting nicely, but not enough to be painful—that must be Presley. The next strike is on the left side, and it's a palm. This one is harder, and it'll leave a nice print that I'll feel for a couple of days—that was Wolfie.

I've never played with so many archetypes and it's intoxicating. Both the docs and I are in submissive positions, but Teddy is letting me top them as well. It's hot as fuck, and we've just started. I didn't realize that indulging both of my sides at once would be so goddamned sexy.

They get a few more strikes in before my chest tightens and I look up at Teddy. Heat flickers through my veins, and I give him a saucy wink. Spinning in his embrace, I turn to Presley. "Tie my darling boy to the bedposts. You'll find hooks on the posts and restraints under the bed."

His grin makes my nipple harden, and I hook my arms around Teddy's neck. His hands slide to my ass, lifting me until I wrap my arms around his waist, pressing our bodies together. With a grunt, he adjusts me again, dropping me onto his cock as I weigh nothing.

A gasp rips from my throat at the sudden intrusion, but I hold on tighter, using my position as leverage to move with him. I'm certain the boys are doing as instructed, so I focus on squeezing Edgar's cock every time his hands lift and lower my hips. I dart my head in to nip his ear and his groan rumbles over my skin.

I continue biting and suckling along the length of his neck until I reach the juncture of his shoulder. My teeth sink in harder there and Teddy rears back, his eyes wild as he stares at me. A darkness flashes there before he turns and strides over to push me against the wall. Once I'm sandwiched between him and the hard surface, his hips piston into me roughly and his big hand pulls my head back to the spot I bit.

"Boone…"

The tone in Presley's voice carries a soft warning, but the stirring deep in my belly pushes me to ignore him. A noise I didn't even know I could make rumbles out of me, and I sink my teeth in as a wave of intense pleasure slams into my gut. Stars fill my vision and the fire I've felt every time I've touched Edgar since I came back wells up in my chest, filling my frame until I throw my head back and let out a howl of triumph. My fingers dig into his biceps, and the smell of sulfur fills the air.

"Holy shit…" Wolfie exclaims.

I hear him, but it's distant, and when I lift my head from Teddy's neck, the sweet tang of coppery blood fills my mouth. It should taste bad, but it doesn't and I can't wrap my head around it. I feel fuzzy like I do when I'm getting ready to black out, but also like something inside of me is in sharp focus. Teddy leans in, whispering something dark and foreign sounding in my ear, and I growl—actually growl—a response.

That tips the scales, and he throws his head back, hips stuttering as the orgasm hits him. A matching bone-chilling howl echoes through the room, and I gasp for breath as my body follows his without pause. An ache I've never felt before starts in my arms and spreads along my frame until I feel like I'm going to burst from my skin like an alien in a movie.

A cool hand on my shoulder soothes it, and I turn my head, eyes narrowing on the intruder. Presley gives me a wink, giving Edgar a push to free me from the confines of his embrace and the wall. He lifts me in his arms, carrying me over to the bed, whispering, "Not yet, Magpie. It's too soon. You're not done gathering your nest, and you can't let it all out until you're ready."

I frown. *What in the hell is he talking about?*

"Come play with us, love. Calm the fire with moonlight and ice."

"Moonlight and ice?" I mumble, looking up at him as he sits me down on the bed next to a deliciously prone vet. "Why am I so damned hot? Teddy, you broke me!"

Masculine chuckles fill the room and I do something I almost never do—I pout. Wolfie just smiles up at me, despite his hands and feet being masterfully cuffed to the posters on my bed. Presley drops a kiss on my temple before handing me a feather from my box. Edgar is still growling and pacing. Crossing my arms over my chest, I dig in stubbornly. The least they could do is react!

"Magpie, get our darling boy ready, and I'll calm the beast," the doctor says. "I haven't had my turn yet."

My lips curve, and I shake off the weird sensations from my primal coupling with Teddy. I crawl up Wolfie's frame, straddling his waist as I twirl the feather between my fingers teasingly. "Only if you're in the mood to kneel, baby."

"For you? Always."

"Isn't that a pretty sight? Tilly, you look scrumptious with your ass in the air like it's begging to be fucked."

I don't look up because I'm busy teasing McBabyVet with my tongue. Edgar sounds like he's back to normal, so whatever my other doc did brought him back. Humming my approval over the sensitive skin of Wolfie's balls, I wiggle my bum to lure them over to the bed. I promised fun for all, and examining Teddy's weird fugue isn't conducive to that. That's a future Jolene problem, and present Jolene isn't worried about it.

The bed dips and I can tell by the hands on my hips that it's Prez. His lithe body presses against mine, cock sliding along the mingled wetness between my legs easily as he leans down to murmur in my ear. "Now that we're all here, love, you can stop torturing our boy. Slide down that ladder of his so we can fill you up from head to toe."

That's exactly what I was hoping for.

Rising from my place between Wolfie's legs, I crawl up his body, pausing for a moment to give him a deep kiss. He's been a *very* good boy, and he should know it. "You've been so good, holding back until the boys got back. It's time for a reward, my darling."

His eyes light up and his hips arch as I hover over his pierced dick, and a long, low moan tumbles out of his mouth when I slide home. The metal rubs all the right spots inside of me and I rock, vaguely hearing the slap of a bottle being caught and the sweet scent of plums fills the air. Cold liquid hits my ass, and I grin to myself, pleased I'd thought ahead after the first night they stayed with me.

Yeah, I'm a complete control freak that ordered plum scented lube, and a variety of my men's favorite enticing shit just in case I needed it. I know I'm a mess with them, but look how it turned out.

"Sugarplum, your crazy is the best fucking crazy I've ever met," Wolfie says, wriggling under me to speed my movements.

"That's lovely of you to say, baby," I reply, giving his thigh a smack to stop his urging. "But you need to hold still until everyone is ready. That's one, little Wolfie."

Presley chooses that moment to slide a finger into my ass, and I growl under my breath. Three sets of eyes burn into me at the sound, and they yanked my chin up to look at Teddy. His cock is hard again, bobbing near my mouth, and for a second, I lose my confident veneer. It's just a flash, but I've never gone down on someone his size before. I won't gag, but I'm not a hundred percent sure how I'll breathe.

"Relax, *drugar*. Feel them inside of you, and focus on the sensations. Now… *Open. Your. Mouth.*"

Ooh, that tone did it for me.

Clenching around Wolfie and Prez, I do an instructed without a snappy retort, and the head slides past my lips. My mouth stretches wider to accommodate him, and he rumbles his approval from above. Each time Edgar thrusts deeper, Presley slips another finger in until he's stretching me enough that Wolfie is whining at the contact between his dick and the fingers. One swift stroke has me deep throating, and before I know it, I'm air-fucking-tight.

Holy Britney, queen of pop, with all of them inside of me, I'm so full I don't know what to do with myself.

Closing my eyes, I focus on finding a pleasurable rhythm. My hands grip Teddy's hips, helping him slide in and out as I lick, nibble, and yes, drool my way through, blowing him like a pro. Prez does the same to me, guiding me back and forth between him and my vet with expert hands. The fire doesn't rise in my belly like it did last time when the doc slips two fingers down to pinch my clit. This time, I feel ice travel up my veins, and a darkness blooms in my chest.

"Embrace it, magpie. We have you. Let go again, and feel the weight lift from your mind," Presley whispers.

My brain shuts off as I give in to the orgasm that rips through me, and though I know I'm going to pass out again, for the first time I can remember, I'm not scared that I'll wake up alone and confused. The boys will be here to catch me. A chorus of shouts echoes as they find their own climaxes, and I see stars as I come again, and then... there's nothing.

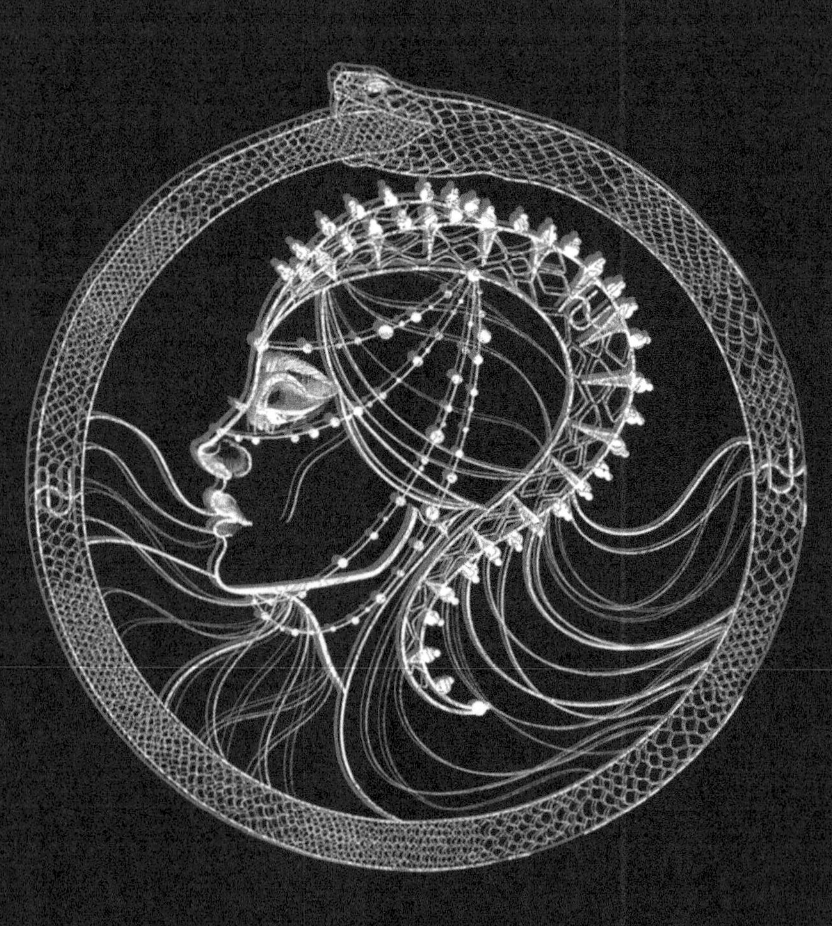

Wings

"Be careful with that, Seer!" I holler across the room. My friend is swishing around the now complete studio, delivering coffees from the diner to the crew of misfits working to get me ready for the grand opening.

Teddy is on a ladder with one leg hooked around the side as he uses his long limbs to hang the banner in the front window. He nearly gave me a heart attack four times today as he climbed around the room, and every time he strikes a dangerous pose, I feel panic grip my chest. Wolfie laughs from where he's meticulously checking every piece of art hanging to ensure its level. The labels are correct, and the lighting is showcasing the work appropriately.

"Magpie, she's nowhere near the art. Don't worry; we all know the rules about drinks in the gallery," Prez says, coming up behind me and rubbing my shoulders reassuringly.

"I know. I can't help being nervous, though. This is a big event, and I know there will be people here who will actively work against me. It's making me a little compulsive," I reply, turning to steal a quick kiss.

After we set our boundaries and had mind-blowing sex, the four of us found a day-to-day routine that surprised the hell out of me. They almost never go home, which I thought would make me feel crowded, but with Seer camped out in her own place, it feels right.

Wolfie helped me move all the fabulous clothes belonging to my mom into the master bedroom closet, and they've taken over the one in the guest room. Luckily, it was also a walk-in, and they had everything from scrubs to suits stored in their sections. Again, I thought it would make me panic to see it, but I just smiled and threw my hands around the vet's neck to kiss him breathlessly.

I don't know where lone wolf Jolene went, but I guess when I woke up in my bed with three men snuggled against me and a corset biting into my ribs, she took an extended vacation.

Outside of ribbing my guys about abandoning their homes, I've accepted the routine of having breakfast together after our early morning run, parting ways to head to work, and meeting for dinner. We're not always all together because of various appointments, practices, or commitments, but we fall into bed in my room when we arrive home. It's comfortable, and just thinking about it makes my heart thump a little.

"Sugarplum, are you thinking about something naughty?" Wolfie says, sidling up to Prez and me with a grin. "Your cheeks are the most adorable shade of primrose I've ever seen."

Wrinkling my nose, I swat him playfully. "Wouldn't you like to know?"

"La, la, la, la, la!" Seer shouts, handing Prez his chai tea and Wolfie his fruity pink drink. "Peanut, I know I've been part of the festivities in the past, but you're going to burn me virgin eyes if you keep going!"

"Her eyes are the only thing virgin about her then," Teddy mutters loudly enough that we can all hear him.

Seer's expression shifts to glare and she turns on her heel and stomps over to the man monkeying around the window. "Aye, lad. It'd be true, but I doubt you want me to recount all the non-virgin things

I've seen your precious Tilly do, eh? There was this one time, in Bangkok, where we decided to…"

"Enough, you demented leprechaun!" he growls, jumping down from the top of the ladder with the grace of a fucking panther. "Haven't you reached your 'Edgar torture' quota for the day?"

My bestie cackles, putting her hands on her hips. "Never! I'll never reach that quota, even if I live a million years!"

Teddy ignores her, striding over to swoop me into his arms and kiss the shit out of me. When he pulls away to allow us to breathe, I run my fingers through his hair with a soft smile. "She's baiting you, silly man. Don't let her get under your skin. The past is the past."

He grumbles under his breath, and I hold my arm up, showcasing the ridiculously expensive jadeite and black opal cuff. They set the stones in a wide platinum band in a shape that looks like a snake winding its way around my wrist. It was a surprise gift the boys brought home two weeks ago, claiming it was our one-month anniversary.

After scolding them for not telling me, this was an important date—because when the hell had I ever kept someone this long—I ordered three matching bands for their Apple watches from a master jeweler I worked for.

"I know, Tilly. I'm an asshole at heart, though. I can't help it."

"You got that in one," Presley says, lifting me out of his arms to spin me around. "When are the caterers coming to set up, magpie?"

I check my watch and sigh. "In two hours. Are you going to pick up the animals on your way home, Teddy?"

Wolfie laughs, shaking his head. "No, I am. Jekyll and Hyde won't get in his car, even if Kali and Hecate try to push them in. It's pretty funny to watch."

"I don't blame them. He drives like a maniac," I grin, squealing when Teddy delivers a firm smack on my ass in retaliation.

"We reconvene here in two hours, dressed to kill. That's the plan, aye, Peanut?" Seer asks.

I nod, looking at the boys. "Prez, if you could grab dinner, we can eat while we dress. Teddy, you can get the flowers from... WAP." I frown, hating that name every time I say it. It doesn't help that it's owned by Dorothy Elizabeth Hale—the crusty old bat who gave birth to Jillian Marie Remington. Much like Zelda, she's made it her mission to be shitty with me, although I gave her my business.

"I love the face you make when you're forced to say that name. I wish Doyle was around to see it," Edgar says, giving me a wink. "I'll see if I can charm her."

"Alright, team. Break!" I clap my hands like Teddy does at practice and everyone groans.

What? I thought it was cute.

"Jolene! You look lovely, as always. They have transformed the space since I last visited," Mayor Cornelia Sykes says, sipping her champagne delicately. She's looking rather resplendent in a brightly colored caftan and sandals, her long hair threaded with colors and swinging at her waist.

I smile brightly, tugging at the lapels of the black satin Armani tux jacket. Seer had her way with some pieces of the couture that belonged to my mom last week, and she insisted this suit paired with the five inch Louboutins would blow the faces off my critics. I'm not so sure, given that she tailored the jacket with boning and forbade me to wear a shirt underneath.

"Thank you, Nelia. It's a hand-me-down from my mother, and she always encouraged my art. I feel it's a nice tribute for this evening."

Nelia arches her brow at me. "Jolene Whitley, I knew your mother and if anyone encouraged your artistic side, it was Andrew. But I appreciate your manners in not saying so. Eloise had a stunning wardrobe for official events and I'm pleased to see it serving you well."

Zareb tosses his mane next to her, and I watch him. He walks forward, bending at the front paws and putting his head down at my feet. What the hell? I look at Nelia in a panic, but she only laughs. Edgar chooses that moment to walk up behind me and place his enormous hands on my shoulders. His proximity calms me, and I take a slow breath.

"Don't worry, Miss Whitley. Zareb is only showing you he won't harm you. In fact, this position shows deference. I've never seen him do it for anyone but me before."

I gape at the Mayor, unsure what to say to that. Why on earth would her companion show me deference? Jekyll and Hyde stroll up, brushing my fingertips on either side, dropping into a similar position facing Zareb.

Okay, this is getting weird.

"Looks like we've found allies, *drugar*," Teddy says, his chest rumbling against my back. "I'd never turn down such a gracious offer, Mayor, nor would my lovely girlfriend."

Is there a shock quotient for less than five minutes? I may be at mine. I hear a gasp from across the room, then the buzz of people talking in the crowd. Teddy just dropped a gossip bomb in the loudest, clearest voice possible. The animals stand, and Euryale screeches from the perch Wolfie made for her high in the corner across the room. Kali and Hecate join the animals crowded around us with a low 'woof', and I feel claustrophobic.

A loud whistle sounds from the door to the back room, and I see Prez wink. For someone so quiet, he seems to always have a bead on how I'm feeling. I give him a grateful smile, watching the cats and dogs wind their way to the back for treats.

The Mayor smiles at me, her eyes knowing. "I see you've found admirers. That's good—a lady should never be without a cadre of trusted associates who would burn the world for her."

I tilt my head, studying her for a moment. "You seem to do well on your own, Nelia."

Her laugh is rich as her eyes twinkle. "My polycule is never far, but seldom seen. They move with the shadows, so no one mistakes my femininity with weakness. Perhaps I will invite you to dinner one night once you've assembled your consorts."

"Her what?" Teddy cuts in, his hands tightening on my shoulders.

"Young Boone, you may have a name, money, and a title, but you'd do well to remember who I am." Her reproachful stare makes him shrink the tiniest bit, but I don't comment on it. "However, I understand not everyone present knows the same amount of information as me, so I'll forgive your impertinence—this time."

With that, she swishes away with Zareb in tow, and I watch her with interest. I swear, I didn't think there was a person alive who could make Edgar Olivier Boone III cringe. But he's muttering under his breath, so I turn to drop a kiss on his jaw. He calms slightly, and I wrap my arms around him.

I know there are eyes on us; I can feel them. I can't find it in me to care what people think about my unconventional home life anymore. Teddy chuckles and presses a kiss into my hair, rubbing his cheek against it for a moment before speaking.

"You realize this is going to paint a target on your back even bigger than before? So far, the harpies have seen you kiss me, snuggle with the vet, and watched the doc tame our pets. It's going to get around."

I shrug. "Let them talk. It's what people here do best."

Laughing softly, he lets go of me. "I'll remember you said that. For now, go schedule classes at the desk. Some ladies are lingering there with claws at the ready. Best get them settled before blood is drawn."

"I do NOT promise to keep Eury from pecking them to death."

"Well, as long as you have a plan…"

Good Girl

"I'd like to put all three of my children in lessons," Ophelia Jane Longworth says.

She's sitting on the chair primly, her knees together and a small cocktail purse balanced in her lap. Her entire demeanor is like someone who's afraid to catch a disease from the place they're in, and it pisses me off. Ophelia was the duchess in charge after Amy Matilda Behle, and she carried out the most heinous of the punishments when we were in high school.

OJ wasn't afraid of getting her hands dirty back then, and she hasn't grown up a whit if you ask me.

"I can do that, Ophelia. I'll need to put them in different age groups—which means they'll have lessons on different days. If you need to check their current activities against the open lesson grid, you can use the website to request their day and time."

My smile is sunny, but inside, I can't wait to get this viper away from me. She glared at me hard when she saw Teddy with his arms around me. I'm not sure if she's holding a torch from high school or if she's acting in defense of a friend, but she's been an icicle from the second she perched her malnourished bum in my chair.

"Outrageous! I've been waiting in this dump for over an hour while you climbed on every bachelor in town like a cat in heat. Now you tell me you can't register my children tonight? Wasn't that your line at Parent's Night, too?"

I whip a piece of paper out of the file folder, planting a pen on it a bit more firmly than I need to. "Ophelia, if you have all the information on all three of your children's activities memorized, please fill out the request now. Note the line that says all spots are final once claimed, and if the child can't attend a class, you will get charged. My time is valuable, and I do not wait for students who cannot be on time and prepared to learn. There is also a non-refundable fifty percent down payment due at registration."

Her eyes narrow. I can see the wheels turning in her brain, trying to figure out whether I've written my paperwork well enough to keep her from fighting it if she risks it. I bat my lashes at her, waiting patiently. Jackson drafted all of my forms and paperwork for the gallery, and this weekend, Edgar and the boys helped me 'Hollow Proof' it. They're all aware of how the snooty assholes in this town wiggle out of contracts and paying their debts, so I'm confident OJ can't find a loophole.

"Fine. I will consult my calendar, the nanny, and our staff. Once I'm certain, I assume I can sign them up without having to waste time coming here, yes?" she snarls, curling her lip.

"Yes. On the website, Ophelia. It's listed on every page of every form you're holding," I reply sweetly. She's not the first socialite I've had this conversation with tonight, but she's the least brilliant. Like father, like daughter, I suppose. Aldous may be cunning, but that's a survival instinct.

"If I have any issues with this ridiculous process, I will let Mayor Sykes know of my displeasure."

"Say hello to your father, Ophelia. We were so hoping he'd attend this evening," I reply, trying to look innocent as I call her bluff about the Mayor. She's used to people knowing that Aldous has the Mayor's ear, and her angry expression betrays her intentions. My dig prevented her from using that connection surreptitiously—good. If OJ wants to come at me, she'll have to do it directly.

She's not the Queen Bee I'm worried about... not anymore.

When she stomps away, I breathe a sigh of relief. Since I moved home, I've had to confront a lot of demons from my past. Starting with Edgar, I've been working my way through the elites one by one. The boys may have grown up, but the girls have not. I still haven't seen Jillian Marie Remington, Reese Emily Barrington, or the head mean girl, Amy Matilda Behle. Since I've had to deal with their parents in town and the next generation at school, I'm not eager to remedy that situation.

"They've been rough, eh, Peanut?" Seer remarks, coming up beside me to hand me a glass of champagne.

I gulp it down in one swig, turning to give her a grateful look. "At least none of them has called me a whore yet. I know they all saw Edgar's little show, and trust me, it wasn't received well. I'll make a tidy sum with lessons and classes, but it won't come easily. These bitches will make certain of that."

Her lips quirk, and she tilts her head at me, giving me a mischievous grin. "Good thing I've got a plan to make everything better, innit?"

Arching a brow, I frown. "No retaliation for the moment, Seer. As much as I'd love to botch someone's Botox or whatever crazy revenge you've got planned, I don't think it's time for Def-Con Seer yet. They're spiteful witches, but they have done nothing but remind me why I stayed away from this town for so long."

"Ah, Peanut. You mistake the source of my excitement. There'll be no arguments once I tell you, right?"

"That's not a suspicious request at *all*," I retort. "But I trust you. What do you have planned?"

Her grin widens, and she vibrates with excitement. "I've already told your lads to shove off because we're driving to the city to have a girls' night. I have all the shite to take off in an hour, and they're going home to man the animals. It's you, me, alcohol, and the dance floor tonight, just like old times."

My bestie is so excited about her plan; I can't tell her I'd rather go home, down a couple of milkshakes, and let the boys coddle me until I fall asleep. It's not a school night, and I'm not scheduled for the farm tomorrow. I don't have even a hint of an excuse to pawn her off. She's clearly had this plan in motion for most of the evening, and I'll hurt her feelings if I refuse. So I muster up as much enthusiasm as I can and give her a bright smile.

"The Terror Twins of Tripoli ride again!"

Seer whoops loud enough to turn more than a few heads our way, which she silences with a glare that could freeze a flame in place. "Aye, that's my girl! Now, get these women settled, and we can shut this down on time. I can't wait for you to see what I've got planned for our entrance."

Oh, sweet baby Hercules and the minions of Hades. I gave her another reason to dress me up.

◯

"*SEER*! MY ASS IS HANGING OUT OF THIS. I HAVE ENOUGH DUDES clogging up my kitchen in the morning!"

Her laughter is contagious, despite the insanity she has me strapped into. She insisted we drive into the city to go dancing at a club she found online, and if what I'm wearing is any sign, the boys are gonna be *pissed* we didn't invite them. I tug on the bottom of the tux jacket a bit as we walk, finally understanding why she insisted on leaving it a shade longer than I would have preferred.

She intended the damned thing to be a mini-dress for this outing.

Saoirse O' Flanagan could have built her own fashion house from the ground up, even without her family name, but she chose the avant garde route as a personal costumer instead. The fashion world should both weep and be glad she decided her talents were better used for individual designs rather than the mass market.

I watch her stride up to the bouncer in the white corset with a fluffy bustle that trails over her matching fishnets to the heels of her knee-high raver boots. His eyes widen at the shock of flaming hair, wild fairy makeup, and leather accessories on her thighs, wrists, and neck. She could be the bait in a bondage themed paranormal romance, and she knows it.

The dude rakes his eyes over me as well and I glare, holding up the cuffed wrist with a haughty smirk. "Sorry, bud. Not on the menu."

"Shame," he mutters, lifting the rope in front of the line so we can slip in. "The Boss would like you—both of you."

I share a look with Seer, and she giggles. There was a time where we would have taken Gigantor here up on that offer. But, alas, no more. No matter how many people tell me 'I'm gathering', I'm content with the amount of people demanding my attention at the moment. I don't care if his boss is Jason Momoa; I'm good.

"Keep yer shorts on, bruiser. I might be free later," Seer says, winking as we walk into the dark club.

A swift yank on her train stops her, and when she turns to look at me, I hiss, "I'm not running around here alone while you pick out your favorite sausage or taco for the evening, you know. You said this was a girls' night."

"We won't be alone, Peanut. We came to see the show. You're going to *love* it." Seer grabs my hand and I sigh, letting her pull me deeper into the club.

The inside of this place isn't at all what I would have imagined based on the name. Howl isn't some trendy Goth disco, or even a warehouse rave—it's a velvet seating, crystal chandeliered room with modular seating facing small stages. They dressed the staff like it's the roaring 20s, and the bar is mahogany.

A few of the areas have curtains drawn around them, and the ones that don't have darkened prosceniums. They dressed patrons in everything from cocktail gowns to bondage gear to what appear to be period costumes. The one thing the clientele of... whatever the hell this place is... have in common is they're all ridiculously good looking and almost certainly wealthy.

"Saoirse Viola O'Flanagan, where the goat slaughtering hell are we?" I mutter under my breath. I don't expect her to answer; she's too far ahead to hear me. However, even when we were gallivanting around the world, we never came to a place like this. It's... otherworldly. There's just no better word to describe it.

We stop in front of a section near the back that looks half filled. Seer drops into one of the fancy booths meant for a smaller group and gives me a cheerful grin. Rolling my eyes, I slide in next to her with my hand over the back of the tux dress so I don't flash anyone nearby. A server in a flapper dress appears, and we order drinks. My friend ignores my anxiety, humming under her breath as she looks at a menu to decide what she wants to eat. When I can't take it anymore, I slam my fist on the table, making her jump.

Oddly, no one even looks in our direction.

"I need an explanation. *Now*," I growl softly. "Where are we? What is this place? I thought we were going clubbing."

"We are, lass. But first, we're meeting up with a few of my friends. They haven't been to this side of the pond for a long time, and I'm up to high doh for them to meet you."

The server reappears with our drinks—a Blanton's neat for me and Ocean Water for Seer—then disappears once she places the food order. I'm not sure what the hell she ordered because it had weird names, but my BFF knows good food and she hasn't steered me wrong in the past. Sipping my drink, I look at the stage for a moment before I sigh. "Seer, I'm happy you're here, and I love going on adventures with you, but you need to tell me who—"

"There's the bawdy lass who always has a glass!"

Turning towards the sound of the booming voice, my jaw drops. Three impossibly hot people are making their way to our table, and behind them, the curtain around our module is closing as if it was waiting for their arrival. The woman is tall and pale, with silver and rainbow colored hair shaved into a rakish faux hawk.

There are designs shaved on the sides, and she's dressed in skintight leather matching the streaks in her hair. Her companions are a brute who would give Benjy a run for his money in a 'stuck in the doorway' contest and a lithe, long-haired guy who could audition for an ACOTAR movie. It charges the surrounding energy as they approach, and I can't help but wonder why I've never met them before.

"Aye!" Seer shouts, jarring the table in her enthusiasm. "Julia, Tharin, Zasha… this is Jolene Athena Whitley."

I watch the motley trio, not sure why something inside of me is wary of their presence. I'm not one to be jealous of my friend, but I've also had a *lot* of reasons to suspect Trojans bearing gifts, so to speak. "Hello. It's nice to meet you. Seer has told me absolutely *nothing* about you," I snark, giving them my best Southern belle smile.

"She *is* a pip," Julia murmurs, her eyes dancing. "I can see why you're so attached to her, O'Flanagan."

It's hard not to bristle at that. People seem to equate my ability to stand up for myself with cutesy spunk of late, and it's grating on my nerves. I know not *all* of them are being condescending, but it damn sure feels like it. "*She* has a name, and *she* is sitting in front of you, Julia."

Seer winces when speakers in the club squeal with interference, her gaze cutting to mine with a panicked look. "Now, ladies. Let's not be a cliche trope. There's more than enough of me to share."

"That's been true many a time in the past," the big dude says with a knowing smirk.

Assholes.

Seer's friends are assholes, and she's giving me the 'make nice with the scary people' expression she patented years ago. Her penchant for finding the ne'er-do-wells in every crowd is legendary, and if she's trying to get me to behave, I guess I'll go along for now. "Yes, well, since we're all aware of how flexible my bestie's proclivities are, would you like to let me know which one of you is Tharin and which is Zasha?"

The smaller man drops into the booth next to me, flashing a toothy grin. "I'm Zasha, love. It's lovely to make your acquaintance."

Ah, I get it now. Julia is traveling with a grumpy asshole and a smooth talker. I can relate. "That would make Mr. Personality here Tharin, I suppose."

Julia climbs into the booth, scooting in next to Seer, and motions for Tharin to follow. After a moment of watching him struggle to wedge himself in, she gives me a wink. "That's spot on. We took a job that brought us back to the States, and when we heard it was near where Saoirse was living, we had to drop in. Apologies for the last minute notice."

That was vaguely specific. Hm. "Will you be in the area long? I could recommend some hotels here if you need."

Tharin coughs, and Zasha lets out a booming laugh. "Unnecessary, Miss Jolene. Saoirse has graciously agreed to host us while we consult throughout the state. We'll be in and out as our contract dictates, but you will definitely see us."

Frowning, I narrow my eyes at the server as she returns with a huge tray. Now I get why Seer ordered enough to feed an army—Tharin alone could probably eat all of it and us without getting full. I pick up something that smells delicious and looks fried, holding my glass up to the woman before she leaves again. I'm certain I'll need more alcohol and a lot of terrible food to get through this evening.

Let the show begin.

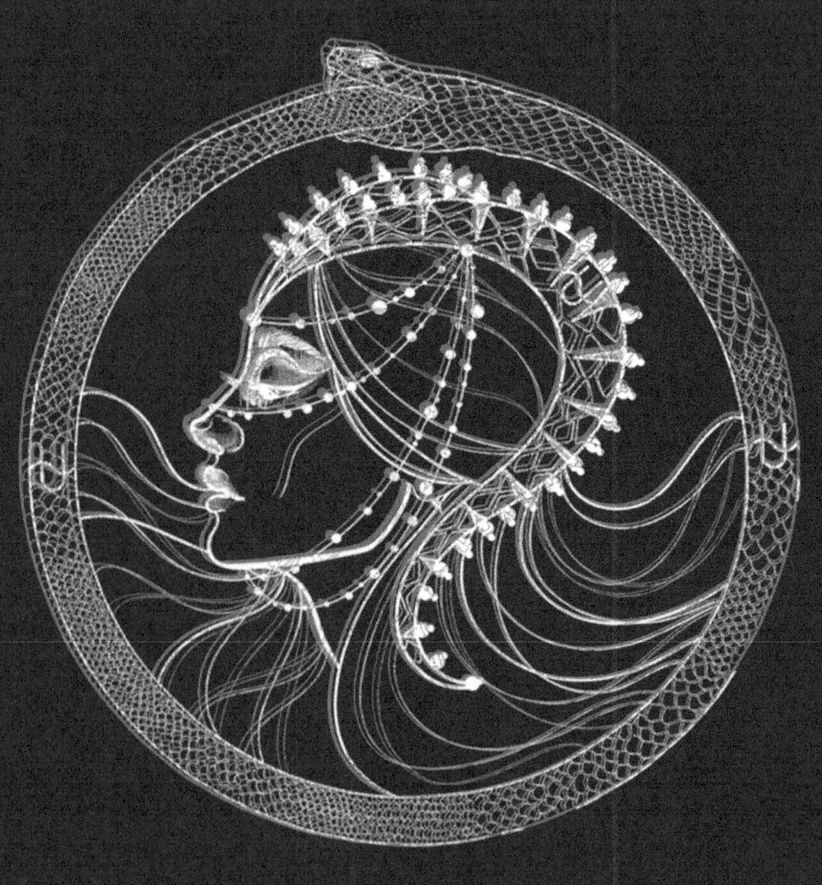

Wishes

The curtain rises on the stage right after my drink arrives, and I watch with morbid fascination. Seer still hasn't told me what kind of club this is, though I find it much more obvious why we're here. She wanted to meet up with old friends in the place they're all comfortable in.

I'm not sure why she and I never visited anything like this all those years, and the thought Seer has held parts of herself back pinches. I've shared some of the deepest, darkest events in my life with her, and now I wonder if that's been reciprocated or if our instant connection simply fooled me. A vaguely unsettled feeling sinks into my gut and I sip the bourbon to cover my discomfort.

"This should be good," Julia murmurs to Seer. "I heard through the grapevine the entertainment was a previously lost one who just blew through town. Likes to perform in anonymity."

Seer claps her hands, and the guys laugh. "Class! Overseas or home-grown? Number?"

Tharin stops tearing into the chicken wings like a wildebeest to answer her with a sauce-covered grin. "Overseas. No number. His family kept it hidden, but benefited during their lives."

What an odd way to say that.

I mean, lots of parents live off their talented offspring through child acting or Disney channel deals—not that it makes it right. I'm one hundred percent Team #freeBritney, but Tharin didn't make it sound like this person was famous or anything. In fact, Julia said 'lost one' as if that meant something they all understood. I rub my temples, trying to decide if getting hammered might make the ugliness earlier in the evening and the encroaching fear of losing my only friend easier to swallow.

Why the fuck not?

I haven't been able to let go since I moved back to the States. The closest I've come is with the boys, and they're not here. I wish they were, honestly, and that's scary, too. My life is a writhing snake pit of things that might destroy me at the moment, and I'm no closer to finding out why I got the kiss off from the FBI, either. One might say I'm a veritable cornucopia of failure, and they'd be right.

I slam the rest of my drink back, catching the server's eye to hold up two fingers. She needs to make it a double this time. "Is it starting or what?"

Zasha narrows his eyes at me. "It is, love. Just wait. Some people like to make an entrance."

"I wouldn't know anyone like that," I mutter, leaning back against the plush cushions of the booth as I nibble on some weird fried concoction.

Seer gives me a playful glare. "Careful, Peanut, your grumpy side is showing."

Rolling my eyes, I continue nibbling at the array of snacks. When the overhead lights flash three times, then go dark, I blink. What in the merry fuck is this? My eyes adjust to the dark, and I look around to see various tables of people whispering to each other. A crack of lightning illuminates the stage and smoke fills the space. Damn, these people have some good special effects for a small club. When it clears, one of the hottest dudes I've ever seen in my entire life steps out of it like he just... appeared.

Are we here for a magic show?

The olive-skinned performer flashes impossibly white teeth, his expression looking more hungry than welcoming. Raising his hands as if encouraging the crowd to applaud, the good-looking magician walks—no, struts—across the stage. His dark eyes search the crowd as they clap and hoot, a smirk gracing his full lips. When he lowers his arms, he unbuttons the cuffs on his sleeves, rolling the obsidian dress shirt up to his elbows. I can almost hear the sighs from the audience, and his expression only grows more devilish.

Okay, Edgar knows he's hot, but this guy?

He basks in the adoration of men and women alike as he peacocks around the proscenium. Ugh. I could never deal with an ego this big —it'd knock us all off the bed and mine's pretty damned huge. Why does everyone think megalomaniacs are so attractive?

"See something you like, Peanut?" Seer whispers in a not very subtle voice.

Tharin and Zasha snort, and I turn to shoot a sneer their way. Men are nothing if not predictable, even ones traveling with a mystery woman I just met. "Definitely not, Seer. He's lucky he's not sprouting tail feathers or falling in love with his image in a martini glass. Gross."

She opens her mouth to respond, but a poof of smoke explodes on the stage and the sexy dude disappears again. When he reappears, his hair is pulled into a loose topknot instead of falling loosely over his shoulder. His grin is even more self-satisfied, and for the first time, he speaks.

"Good evening, my illustrious friends! The Theopoulous family graciously ceded one of their stages tonight to allow me to indulge my penchant for theatrics while in town. I am honored to be granted the opportunity." Mysterious dude smiles again, then continues. "My name is Dhameer Mirza Al Sharqi and I will grant your deepest desires."

I snort. No, I snort hard enough for it to hurt. Could this guy be any more into himself? He should just make out with his hand on stage and get it over with it.

"Shhh!" Julia admonishes, her expression disapproving. "It's impolite to scoff at royalty."

"Uh. Royalty?" I whisper.

"There! You! The girl who cannot be arsed to pay attention to my magnificent show. You will be the first participant," the asshole booms into the audience.

Fuck. Me.

I look to my friend for help and she looks away while her companions snicker like elementary school kids. "A little help, guys?"

"You're the one who snorted at the Crown Prince, my lady. You'll have to pay the price," Zasha smirks, shrugging his shoulders. "Sarcasm isn't always free, you know."

Great. I didn't even want to come here. Hell, I don't even know where this is!

It's apparent I won't have a choice, though, so I stand. Before I move, I smooth the jacket dress and my fishnets down, trying to make sure I'm not flashing anyone on my hike to the stage. I don't have the foggiest how he heard or saw me through the smoky haze at that distance, but my mom's insistence that one day I'd regret muttering under my breath is echoing in my mind.

At least she was right about one thing.

When I reach the front, I take the stairs at the side and walk towards the spotlight. Dhameer gestures impatiently, and I walk up to him with an irritated look. His smile only grows wider as he turns to the crowd, stepping back to hold his arms out.

"I know nothing about this woman—save she has no patience for prideful wretches such as myself." The titters echo across the room and I cross my arms over my chest. He walks to stage right, pulling a chair from the wings and placing it downstage center. "But tonight, for your viewing pleasure, I will uncover her deepest desires and grant her the ability to realize them."

Mmm. One part magician, one part con artist, I suppose. He will not hypnotize me or put me in a trance; many have tried and failed in the past. "If you say so, dude."

"A skeptic! How wonderful!" He claps his hands, actual delight flashing over his features. "Sit down, Miss…?"

"Whitley. Jolene Whitley," I sigh before perching on the chair.

His eyes widen, and he tilts his head, studying me carefully. "A lovely name, to be sure. If you could close your eyes and try to relax, I will ask you a few more questions."

"Okay." I close my eyes, mentally swearing at Seer for bringing me to this farce. I can hear the boards creak as he walks around me in a slow circle. A soft breeze coasts over my skin, but he doesn't touch me. The distance helps me relax and when my shoulders slump, I hear a pleased sound.

"Miss Jolene. Tell me what your fondest memory is."

I shrug. "I don't know. My memory is an issue."

Another sound, a few steps, and a pause. "Can you tell me what makes you happy?"

That hits me. It's changed so much since I came back, and I haven't had time to sort through all of those feelings. My hand moves to my breastbone of its own volition, and I rub my palm there as I consider his royal dickface's question.

What makes me happy?

Definitely not what I thought made me happy before I moved home to the Hollow. I intend to solve the mystery of my background check, and whatever my parents had going on, but I don't think I'd move to Richmond to pick up where I left off.

In the past month, I've unintentionally put down roots, and I want to see where my little cadre is going. I enjoy working with the kids and in my studio. I love having the guys and my companions around. Even having Seer down the road has become part of the fabric of my daily routine. I couldn't give any of it up to go back to a lonely apartment and weekends on the gun range.

"My new life," I whisper as my heart squeezes in my chest. "My friends and family make me happy."

Footsteps stop in front of me, and I can only assume he's looking down at me. The crowd gasps at something I can't see, but I feel a rush of cold air before a warm breath near my face. "Then a family you shall have. It is done."

My brows furrow as I frown, confused at the murmured words. After a few moments, the crowd claps and I can't resist opening my eyes. Looking around, I peer into the darkened room, trying to see what they're applauding for, but I only see patrons. I turn to look up at the handsome jerk smirking at me, rolling my eyes. "Well, that was anti-climactic."

"Was it?" he replies. "We shall see."

"If you say so, dude." I stand, stomping over to the stairs and heading for my group. I don't know what kind of magic this dude was flogging, but he didn't pull the wool over my eyes. I didn't feel a thing, nor do I have an urge to cluck like a chicken.

Chicanery, that's what this was.

"How do you feel, Peanut?" Seer asks, cocking a brow at me.

"Ugh. Fine. Let's get out of here before I have to survive another round of this idiot's lame magic."

Tharin and Zasha look at one another as if they know something I don't, and I'm too irritated to ask. The list of what they know I don't is miles long, given that I just met them. Julia clucks her tongue at me and gives Seer a look like I'm the crazy one. I tap my foot, waiting for them all to move their asses, and they scoot out of the booth.

It's about time. I need more booze and a LOT of dancing to wash the ick from my mind. That guy is a con and an asshat; thank fuck I never have to see him again. I don't care if Julia's royalty comment is true—I want nothing to do with that arrogant fuckwad.

"Are you leading us to an underground place where the youths get jiggy?" Julia asks, giving Seer another one of those annoying wordless conversation looks.

I choke. "Youths... get.. jiggy?"

Hell, even I'm not *that* out of touch. God help this woman if she gets within four feet of any teenager in town. They're going to destroy her, and I'm going to laugh until I suffocate.

That's my *prediction.*

Wake Me Up When It's All Over

Wolfgang

Sugarplum needs some blackout curtains in this room. The sun damn near fried my eyeballs in the sockets when I opened them. Yawning, I frown when I stretch my limbs and notice how empty the bed feels.

Rolling to my side, I look over at Presley sprawled like a starfish. He was the most vocal about our lady's absence when we headed to bed. Boone pouted like a toddler and stormed to his house, and I checked my phone more than I have in years, but Prez…

He spent a good portion of the evening wearing a tread on the living room carpet. It's not that he thinks Jolene can't take care of herself; he's worried about her emerging powers and Saoirse's cavalier attitude. The Irish lass isn't a bad Guardian, but her personal connection to Sugarplum makes it harder for her to do her job.

It's obvious she's allowed her to take risks most Guardians wouldn't have over the years, and Prez can't stand things outside of his sphere of control. His gifts make him certain of his ability to help if something goes very wrong, but since they kept us in the dark about their plans, he fretted all night that he might not make it in time.

The weird presence that's been lurking around the house has us all on edge, I s'pose.

I tried contacting my old Guardian, but she's incommunicado. The same goes for Andromeda from the school, and when I had Boone text Nelia, she was 'disinclined to acquiesce to our paranoia'. Fancy words for 'mind your business', but that's our mayor in a nutshell.

"What time is it? Is Magpie home?"

My lips curve as I look at one of the best things to happen to my life since I graduated from vet school. "No, love, she's not here." I brush his hair out of his eyes, cupping his cheek. "Unless they're passed out downstairs, which seems unlikely. I just woke up and hadn't gone looking yet."

He sits up, fumbling around for his glasses before turning to me. "Why didn't you wake me? It doesn't feel right; she's not the type to not come home."

"At some point she was, babe. We've heard her and Saoirse talk about their wild days. Maybe it's like a reunion, and they're curled up somewhere sleeping off hangovers," I reply, trying to soothe him. I didn't realize how close he was to the bond—that's the only thing that would cause such a panic. I'm not saying mine isn't pinching, and I'm sure Boone is as well.

In fact, it's strange that he hasn't—

"Where is she?!"

Yep, that's about what I expected. Guess I won't be distracting Prez with breakfast in bed now. Sighing, I roll to my feet and head for the bathroom. I'm not worried about being naked; hell, he's seen almost as much of my ass as Prez has by now. "You both need to calm down. It's making me fritz. Too much emotion, and it's too naked in here to get frosty."

"Focus, Lucy. Your mother will make an appearance if your control slips. The real one, not poor Aurelia. She's the last thing we need right now."

"Is no one listening?"

I blow a kiss at my love before I close the door, chuckling under my breath. He's not wrong—my mother loves to use a substantial power burst as a reason to break her promise to my father. She's not supposed to come here because she lacks the ability or will to blend in with modern society. With Boone losing his mind, Sugarplum not yet emerged, and the gossip in this town, a visit could blow up in our faces in a million ways.

But I am concerned our girl hasn't called. I don't want to fan the flames of the other two—especially Edgar—so I'm trying to remain calm. However, their panic is feeding my powers, and well… It'd be nice if we had Jolene to balance us all out. She brings out the best in all of us, and I feel like we're missing a piece with her not here.

That's odd, right? Is the connection between us so strong this soon?

Hell, if I know how this bond thing works. There's book learning, which we all get in school from Andromeda, but there's practical application. I'm not sure the stuff we covered really prepared me for how it would feel to have that connection—much less with two people. I'm sure it's part of what's ruffling Prez' feathers, too.

I step into the shower, grinning to myself as I pick up their conversation through the wall. It's the ears—fashionable and functional, that's my heritage.

"Hamilton, I don't care what we have to do. I need to know she's okay!"

"Take a benzo, Boone. Magpie's a big girl. She can handle herself."

That wasn't his attitude earlier. Huh. I smile to myself, feeling Prez self-soothing through our bond as he tries to talk Edgar out of his hysterical fit. It must be the switch in him needing to take care of our panicked third. His own emotions smooth out, and that helps me keep control of the ice that was crawling up my spine.

I close my eyes and let the warm water sluice over me as I lean my head against the shower wall. The magnolia body wash Sugarplum uses is on the hanging shelf, so I pour some in my palm, inhaling the scent. It makes me feel closer to her, and I used it in my hair as well. I frown when I run my fingertips past my ears, cursing under my breath. Maybe I'm not as calm as I thought, and I gotta figure this out before she comes home.

Until she emerges, the three of us have to keep the other sides of ourselves quiet. Boone almost fucked it up the first day we were all together, but Prez helped talk him down. Of course, neither of us has triplásia, so who knows how hard it is to control three dominant sides in that kind of situation?

I'm only dual myself—like most of the 'special' residents here—and my darling doc has only one known contribution. Since no one knows who his father is, that may not be accurate, but he's never once shifted or displayed an affinity for anything outside of his feathered alter ego.

We're outcasts from the larger supe society because of our 'mixed' genetics, whether we come from the Hollow enclave, the Tsuihō-sha enclave in Asia, or the Mínádúrtha compound in Ireland. There are a few smaller communities in places like Hawaii, Greece, and Thailand, but those are where the more... water-minded kids are placed.

By the time we're middle schoolers, we all know why we've been placed in our adoptive homes, and if possible, our lineage, so the town doctor can help the schools manage our emergence. How Jolene made it through her childhood and the first half of adulthood without a single sign, I don't know.

I suppose Andromeda and her parents were shocked as well. It happens—there are 'lost ones' and those who never realize their powers, but it's infrequent enough that they still assign every unemerged hybrid a Guardian until it's proved beyond the shadow of a doubt that they will not realize their potential. That Sugarplum's Guardian is still with her after thirteen years makes me certain she's dedicated to our girl's happiness.

Son of a bitch. I know where they are.

I turn off the water, rubbing a towel through my hair as I rush into the bedroom. "Guardian. Seer. Is. A. Guardian."

Edgar blinks at me, rubbing the back of his neck with his large hand slowly. "Uh, yeah, pup. She is. What's that got to do with the war tax on whiskey?"

Prez blinks, then I see the realization dawn on his handsome features. He beams at me, leaning in to kiss me softly, and my whole body flushes with pleasure. "It means that she wouldn't ever let our magpie be in danger, no matter how blasted they got. My darling Wolfie is trying to tell us the Irish lass probably took her to her house to crash."

"Fuck. Why in the hell didn't I think of that? I helped get that place built!" Boone growls low, pointing his finger at us. "Clothes. Now, gentleman. We have a lady to rescue from a fiery-haired warrior."

Yes, sir.

PRESLEY IS A BIT OF A DAREDEVIL.

That probably comes from the whole soaring in the clouds shit, but he insisted we sit on top of the seats in the back of Edgar's drop top Cobra. The wind in my hair is nice, and it's not a long drive—we didn't *need* to drive at all—but unlike being on a horse, this is terrifying. Prez squeezes my hand as we pull up the drive and murmurs in my ear, making my cheeks heat, and I swat him.

"You realize that I'm having control issues this morning, and when you say things like that, growly and full of praise, you make the pointies flare," I scold. "Sugarplum isn't there yet. Help me put it away."

Boone snorts from the driver's seat, waving his hand. "Don't mind me. I'm the only supe in this car who can deal with his shit. Nothing to look at here."

"Oh? Have either of us marked her three times without her knowing, or did I imagine pulling the hound off her a few weeks ago?" Prez shoots back, giving him a dirty look. "Seems like I'm the only one who's in control of my powers, you tool."

I snicker, enjoying their banter. After my adoptive father died and they committed Aurelia, I didn't have any family left. My Guardian was reassigned after I emerged, graduated, and was inducted, so until I met Presley, I was on my own. The sense of family the four of us are building is filling a need I didn't know I had, and I don't know how to explain it to any of them. Maybe Sugarplum can help me find the words—that is, if my guess that Saoirse brought her here after their night of debauchery is correct.

Glaring at us, Edgar hops out of the car, moving with the grace of his kind. He doesn't look back, but the raised middle finger tells me our conversation is over. Prez and I jump out, following him into the enormous house. I'll never tell him, but whatever he and Jamie used to get the elves to bust their asses in this place was a miracle. Before we can catch up, he's pounding on the front door like a federal marshal, and I groan. That will not make us any friends if the girls are hungover or sleeping.

When the door swings open, he turns to look at us and I don't think I've ever seen him look so terrified. He puts on a rough, assholish exterior as the Boone family heir, a judge, the son of a senator, and bookie extraordinaire, but at this moment, his facade falls apart. We all know that neither Sugarplum nor a Guardian would leave their residence unprotected with the threats we perceive.

"Take it easy. Maybe they were drunk enough that caution went with the wind," Presley murmurs as he clamps a hand on his shoulder. "Let Wolfie do a little scan before we come in, guns blazing. He should at least be able to feel if there's been something sinister in the house, so we don't walk face first into some kind of trap."

I give Edgar the most positive smile I can muster before I nod. "Of course, if they *are* in there drunk off their asses, you'll need to let me...cool down before I come in to help scold them. No paddling without me," I warn, shaking my finger at them with a playful tone I don't feel.

Closing my eyes, I look deep within, ignoring the chill from my mother's heritage to find the dark night of my father. The hum zips over my skin as my skin, my body, and even my hair change as power flows through me. Julia told me once that she'd never seen a hybrid change as fully as me, and it had to mean that my real father—whomever he is—is royalty. I don't know if she said that to make me feel better as a kid or if it's true.

No one has ever gotten my mother to admit which consort produced me was. She likes to dangle it to bend people to whims, especially me, but I doubt she'll ever tell anyone. Her heart is as icy as her powers, but something about the way she guards the secret makes me think it's about keeping the man who fathered me safe. She's just not above using it as a bargaining chip when it's useful, either.

Presley smiles at me, reaching up to tuck one of the long strands behind my ear. "It's not fair you get a billion times hotter when you change. Sure, I'm pretty when I shift. Boone's scary and sexy and terrifying, but you, my darling, are so gorgeous it hurts to look at you."

"Are you two done fawning? Because I'd like to see if my drugar has been abducted or injured or…"

Now that I'm changed, it's a very simple thing to lay a hand on his shoulder and murmur, "You must calm, Edgar. We will find her. But you must be calm."

His posture wilts, and the fear and anger melt from his form in response to my soft words. "You're right, pup. I… lost her once because I was a coward. I can't lose her again; not now, not after…"

"I know." I smile and face the house, letting the auras and traces of power and emotion soak into me. It always makes me feel as though I'm floating between time and space as the images and sensations pour through me until I can sense the signatures. There's a lot to sift out because the elves are still finishing some of the interior and their magick lingers the longer they stay at a dwelling.

"What do you feel, love?"

I open my eyes and look at Presley, my expression troubled. "Nothing good. There isn't danger lurking inside, but something isn't right. The energy coming from the house feels wrong."

Edgar growls low, and the heat rolls off him as he spears us with his gaze. "We go in. The doc stays in the back. He doesn't have offensive gifts, and you can keep him safe if I have to shift. No arguing. Understand?"

Holding up my hand to keep Prez from spouting something witty but ultimately unhelpful, I nod. We all have powers, but his are more suited to fighting than my bird-loving mate. "Understood."

"He's no more powerful than you; he's just an asshole," Prez mutters.

Boone turns and flashes us a toothy grin. "I heard that."

Before either of us can answer, he's barreling through the open door like a kamikaze trench runner, and I sigh. "Well, let's go cannon fodder. The alpha is on the hunt."

Waking Up in Vegas

Jolene

"**I** can't get her to wake up!"

I hear people talking, but it's like they're at the end of a tunnel, and I can't see how long it is. I try moving, but hands press me down, causing me to panic. Every woman's secret nightmare is waking up to someone holding you down. I'm pretty sure I say something in protest, but I can't be certain if it's out loud or in my head.

Jesus line dancing Christ, I'm a trained fighter and I can hit a flea on a dog's ass at fifteen hundred feet, but here I am, as useless as a trap-door on a canoe.

How in the donkey fucking hell did some asshole corner me?

My limbs feel like they're filled with sand, and I frown as I try to wiggle out of the firm grasp again. Something isn't right. I can't seem to move like I should be able to. My brain feels like it's filled with cobwebs, and when I attempt to scream, it echoes in my head like a gong in a bomb shelter.

Holy fuck, they drugged me.

Panic sets in and I struggle, forcing my eyes to open. It isn't easy, as fear and exhaustion are weighing every part of my frame down, but I pry my lids open. Everything is blurry, and the light is so bright that I might as well be in a Siberian interrogation camp.

Son of a bitch! Did those assholes from Thailand catch up to me?

Wouldn't *that* be an ironic way to die? Find a place I can finally call home, make genuine connections with people, and end up getting plugged because I couldn't save some tin pot general who supported the wrong side of a revolution. Never mind that I was only there to…

Focus, Jolene. Figure out where you are and how you're going to purge this shit from your system so you can escape.

Vomit. I'd play a fiddle of gold against the Devil if it meant I could get out of this without having to make myself puke.

"Why is she muttering about puke? O' Flanagan, you better have answers!"

Do they have Seer, too? Fuck me with a tire iron, now I've got to save my sorry ass *and* rescue a damsel. If the chimps in my head would quit playing bass drums, it would go a long way to allowing my brain to function. I close my eyes again, lifting my hand towards my face. I'm ninety percent certain I'm going to toss sidewalk pizza to get the effects of this shit to wear off. Might as well start with the old tried and true from the popular girls in high school…

"No! She's going to choke herself. Christ, Hamilton, *do something*. This is your moment to shine, you feathered freeloader."

A hand lifts from my shoulder, sliding down my arm gently to grasp my wrist. They pull my hand away from my face and I whimper pitifully. For a moment, I think all is lost, but I realize that holding my hand freed up one side of my body. I'm not fully pinioned, so if I have an opening, I might get free. I can't feel much below my ribs, but I concentrate hard on wiggling my hips. I don't know if it will work, but if I can get this asshole to lean in, it opens up some options.

This would be a lot easier if I had an operational brain box. I may never drink again, just so you know. Okay, that was a straight up lie, but give me a break. I'm drugged and may be a prisoner. My headspace is pretty fucked up at the moment.

"Is she crying? Fuck, I thought you were going to help her, not make her cry, Hamilton!"

The dude on top of me seems to have a friend. I keep hearing bits and pieces of conversation that I can't process, but whatever the last bit meant spooked my captor. Fingers unwind from my wrist and move to wipe what I guess are tears off my cheeks. Now they've done it... I never let people see me cry. It's a taboo subject in the Jolene handbook, and I'm well and truly pissed now.

When my captor leans in to make soothing noises, I strike. Forcing my noodle arm around his neck, I summon every bit of strength I have to push their head into my armpit. I lock that arm around their throat, creating a chokehold with my hands interlaced. Wheezing sounds echo in my head, and I'm not sure if it's the asshole or me, but I wing a prayer to the wine god as I send a message to my leg to wrap around his back.

If I can keep this fucker in the Guillotine, I may make him pass him out. Then I'll have to figure out how to move and find Seer.

"Holy fuck! Where did she learn Brazilian Jujitsu?"

"In Brazil, ya knob. Stop yelling; my feckin' head feels like gremlins have a brass band in it."

Wait, a minute. Seer doesn't sound scared; she sounds annoyed and... maybe hungover? What in the fiddling fuck is going on?

The arms of the asshole I've got choked are flailing, and I can't seem to figure out what is going on, so I ease up on the pressure. It takes a momentous effort, but I lift my head and lean in to smell the grabby dickface. When I smell the scent of my body wash, I gasp, letting go of the person on top of me. My eyes open and I squint hard, the images swimming as they float over my field of vision.

"Presley?"

"Thank Zombie Jaysus! She's coming round, boys!"

I turn my head, forcing myself to focus until I can see my best friend standing next to a furious-looking Teddy and a... Smurf? Man, whatever I got dosed with is strong. I don't even know what day it is, and I'm seeing imaginary cartoon people. I lick my lips, realizing that my mouth feels like an old sock. "Seer? What the hell happened? Where are we? Who brought the Avatar guy?"

A curse rumbles out of the walking blueberry, and it heads for the hills. Teddy bursts out laughing, and Seer even giggles. I look down at McSteamy in confusion, but he just gives me a broad smile. Feeling bad for almost choking him out, I reach up to straighten his glasses. I knocked them askew when I was shoving his face into my armpit, and the thought makes me flush with embarrassment.

Who knows what it smelled like in there after the hot lights at the show, the dancing, and... whatever else happened after that?

"I remember nothing after the first round of drinks and dancing in the club. We went to the bathroom and then... everything is blank," I admit, feeling like a fool. Some FBI agent I would have made. Hoisted on my petard by some college roofie distributor—I'll never hear the end.

"Aye, Peanut. All in good time. We seem to have ended up at my place, though I don't know where…"

"Do you chits make a habit of drugging your friends with fairy dust, or is that a special treat for us?" The voice lilts as the handsome fantasy novel hero walks in, rubbing his temples.

"Who is this?!"

I blink, squinting again at Teddy as he thunders like a volcano ready to erupt. Presley snorts, burying his face in my side, and I'm pretty sure I swat him in response. "This… this is… did you say fairy dust?"

"Zasha Fydor Petrov, at your service. At least I would be if the evil sprites in my skull would stop banging pots like a poltergeist," he mutters.

"That doesn't explain a goddamned thing," Teddy snarls, stalking up to him.

"Mr. Boone, I don't think you want to tangle with Zasha this morning. Tharin gets so overprotective when we aren't well, and Zasha seems to have the worst time."

My nose wrinkles when I hear Seer's friend Julia step into the fray. I can't decide if I like her, and now I'm trapped in the middle of my guys being weird and her trio of terror. How in the hell could this morning get worse?

"*Julia*! I missed you so much!"

I should quit tempting the Universe to fuck with me, right?

Wolfie's shout follows my ill-advised statement, and I don't know where he popped out from, but he's bounding toward my new least favorite person like a happy puppy. She smiles at him fondly, and something heavy and gross settles in my gut. They know one another, and my little Wolfie is brimming with excitement at her presence.

"Tharin, Zasha... it's been years. You settled in with Juju, huh?"

Gag me with a spoon. Juju? Christ, I'm wishing this fairy dust shit had killed me.

I'm going to barf on Prez, and that won't end this humiliation any faster. It might prolong it because... vomit. Ugh, everything about today makes Thailand look like a weekend romp in the Hamptons. "Can't I pass out again?" I mutter to myself.

"No, Magpie, you can't. If you feel sick, I can help you to the bathroom, though."

Presley's eyes roam over my face and warmth floods my skin. It's a weird time to be horny, and I frown at myself for being super inappropriate. I shake my head a little, turning my gaze to Teddy with a pleading look as the trio, Wolfie, and Seer jabber on the other side of the room. I can't find the right words to respond to anything, and my emotions are caught in my throat as I watch the animated gestures in the little group.

"Sorry, folks. No time for introductions. I'm going to take Tilly home to get cleaned up and see if she can sleep the rest of this off. The rest of you can fuck off until I call you."

Ignoring the puzzled and irritated looks, Edgar walks over, lifts me out from under Prez, and tucks me against his chest. I hate myself for doing it, but I rest my cheek against his firm muscles and close my eyes. His lips brush my temple, and he heads for the door without another word. When we get to his car, he buckles me into the passenger seat quietly before hopping into his side. The engine purrs as he starts it, pulling out of the driveway and heading towards my house in silence.

It occurs to me that for the first time in his life, Teddy didn't put his fat foot in his mouth, and for the first time in mine, I let him rescue me without a fight.

That's what the old timers call progress, folks.

Breakaway

If past Jolene told me Edgar Olivier Boone III would end up sitting next to my whirlpool tub while I soak away a night of debauchery, I would have laughed in her face. Yet he's reading me some spicy romance novel he found on his Kindle app in an array of accents as I wash the club glitter from my hair. Life is weird sometimes, especially since I moved home to the Hollow. He pauses occasionally to make sure I'm awake, but I'd swear he's enjoying this.

What is it biologists say?

Pop culture gets it wrong—true alphas care for their packs like a den mother, not run around snarling and being giant dickwhistles? If that's true, Teddy is proving his alpha status today. He was gentle as hell when he pulled me out of his car and carried me inside—despite my vocal protests—and sat me on the bed. Water was run, clothes were laid out, and he even undressed me without a single innuendo. Miracles like this don't happen every day, so I let him baby me.

A girl likes to be taken care of sometimes, even if she can take care of herself.

After his quiet interrogation about the events of the evening, Teddy let me soak for a bit while he texted. Then he settled in on the steps and started reading in that rich voice of his, and I was a goner. I haven't even asked his opinion of what happened; I figure that's a conversation we can have once all the unusual fog lifts from my brain. My memory is another story altogether, and I don't expect to solve that riddle soon.

"Are you listening, *drugar*, or are you falling asleep again?"

My lips curve as I turn my head to look at him. I lift my hand to brush the stylish shaggy strands out of his eyes, feeling that bizarre squishing in my chest. "I'm listening, Teddy, but I was also thinking about what past us would think about present us. I don't think I could have imagined this in my wildest dreams as a teen. I was certain you hated me. After the cotillion…" I let my words drift off because it still aches to think about the details of that night and what happened at school in the weeks following.

Sitting his phone on the end of the steps, he leans into my hand for a moment. "Ah, Tilly. We were kids—stupid ones, at that. The way our parents pushed us to associate with children of those they considered social equals, the intense expectations of being one of the 'named families', and the sheer idiocy of youth all contributed to poor decision making. I could say those are the only factors, but I'd be lying and I don't want to do that to you. There was a significant amount of outrage in our group because not only did you never *care* what or whom we were doing, you actively fought against our petty tyrannies. You were a fucking Katniss, and you didn't know it."

I blink. I was what? Where the hell did that comparison come from? "Teddy, I don't understand. I spent most of middle and high school actively avoiding your crowd unless I had to save someone from one of your torturous 'pranks'. I didn't engage with y'all. How could I have been some YA resistance leader?"

His chuckle rumbles as he gives me a lop-sided smile. "*Drugar*, you didn't avoid us. You snubbed us at every turn. If we were holding court somewhere, you'd walk away, head held high. When we bullied someone, you intervened. Those we had vendettas against you protected. All the while, you acted like our influence and power didn't exist in your world. The girls wanted to do so much worse than the Cotillion shit; the guys and I had to back them off a couple times because their ideas would have been impossible to cover up. Threats of ruined records and college admissions were the only thing that kept you from being traumatized. Trust me."

The truth in his words is clear by his earnest expression, but I can't believe I survived six years of what I *thought* was hell only to find out that Teddy, Benjy, and their cohorts prevented the mean girls from making it immeasurably worse. It upends my world, and I sit in the warm bubbles, just gaping like a landed trout. What in Hera's name could they have wanted to do that even the bully boys thought was too far? I can't fathom it, but his admission about the threats of college admissions problems let me know it was likely illegal.

"Don't look so shocked, Tilly. You know what we planned the night of the cotillion? It wasn't meant for you, and you took the brunt of it. The girls had much more emotionally and possibly physically scarring ideas for you, just not in public arenas." He pauses and murmurs, "Even then, I was too fond of you to let them destroy your spirit. I liked when you fought us then, as much as I like you fighting me now."

"Edgar Olivier Boone III, you want a brat. I'll have you know that's not my style, buddy," I say, giving his hair a tug as I try to smile.

The timbre of his voice drops and he growls low. "Tilly, I hate to break it to you, but even switches can be alpha brats. You might as well knock things off my table and living on iced coffee."

A laugh breaks free, and I shake my head. "That's it. I'm having Wolfie put a parental lock on your phone. Seer helping you sign up for TikTok is an absolute nightmare and I hate it. You've already got Jekyll and Hyde addicted to the animal video hashtags you play on the TV for them at night."

"That's me—bad influence and scoundrel extraordinaire. I wonder if being a crooked alphahole judge makes me some kind of trope in this book?" He grins, picking up his phone and tapping keys. "I should search up more shit like this because you were so relaxed when I read to you. I think you *like* smutty bedtime stories. Maybe the boys can act out scenes? I bet I could get Dr. Birdman to convince your pup to do it."

Wrinkling my nose, I splash bubbles at him, and he sputters as he rolls to the side to keep his phone dry. "Jesus, Tilly. A little warning next time." Using a towel to meticulously dry it off, he frowns and clears his throat, "Siri, notes. Order waterproof case for phone."

I rise to my feet while I roll my eyes at him. "Okay, Judge Boone. I see you planning for every eventuality; I get it. However, whatever happened to me last night was not planned. Do we need to call the boys and meet them at Prez' office? I don't know if he can test for anything, but…" I shrug, feeling exposed and unsure. "I guess we should find out if anything… bad… happened?"

His eyes darken and I could swear they turn pitch black. "We should, because if someone harmed a hair on your head, I'm going to make their deaths very painful."

"Don't be so dramatic, Teddy. We'll have to track them down in that big city, and I don't have a clue what happened. Neither does Seer. The police won't even be able to do much because we waited so long to report. You will not hunt them down on your own."

"Not on my own," he echoes, picking me up with the towel he's holding. "But it will definitely be a hunt, and they don't stand a chance."

Why are men so freaking *weird*?

"IT'S ABOUT TIME, BOONE," PREZ GRUMBLES AS WE WALK IN THE front door of the adorable building that sits on the edge of his property.

He lives at the other end of town from both me and his practice, but Teddy insisted he have an emergency office set up here. From the looks of the quaint waiting area, I guess he's right. Presley is one of those old timey town doctors who do house calls and take emergency calls in the middle of the night.

The closest thing I've ever seen to that is the 'concierge doctors' the wealthy contract in the Hamptons, and I just figured those people were shysters bilking the Uber-wealthy. This place seems much more geared to treating actual patients rather than writing a script to make the problem go away.

These men constantly amaze me, and I hope it never stops.

"Do you see patients here often?" I ask, looking up at him. His eyes soften, so he must see the discomfort the thought of this visit is causing me.

"Rarely, but it's here for emergencies and last minute scheduling. Are you uncomfortable with me looking you over, magpie? If so, we can take you to a doc in the city."

I shake my head. "No, it's fine. I know there isn't a need for any kind of... assault kit... so I'm fine with you taking blood or whatever."

Edgar lets out a dark snarl at my words, and I reach over to grasp his hand. The sound abates a bit, and Presley chuckles, reaching out to tuck a hair behind my ear. "If you're sure, love. However, I believe the guard dog needs to wait in the front. Can't have him losing his cool every time I need to poke you."

That little shit. He said those exact words to provoke Teddy, and before I can react, he grabs McSteamy by the shirt and pins him to the wall. My head drops back on my shoulders and I stare at the ceiling, willing the testosterone to drop into the room so we can get this indignity over with.

"Tut, tut, Boone," Presley says, letting my growly ex-bully pin him. "If you keep pushing me against things, I'm going to get ideas you aren't ready for."

A snort escapes my lips before I can help it, and a giggle follows. Wrapping my arms around myself, I laugh until my sides hurt, not caring if I look completely insane. Presley is the biggest troll of all, and he's sniffed out an ambivalence in Edgar he doesn't even know about. The situation tickles me because if Teddy thinks Prez is bad, wait until little Wolfie catches the scent. The two of them are irresistible together, and I can't say I'll complain when they figure out a plan of action.

"Fuck off, featherhead. I'll go wait in the front, but only because it will make my drugar more comfortable. Don't make me regret it; do what is needed." He glares at my laid-back doc as if trying to communicate with his eyes, and lets go of his shirt, backing away.

Once he leaves, I tilt my head at Prez. "I thought you guys were all doing so well. What's with the theatrics?"

"Ah, Magpie. Men like Edgar have serious issues when people dare to mess with what they consider theirs. This incident has pushed a primal button that he's having trouble shutting off. He's not angry at me, and I know it. He brought you here because he trusts me to take care of you."

"I guess so," I murmur, glancing out at Teddy stuffed into a tiny chair with his long legs stretched out. "So, tell me... what kind of nasty things are you going to do to me while you have me alone?"

Presley grins, his eyes dancing at my unexpected innuendo. "Why, Jolene Whitley, I believe you intend to test my professional integrity. I'll have you know that I'm not that kind of doctor."

His grin makes the tension in my frame melt, and I look up from under my lashes. "I'll guess we'll have to see about that, doctor."

Rich Girl

Jolene

After a weekend filled with overprotective guys and an absent Seer, I thought coming back to school would take my mind off of the results from the bloodwork Prez took. Instead, I walked into a fretting Bobbi Jo, who had to sit me down to talk to me about my 'inappropriate curriculum'.

That turned out to be a rumor spread by unidentified staff members about the sculpture unit we're working on. It seems they 'mistook' the statue of David for some kind of crazy 'avant garde, NEA funded pornography'.

Mmm-hmmm.

Once I settled that nonsense, I headed for my room to find that the entrance to the art room mysteriously had a new lock on the door. There wasn't a janitor in sight, and I'm sure that was on purpose. I had to go find Hugo to teach me his secret entrance through the back room, which he wasn't ecstatic about giving up. I guess it's been a way for him to disappear before I came along, and after meeting our colleagues, I don't blame him.

Apparently, the boys don't have control over the mean girls now that some of them married or date them as adults. I've also learned that

Bobbi Jo is beyond oblivious and has zero control over anything in the school because of a suspiciously worded school board law put in place thirteen years ago.

That doesn't seem weird or anything—it went into effect right about the time where the events of my famous catastrophe took place, the rich assholes in this town made it so they were the only ones who could vote to suspend, expel, or fire students and staff from WHFS.

Color me amazed that this wasn't in the staff code of conduct, nor is it in the student handbook.

Sighing as I clean up the classroom from a day full of beginning sculpting, I consider the lessons I have tonight. The boys know I'll be late, so we're ordering takeout Chinese. I haven't gotten to discuss the weird crush-y vibe I got from Wolfie when he saw Julia was in town, nor have I been able to talk to Seer about her 'friends'. It's left me unsettled, and this bullying nonsense doesn't help my frazzled nerves.

Once I put the last piece in the cabinet to ensure no one 'accidentally' destroys a student's project, I gather my bag and my glasses to head out to the companion area.

Kali and Hecate insisted on joining my guys this morning, so I whistled for Eury as I herd the crew of canines and felines from their spots. They don't seem to like the other animals, instead choosing to perch on a craggy rock fixture like they rule the roost as they glare at the assorted companions belonging to students and staff alike. I'm not a fan of the bigger predators that some folks kennel there for the day, so I hope they never get into a rumble.

I don't think two King Danes and two servals can take a fucking mountain Lion and a lowland gorilla, even with the help of a pissed off harpy eagle.

"Have fun today, dudes?" I ask, adjusting my sunglasses before I start the engine. An indignant 'mow!' and matching growls echo out of the backseat. Hyde looks at me sheepishly from the front, as if explaining that she can't control the others, and I frown.

I wonder if my companions are being bullied as well. Teddy might know who some of the more aggressive animals belong to. If so, a conversation might be in order. I'll end up in the principal's office again if some asswipe is having their companions try to hurt mine.

Shaking my head at the sheer lunacy of my colleagues or students ordering fights like we're at a *palenque* rather than a damned school is over my fucking line. I'll have their guts for garters and them some.

This fucking town is a snake pit, I swear.

My studio is dark when I arrive, and I'm glad to see the motion sensor lights on the front wall work when I walk by. It's not dark out yet, but after the events at the club, the guys are certain the stalker is a bigger threat than we assumed.

I still believe the movement outside my house was wildlife, and what-ever happened to us at the club was coincidental—college areas are rife with assholes trying to score with chicks in bars. Chemical help in that effort has become a one in five statistic in the U.S. and we simply ran afoul of a would-be date rapist.

That doesn't make it less disgusting, but it's not as scary as assuming that I have a stalker obsessed enough to follow me for an hour to the city, poison me, and lug five people home instead of harming us. Tharin's size alone would take a goddamned Hulk or a team, and I'm not ready to concede I've got an entire crew of motherfuckers trying to hurt me.

Besides, if it was the asshole from Thailand, they wouldn't bother with Julia and her guys. They would have killed Seer and me, maybe posted some revenge video, and gotten the hell out of Dodge. The General doesn't have a beef with them, and I can't see why he'd risk leaving any of us alive and relatively unharmed.

Psychological games are way above his IQ and his pay grade.

Impatient yips from Hecate draw me out of my musings and I open the back door, letting all the furry folk in before I flip on the lights.

Kali comes rocketing in—followed by Jekyll, Hyde, and shrieking Eury—and barrels past us into the studio like her ass is on fire. Dropping my bag, I run after her to find her in the main gallery, snarling at a large chest.

A chest that was not there when we left the gallery after the event last week.

I approach the ancient-looking thing carefully, pulling my phone out of my pocket. Pressing the speed dial for Teddy, I wait for his voice to come out of my AirPods before I speak. "Teddy, where are you?"

"I'm in Burkettsville meeting with clients, drugar. Don't you have lessons this evening?"

"Yes, but the kids and I just arrived at my studio to set up and there's a mysterious-looking pirate chest in the middle of the fucking floor!" I hiss, moving closer to the small pack of angry animals as they make threatening noises at it.

The panic in his voice is clear as day, though I'm sure he's trying to hide it. "I can't be there in a reasonable time frame, Tilly. The doc went to the city to meet the lab techs about the tests, and the pup was on the farm with that fancy pants Sheikh. None of us are available. Do you have a weapon?"

I roll my eyes inward. Of course, he thinks I need someone to ride to the rescue. What I really wanted was to make sure none of them left this thing and once I verified it wasn't, ask if they'd come open it with me. "Teddy, I'm always armed, even if it's my fists. I don't need you idiots to save me; I just wanted to make sure it wasn't some big surprise. Now that I know it isn't, I'll leave the pack in here to guard it and open the side door for the kids. We can deal with it after I'm done."

"What if it's set to explode? Get out of there!" he shouts, his voice clanging in my head like a bass drum.

I walk a little closer, taking one pod out to listen. "Doesn't seem to tick, Captain Hook. I think we're okay."

"For fuck's sake, Tilly, they trained you for the FBI. You know bombs don't tick anymore!"

This shouldn't be funny, and I shouldn't start laughing, but his exasperation is tickling me. Edgar Olivier Boone III is like a hysterical chick in a hostage situation, and I'm standing three feet from a metaphorical dead man's chest. Also, my eagle is swooping around like it's going to land on my head to protect me.

The whole thing is out of a Mel Brooks movie.

"Teddy… I… I… don't think… it's dangerous," I wheeze.

"You have lost your mind, *drugar*, and I don't have time to argue. Get the animals out of the room and post them by the door to keep people from going in. Teach your lessons, and when we arrive, we're having a serious conversation about your cavalier attitude about your safety."

"Yes, Dad," I deadpan, glaring at the picture of him on my phone as if he can feel my irritation.

"I told you I prefer Daddy, Tilly. We can't play that game if you don't say it right," he practically purrs.

I snort, shaking my head as I walk away from the chest. "I'll slit my own wrists first, Boone. Get bent, you perv."

Clicking the end button before he can respond, I grin to myself. I'm playing a dangerous game, taunting him like that, but it makes the muscles in my abdomen clench, so I'll keep doing it.

Maybe I am a brat, after all.

"My mother says you were a loser in high school. How are you qualified to teach me?"

Sucking in a deep, calming breath, I look at the petite blond middle schooler with a fake smile. "Britannia, it's not appropriate to speak to me like that, nor is it good manners to repeat rumors."

She pops her gum for the fiftieth time, her eyes sharp behind her ridiculously oversized glasses. I'm certain they're not real, and that she wears them when she doesn't need them to see tests my ability to control my eye roll.

Ophelia Jane Longworth's eldest daughter is a carbon copy of her mother in everything but looks. Her expensive hipster clothing, top of the line supplies, and shitty attitude scream privileged teen, but her talent is real. I could help her advance her innate skill more than any student I've encountered in the Hollow, but her mother has filled her head with garbage.

"I asked a question. I'm not looking for crappy Dr. Phil witticisms. My therapist bills four hundred dollars an hour and her degree is from Stanford. Just tell me what I want to know," she replies as she turns back to her easel with a shrug.

Christ, I want to punch this little shit in the mouth.

"My BAs in illustration and business are from State U, but my masters in education is from Cornell. However, if you're fishing for higher status, it will please you to know that my doctorate in abnormal psychology is from Harvard. I also took a year of painting at the Sorbonne, and a year of sculpting at *Sapienza* in Rome. Does that satisfy your curiosity?" I can't help but grin when her facade drops a bit, clearly impressed by the credentials I worked so hard to attain over the years.

Her shoulder lifts nonchalantly, and she sighs. "I suppose so. Beggars can't be choosers in this backwater hell hole."

I've never been so glad I don't teach middle school in my entire life. The split between the Formative and Finishing schools cuts off after seventh grade and this darling witch is a seventh grader. It doesn't help me for next year, but by then, I hope she's convinced her parents to send her to some rich bitch boarding school like Miyako or Swallowtail.

Good riddance to bad rubbish, Niecy would say.

"Glad you feel comfortable settling. Now, it's almost time to end our session. You need to clean up your supplies and put your work on the rack for next week. After that, you can go find your companions."

"It's bullshit that they have to stay in that room with your mangy bird and those raggedy cats. At least they have Coach Edgar's purebreds to keep them company."

I take another calming breath, willing myself not to give in and snap at the snarky Ophelia clone. That was OJ's favorite schtick in high school—anyone not as rich as the elites were trashy and beneath her. Low bred was the term she preferred, and it takes as much effort not to smack her kid as it did her.

"I don't allow companions in the lesson rooms, Britannia. I kicked them out of my space and I had every right to do so. Why I choose that rule is not something I have to explain to you, no matter what you think you're owed in life."

Ha! Eat that, you rude pre-pubescent Regina in training.

She sniffs and packs up her supplies before standing with her drawing. I open the door to allow her access to the back room, rubbing my shoulder when she bumps into me like a fucking pro. Goddamnit, did OJ teach her ALL of her assholery or is it in their DNA?

"Hey! That hurt Britannia. You can't just attack people you don't like because someone told you they were bad."

Her expression is one of pure disdain as she looks over her shoulder. "Clean up the mess. Employees should be seen and not heard."

White rage floods my entire body and I feel the worst possible thing coming over me—it's going to go black and I'm alone with a weird box and bitchy teenager. This can't happen right now; it just can't.

"*Britannia*! That behavior is *unacceptable* for a young lady from your family. Apologize to Miss Whitley *immediately*!"

The voice that booms out from the doorway is familiar and the mere knowledge that he's here seems to push the blackness from my mind a little. "Teddy?"

Britannia shoots me a look full of venom as my sharply dressed lover comes rushing across the room. He cups my face in his hands, murmuring low as he looks into my eyes. "You were going to go down; I could feel it. Hell, Tilly, I could see it on your face."

I nod, putting my hands on his chest as I murmur, "Too much in one day. Just tired, I think."

His growl is an argument, and I dip my chin. He's not wrong, but I can't show weakness to Britannia anymore than I could her mother. It would diminish what little authority I have left and I have an entire year of this girl to contend with. Edgar drops his hands, tucks me against his side, and gives her the same fierce glare he used on his players that first day.

"You will take your companions and leave once you've apologized. Your mother is waiting outside, and if you think I won't be addressing this outrageous behavior with her, you're delusional. Now *go!*"

My thighs clench as he orders the tween around like she's not worth his time, and I realize I *might* have a wee damsel fantasy that I've never allowed myself to voice. Every time one of these guys steps in and tells people to fuck off, my vagina flutters like butterfly wings. It's baffling and hot at the same time.

Not that I'm ever going to tell *them that.*

"Whatever, Coach. Sorry, Jolene," the girl mutters as she hangs up her artwork. She scoops up her supplies with a sneer at me, and heads for the hills, not bothering to do the cleanup needed in the lesson room.

I sigh, knowing it was on purpose and now I'm stuck being her maid, just like she wanted. "You didn't have to do that, Teddy."

He grins and leans down to give me a soft kiss. "Of course I did, Tilly. Kids need boundaries and she was way the fuck over hers. Let me help you clean up the mess she left while we wait for Prez and the pup. They can't wait to figure out if you've been teaching in a building rigged to blow."

"Christ. You guys need to stop watching so many crime shows. It's just a creepy box, and it probably doesn't even have a head in it."

His laugh rumbles over me like a big cat. "You say that now, but when it leaks rancid people juice on your new floor, don't expect me not to say I told you so."

Who would ever expect that?

Here's to Never Growing Up

N *ot telling her what we know was hard as fuck.*

When Wolfie and I arrived, we had his portable x-ray in tow. Boone was worried about the escalation from outdoor spying to direct attacks, and though I didn't believe that big ass treasure chest was booby-trapped, I agreed we should approach it with caution. There are plenty of ways to harm someone that don't go boom, and since Magpie rolled into town, the hornets' nest has been stirred.

The x-ray showed a trove of books and papers, but no wiring or mechanisms to rig the lid or anywhere else. We hauled the thing back to the house and examine the contents piece by piece instead of pulling it out in the studio, only to cart it home afterward. Magpie wanted to dig in, but sharing the results from the blood work was more pressing, so we stowed it in her garage for safekeeping.

That was two weeks and what feels like a lifetime of bullshit ago.

Jolene was furious that the blood we drew showed signs they were dosed. To keep it simple, I had my lab rat ex-girlfriend dummy up a report showing that it was Rohypnol. Unfortunately, I had to add a lie to the pile to avoid questions; it wasn't my first choice, but once I showed the guys the real one, we agreed it had to go to the Society.

The drug they were given isn't one we've ever seen before. It was powerful enough to take out four Guardians, so it's dangerous. They confiscated all the samples and paperwork from my source so they can analyze it further. Whoever made it—human or supe—knows enough about our physiology to tailor make a knock out liquid to transcend species-specific resistances.

Someone isn't just dosing college girls to get laid or targeting Jolene because of her work overseas; this was a well planned, coordinated test run. The clubs Seer took magpie to are extranormals only, and it's impossible to know if they hit her group on purpose or at random. What we know is that there is an enemy looking to do harm to supes.

And they know where our girl lives.

Boone damn near lost his mind. He called his father and his mother —a miracle—and the mayor. After they promised to look into it with their contacts in DC and abroad, he spent hours looking at the lab reports as if his degree was going to magically change from law to biomedical engineering. His supe sides have been in overdrive so badly that Prez gave him some of the suppressant they give the kids until puberty.

Conversely, Magpie has been burning the midnight oil after classes pouring over the contents of the trunk. She seems convinced they left it as a clue to the mystery of her background check. That little tidbit came out when she had to ask us to move her boards from the basement to the garage so she could work in one place.

It breaks my heart that we can't tell her we know why she couldn't join the FBI. Anyone with a birth certificate registered to Whistler's Hollow is forbidden to work in the military or law enforcement. It's part of a deal the council made with various governments hundreds of years ago to keep supes out of positions where they could lose control and hurt someone. Every location we have enclaves—hybrids or not—have specific coding in their birth or adoption records to indicate the person is banned from those careers.

That's why she passed security checks, but not this search.

Boone's father is part of the coalition in the Society that got our kind allowed to have any security clearance at all when he first got elected. Until then, we couldn't hold office, work for agencies or get licenses for a lot of jobs. Edgar Two may be a randy old jackass, but he's always worked hard to give supes more freedom.

Hybrids are another story, and Teddy struggles with being a disappointment to the asshole all the time. His mother is no better, but at least she favors him in public.

Jekyll comes running up to her with a tennis ball, pulling me out of my meanderings. I scoot my chair back—my natural aversion to felines puzzles the hell out of Jolene, but she gives me a crooked smile as she lobs the ball out the open garage door. I shrug, continuing to organize the papers in my stack by year.

"I'd love to know who sent me this treasure trove. It's full of information I think got scrubbed from town records. So much history… I'll be at this for weeks," she murmurs, holding up a faded world map that has to be almost a hundred years old.

I wince. The map is full of Society markings and both abandoned and current enclaves are marked with symbols that won't be hard for her to research. "It may be old junk from someone's estate sale. You're an artist; maybe they thought you could create something with this crap."

Her brow furrows, and she narrows her eyes. "So they broke into my studio, reset the alarm, and left it without a note? I don't buy it, Prez. Also, you don't either."

Sighing, I tug my glasses off and clean the dust off of them as I blink. "Okay, you're right, my little detective. But I also don't think it's as sinister as an obsessed stalker following you from city to city."

My words are only partially true, but I don't want her to lose herself in this unnecessary sleuthing. Once she emerges, we'll be able to tell her what all of this means and why she didn't get to follow her dreams to the behavioral unit like she planned. Though, to be honest, I couldn't be less concerned about our heritage buggering up her original plans. If we weren't on lists, she might never have come back here and we'd all be poorer for it.

"Do you guys know where Seer has been taking off to with her friends all the time?" she asks. Her tone is offhand, but I can tell by the way she won't meet my eyes and the teeth tugging at her lower lip that it bothers her.

"No," I admit. "She's been mysterious of late. Julia wouldn't let her get into trouble, though. She's very conscientious and so are her consorts."

My magpie looks up at me with an arched brow. "So much so that they allowed us to get roofied? Forgive me if it doesn't inspire confidence."

"That's true," I nod my agreement, but since she doesn't have all the details, I can't correct her. Wolfie talked about his old Guardian as if she could destroy the universe in a single blow for years, and he's one of the more powerful supes I know. Julia, Zasha, and Tharin are a deadly triad, and under normal circumstances, they would have left very few pieces of the person who dared to cross them.

"I don't trust her or like her. Her guys are okay, but she's got an air about her that says she's hiding something. I hate people who lie when it wouldn't cost anything to tell the truth," she mutters, tacking the map on the board and rearranging some pictures around it.

Her words hit me like a ton of birdseed and I snap my mouth closed before I blow it. I don't want to lie to her, but I know why we have to. I'm not sure any of us will be forgiven, though. Jolene has become an integral part of our lives and I can't imagine Wolfie or Boone feeling any different. In fact, for them it has to be worse because…

"Prez, can you hand me that stack of journal entries on the bench?"

I grin as I look over at her. Magpie has her hair in a messy bun with three pens sticking out of it, and an adorable pair of glasses perched on her nose. I didn't know she wore them until I walked out here to help her with sorting. She told me they were only for reading, but her eagle eye marksmanship tells me she doesn't need them much. After her long week of lessons, school, horse training, and research in here, she's probably strained her eyes a bit. I should pull her chart from the office records to get more familiar with her particular physical quirks given it might have hints why she hasn't emerged or even what she's going to emerge as.

The Council sure as fuck hasn't been forthcoming about their thoughts on the subject. Boone, Wolfie, Seer, and I have all made separate requests to access her Society files, but they have blocked us at every turn. It's like someone is actively hiding her true parentage. That's weird because usually the docs and Guardians have unrestricted access to their charges.

However, since Andromeda isn't back yet from whatever assignment she's been on, we can't talk to the one person who helped guide Jolene when she was a young shifter. Paired with the fact that she's mated with one side of my darling vet and three of Edgar's, it's not a leap to believe that we're being kept in the dark on purpose.

Supes can mate with more than one person depending on species, but I've never heard of an unemerged supe mating with four vastly different species.

We won't discuss my insecurities about her not triggering my supe side yet. I'm not a hybrid like the others, and I'm a little terrified that whatever she has lurking inside won't choose me. I don't want to mention it, though, because I don't know if I could handle their platitudes. The one woman I loved before I came to the Hollow and met Wolfie left because our inner selves didn't mate.

It's a sore spot, and one I've never had to worry about with him. His sides seem to click with mine, even if that step hasn't happened yet.

I'm confident that it will. In fact, I wonder if Jolene is the catalyst to awakening that part of me. But that may be dreaming—my creature is so different from your average shifter or mage. I'm more rare than a fae or even a phoenix. I only know of a few of my kind because we are solitary and get deployed by the Society to care for enclaves of supes both big and small throughout the world. Our gifts make us perfect candidates for the position I'm currently holding, though a few other types can handle it as well.

"Hello! Earth to Prez!"

Blinking, I give Jolene a sheepish smile, pushing my glasses up. "Sorry, love. I got lost in thought, it seems."

"I wanted to know if you were ready to break for lunch."

"Hell, yes. I'm ready to eat my hand. Would you like to accompany me to pick up food from the diner and then we can stop at my place to feed my clan?"

She looks at me with a puzzled expression. "Your clan? I didn't see anyone else living at your house when Edgar and I came to the mini office."

I grin, shaking my head. "Not people, love. I have an entire building of friends I'd like you to meet. We were too worried about you to take a tour after the drugging. I'd like to introduce you to—well, not a hobby, but a passion of mine. Are you game?"

Her face lights up as if I've asked her to adopt a barrel of adorable puppies. "I *absolutely* want to! You're always so reserved outside of the bedroom, McSteamy. I can't wait to learn more about what makes you tick."

Holy fuck. Why didn't I do this earlier? I'm an idiot.

MY MAGPIE WALKS THROUGH THE LARGE AVIARY WITH WIDE EYES AND coos of joy as she greets every bird. She asks about their species, where I got them, and what makes them special. I've had no one take such an intense interest in my clan, and it's making my stomach flutter with happiness. Wolfie always helps me feed them and even clean, but he's not fascinated by every feather and fowl I house.

Jolene is. She's like a kid in a candy store, and she lets them land on her hands, shoulders, and head as much as they please, even giggling when some of the bigger species try to groom her. I should have known by the way she is with Eurayle, but I assumed her fondness was because that companion chose her. Now I realize that our girl simply adores animals of all kinds, and she seems to have a knack for getting them to trust her.

I wish that was a clue to her nature, but it isn't. Quite a few common species of supes have animal affinities, and even more rare types bond with non-humans easily.

For now, I'm going to enjoy watching her chitter and play with my babies. This little side quest was exactly what I needed to quell my worries about where I stand with my magpie.

If she can charm my aviary, she can charm my inner fellow, guaranteed.

Timber

T he adults-only Homecoming party at the Speakeasy is in full swing.

Henry is slinging drinks like nobody's business. The exhausted staff of WHFS are unwinding from weeks of floats, court elections, student infighting, angry parents, and inter-school rivalry. Every single teacher and administrator has withstood outrage and wrath over pranks and hair pulling—both literal and figurative.

"Nice job, Boone! Our boys took those Rebels downtown tonight," says the shop teacher.

I haven't bothered to learn his name, and I feel bad about that, but most of the teachers have sided with my choir of detractors. It hasn't made for a lot of friendly relations with my colleagues. I eat lunch in my classroom and use the staff lounge to prepare copies when everyone has left for the day. When I was young, alienation from the surrounding people would have made me sad and lonely, but now I have support.

Or I did.

Jekyll butts my hand with his head as if he heard my thoughts, and I hear a laugh across the room that makes me smile. Presley and Wolfie have the rest of the pack over at our usual booth, holding court over a group of people from work who won't talk to me most days. I watch Teddy chat with the weasly auto repair guy. His stubbled jaw stretched as he takes his praise and back slaps with a grin.

Grabbing my bourbon, I toss it back, letting the burn warm my insides. It's my fourth—no, fifth—since we arrived. The haze of alcohol is soothing the sharp edges from the past month.

Despite the efforts of my lovers, I'm feeling the pinch of being berated by students, dismissed by parents, and abandoned by my best friend. I still don't know why Wolfie is so enamored with the mysterious chick who stole my only confidant, and I'm no closer to figuring out what the hell any of the shit in the trunk means. While Teddy's team is a success, the school is victorious, and those closest to me are celebrating, I'm an utter failure.

I sit the rocks glass on the bar, shooing Jekyll back to the crowd as I walk towards the door. A little fresh air might help my morose attitude. I don't want to ruin the night for my sexy Coach or drag down my doc sandwich by telling them how low I've been feeling. They deserve a night of fun, especially because they've been working so hard.

Teddy's been practicing with the team every free second to earn this win. The sheikh has had Wolfie focused on Mehdi at the farm, as his visit seems to stretch on forever. Presley has had a parade of young patients, waking him at all hours of the day and night with some bacterial infection that's making them act insane.

That's why I haven't told them about the problems at the school or my studio. They've been working so hard, and my petty grievances with my friend or colleagues aren't worth whining about. Besides, I don't want them—or anyone—to feel sorry for me.

I just want things to go back to normal.

Walking out into the crisp fall air, I wonder how such a picturesque town can be so full of hidden pitfalls and venom. The quaint street, gas lamp streetlights, and cobblestones would make a visitor think this is the perfect little American town full of happy, friendly people with matching lives. But like everything else in the world, the gorgeous outer layer hides an insidious rot underneath.

Apparently, I'm a morose idiot when I don't get laid often enough because of scheduling conflicts.

A wry chuckle escapes my lips as I walk down the street, studying the storefronts absently. The silly names don't phase me anymore, so I pass by without a thought until I come to the space with the blacked-out windows. No one has ever mentioned what this place is or why it remains empty in such a prime location. I wonder why it's here and who owns it. Like so many things I've seen or heard since I moved home, it's an unspoken mystery.

"Evenin' Tíogair. Out for a wee constitutional? Where's your entourage?"

The lilting voice echoes out of the alley between the blacked-out window space and *Bound Together*. A plume of spicy scented smoke leads me into the shadows of the small access area, and when my eyes finally adjust, I see my grocery store leprechaun smirking as he leans against the bricks. He's staring at me with an intense emerald stare I could swear is glowing in the dim light.

"Did anyone ever tell you it's creepy as fuck to lurk in dark alleys?" I ask, crossing my arms over my chest.

"I'm sure they have, lass. It's not a day ending in 'y' if someone hadn't scolded me at least once. Pity for them; I enjoy it."

A throaty chuckle escapes before I can stop it, and I toss my hair over my shoulder. "Ah, I see. Naughty boy doing bad things for attention. Well, you're not the first, and definitely not the best I've known…" I let my sentence trail because he never gave me his name.

Clutching his chest dramatically, he gives me a pained look. "You wound me, Tíogair. I would have thought my reputation preceded me." At my blank look, he winces again. "Doyle Aloysius Haggerty, at your service, milady."

I blink. People have mentioned Doyle to me in passing——he's responsible for the crazy business names—but I didn't realize I'd met him. I can't think of a thing to say except, "I don't have an entourage."

"You have felines and birds and dogs and bullies and white coats, lass. The trail of admirers behind you is longer than the Queen's attendants."

"Oh, piss off," I grumble, walking closer as he draws on the thin cigarette in his long fingers. "And who smokes cloves unironically? Those things are the worst."

He shrugs, his eyes flashing as he grins. "Just another one of my bad habits, I'm afraid. I'm too old to be taught new tricks—many have tried."

Something about the way he says it feels like a dare, and it makes my stomach tighten. The fire in my veins rushes forward, and I stalk closer, plucking the clove from his fingertips. Pitching it, I watch the cherry skitter across the pavement before I lean in to look directly into his eyes. "You, Doyle Aloysius Haggerty, couldn't *handle* my efforts were I to try. There's…" I inhale for a moment, closing my eyes to feel the sensations running through me. "… fear running through you right now. I scare the hell out of you, but you like it."

The redhead doesn't move, save for his smirk deepening. "Aye, Tíogair. You've got me nailed like a fence post. The question is, what are ye planning to do with that information? What scares *you*?"

I'm not scared of much, but I doubt he means things like spiders or gang violence. No, Doyle is asking me about my deepest insecurities, and it's not something I share with people.

In all my years of friendship with Seer, I've never admitted to feeling like a stranger in my home as a child or the gnawing pit in my stomach when I think I'll lose someone I care enough about to consider an ally. Alienation and abandonment are root causes of the path my life took once I left the Hollow, and I'll be damned if this cocky asshat is going to get that out of me with a sexy pout. "I'm not afraid of anything."

"Liar," he hisses, reaching out to brush a hair off of my face. "You, Jolene Athena Whitley, project an air of untouchable confidence, but underneath, you're hiding rage, fear, and heartbreak. Your armor may fool the Dublin heiress and the platoon of gooey centered boys who follow you like lost pups, but not me. I've been around far too long and seen more than you can imagine—I can practically *taste* your desires."

Inching closer to him, I force his body against the brick he was lounging against, and my hand comes up to rest on his throat. The claws in my gut dig deeper, and I squeeze hard with my thumb and forefinger on the column of his neck. I can feel his pulse jumping in his carotid—which I'm careful to avoid because I don't *think* I want him dead at the moment. "You don't know a damn thing about me, Lucky. What gives you the right to play armchair therapist?"

His laugh is full of delight. There's not a trace of fear in his expression as I continue to put pressure on his airway, only hooded eyes and that fucking smirk I'd like to knock off his pretty face with my fist. "I don't ask for permission, Tíogair—never. If you want me to kneel, you'll have to do better than a snarl and a mean face. Give me the heat, and I'll consider it."

I open my mouth to respond, but a rush of cold fury fills me. No one tells me what to do without my permission, and he's giving me orders like he owns my ass. My breath escapes in a sibilant sound as I increase the pressure on his throat reflexively. A sexy rumble vibrates in his chest, and my lips curve up a bit before I smash our bodies together, using the wall for support. "I don't take orders; I give them."

"Ah, *there* she is," he croaks. "I've been waiting. Go on, then. Let it take charge—do it."

The words make little sense through the red haze in my mind, and I tilt my head as I try to puzzle them out. Leaning in, I run my nose over his Adam's apple, and the scent of his skin triggers another flood of energy that shoots straight to my pussy.

A fleeting thought about the boys whispers in my head, but my body overrides my brain. Something dark and hungry and icy is slowly taking over, and I don't know how to stop it anymore than I do the black outs. Before I can even process that, his hand snakes around me to squeeze my ass, and I'm done.

There is no Jolene, only a horny Domme.

Holding his throat, I hook my ankle around his and use my shoulder to flip us around. The bricks scrape my skin as our position changes and I'm flush to the wall, but the scratches will be worth it. His eyes glow that eerie green as he waits, not giving up his power because I was rough. My eyebrow arches and I push harder, using my free hand to put pressure on his shoulder as well. The command comes from the bottoms of my feet when I growl at him. "Kneel!"

A satisfied smirk stretches across his handsome face as he slowly lowers to his knees, looking up at me with a mixture of defiance and compliance that is both hot as hell and infuriating at the same time. He tucks his hands behind his back, spine straight and chin up despite my continuing kung fu grip. I only have a few more seconds before that becomes dangerous and we both know it. It's time for me to make a bigger decision than playing chicken with a hot guy in a dark alley.

"Tíogair, I'm waiting."

His voice is raspy, and I relax my hand before I do unintended damage. The weird lusty rage slithering through me doesn't like my choice, but I ignore it. I've been in the scene far too long to ever let my weird psychological problems cause me to damage another player in the game. "What are you waiting for? An engraved invitation?"

"There's what I needed—voiced assent, milady." His hands grip my hips roughly, yanking them forward as he buries his face in my stomach and inhales.

The hungry thing inside of me practically shivers with pleasure and I groan.

I think this is going to be a rough ride.

Savage

The scent of her excitement is sodding intoxicating.

It's in my nature to be, shall we say, *flexible* regarding my preferences. Beings like myself have been around long enough to dabble in every paint pot and art bin available. The narrow strokes humans and even most supes paint themselves with are amusing. Unlike her current trio of lovers, I've clued into the fact that Jolene will not emerge as a singular entity, and her varied tastes tie to the parts of her struggling to the surface.

Whatever put the mojo on her is someone I want to meet.

It's by far one of the strongest suppression spells I've encountered in my lifetime, but since I'm not a Guardian, I can't declare it beyond the capability of those on this plane. She's locked up tighter than a drum, and it's no wonder the Society and the councils are eager to discover her lineage.

However, I'm not their errand boy or acolyte, so I'm only interested in the woman looking down at me. Her eyes are swirling with colors and I would bet a Rembrandt she's never seen what happens when her hidden natures push through the veil of magic. The fierce look on her face, the throaty command, and the hold she had on me were enough to make me disregard the clear danger in getting intimate with her.

I know I'm dancing in the fire, but I don't care.

She gives my shoulder an impatient tap and I chuckle against the fabric of her skirt. I adore a woman who knows what she wants and isn't afraid to ask for it. My fingers slip under the hem, inching it up as I kiss my way over her curvy thighs. The tiny growls she lets out every time I nip her skin make me shiver, and I continue doing it just to see what will happen. At the next bite, her hands bury in my hair and she snarls at me.

There's unquestionably some sort of shifter in the mix, and it's been a while since I've been with one. I hope she accidentally shifts for the first time when we're in flagrante—the chaos will be delicious.

"Stop fucking around, Lucky," she says, her fingers tightening in my hair as she pulls me towards her pussy.

I look up, shooting her a mischievous wink and lift her thighs onto my shoulders. As soon as she finds her balance, I dive into her spread legs like a starving man. She's practically dripping down my face already, but I slowly lap a trail around her sex, cleaning that up before I direct my attention where she clearly wants it.

Her ass wriggles impatiently in my hands, and I'm sure I'll pay for this later, but I can't help but tease her. Blowing a puff of air over her clit, I wait for the whine, and then suckle. One of my fingers traces her opening lightly, and she tries to force it to slide inside. A quick nip redirects her attention, and I smirk against her heat.

After all, if I'm not misbehaving, life is no fun.

"Doyle, if you don't—ahhh!"

That's better. I prefer her to be screaming if she's invoking my name.

Done with games, I slip three fingers inside of her, pumping them in rhythm with the movements of my tongue. I close my eyes, letting the taste and feel of her surround me. The noises she makes are almost musical and I can sense where to be fierce and when to soothe. The power inside of me swells in unison with my cock, and though it's unusual, I allow it to flow over me. When her hips rock faster, I slip another finger in, feeling her muscles tighten around my digits like she's trying to break them.

This girl is going to explode at some point and I cannot wait to see it happen.

Shivers crawl up her limbs as she rides my face and hand, but I keep licking, sucking, and thrusting into her until she screams loud enough to rattle the darkened windows on the building we're defiling. When her thighs go limp, I withdraw, lapping up the evidence of her orgasm. She's still panting above me, so I shift to hold her weight in my palms as I raise my eyes to meet hers. The fire there hits me like a brick to the face, and before I can comprehend what it means, I'm on my feet with her back pressed to the rough wall.

"I'm adding the noise you make when you come to my mental playlist, Tíogair," I murmur against the shell of her ear. Both of my inherited natures are awake, and for once, they're twined together, focused on the girl in front of me. In all the years I've walked this world, I've never felt my entire being funnel into one desire that isn't based on my raison d'être. I'm in uncharted waters, and I'm uncertain if I should keep sailing or try to make it back to shore.

"Lucky, your mouth is *so* much better when it's occupied. Just fuck me already."

Her teeth sink into my shoulder, and it's almost impossible not to let the energy welling up inside of me escape. The last time I did that, I started a chain reaction that led to an orangutan leading the humans. The hilarity of the situation escaped my relatives and the rest of the boring people in charge. This time, though, I think I'm aimed in the right direction. So I hold her hair in my fist, enjoying the sting of her blunt teeth while my free hand undoes the buttons on my jeans. It takes every bit of my waning focus, but I situate our bodies in the right position.

I lift her head and look into her eyes, startling at what I see. It can't be...

"Tíogair, tell me what you need," I whisper, gritting my teeth.

Her lips curve as she rolls her hips, sliding against my cock. "I need you to fuck me until I scream your name, you bratty asshole." That said, she pushes down, impaling herself on me until I'm balls deep.

Holy mother of Hercules. My aunt was right and I owe her a bloody library.

Shaking my head, I turn my attention back to the woman in my arms. Her limbs are wrapped around me like tentacles, and my hips grind into her with each thrust as our bodies move together. The tendrils of power within me spiral up, around, and over us as I pound her into the wall, the pace picking up every second that my true nature is unleashed. I dip my head, taking her lips for the first time since this began. Kissing deepens the intimacy of the connection between us, and I groan into her mouth as I feel the impossible continue to happen.

My magic, my power, my essence—mighty and ethereal as it is—are merging with something I can't identify. I have no idea what part of Jolene's lineage is calling to the immortals inside of me, but as our hips buck and bodies heat with sweat, our inner beings are twining together. It's not supposed to happen with beings like me, and as pleasure takes over my consciousness, I realize why she's been keeping a secret for so long.

Jolene has the blood of the ancients in her line, and there are people who will want her dead.

I lift my head, breaking the kiss to look at her as we rocket towards our climaxes together. "I won't let them hurt you, Tíogair."

Her whine makes my cock twitch and I know I don't have long. "Whoooooo?"

"Anyone. Everyone. Ever," I growl. "Hold on to me."

The glow that surrounds us as I unleash the entirety of my being is emerald, like the hills of the land I grew up in, and the boom of unleashed power echoes down the street as her body clenches around me. I throw my head back as my orgasm slams into my gut like a freight train, holding her quivering body so tightly that she digs her nails into my arms and screams.

I have no idea what I just unleashed into the world, but it's worth every ass-kissing moment of penance I'll have to do to have this moment with her.

THE END OF MY CLOVE GLOWS AS I GAZE OUT INTO THE NIGHT. Taking a deep drag, I consider the implications of tonight's activities. I'll be called in for a verbal lashing, but that's nothing new. It will only be from the mother's supposed relatives; my father's have never been an issue. It's rather amazing that the entire extra normal world kept trysts like those of my parents and Jolene's hidden in the shadows for as long as they did.

Humans think they have a lock on prejudice within their species, but they don't have a glimmer of what supe society was as recently as forty years ago. Shifters, magic users, the fair, the demi and full ancients, and even legendary beasts didn't intermingle, much less cohabitate. Hybrids like those who live in the enclaves worldwide were dark familial secrets, and if discovered, could be killed before they could 'dilute' their lineage.

Hell, I'm old enough to have watched supes evolve from literal and figurative witch hunts to where we are today.

The Society was started in the dark times—the purges—and has worked tirelessly to protect and care for those whose parents couldn't or wouldn't raise them as their own. Children of interspecies mating no longer suffer as they once did, but some supe communities are less progressive than others.

It's easy to judge the parents who turn their progeny over to the Society, but if your choice is to be exterminated, shunned, or sent to a freak show, you'd be surprised how that changes perspective.

The other reason hybrids are sent to the enclaves to be adopted by childless supes is they're abandoned. The official term is 'enrolled' if you ask, but some supes are so infamous or powerful that even the hint of a child with their powers mixed with another's puts them on hit lists. Most hybrids only have two donors in their genetic or magical lineage, but occasionally, a third emerges. These kids are powerful and if a mother believes it's a possibility, she might protect her child by keeping their heritage secret.

Yeah, some very naughty deities, high Fae or alpha shifters use the enclaves like a baby laundering service, especially if the kids aren't a result of their mate bonds or marriages. Enter me; that's how I started as a kid at Swallowtail. (Mind you, they'd barely opened it when I matriculated through, but I attended just the same.)

My mother and my unnamed father had a lovely brief affair and dumped me there as a toddler. I met my dear auntie later, but I've never had contact with my father's side. Hell, I don't even know who he is, save his species, but that alone tells me why my mother fell for him. Their powers compliment one another, and they had some lively encounters—much like the one I had this evening.

My Tíogair took off like a bat out of Hades once we came to, and I can't say I blame her. The parts of her trying to claw their way through the suppression spell are getting stronger, and she seems to collect us like a miniature army as they push the bounds of the magic. Much like my favorite frenemy, Boone, I can only assume my lass has a complicated parentage once we peel the layers of her adoption away.

She's not quite ready to hear that her dead parents weren't her parents at all.

That's an assumption, but it's likely the truth. Her parents aren't some penny ante wolf and wizard combo or even a mix of a rare supe and a common. There's power lurking under that milky skin, and I'm going to find out everything I can to help protect her. I might even tap that insufferable self-sacrificing git that works at her school. Hugo's kind doesn't reveal much because their powers are both a gift and curse to bear—one that has been forbidden from sharing their knowledge with anyone but one ancient one who spawned their line.

Fortunately for me, I have a bit of sway in that arena.

Sighing, I stomp the remnants of the smoke on the ground and inhale the scents of our couplings from earlier. I wish she'd been brave enough to stay, but I know the part of her that believes she's human feels like she's done something wrong. She had to process it and make amends to those she thought she's betrayed. I could have told her she didn't have to worry about it, but it would have involved things she's not aware of.

Her boys will understand, and though it'll be a helluva fun time figuring out how I fit into that dynamic, she won't be disparaged for our playtime.

At least, she'd better not be. I'll show her wee young-uns what it feels like to incur the wrath of a demigod.

That I can guarantee.

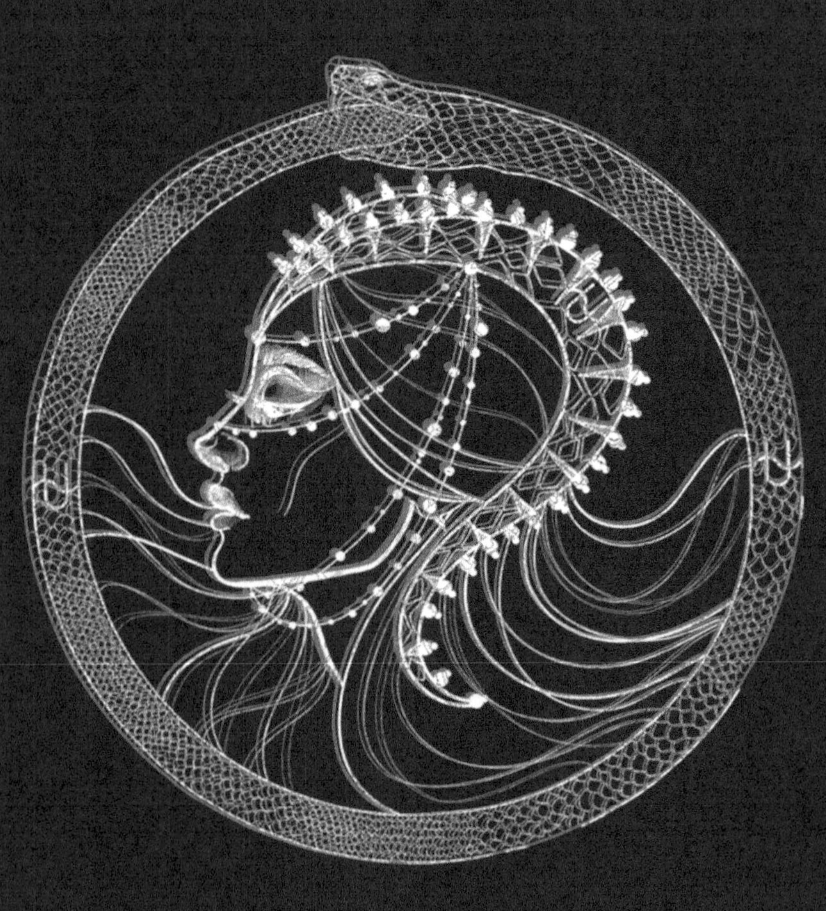

I Did A Bad Thing

Jolene

The thundering of paws and a screech wake me as the entire cadre of animals comes bounding into the bedroom, trampling over us as the dogs chase the cats and the eagle swoops behind them with a scream of fury. Multiple boob crushing stomps force me to pry my eyes open, looking around with a grunt of anger. I'm about to howl with anger when another intruder comes crashing in.

"*Holy feck*, ye bloody fools, you're going to wake up the entire…" Seer's snicker is followed by snort, and within moments, she's lost it.

This is *not* how I wanted to start my morning.

"Seer!" I hiss-whisper. "What in the hell are you doing and when did you get back?" I pinch the bridge of my nose as she continues to cackle. Teddy shifts on my left, his face buried in my neck, and Prez grumbles something sleepy in my right ear. I don't bother asking why she feels the need to come barging into my room without knocking all the time. The boys have begrudgingly gotten used to her doing it, and none of us are shy.

"I got back last night, and I came over to play with the kiddos. No one was up, so I did the food and exercise thing, but they were so hyped up when I opened the door…"

Uh-huh. She *definitely* unleashed the beasts, hoping they'd wake us all up. I know my friend better than that. "We don't have a kitchen full of strangers, do we?"

Rolling her eyes, Seer shakes her long ponytails like an anime character. "No, Peanut. Julia and the guys are at my place. I don't think we're comfortable enough as a pair of polycules to wake up in the same place."

Wolfie's head pops up from under the cover when I groan. "If you're going to make her sound like that, we'll need an hour before we join you. And you, pumpkin, will need to evacuate the premises."

My eyes open and I glare down at him. "I think she buried the lead here, my darling boy. She said *pair* of polycules. Since when is she shacking up with the trio of doom versus letting them stink up her space?"

"Aw, sugarplum, I didn't miss it. I think it's cute. We've got groupies."

His adorable smile defeats my dislike for the interlopers. Wolfie has known them for a long time, and he seems happy. I should be glad because it means Julia won't be triggering my Trevor-based insecurities, right? But it also means those idiots aren't going away soon, and they'll move to monopolizing Seer.

Teddy leans in and nips my ear, proving once again that he has some sort of Vulcan mind meld with my insecurities. Every time I feel bothered or an old wound aches, he seems to know almost simultaneously that he should distract me. It's freaky.

"Well, I suppose we are pretty fucking cool," I mutter. Prez chuckles softly, his arm snaking across the puppy pile to pull us all closer. The warmth draws a soft sigh of satisfaction from me, and I feel all the sharp edges of irritation that were spiking inside of me fade.

"Ahem!"

Teddy lifts his head, propping himself up on one arm as he glares over at my bestie. "O'Flanagan, I'm going to count to five and if you aren't gone by the time I finish, you'd better be okay with my bare ass. I have to piss, and I'll be damned if I'm going to hold it while you act like a five-year-old."

"Oooh, scary man. I'll have you know I've got plenty of arse of me own at the moment, and though I'm disinclined to acquiesce to your command, I ate this morning. It'd be a pity to have brekkie all over the lovely hardwoods."

Presley gives in first, snorting as he hides his face from our early morning grouch. I wink at Wolfie, who ducks under the cover to muffle his laughs against my tummy. I just bat my lashes at Edgar, watching the fury flash across his face with a look of fake innocence. The two of them spar like this all the time, and I find it cute, though he'd tan my hide vermillion for saying it out loud. Seer knows exactly how to get his goat, and he knows how to send off into a half-intelligible Irish rant.

I've considered popcorn before. It's a meme worthy event.

"That's it!" Teddy flings the covers off the lot of us, rolling to his feet with the grace of a panther as he heads to the bathroom.

Shrieking as cold air hits me, I scrabble the blanket back enough to keep my bits from shriveling. I know he can hear me, so I shout, "Way to shoot the messenger, you asshole!"

"Children," Presley says with a fond smile. "Can we stop bickering long enough to get showered? None of us have work or lessons this weekend. We have a break and I, for one, would like to enjoy it without the squabbling."

"He's right. We don't have a bunch of commitments, and since no one is hungover after the party, we should have a lazy Saturday," Wolfie murmurs, looking up at me with a shy smile.

My heart jumps in my chest, and I wriggle out of the pile as reality hits me like a stinky trout to the schnoz. Gripping the blanket around my chest, I walk to the closet to get out of the open space. The small, dark space helps me catch my breath and I stare blankly at the wall as my mind races.

I was so surprised by the morning trampling and Seer being back that I almost forgot what I did. Chewing my lower lip, I dig my fingers into the soft faux fur of the comforter. I should have spoken up last night when I came running in from the dirty trust in the alley, but I didn't know what to say. Everyone was talking and laughing and celebrating—how could I ruin that by confessing my sins? I'm not even sure if they are sins, to be honest, because the boys kept saying things about the crew getting bigger.

But I'm supposed to discuss it with them first, right?

Argh! I know how to navigate so many situations with the aplomb of a true debutante or diplomat, but this relationship shit is for the birds. I haven't been tied to any one person since Trevor, and now I'm in this lovely little square with three men who have been nothing but amazing. What do I do? I decide to find the town troublemaker and hump his face against a wall in a dirty alley. I'm my worst enemy, I swear to Hera.

The tap on my shoulder makes me jump, and I whirl around, putting my fists up out of habit. When I see it's Wolfie, I drop my stance and wrap my arms around myself. "Hi, baby."

"Sugarplum…" he hesitates for a second, reaching up to brush his thumb over my cheekbone. "You never have to hide anything from us. You know that, right?"

I blink, gob smacked. Yet again, one of them has done some sort of hot guy bullshit and figured out that I'm standing in here kicking my ass. "I mean… I do. But what if I messed up? What happens then?"

He leans in and brushes a kiss over my lips. "Then we all have a chat and work it out. We'd do that if anyone made a mistake. That's how relationships work."

My head drops and I look at my feet, feeling rotten because I don't know how to explain what happened last night. "I…"

Teddy bursts in before I can finish, looking at his side of the closet for clothes. He's naked, wet, and looking delicious, which confuses my idiotic mind and body even further. As if he can read my thoughts, he turns to give me a cocky grin. "When you finish telling the pup that you let the Irish knob dive through your pot of gold, I've a mind to grab pizza."

My head turns towards him like I'm stuck in slow motion, mouth gaping at his words. A few indignant sounds break free, but I'm so completely shocked I can't do more than squeak. The jackass just winks and tilts his head at Wolfie, who looks sheepish. I drop the blanket with a huff. Striding over to grab a pair of paint splattered jeans and a jean jacket, I give them both a reproachful look.

"If you knew, you should have said something when we got home last night. I worried myself to sleep, and I was just contemplating what I'd look like in the stupid stocks."

His shrug is nonchalant as he yanks sweatpants and a white tee off the rack. "Tilly, you wouldn't have worried if you'd just told us. We promised you we were in it for the long run, even if it means that an irksome idiot is going to tag along. You did nothing wrong. People like us…"

"Edgar, your phone is buzzing!" Presley shouts from the bathroom.

"Come on, sugarplum. Let's get dressed and go find something to eat. You can be pissy with us while we inhale a slice or two," Wolfie says. He grabs a pair of sweats as well, winking at me as he trots back into the bedroom.

You know, I feel as though they might butter me up for something. There's an awful lot of 'hot dudes in tight pants and tees' going around this morning.

"JESUS CHRIST. WHO WOULD HAVE THOUGHT SHERILYNN WOULD RUN a pizza joint with slices so good that it reminds me of New York?" I mumble around a huge bite. "I mean, the pie names are weird because… horses... but damn, this shit is good."

Teddy grins. "Ah, well, that's easy, drugar. Benjy flew to the city and stole a Michelin rated git who wanted out of the fast lane for a slower, more provincial life. Sherilynn hated the idea of hiring 'an outsider', but Guillermo is the best Italian chef in the region. I don't know if he'll stay, what with…"

"Ugh, don't remind me. I don't know what the hell is going with that separation, but I've already stepped in it with Sherilynn. My 'stay off of their radar' plan is decimated between her, OJ, and their minions at school." I reach over and swipe Teddy's bourbon, tossing it back with a sigh of pleasure.

"Benjy's been one of my best friends since high school and he won't say a word, even if I poke at him. The dude's usually so upbeat when he's in the store or the Speakeasy, but since that night, he's locked up like a bank vault," Edgar muses. He swipes some of Wolfie's garlic bread and gives me a smirk.

Presley sighs. "You know, I often wonder how I became the mature one in this quadrilateral. Give me the pepper flakes, Boone."

The shaker flies across the table, and McSteamy catches it easily, shrugging as Teddy gapes. "Uni soccer, mate. Goalies are quick on their feet."

"*You* played on the Miyako soccer team as goalie? You?!"

I lean my head back on my shoulder, settling in for a bunch of male posturing. Sports are about as exciting as tax forms, and though I love watching the boys squabble, I'm not the least bit interested in their dick swinging when we aren't naked.

"Mow!" Jekyll's head pops up between my legs as he looks up from under the table.

"I know, buddy. Sports are a snooze fest. Where are the rest of the motley crew?"

"Mow?"

That means he doesn't know—I think. I ruffle the fur on his head as Prez and Teddy continue arguing about collegiate sports at State U— that's where Presley went as well. Wolfie joins in once it turns to State U talk, and eventually Teddy pulls out his phone to do that sabermetrics shit he uses to help set the line for his book. I vaguely understand it, but again, math is also not one of my favorite subjects.

Putting on a bright smile to hide my boredom, I turn to them. "Boys? I'm going to take the kiddos for a walk down Meanwhile you... whatever it is you're doing. Be men or whatever. Maybe I'll pop in to the bookstore, too."

Grunts of assent are all I get as they talk players, positions, and stats that would make an actuary bang their head on the table as they feel asleep.

I wriggle out under the tall table, bending and twisting until I'm standing, then whistle for animals. If I'm going for another walk on my own, this time I'm taking bad decision deterrents. My track record with taking a simple walk without getting into trouble is becoming embarrassing.

"C'mon, cats and doggies. Let's blow this joint."

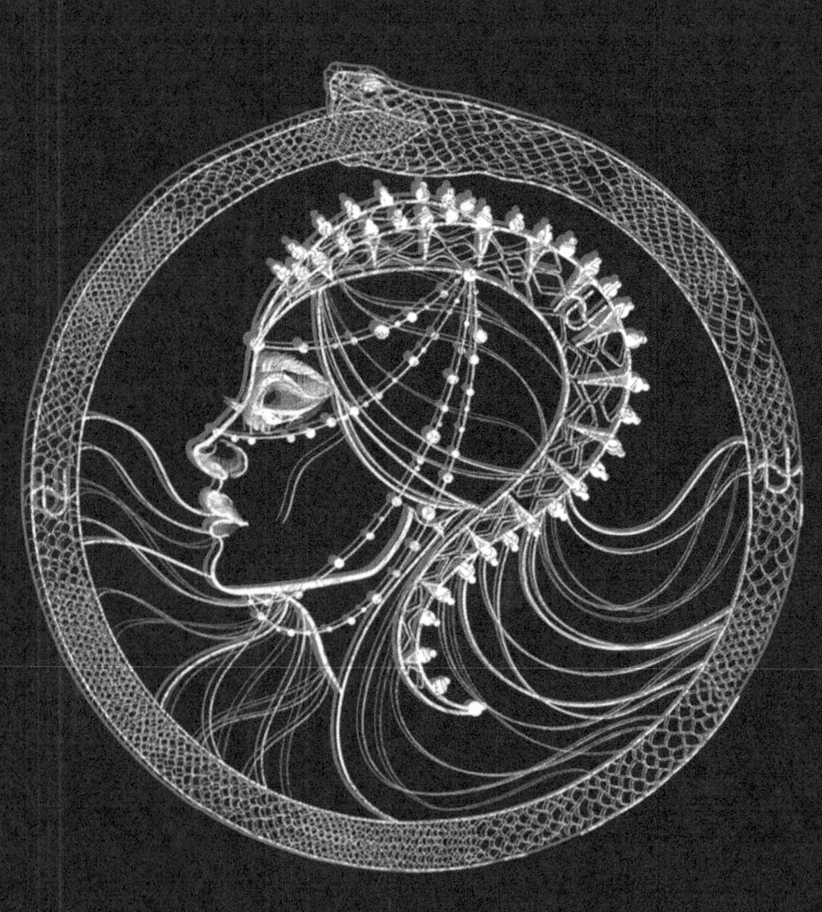

Backstabber

I walk down the street with Jekyll, Hyde, and the dogs following along. Eurayle stayed behind with the boys. Prez is its favorite, and Eury rarely allows any of us to travel without an escort after the drug incident. My tryst with the Irishman was an anomaly that isn't likely to be repeated. Both my companions and Edgar's have been on high alert, as if they realize I was in danger and they weren't around to protect me.

Of course, the boys would be a lot more worried if they'd seen the video feed of that shadowy movement in the yard last night. Their overprotectiveness is why I had Jackson's people set them up to feed to an app on my phone. I didn't want anyone reviewing a tape while I was out and deciding I'm in too much danger to live my life. I appreciate their concern, but I also know I've been trained to take care of myself.

"Mow!"

Hyde's cry draws my attention, and I watch as a group of women snicker in a closed circle in front of the diner. One of them turns her head, pretending to look past me for something, and I roll my eyes.

Women are the absolute *worst* with shit like that. The old 'I'm not looking at you' trick isn't fooling anyone outside of an elementary playground, but we just keep doing it our whole lives. Freya forbid we just fucking *ask* someone whatever the hell it is we want to know. Shaking my head, I stride over to the group, feeling a rush of annoyance as they jabber loudly, as if they weren't whispering about me from across the street.

"Hello, ladies. Can I help you with something? My name is Jolene Whitley. I don't believe we've met." The smile I plaster on is only for show. These women know something I don't, and I'll be damned if I'm not going to find out what it is.

They turn to look at me in unison like some sort of Stepford lizard people. The blonde bats her fake lashes, perfectly plump pink lips in a moue of faux surprise. Her brunette and strawberry haired friends titter behind their manicured hands, waiting for the obvious ringleader to respond. She has a newspaper in her hand, but she doesn't speak as she stares at me.

Rolling my eyes, I reach over and snatch the paper with a growl of annoyance. Jekyll bounds over, leaping in front of me and making a low, angry noise in his throat. The wannabe socialites sneer at my companion until Kali joins him, her sheer bulk forcing the women to back up a little. Now that I've got space, I flick the paper open and if the headline was a punch, I'd be KO'd.

I stagger backward; the shock making my chest tighten and sparkles dance in front of my eyes. Fury burns its way from my gut to every inch of my frame, like liquid fire running through my veins. The darkness creeps in the edges of my vision and I know I'm going to lose time again if I don't stop it. Kali butts her gigantic head against my hand and Jekyll does the same on the other side. Their presence helps a bit, but even my animal friends aren't going to help me curb my break.

"Is she gonna lose her lunch? I can't say I'm surprised. Trash is as trash does, my momma always said," the red-haired one says,

"Don't be ugly, Aprilynn. I swear, you could start an argument in an empty house," the brunette scolds, swatting her arm. "It would appall your mama."

"Rebekkah, don't pitch a hissy. Even if her parents didn't have a pot to piss in and she's currently the village bicycle, that doesn't mean we can forget our manners."

I'd respond, but all I can hear is the pumping of blood in my ears as the rage takes over. The only thing that saves the random bitches on the street is me not knowing them. I wouldn't recognize them in a three person line-up, so I know they weren't involved in this outrage. The person responsible is the former ringleader of my personal torture brigade—Amy Matilda Behle.

She owns this fucking paper, and I don't know how she got this picture or why she began her offensive today. I know she's been pulling the strings on the women at work and the remaining members of her clique from high school. Before today, I truly believed she might eventually leave me alone if I ignored their petty machinations.

Ignoring bullies has never been good advice, and giving it to myself was stupid.

"Come!" I snarl at the animals as I turn on my heel, leaving the babbling twits to stare as I stalk down the street towards the Hollow Hollar office.

I'm going to end this right here and now. Coming home was about solving the mystery of my FBI failure, not healing the war wounds of the past. The weird stalker, clues in a box, and endless questions that lead to more riddles make accomplishing my goal more complex every day. I don't have time to play games with these bitches who never outgrew mean girl bullshit.

Arriving at the office faster than I thought possible, I yank the door open and watch it slam against the wall hard enough to shatter glass. Every fiber of my being is screaming for blood, and Seer would be the first to admit she's had to pull me off someone when I got like this. People are talking or yelling—I'm not sure which—but everything is a low buzz in my ears. I can see their mouths moving, but nothing registers as I stalk over to one of the few people on this planet that I'd unironically call my nemesis.

"*Amy Matilda Behle!*" I shout, dropping a palm on Kali's and Jekyll's heads. Hyde and Hecate hang back at the doorway, forming a perfect block for anyone who thinks they'll escape my wrath by running out. "Show yourself, you spineless twit."

The Queen Bee emerges from an office near the back, arms crossed over her chest as she stalks towards me. Her platinum hair is natural, as are the perfect button nose, wide blue eyes, and bow shaped mouth. Amy won the genetic lottery in her family as she's naturally built like pinup Barbie while her sisters, Henrietta and Jasmin, had to have surgery to achieve the same look. Her father is also ethereally beautiful, a fact that couldn't have hurt him in his career as a diplomat.

"Well, well. If it isn't the Hester Prynne of Whistler's Hollow." She looks over at the entirely female, extremely chic staff of her tiny hometown paper as if they're the editorial department of the Times. "Ladies, it isn't often we have such an infamous visitor. Did you make her feel welcome?"

"None of us have a dick, so doubtful," mutters another blonde, standing immediately to Amy's right.

My eyes narrow. That's her lieutenant—just as Reese was in high school. This woman serves as the right-hand toady to Amy's army of Skippers. I haven't seen her ex-capo since I arrived, but I assume that much like OJ and Sherilynn, Reese and Jillian will make themselves known eventually, probably with their own little cadre of sycophants. "I have no idea who this flea is, Amy, but you've made a grievous error with this stunt. I'll have your paper, your family fortune, and everything you've ever held dear by the time I'm finished with you. I am *not* the powerless girl you tortured in the past."

Her laugh tinkles like a vicious fairy as she strides forward to stand less than a foot from me. Amy ignores Kali's escalating snarls and Jekyll's angry cat noises; instead, she bats her lashes at me. "Jolene Whitley, you are and always have been an overfed peon. Your love affair with undesirables put you on my radar, but I've enjoyed every moment of your comeuppance. Today's headlines are just the beginning of a delicious campaign to run you out of my town for good."

That does it.

My vision goes black and the fury inside of me feels like it's bursting free. Before I can pass out, shrieks fill the air and I blink, clearing my eyes enough to see an enormous black constrictor snake with almost metallic looking scales fall from the ceiling onto Amy. The women around her scatter, too chickenshit to help as they scream loud enough to wake the dead generals. I watch as the snake coils itself around her from head to toe—putting its length at a minimum six feet with a body as thick as my thighs—and her horrified pleas turn to gasps and choking.

Goddamnit, the fucking thing is going to kill her and I'm going to get blamed for sure.

Considering she printed a headline in this morning's paper declaring me a 'Southern madam' running a 'cathouse' who is a danger to the morality of our town and its children, there's not a snowball's chance in Hell that people aren't going to light pitchforks to come after me. I shake my head, trying to clear the burning rage so I can focus on the situation at hand.

Snakes can't 'hear' externally, so to speak, but they sense vibration through their jaws. Or, that's what the yogi in India taught Seer and me, and I'm hoping he wasn't full of shit. Amy's screams are loud enough to make it panic and squeeze tighter, and I'm not even addressing the choir of women plastered against the walls or standing on desks yelling. We'll never get this thing to let her loose before she suffocates if they don't shut the fuck up and let this large exotic animal have some goddamn space and quiet.

"Hey, buddy," I say, taking a cautious step towards my idiotic enemy. "She's not worth it. Someone will insist you be euthanized if you kill her. You gotta loosen up so she can breathe."

"What... what... is... she..." Amy gurgles, but I ignore her as I focus on the serpent, studying me curiously.

Another step, followed by another, has me close enough to look into its reptilian eyes. I lay my hand on one of the thick coils gently, trying not to spook it. I'm hoping the vibration from my voice will transfer through my fingertips because Amy is damn near blue in the lips. I have little time and it doesn't seem like anyone is coming to save me.

"Release her. Let her go and I will deal with her nastiness. She hasn't harmed you and her words no longer hurt me. The bike inside of people like this eats them from the inside out, much like your venomous relatives," I murmur to it.

I have no idea why I feel like I should justify myself to this random murderous snake, but I have a soft spot for almost any animal, and I'm worried that this attack will get it killed. I can't prove it crashed through the vent to defend me, but the timing is hard to ignore.

"Is she some sort of Harry Potter reject? What is *going on?* Get the mayor! Get Chief Barrington to throw her ass in jail and shoot this thing!" one of the Skippers shrieks.

Before I can tell her to shut her fucking yap, the door bursts open and my guards let out territorial snarls and yowls. My head whips around, hoping it's Teddy or one of my boys—hell, even Seer would be helpful at this point—but it's Doyle. The hero of the hour *would* be the snarky Irish asshat that got me into this bloody mess. The picture of us isn't pornographic, but it's detailed enough for everyone who reads this godsforsaken paper to know what we were up to in that alley. His arrival doesn't do a damn thing to quell the rumor reported as fact in this paper, and I want to kick him in the balls for not being smarter.

"Aye, lass. Looks as though you've got a bit of a cat on a melodeon here. Allow me to assist," he says, giving me an infuriating, mischievous grin.

Ugh, why, oh why, do I always attract trouble like a magnet?

"Doyle, baby, stop this freak from killing Amy!" the annoyingly brave Skipper shrieks.

His brow arches in that way that only those of us with the dominant gene seem to as he looks at her. "Bambi, I am not, nor have I ever been, your baby. I wasn't even my mum's baby for very long. Now shut up and let the adults handle this, you twit."

I have to struggle with whether I should laugh that this idiot is actually named Bambi or that he basically sent her to the kiddie table in front of everyone. My smug delight wins the war and I smirk at her, turning to my reluctant savior. "Well, Lucky, I woke up this morning, and decided since the paper called me everything short of a snake charmer, I'd try my hand at the hat trick."

His laugh booms through the room as he comes over and whispers in my ear, "I believe you already know exactly how to accomplish that feat, but let's try it on the real one together, aye? Talk to the git before the melters in here get their friend killed."

I wrinkle my nose, wondering why he thinks my voice is going to soothe this fifty-pound monster. Humoring him seems to be the best way to stall for time, so I nod. "Come on, dude. Amy won't even taste good. You're not going to squeeze the bitter out of her, and when you go to chow down, she's gonna give you indigestion. Hell, she gives me an ulcer and I'm not even trying to digest her mean ass."

The serpent tilts its head, bobbing it back and forth for a moment as its tongue flicks in the air. I know that means it's scenting because snakes use taste as one of their main hunting tools. One coil at a time loosens after it dances for us, slowly letting go of my childhood nemesis until her lips pink up. Eventually, the shiny black and rainbow python lets go of her completely and slithers over to me. It winds its way around my left leg and up my body until it's wrapped around me like I'm in a Brittany Spears video.

Oh, just fucking great.

"Looks like ye found another admirer, Tíogair. I have to admit; I'm a lot more fond of this one than the giant feathered git or the doggies," Doyle murmurs, his eyes dancing with mirth.

"Of course you like the snake and cats. If you were some sort of Wuzzle, you'd be a mix of those animals, Lucky." I sigh, looking back at the gasping Amy and her fawning Skippers. The thought of dealing with her or the fallout of this is exhausting.

"*Why hasn't anyone told this bitch*? She's dangerous!" Amy shouts, pointing a shaking finger at me. "The Mayor should have her *locked up like a zoo animal!*"

The rage builds again, and Doyle takes my hand, squeezing it as if to calm me. I don't know that his presence is so effective just yet, and I open my mouth only to close it immediately when Teddy comes barreling through the door with Wolfie, Presley, and Benjy. I don't know who called my guys or why in the hell they brought the biggest dude in the entire town with them, but I'll take it.

"Amy Behle, you need to… Shut. Your. Mouth. *Now*," Teddy growls in a dark voice that makes my girly bits tingle with excitement.

You'd think I'd be too distracted by the giant snake, half-dead bully, Skippers, or the appearance of my Harvey Wallbang to register that, but nope. My vagina is just trampy enough to flutter in excitement at the cavalry and Teddy's booming command.

I'm fairly certain I have an illness. Is nymphomania communicable? Never mind, I know it's not, but if it was, this town definitely gave it to me.

"But, *Edgar*, her stupid snake tried to *kill me!*"

His brow arches and I swallow hard again. I almost wish someone would kill me now—that or fuck me senseless because despite the wailing moron over there, this whole rescue bit it fucking hot.

"Amy, your father and the Mayor need to see you immediately. Your stunt in the paper has triggered a protocol and they need to speak with you," Wolfie says softly, giving her an angry look. "Don't dig the hole deeper; you'll be lucky if you get out of this one without a lot of groveling."

Presley looks at the Skippers with disgust. "Get her out of here and to Town Hall. Lock this place up and go home—all of you. I'd suggest looking for jobs, as you may not have one when this is over."

"They won't if I have the Mayor's ear on the topic," Doyle drawls, his lips curved in a malicious grin. "They'll be lucky if they aren't re—"

"That's enough, Haggerty." Teddy glares at him and he rolls his eyes as if all of his fun for the day has been spoiled.

"C'mon, Jolene. Why don't you and the guys come down to the store and I'll take you in the Speakeasy early?" Benjy murmurs. "I have the feeling you could all use a drink, and I'm happy to help."

I nod, running my hand over the smooth scales of the giant snake that seems to have no inclination to let go of me. "I'm going to need another form, Doyle."

"Aye, milady. I'll get one and come back to join you."

That said, I turn on my heel, whistle for my companions, and walk out of the Hollow Hollar for the first and last time.

I'll never step foot in this building again if I can help it.

Enemy Fire

The hometown-style diner in the middle of the bustling city I'm sitting in is just off State U's campus. Belle's is an institution, and as always, it's packed even after lunchtime.

I agreed to meet Jackson here after he texted about a potential source. My useless fishing expedition on the darknet didn't yield solid information and, with the chaos surrounding my life in the Hollow, I haven't had time to dive in again. I reluctantly handed my contacts and digital breadcrumbs over to him after the drugging incident because I knew we needed answers more quickly than I could manage on my own. I didn't think he'd get a hit this fast, but when he messaged me, I had to come.

I'm here without my 'entourage' because despite their fury at the blow-up at the Hollar yesterday, every single one of my boyfriends, friends, and the stupid freeloaders had conflicts. Their absence is a bit sus after the scolding I got at home last night, but it's not like they're all off together at some secret 'Jolene Protection Society' meeting.

Presley had a full schedule at the office, Wolfie had to go to the farm to check a foal, Teddy had to see someone called 'The Hook', and Seer went off with her new playmates. I didn't ask for more details because while it's sweet that they're protective, I won't complain when they decide *not* to smother me after a day like yesterday. I'm still processing my emotions and I can't keep analyzing the motivations of my old bullies.

Besides, I have the animal contingent with me. Euryale had to wait outside because of her size, but the cats, dogs, and this blasted snake are all at the table. Jekyll and Hyde are perched on the chair with Kali and Hecate flanking them on the floor. The snake—who I haven't named yet, but can seldom get to stay more than a couple of feet from me—is coiled around one leg and up to my waist with its head resting on the table. I must look like a reject from a Steve Irwin special to passersby, but Belle and her family have ties to the Hollow.

How do I know?

The cute freckled girl at the hostess stand damn near kicked someone out of their table to seat me without batting a lash at the menagerie following me. Then Belle herself trotted out of the kitchen to coo at my servals and promised I didn't need to order because she knew what I needed to eat. I just nodded at her, deciding I'd had enough drama to last a month and I'll just eat whatever the hell she brings. I wouldn't even be in public today if it weren't for Jackson's text and my gut deep belief that all of this weirdness starting from my background check to the latest bullshit is tied together somehow.

Whistler's Hollow is the key to everything; I know it.

"How's it hangin', J-Dawg?"

I chuckle, looking up at my old college friend and the least lawyerly looking attorney this side of the Mississippi. "Jackson, it's been a while. You look relaxed as hell."

Tossing his blond surfer style hair out of his eyes, Jackson Ellison Thorn IV gives me a megawatt grin. "I sure as fuck do, doll. Since my dad finally kicked it, I restructured the firm and I have all the sibs handling the drudgery. Taxes, estates, civil class action, corporate—I only handle the bloody stuff besides you. Litigation keeps my blood pumping, and I only take the ugliest shit I can find."

My lips curve. "And you take it via sandy beaches, I'd assume? You're so tan that you might as well open a bar and serve umbrella drinks in Bermuda, dude."

"Ah, well. I do like to plan my legal assassinations in locales that suit my temperament, Jojo. My dad would never let me move to the coast and be a surfing bum, so now I get to do both. It's a win-win—much like everything I do."

I roll my eyes at his arrogance. Jackson was the one who found me after Trevor left. I was holed up in my room, doing nothing but studying and homework for weeks. He was the RA on my floor, and when someone reported to him they hadn't seen me leave for almost a month, he came barging in.

I was a stinky, malnourished, snotty mess he threw into a shower fully clothed. Once I stopped screaming at him, he helped me get back on my feet for the next few days and booked me in with one of the school therapists. He sort of saved my life, and we've been accountability buddies ever since.

Notice I didn't say friends?

We are friends, but casual ones. He helped me because he recognized the broken pieces I had on full display. Jackson will always be a recovering drug addict—rich kid, overbearing dad, drunk mom, family legacy shit—but he pulled himself out of the hole and stay clean. While we didn't share our darkest thoughts and pain, our relationship has always been an anchor point for us both. When he graduated from law school, I was his first client. He's never let me down, and I never let him forget how grateful I am.

"Are you going to sit down or stand there posing all day?" I grumble, giving the group of giggly Alpha Phi girls staring at him with the stank eye.

"The ladies love a Thorn, Jojo. It's in our blood." He plops into the chair, sprawling like it's a couch and he's on a Vanity Fair photoshoot for eligible bachelors.

Too bad for all the ladies because the Thorn sitting in front of me likes dicks as much as I do. "Don't be gross. You called me here because you have information, and we're working. Show me what this hacker found."

"Right. Business Jojo in the house. Okay, so I hired this delicious little emo boy I found at a drum and bass rave. Who on *Earth* knows why he was there, but when we got to his place and saw he stocked it like a hotel room at DEFCON, I knew I'd gotten a two-fer."

Pulling the messenger bag off his shoulder, he opens it and pulls out a stack of accordion files and two hard drives. "The kid wrote a program to trawl for specific keywords and phrases—a spider bot or something—through four different darknets while he gave me the most amazing bl—"

"Jesus Christ in a sweet potato pie, Jackson!" I glare at him, grabbing the first file as he smirks. "Boundaries, asshole."

"Aw, Jojo, I just wanted to *share*. You're no fun since you crossed the pond. All you've done is work yourself into a hole for that FBI thing, and now that it's shot to hell, you went and buried yourself in that toxic wasteland you call a hometown." He pauses, arching a brow at me. "And *what* is with the zoo, Doolittle? Those dogs look like short chicks could ride them."

"*Don't* call me Jojo," I murmur as I read the page. It's a police report, but not one I've ever seen before. It was taken by a Statie the night of my parents' car crash—it doesn't match *any* of the official records they sent me after they died. In fact, it doesn't read like any report, news story, or even medical chart Jackson sent.

His brown eyes soften as I pick up the glass of bourbon and take a shaky sip. "This is pretty out there, right? When I looked up this dude, I found out that he was a rookie when the accident happened. Fresh out of the academy and working the corridor in a speed trap. Want to know what else?"

I take another swig of the Booker's, knowing in my gut this information is going to change everything. "Yeah. Tell me more, Jax."

"After the inquest and all of that, this dude retired with his wife and two kids to fucking Istanbul. He's a cultural attaché to some fancy pants charity organization as far as the paper trail shows. Now, I may have fried my grey matter with way too much coke and X in the day, but I'm still smart enough to realize that a Statie with an associate's in crim jus doesn't have the money, the experience, or the language skills to move to a foreign country for that job." Jax stacks his hands behind his head and grins. "So I had cutie Ely dig in further, and that rube cop is living in one hell of a fancy fucking house with a goddamned Jag in the driveway. The job is bullshit—the charity doesn't exist."

The coils of my new companion tighten and relax around my midsection and I realize that I'm sitting ramrod straight, tension flooding my body as I digest the news. "You think someone buried this and whisked his family as far away as possible to keep it from coming out?"

"Jojo, that report says there was no drunk driver on the road. It says it was a single vehicle when he arrived, and the scene looked like someone had set a bomb off. Yeah, I think it's shady as fuck. This is the scent that makes predators like me hold their heads up and start tracking."

Closing my eyes, I try to reconcile that my parents may have been murdered, and they covered it up. Why? Two college professors with a paid off home, no connections to any weird criminals, and a boring lifestyle in a small town are *not* assassination targets.

It's like aiming for the goddamned Cleavers, for fuck's sake. Who in the nine realms of Valhalla would put a hit on two middle-class teachers?

"Jax, I don't... I don't know what to say. I can't wrap my mind around this. It makes little sense. My parents were as small town, plain Jane as two people could be. Imagining someone being angry enough at them to take out a hit is almost laughable."

"I know, but everything Ely found points to a massive cover-up. It doesn't point to *who* covered it up, but you assume that Chief Barrington's dad, Dr. Bennett, Grayson Parks, and Aurelia Fletcher were in on it. Obviously, to achieve something like this, you'd need the Chief of Police, the town doctor, the coroner, and the nurse to start. Given that it happened on Statie territory, not in town, you'd probably need someone with governmental sway, so I'm going to point a finger at the local senator, and possibly whoever handles burials in town," he muses.

Belle walks up with a big tray and we pause, flicking our eyes around guiltily. She places bowls of spoon bread, greens, fritters, fried green tomatoes, and a basket of crawdads on the table with a flourish. "Y'all eat up. This is just the beginning."

I groan, knowing that I'm going to gorge myself and have to roll my ass into the Impala to drive home. Making a mental note to talk to Teddy about that damn gym, I shove a fritter in my mouth and almost pass out in a food related orgasm. "I said god*damn*," I mutter as I pick at the tomatoes. "Nothing like home cooking, no matter where in the world you go."

Jax chuckles, nodding his head. "You just can't get it like this outside of the South, Jojo. Trust me, I've tried."

"Tell me about the rest of the stuff in these files," I say, reaching for the salt. "Is it all related to the accident?"

He peels one of the crayfish, sucking the shell clean and shakes his head. "Nope. It's also a pretty detailed path from the college to some sort of shadowy recruitment. I don't really understand it, but maybe with all your secret agent shit, you'll be able to figure it out."

"If it's about basketball, I'm not interested. Everyone knows that State U and Pointe do shady shit to get recruits to the teams. Scandals at the NCAA level aren't my focus," I reply as I spear some greens. "It's gross, but not something I need to look into."

"No, Jojo. You don't get it. This seems to indicate that State is paired up with some untraceable... thing... or group... that it funnels grads towards. Like some Skull and Bones shit. If either of your folks was wrapped up in it, maybe that's a reason..."

Oh. Now I feel stupid. Who's the brilliant profiler now?

Getting laid is making my brain soft, I fucking swear. "I see. Do you think if I scan a bunch of old crap that I found in a mysterious trunk, Eli could try to...do his thing?" His eyebrows bob and I make a disgusted face. "Ugh, not *that* thing, you pervert. The hacker shit. Goddess, you are *so* fucking nasty."

"Jojo, you've never been a prude before now! Why don't you want to indulge my... sweet tooth?" His eyes sparkle as he waves an aptly shaped fritter at me and he bites the end off with a satisfied smirk.

"Because… because… because I just don't!" It's not the best retort in the world, but I'm not prepared to share my alternative lifestyle with him, especially since I avoided the animal question. "Now, can he do it or not?"

"I'm pretty sure that boy could launch the nukes at CENTCOM if he felt like it. Send me the files through the encrypted drops, and I'll talk to him." Jackson tilts his head and eyes me carefully. "Oh, I get it! You're getting *laid*. And it's not just a fling-a-ling like in Europe, so you're being all provincial about it. Tsk tsk, Jojo. I'm hurt."

I sigh, stopping my inhalation of the fried food at the table to look at him seriously. "It's...it's… You know what happened with Trevor; you were there. This is the first real thing since then, and I'm not ready to open that wound and let it bleed today."

"I'm not asking if you're gonna *wife* anyone, doll. I just want the long story, and I'm not going anywhere until I get it. Settle in kitties," he says, looking at Jekyll. "Your mama's gonna keep her ass in this chair until she spills the beans."

Kali lets out a howl, and I press my thumbs into my temples. Just what I fucking needed today—traitorous companions and a gossip mongering lawyer.

I wonder if the boys are faring any better.

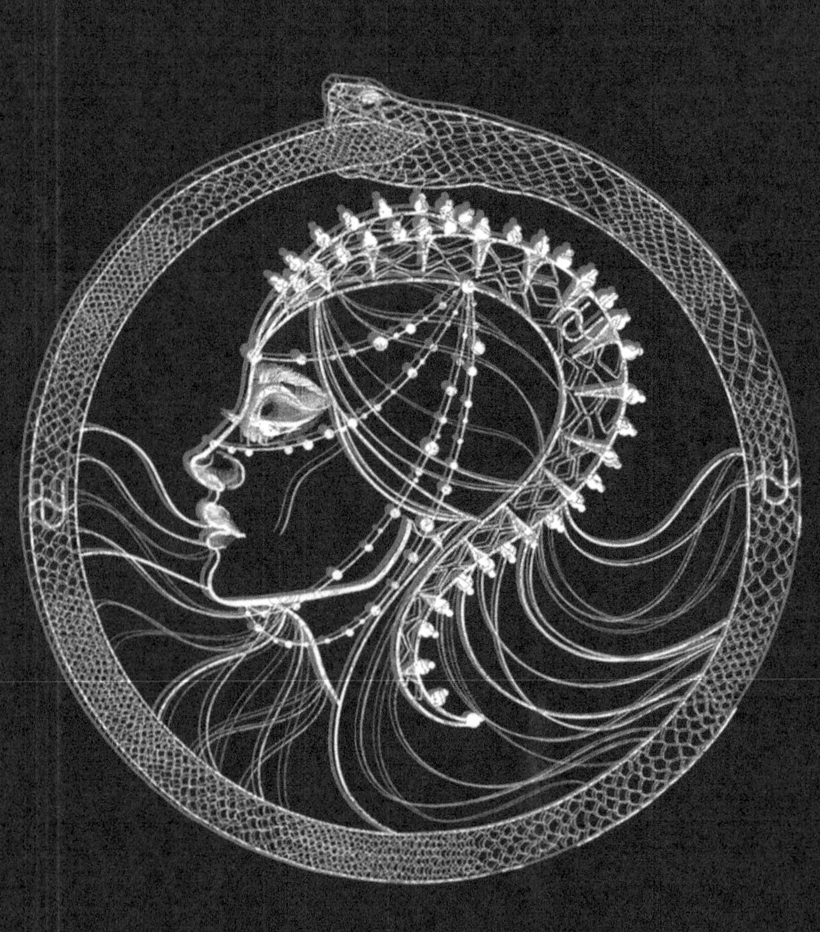

Seven Nation Army

Edgar

My drugar is occupied for the rest of the evening.

The message from Thorn was enough to send her barreling towards the city with the animals, and his timing couldn't have been better if I'd planned it. I know it shocked her when we all came up with excuses not to accompany her, but the glint in her bratty eyes was also triumphant. Jolene isn't one to be caged—not that I'm trying to—and she was pleased as punch to go hunting clues on her own.

We have to monitor her progress, though, which is why the doc has been helping her set up the 'war room' in the garage. Re-locating it from her bolt hole in the basement means any of us can pop out there to check up on her sleuthing without having to take drastic measures to get in. When she moved the armory to the basement, I didn't expect her installing biometrics for the storage area, and without the Irish car bomb along, we wouldn't be able to keep tabs on her research.

Since the bloody councils both want updates on her progress once a week, I find it necessary to know what she's discovered about Whistler's Hollow. The smallest memory or flashback triggered by something in the mysterious box could awaken a part of her and once she shifts, breaking the magic bonding, her inner beasts will begin.

I should know.

My first merged near the end of high school. Bane helped me along —as is her job—but the transition from knowing that the world was solely human and regular animals to discovering the breadth of extranormal society is rough.

Learning that my parents aren't my parents, I have a destiny that I cannot change, and the level of disappointment my adoptive parents felt when I seemed to scorn their ambitions for me facilitated several poor decisions. Tilly suffered because of my self-centered egotism back then, and I didn't even understand how much until she strolled into town two months ago.

Boones don't regret things, but if I did, her shame would be the one thing I'd carry that burden for.

Logically, I realize a teenage boy who had his entire world flipped upside down, filled with raging hormones and hellfire, could not have comprehended the consequences of his actions. However, every time I look at her when she thinks no one is watching and every small moment of self-doubt I feel through our bond floods my heart with guilt and shame. The founding children of this town broke that girl so effectively that she would never have returned if not for the background check snafu.

"Boone, are you ready to go or are you going to stand at the window with your bourbon and brood? If it's the latter, let me know what lighting you'd prefer. I think we can post it on *OnlyFans* and make some dough."

I whip around to glare at Prez, only to be greeted by the entire cadre outfitted to the nines for the trial. "Hamilton, if I were to let you, we could build you a new aviary without touching the first month's fees. Nice leather, by the way."

He smirks, adjusting the collar of the black leather jacket he's wearing with low-slung jeans, a-line tank and combat boots. Given his species, he's not likely to show up completely revealed; They use his kind for shifter care in all the enclaves and towns, but they're also hunted by poachers because of their rarity. Revealing himself wasn't a worry here until stalkers showed up looking for my *drugar*—we have no idea what this person or people are capable of. "I dirty up good and you know it. Go ahead; admire my ass. It looks fantastic."

I glare at his antics, turning to the unusually quiet Irish lass that watches over Tilly. "And you? Thought you were going to a party east o' the sun and west o' the moon?"

Saoirse shakes her bright red locks, making the fluffy mound of braids and ties and trinkets crowning her head tinkle. "Aye, doggy. I thought I'd find out if yer pet could give me a tour. I hear it's almost comparable to our lands."

Snorting, I sip my bourbon, studying her before I respond. Of course, she doesn't mean England—that dreary rain-soaked castle her adoptive parents live in isn't the true home of her people, either. It doesn't matter *which* of her people she means, she's not wrong that their lands would give Wolfie's father's kingdom a run for its money. As she squirms in the silence, I grin a little. She's made it her own, but the aquamarine and cerulean garb under the shiny armor of her father's side paired with the glinting knives and weapons of her mother's make her look fierce.

She'll need to be; we all will. Going against the will of the founding families over the incident last week will require us to appear loyal to the councils and the society, but also outraged at some of its favored townsfolk.

My gaze cuts to the hulking man and his two companions. Tharin and Julia aren't hybrids; I scented their creatures from the moment I met them. They're also dressed in the flowing garments and armor of their species. Zasha, however, matches Saoirse, but less stabby and more... regal.

Christ help me.

Children of royals and upper tier extranormals should help our case, but given half of them are dirty secrets and the other half's relatives spend all of their time squabbling, it's likely to be a hindrance rather than useful. Sometimes, I think it's better when the Society has no records at all about birth heritage—like with Jolene and I. It means there are fewer worries about interference and less petty grievances that can be used against you.

Except that someone is clearly coming after our girl, and none of us can figure out who or why.

"Edgar, are we ready to go?"

I turn and my lips curl up as I walk to the counter in Tilly's kitchen and sit my bourbon down. If only she were here to see this, she'd lose her goddamn mind. My *drugar* has *no idea* what her pup looks like when he drops all the shields and glamours, and when she sees it, I have to be there. I'm no slouch in my dark blue Armani suit and Society silk tie, but Wolfie is… ethereal. Even the doc and the merry men shut up to stare as he walks in. "We are, pup. You clean up good."

He ducks his head, making the waterfall of sparkling silver hair slide over his iridescent skin. I notice he's kept his ears but is controlling the rest carefully so he can wear a stylish sharkskin suit rather than the garb his mother would expect. "I miss her, too, T," he murmurs.

"C'mere, Lucy. You can ride with me in my car and the rest of these clowns can find their own way to the sanctuary. You look hot as hell, and I don't get to see the sparkly bits very often," Prez growls, crooking his finger.

Humph.

I was doing a perfectly fine job of calming the pup down. Hamilton is such an ass when he decides he wants to mark his bloody territory. I'll show him later, though, when Tilly gets back. I order some brand new—

"Oi, mutt!"

I turn, feeling the fire dance in my veins as the usually silent brick wall yells at me from across the room. "Ah, so he *can* speak. I wondered."

Zasha rushes forward, ever the diplomat. "Now, boys. No need to get in a scrap. We have to present a united front at the trial. Otherwise, we won't be able to win any of the wildcards over."

Blinking, I look at him and then the nodding behemoth. "Since when do wildcards show up for a small town trial over a fight in the newspaper?"

"Since the small town bitches posted their idiocy to their *blogs* for the paper before the fight and now it's not about an internal struggle in town. It's a breach of protocol. Wildcards from surrounding areas will be at the meeting to help keep the vote from being swayed by personal relationships," Julia says. Her gold and green gaze holds mine for a moment, and I shake my head, breaking the contact.

Fucking snakes. It's bad enough I have to deal with Tilly's clingy ass new companion, but adding in O'Flanagan's scaly consort is not my idea of a good time.

"Then we discuss strategy in the car as we head to the entrance. Haggerty is meeting us at the door. O'Flanagan, make sure we have enough earwigs from my drugar's stash downstairs for everyone to be wired. We may have to split up during the cocktail hour to curry votes from all the old farts they brought in to sway the proceedings. Everyone clear?"

You'd think the general would get salutes or even choruses of agreement, but all I get are grumbles and middle fingers.

Have I mentioned how much I hate fucking brats that aren't Jolene?

"I can't believe we're having a trial at all," the jowly man in an ancient, tight dress uniform of some type grumbles around the brandy he's sharing with several other founding family patriarchs. "The girl got distraught and made a terrible decision. Womenfolk do that. And this Whitley girl needs to remember her place. She's the disgrace here, if you ask me. You all remember the Catastrophe…"

Rage surges through me and I feel every bit of me pushing to get out all at once at Reginald Whitman Behle's snide commentary. I stalk over to him and let him get a taste of whichever side wins the battle as I cross the floor. That is until a hand grabs my shirt and yanks me aside.

"Look, you tosser. I'm no more fond of you than you are of me, and we haven't had our words yet about my Tíogair. But if you attack an ex-diplomat and the accused's father during cocktails, we won't make any friends. Leave him to his crusty old misogyny."

I snort, shaking my head as he eases his grip. "No wonder his wife is schtupping her cameraman."

The red-haired git grins and shrugs. "Well, he didn't produce a male heir, and Amy came out human. She had to come from somewhere and it wasn't a mage and warlock."

Now *that* would be a wonderful secret to expose. Knowing it would make Tilly giggle—if I could tell her. Ah, well. I'll save it for later. A woman as stupid as Amy Matilda Behle is bound to fuck up again if she survives this process. "How are the others doing with vote counting, Haggerty?"

"Well… it helps that your bottom is so feckin' pretty. Every female in the room is dying just by looking at him. Knowing our girl owns his leash doesn't help much, but the charming grin and the occasional flourish he's giving with his power is helping. I'm certain he's charmed a few of the tourists into hearing our side."

Rolling my eyes, I mutter, "Not. My. Bottom." His eyes dance and I look up at the ceiling, wondering what grievous sin I committed to have to deal with the inordinate amount of fucking sass I now get daily. My life was fairly squared away before Tilly came crashing in, bringing all of this chaos with her. People did what I said, and I didn't get all this lip.

"You can stand here and tell tragic lies to yourself or we can go find out who the voodoo queen in the corner is. She might be a guardian, but since those bastards are like rabbits breeding, I don't know them all anymore," Haggerty chuckles, downing the last of his Jameson.

I sigh, knowing there isn't time to argue if we're going to curry favor before they call us downstairs to proceed with the main event of the evening. We need to make sure this shit doesn't swing in the other direction and possibly earn Tilly a forced emergence. That never goes well, and it usually breaks the supe so severely that they either go insane or they refuse to accept their supe side.

A gong rings before I can muse further, and everything in my body tenses. We're too late.

"Ladies and gentleman, it is time to make your way to your seats for the trial. The Honorable Senator Edgar Olivier Boone II and The Honorable Mayor Cornelia Sykes will be presiding. You have five minutes to get situated."

Thanks, Pop. You're a real mensch.

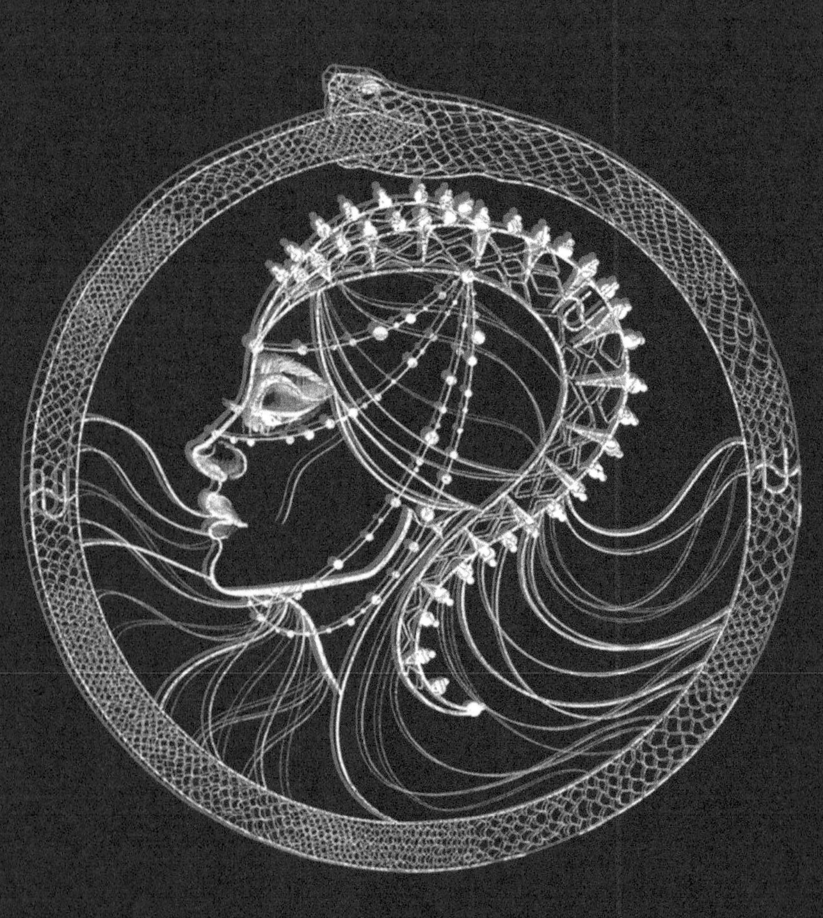

I Can Buy My Own Drinks

Jax is thrashed.

He's been flirting with every guy in the bar like they're a ten, but even by small town standards, we haven't been approached by better than a six.

I don't know why he insisted we go for drinks after our gossip sesh; his heart isn't in this. I suspect the frequently mentioned Eli is part of his reluctance, but his stories are also peppered with names of other guys I've never heard of, so maybe his plate is full at the moment.

Why the bar crawl?

I sure as hell don't need to be fixed up, and he knows it. The conversation about my small town sexual hijinks had him rolling, and he knows I'm in over my head with four dudes. I've tried to call it a night several times since we arrived at this dive he swears by, and every time, he orders another round. I can't figure out if he's working up to telling me something or if he's just missed me.

I have to drive home, though, so I used my bartender hand signal skills to let the burly dude pouring know I don't want liquor in my glass anymore. He seemed to get it because while Jackson is still slugging back Manhattans, I've been getting cherry cokes for the past two hours. Jekyll and Hyde are perched on stools next to me, slurping cream out of martini glasses like royalty. I draped the damn snake around my neck, letting it lifting its head occasionally to taste the air.

No one has remarked on the menagerie surrounding us, and again, it's strange that I'm hanging out in a place with no rules about random pets tagging along. Did the US get way cooler while I was squirreled away studying for my FBI evals or am I crazy? Everywhere I go since I moved has a bizarre set of unwritten rules that everyone but me knows. If I were the tin foil hat type, I'd think there was a conspiracy to keep me in the dark.

But that can't be true, can it?

"This is a safe space, dear. You do not need to be afraid."

The voice startles me out of my head and I turn to speak to the woman who reads my mind, but a rumbling growl distracts me. Kali and Hecate rise from their places on either side of my stool, ears pinned back as they glare at the biggest black wolf I've ever seen. It doesn't move, it simply stands its ground in front of her with unblinking sea-blue eyes. Where did these weirdos come from and why do I always attract them?

"Sweet fancy Moses on buttered toast, lady! Who the fuck are you and why is your wolf threatening my dogs?" The snake moves, coiling around my waist and up my left arm as I point at the closest thing to the Hound of the Baskervilles that I've ever seen in person. How is it even allowed in this place? I look around, but not one patron seems to even notice their presence.

Why is my life so ever loving bizarre? Did I call a disguised goddess ugly in a past life? Am I facing the consequences of an ill-fated wish on the hand of a primate? Was I born under the proverbial 'bad sign'? I'm really wondering.

Her laugh tinkles like wind chimes and the wolf tosses its head, making a sound that might be the dog version of a chuckle. "He is not threatening your hounds, young one. If Argus wanted to show his dominance, your tiny pack could not resist. They are far too new to withstand the pull of an alpha companion."

Arching my brow, I cross my arms over my chest and give her a look of irritation. Again, who in the sainted name of Dolly Parton does this random hippie think she is? "Lady, I'm in no mood to go to war with Miss Mitchell tonight. Back off before we have to draw lines."

"Yes, I can see you are troubled. I am not here to exacerbate your turmoil—I'm here to prevent a terrible miscarriage of justice." She pauses, her lips quirking as she studies me. "However, I must admit you are not what I expected when I granted this boon."

I narrow my gaze on the sparkling sheen of her dark skin, long box braids decorated with baubles and trinkets, and the flowing wrapper and matching gele. The silver and pastel colors are not traditional, but they match the bangles, beads, armbands, and sandals she's sporting. Her bearing screams wealthy foreigner and her attire is curated to project that image. "You're a hissy fit with a tail on it yourself. I swear, I'm a magnet for mysterious crazies," I mutter.

"*Mow!*" Jekyll cries, bobbing his head.

"No need to agree, you traitor." I look down at Kali and Hecate, mentally willing then *not* to attack this Argus if I get upset. Eurayle is off hunting, and the cats are more attuned to my whims than Teddy's dogs, but I don't want to explain how I let them become wolf kibble over some con artist approaching me in a bar. The exotic stranger laughs again at my vexation, and I slam my glass down. "I asked you a question. Where I come from, it's only polite to answer. I don't see what's so amusing."

"There are many things about this situation you do not understand, but if you did, you would laugh with me. Alas, I cannot reveal them, so you will need to trust me. I mean you no harm, Jolene Athena Whitley."

Is the Universe kidding me?! How does this whack job know my name? How many stalkers can one gal have?

"Look, I don't know if you're a stalker or a garden variety kook who can cold read, but I really—"

She holds up her hand, shaking her head. "We do not have time for me to explain who or what I am. I stopped in this place to verify the information given to me by an old friend. She asked me to vote in her stead and I could not in good conscience do so until I could see you through my own eyes."

I snort. "See me do what with your own eyes? Vote for whom?" Leaning forward, I whisper, "Is this person here now? Is she telling you to creep me out?"

Argus lifts his head and howls, the collar of feathers and bells on his neck jingling. The mystery woman nods solemnly as she looks down at the black wolf, her expression serious. "Yes, my darling. We must go or we will miss our chance."

A feeling of warmth and safety slides over my skin as my scaly companion constricts and releases, soothing the rapid thrum of my pulse as my anger rises. "Please do. I don't know what your con is, but I don't need my cards or palm read. However you figured out my name, forget it and go bother some other mark."

"Destiny comes for us all, Jolene. Accept the gifts you have received, and open your mind to those yet to come. You have much to learn before we meet again. Use your time wisely."

Uh-huh. Whatever, Miss Cleo.

A yell from the crowd catches my ears and I squint as Jackson comes stumbling towards me. His hands clamp on my shoulders and I grunt, bracing myself to catch him. He smells like a distillery and I'm going to drive him home before I head back to the Hollow.

Turning to say goodnight to the looney, I blink when I realize both she and the enormous wolf have disappeared.

Great. A lawyer, a psychic, and a failed FBI agent walk into a bar... the question is, what the hell is the punchline?

By the time I dump Jackson at his place, I've had enough of his drunken sexcapade tales. He wasn't wrong; we used to kibbutz about our conquests all night long, but I can't connect with his party player shit now. It feels lonely and sad, and his current state doesn't do much to dispel that notion.

It's like I've been replaced by a pod person.

The Jolene that scampered around Europe and Asia with Saoirse years ago morphed into a serious workaholic who based her whole life on a career goal. Now, that focused loner is transforming again, and I'm not sure who I'm becoming. It's not that I can't be friends with Jax, but we aren't in the same phase in life anymore.

And I'm okay with that, which is even weirder.

I climb into my Impala, checking to make sure I buckled the cats and hounds in. Whistling, I look up and see Eurayle circling above us. She took off to hunt earlier, and I hoped she'd make her way back before I hit the highway to head home. I know she can find her way on her own, but I'd feel better if we were all together.

As much as I hate to admit it, Creepy McWolfLady wigged me out a bit. Having a random whack-a-doo confront you in public when you were recently poisoned and have a stalker is a lot to take in all at once.

The snake squeezes me again, and I blink. Son of a bitch. Every time I get upset, the damn thing shifts, constricts, and I feel better. I have a motherfucking emotional support python. How many girls can say that?

"I suppose I'm going to name you now," I grumble under my breath. "I can't have you calming me down and shit if I don't know your name." A sharp squeeze on my ribs is my answer, and I roll my eyes.

If I don't stop collecting men and animals, I'm going to have to build an addition on my house.

Speaking of that, I should call the boys and let them know I'm on my way. I've been gone far longer than I intended and I'm a little shocked they haven't blown up my phone checking on me.

"***Text Assholes***," I say, waiting for the Bluetooth to pick up my command. When it beeps, I wink at my servals in the passenger seat. "Hey. I'm on my way home. Should I pick up food?"

The robotic voice repeats my question and I hear the swoosh of a sent message echo. My fingers drum on the wheel and I hum under my breath as I wait for a response. Minutes and miles tick by and I frown. It's not normal for all of them to ignore my text at the same time. What is going on? They usually jump on a group text like flies on shit.

"***Text Assholes***," I say again, pressing my foot down on the pedal to speed up. An odd feeling forms in my gut as I wait with no answer. "Where the hell are you guys? Usually I can't pee without one of you trailing behind me."

Silence stretches as I drive towards the interchange that branches off towards Whistler's Hollow. My phone doesn't buzz, and the animals stare at me as I curse under my breath. How in the hell do I have four idiot boyfriends and not one of them has a second to answer my texts? I mean, I thought it was strange that none of them wanted to accompany me to the city, but now I'm really getting nervous.

The big fight at the Hollar was pretty public. Is it possible someone has cautioned them away from me? I wouldn't put it past Teddy's mom, but I don't know Wolfie's family. Presley and Doyle aren't Hollow natives, but they both work for the town in some fashion. Am I damaged goods now?

Panic floods my system and the python slithers into a position that spreads over more of my torso until its head rests on my shoulder. I wish I knew if it was a boy or a girl, but I didn't, so I sigh. "I'll call you Isis, because that's healing. I don't know if it's accurate or not, but that seems to be your function. You help me

Fine. I'll take my files from Jackson and my contingent of furry, feathered and scaled companions home. If they don't want to talk to me, I can make myself a milkshake and curl up in my big ass bed alone while they do whatever the hell is so important.

Maybe a locked door will get my point across.

"Mrrp?" Hyde says cautiously, poking her head up from the backseat.

"I don't know, buddy. It's been a weird night and I don't understand why everyone's ignoring me. Do you think I should be worried?"

The answering howl from the dogs isn't comforting, so I step on the gas. If something is wrong, I'm not going to waste time following the speed limit.

There's A Reason These Tables Are Numbered, Honey, You Just Haven't Thought of It Yet

Doyle

'*Humans are ridiculous creatures. We should have never allowed them to survive*' could be written on our family crest. At least, on my mother's side, it could be. The vast amount of absolute rot they've come up with to help ease their emotions is astounding, and I didn't think it was possible for anything in the extranormal community to match it in tone deaf self-centered focus—until tonight.

They called us into the antechamber like scuttling mole rats despite the rigid dress code for this evening's three-ring circus. It's damp, poorly lit, and uncomfortable in this cavernous room set up to mirror the human version of a courtroom.

Never mind that we not only have a *real* courtroom down the street we could use; we also have access to some of the nicest country clubs and mansions in the state within minutes, but we're all crowded into a gallery in a fucking cave. Whatever ancient mystical moron who created this process in the burgeoning years of the Society is long dead, but we're all sitting here pretending to be in a rich people cosplay of Harry Potter.

Yawning, I lean my chair back, looking around the room at the assembled codgers and society mavens and Guardians, agents, and inductees. There are a few unfamiliar faces and that must be the 'wildcards' Boone mentioned. He was wound so tight he looked like he was going to spring into the air and rocket to the sun if anyone so much as tapped his shoulder.

I'm not as worried, but then, my kind rarely ends up in the middle of petty squabbles like this. We're not part of the day-to-day bureaucracy of the Society, but my placement in Whistler's Hollow has thrown me into the shallow end of the supe pool.

Just. Fucking. Qware.

If I didn't have a gut deep feeling about my Tíogair, I'd be as far away from here as possible. The fat old goat Boone calls Pop is sitting in the rostrum with Mayor Nelia blathering on about something. She looks bored to tears, and Zareb is squinting at the human as if he'd like to eat him for the offense. I could get into a good old fashion lion eating a Christian thing—it's been over a millennium since I watched a *damnatio ad bestias*. I sit up in my chair a little straighter as I focus on finding something to irritate the big cat. If I can trigger even the slightest provocation from the Senator, I should be able to—

A gavel slams into the lectern, and I jump, catching the Mayor's eye. I'll be a doe-eyed ingenue! She caught me. I knew I liked the old gal for a reason, so I wink at her. I wasn't doing anything out of my purview or even contrary to my nature, so she won't rat me out. Besides, my auntie would send me a case of Jameson if I made Zareb do it. She pretends she doesn't like the chaos my father's side brings, but I've always been her favorite. Every stern, smart lady loves a bad boy, you know.

That brings me back to my Tíogair and her current predicament. I can't possibly explore my fantasies with her in every conceivable spot in this backwater burg if she's being punished by these heavy-handed fools for defending herself. It's their fault the doc can't try to remove the suppression spell; they want it to be natural.

As if putting a spell on a young supe to control when they receive their birthrights is natural in any reality of any dimension. They know it's not, but something about Jolene has them all aflutter. They'd let this slide if that idiot Behle wasn't pushing to reverse the charges his cunt daughter so richly deserves to answer for.

A soft gasp catches my attention and I look over, snorting. The submissive fae is trying—unsuccessfully, I might add—to keep thirsty housewives and unmarried heirs away. He's being far too kind, but I realize that's because he's supposed to be the soft, earnest convincer while the doc flirts and Boone bullies people to our side. I don't have a specific role because the fire breathing asshole doesn't trust me. That's dandy, though, because it means I can sit back and work from the shadows. Almost no one in town has a clue what or who I am, and it was part of the agreement when I was stationed in the town.

Anonymity means I can do far worse than irritate a lion into eating a politician should I choose, and no one will be the wiser. I grin to myself, scanning the room for another target. Now, we're having a grand time, kiddies. I'm hunting for foibles, and once I find them, I'm going to push every single button I can find without lifting a finger.

Jolene has no idea how powerful her friends are. If she did, she'd be afraid of the attention it will bring. Whether through our families or lost parents, all seven of her merry men have enemies lurking at every turn. Once we dispatch with hers, the onslaught of ours will be our next hurdle.

I, for one, can't wait. I never get to have fun anymore.

"My daughter printed the news, as is her purview as editor of the *Hollow Hollar*. We live in the land of the free and home of the brave, Your Honors. The First Amendment is not only applicable to the humans; part of the accords were concessions to staying within the boundaries of their laws, whether we agreed with them," Reginald Whitman Behle argues as he paces in front of the crowd. "Simply because I can both create and destroy with my magic does not mean I can use it to affect the timeline of human history or to cover up violations of their criminal law. By the same token, we also cannot allow our laws and regulations to supersede those of the lands we inhabit secretly."

Aye, this old warlock thinks an awful lot of himself because he was a diplomat during the bloody Revolution, doesn't he? He likes to hear his voice more than Boone and his father put together—a feat I thought to be a theoretical improbability. I roll my eyes, turning my chair to find the specific townsfolk he seems to be speaking to. Those are his plants, I'll bet, and he's not gifted enough in subterfuge to hide what he's doing from a clueless babe, much less me.

A quick flick of my fingers finds what I need, and a loud screech follows. The woman in question is blond (and aren't they all here?), thin, and looks like she dines on martinis for every meal of the day. She's dressed in head to toe Prada, and I have to cover my mouth as she climbs onto her chair, wailing. Her heels are making her totter, and not one of the so-called Southern gentlemen has offered to help. Her screams shut the blowhard up, and Mayor Nelia huffs as she sits back.

"Reese Emily Barrington! Do you think you might tap Amelie so she can hunt down the tiny mouse that is making you wail like a broken ambulance? If not, I could certainly send Zareb to handle it," Nelia says, her tone full of annoyance.

The little witch actually pouts at the bloody mayor of the town like she's trying to get a sugar daddy to buy her a pony. When it doesn't work, she elbows Cantwell's sister, who ducks down under the chairs to take care of the mouse situation with a loud hiss. Titters echo across the chamber and I smirk to myself, feeling like my distractions are much more useful than Boone will ever give me credit for.

"Now that the hysterical women are taken care of, I suggest we get this show on the road. Reggie, you've made your point elegantly, and I think the theory has merit. Your daughter can't be—"

"Point of order, Senator," Nelia says, arching a brow at the puffy old twat. "We cannot accept Councilman Behle's statements—passionate though they may be—as fact without testimony from the parties present at the disturbance. Surely you remember the proper trial procedure from your days on the bench? If not, we can request our sitting judge to remind us."

Oooh. That had to hurt.

Everyone knows Edgar Osiris Boone II is a figurehead in every sense of the word. He was born human in a founding family in the Hollow prior to what those eejits call the 'Hostile Takeover' behind our backs. In reality, we saved a small town from the ravages of changing economies and technology long before their neighboring cities crumbled under automation and corporate gentrification. The bargain was fair, and Boone was one of the wily ones who married into his position by taking an extranormal bride.

Speaking of the literal harpy, I'm pleased to see that Margaret Emily Boone isn't present this evening. When their marriage didn't produce an heir because of the ironic problems the elder Boone had, they adopted a lost baby. Young Boone hasn't turned out the way they'd hoped, and his parents act as if he's the greatest disappointment since Hephaestus. Honestly, I can understand why our *triplásiac* friend hid his true nature. He doesn't want to give those assholes the satisfaction of having a trophy child.

I can respect that kind of nose thumbing, and clearly, so can our intrepid Mayor.

"If my services are needed," Edgar cuts in, smirking through his late evening stubble. "I'd be happy to cover the basics, Pop."

Ouch. Another hard volley at the Senator.

My allies aren't playing gently this evening, and the prospect of an all-out brawl full of extranormals has my blood humming. I haven't been in a real good fight in a while. I wonder if they'll let me use my mother's powers. I'd have to negotiate it, of course, because all supe battles start like good BDSM—with a negotiation of terms.

"I hate to interrupt your provincial power plays, but some of us are needed elsewhere. My fellow wildcards and I were asked to come vote, and so far, we have little information to do so outside of bluster and high-handed propaganda. I would like to hear the facts of the event from those present and take a vote in short order," a short, dark-haired Frenchman with an eye patch interjects.

Who the hell is this Baron Ironblood motherfucker? I've never seen him before in my life.

"The Commandant is correct," Mayor Nelia says. "We are wasting valuable time with this nonsense." Her eyes cut around the crowd until she lands on our feathered cohort. "Presley Hemingway Hamilton, as the town doctor and supe medical advisor, I would like to know what you witnessed."

C'mon you great eejit. Show them…. Ahhh, there it is—the old Razzle Dazzle.

Presley drops his jacket on his chair and steps forward into the round, his form shimmering into a lesser shift. Large white wings appear on his back, and a crest of feathers springs from his head as he faces the lectern and bows. With a dramatic flap as he rises, he tucks the wings back and gives the intricate hand signals to signify fealty to the Society at official gatherings. It's trite as hell, but the git's making a show folks can't take their eyes off, and I'm a little impressed.

"Your Honors, I was not present at the beginning of the altercation. I arrived amid the action with Benjamin and Edgar. Doyle was the first member to arrive who was not directly involved in the turmoil. However, I can attest to the fact that when I stepped into the office, Jolene was attempting to wrangle what appeared to be a new companion—one none of us, including her, had ever seen before. Wolfgang has identified it as a reticulated python and Jolene now has it living with her. I believe she requested Doyle to procure registry paperwork as we exited the building."

The Senator glares at him, his jealousy of the handsome, erudite doctor clear on his piggish features. "How can you provide useful testimony if you did not witness the event, young man?"

For the love of Mother Hera, Mary, and bloody muses!

This idiot is trying to steer the trial for sure. Behle must have made some back alley deal, and if that's the case, I know why the Mayor called in all the wildcards. She's a crafty gal, and I respect the hell out of her for trying to keep corruption from leaking from the human world into ours. Narrowing my eyes, I concentrate on setting an itch in a place he won't like, knowing it will scare the living shit out of the cheating bastard.

"I believe my information is useful. I can verify that Jolene Athena Whitley was not controlling the animal to harm Amy; in fact, she was struggling to communicate with the snake to prevent it from aggressively defending her. Since I am certain she is still held in stasis by a powerful and unfamiliar suppression spell, I know she has not emerged and cannot be held accountable for the bursts of power, as her psyche works to strip the magic." He turns to the crowd, flexing his wings again. "After all, that sort of independent diagnosis is what the Society sent me to medical school to eschew, is it not?"

Get Fucked

Her wolf throws its head back and howls, making my hound itch to burst free.

My father harrumphs in his typical privileged, rich white man fashion. His family name and political clout are the only reason a room full of fearsome extranormals are allowing him to pretend he's even a fraction as powerful as they are. He frequently forgets that in the end, he's nothing but a frail human, and even the weakest species here could destroy him before he could bang his ridiculous gavel.

Mayor Nelia has a schooled expression on her face, but I caught the glimmer of pride in her eyes as our town healer served my father his just desserts. She's been an ally from the beginning, but I understand why she has to appear impartial. Her ability to lead the town hinges on a reputation for fair, even-handed decision making despite the whims of the councils, the Society, and the rich elite that shape our community.

"Thank you, Presley. We will take your expertise into consideration when we call for the vote." Her eyes travel over the crowd as if to instruct us all to do so without saying a word. "Next, I would like to hear from a first on-scene witness. Doyle Aloysius Haggerty, please rise and give your testimony."

Oh, this is going to be good.

If Pop thinks he can talk his way around the Irish jackass, he's got another thing coming. Doyle may not be my favorite citizen, but his gifts trump those of almost every supe in town. No one knows what he is or who he's related to, but the bonny lad schtick is an affectation. He's no more green blooded than I'm blue.

But he has everyone convinced he is. That kind of skill at deception makes him a formidable enemy, one more crafty than my father has yet to face, even in D.C.

The rusty haired idiot rolls to his feet, a bright smile on his lips as he meets the eyes of every person in the chamber. When he reaches the center of the circle, he bows at the Mayor and swears his oath just as Prez did before him. Tucking his hands behind his back, he waits for Nelia to nod before pacing along the edge of the ring.

"I admit, I'm not this involved in the... activities you hold in this building. My duties are vast, and I prefer to focus on the bigger picture." He turns to look at me, his green eyes flashing as they take over our support section. "However, this event has me questioning whether I've been remiss in failing to monitor the wheels of Justice as they turn."

"Son, are you questioning—"

Doyle turns, whipping his hand out as he practically thunders a response. "I am neither your son nor your subordinate, Boone. You have forgotten your place, and I will not be interrupted. Shut. Up."

My father's eyes widen as his mouth clamps closed, and he makes frustrated sounds as he struggles to retort. I could have warned him, I suppose, but I can't help but enjoy seeing him squirm in the most publicly humiliating way possible.

"As I was saying, I believe you were all set to rubber stamp a grave miscarriage of Justice, and I'm more than happy to prevent it." The look on his face is downright creepy now because his smile promises both pain and pleasure. "I was a few doors down visiting the flower shop when I felt a… pulse. It was much like I'm certain MacAuley's visions feel, and though I'm unfamiliar, I gave chase anyway. I'm always up for a little chaos, you see."

I look over at Hugo sitting in the dead center of the crowd, taking in the pallor of his skin. I did not inform him Doyle would reveal his secrets—hell, maybe he thought none of us knew. That's going to be a problem later, and I don't envy the guy for it.

"When I entered the newspaper office, there was a lot of screaming and shrieking. Damn near blew out my eardrums, because unlike some rescuers, I'm not a bloody dog." His smirk makes me close my eyes, and I struggle not to let my temper get the best of me. This fool is going to out half the town before he gets to his point. "The lovely Miss Whitley was calmly speaking to the giant snake to keep it from throttling the accused to death. She was unfamiliar with the animal and despite the imminent danger to herself, she was diligently working to save the bully she came to confront."

Covering my mouth with my hand, I keep the laugh from escaping. None of what he's saying is inaccurate, but he's weaving the tale in such a matter-of-fact way that it's impossible to tell if he's leaving out details. His story lines up with our fluffy doc's without being word for word, and he's telling it while he strolls around the room as if conversing with the attendees.

If we lived in Kansas, I'd think we're getting ready to have trouble in River City.

"Not long after I stepped on scene, the doc, the vet, the bruiser, and his Honor came crashing in the door like a group of aging super-heroes on a mission. They could witness the python release the threat and bond as a companion of Miss Whitley almost instantly. There were some heated words exchanged between all parties, and when we escorted Jolene out, she requested I procure her another companion registry form—which I did and filed the next day."

The mayor smiles, nodding her head. "Indeed, I recall signing the form and having Aldous file it accordingly. The snake in question is officially registered."

"Exactly. The question we are here to answer is not how the events transpired, fellow citizens. Every statement by witnesses who are not employed by the paper or directly involved in the squabble will confirm that we have an accurate timeline." His eyes sparkle as he splays his arms out and spins in a slow circle. "What we need to establish this evening is whether we should punish Amy Matilda Behle for violating one of the Society's oldest rules—the *Supe Secrecy Accords of 1776.*"

The crowd gasps and my father turns red, clawing at his face in vain as he fights the magic, holding his jaws shut. Reginald and his followers surge to their feet, yelling and screaming their outrage at his accusation. I look over at the pup, jerking my chin to indicate that we need the distraction of his pocket ace before this devolves into a brawl.

"People, please!" Wolfie's voice booms through the cavern as his large, glittery Fae wings release from his back and flap gracefully. The dust from them floats through the air, permeating the room with magic only a Royal of his court can wield. "I have testimony to give."

As expected, the fervor dies immediately as the townspeople watch his shimmering, ethereal beauty while inhaling the wing dust. Doyle winks at me, giving us a two-fingered salute as he walks out of the circle and drops into his chair lazily. I roll my eyes and lean back, trying to avoid jumping across the distance and throttling him. There were a thousand ways we could have turned the tables on my father and Behle, but he chose the one that would start a riot.

"I concur with the accounts given by the others. However, I am uniquely qualified to address one aspect of the situation that no one has mentioned—the animals." Our pup flashes pointed white teeth and shakes his silvery hair, using the inescapable beauty of his father's side to distract the naysayers.

"Wolfgang, it would be helpful if you turned down your... youness... and tell us what we've missed. Doyle, release the Senator as well. You've made your point." Nelia winks at me, and I watch as Zareb rises to stalk over to sit between her and my father.

"Of course, Nelia." Wolfie bows to her, his wings collapsing and disappearing from view as he swears his oath. "I only wished to help prevent an unnecessary battle. If my sugarplum had wanted to harm Amy, she didn't need the snake. She was traveling with her servals, a harpy eagle, and Edgar's hounds. Any or all of them could have subdued one angry human without batting a lash."

Well, hell's bells. I didn't even *think* about that. The second half of my drugar's self-anointed doctor panini may not be as aggressive as me or the rabid leprechaun, but his brains more than make up for his gentle nature.

Plus, anyone with wings is okay in my book.

"Mayor Nelia, I hate to interrupt, but I believe it is time for the vote," the tall, ebony skinned woman with an enormous black wolf calls out from the back room. "I am here to stand in for the vote of Guardian Bane, and I have a long journey when we convene the proceedings."

"Yes, Guardian St. James. London is quite far, as is the Commandant's trip back to Argentina. We appreciate you standing in while Andromeda is handling the emergent coven up North," the mayor says, glancing at my father to see if he reacts.

"Argus and I are ever at the disposal of the Society, Your Honor. In time, we hope to have more news for you regarding our mission," the foreign wildcard responds.

"Thank you, Heraclea." Nelia stands and claps her hands. "Members and guests, we will now take a series of votes. After I ask, you will raise your hand only if your answer is 'aye'. Are we clear?"

Murmurs are her response, and the mayor turns to my father, who nods. He's stayed quiet since Doyle handed him his ass, and I can't say I'm disappointed in the slightest. The old geezer has been asking for a comeuppance like this for almost as long as I've been alive.

"The first question being voted on is should we should charge Jolene Athena Whitley with an unprovoked attack on Amy Matilda Behle?"

Hands raise, but they are limited to the Behle family cheering section. Relief floods my chest as Wolfie rejoins our section and leans in to whisper, "That's the most important part, Edgar. Your plan worked well."

I sigh, nodding as Nelia counts the votes and declares the vote has concluded. "I'm glad it did, but it could have gone awry just as easily."

"Since we've cleared Jolene, there will not be a vote on reversing the charges. The ultimate question is should we refer Amy Matilda Behle for further investigation for violating the accords?"

Mayor Cornelia Sykes just sent a warning shot across the bow of the founding families, and the result will change the shape of the town for good. If we'd had a principal in school as strong as her, maybe Tilly wouldn't be as damaged as she is.

Keeping her safe tonight was only a step towards making the mistakes of the past right, but by the look on the faces of my fellow housemates, I'm headed in the right direction.

And my Pop can absolutely get fucked if he doesn't like it.

I See Red

N one of their fucking cars were here when I got home and that put me in an even fouler mood than when I was speeding home like a member of the Andretti family. I stomped into my house with my companions in tow, flicking on lights and tossing my shit left and right. I'm not a slob normally, but I'm too irritated to focus on niceties.

Wanting my guys to see me as a woman who can take care of herself does not mean I'm cool with being ignored. Even a quick emoji would have been better than stony silence, and I'm furious that neither they nor my supposed BFF could make the time to acknowledge my existence tonight.

Fuck all of that.

I was *fine* on my own before they all came traipsing in, demanding my attention and affection, and I'll be fine if they've all gotten bored with it.

After I tore through the house cursing a blue streak, I changed into a comfortable set of yoga clothes and banged my way through, giving the animals their dinner. When I found I wasn't the least bit hungry despite not having 'real food' all day, I let out a screech of frustration and headed for the basement to find weapons.

Precision fury always helps me find my zen.

Knives fly from my fingertips as I aim at the posts with rapid precision. Each one has a blown up vinyl yearbook photo of the bitches who tormented me in high school, and I painted the bullseye right between their stupid eyes. I had Seer set them up a few weeks ago, and I'm glad I did.

Don't judge me; it's therapeutic.

I run out of tossers and with a grunt of irritation; I trudge over to pull the hilts so I can load up another round. Stupid, evil witches. Dumb, bonehead dudes. Flaky, unpredictable friends. Everyone is off doing their own thing while I'm trying to process my parents being murdered, a confrontation with a weirdo in a bar, and that all of this is tied to the very town I'm living in. Not to mention, I just got splashed all over Creation in an article that accused me of being the Whore of Babylon.

It's not like I have a few *things* going on that might require a little *support.*

Jekyll follows me as a line up on the next throwing line—five feet farther than the warm up line I started at—and looks up at me in concern. I don't know if that's because he knows I'm upset or because he knows I'm trying to practice while angry and loaded down with an extra thirty-five pounds of emotional support python coiled around me from ankle to shoulder. I'll admit, it's making my routine harder, and I have to focus on the balance a hell of a lot more keenly when I let my knives fly.

Maybe there's money in training like this? I wonder if Isis would like some friends…

Shaking my head, I return my gaze to the post with Amy's picture. I don't *care* if people want to pass their fifties-esque, Southern Boomer hypocrite moral judgements on my lifestyle—their opinions weren't asked for or needed. However, I *do* care if those articles affect my ability to run my business or investigate, I now have to ramp up. Fitting in is a huge part of the fabric of this community, and in order to work my way into people's confidence, they have to feel they can relate to me.

Pictures naming me the town harlot are going to set me back for weeks, if not longer. I'm going to get called in to the office at school again, and I'll spend far too much time issuing whatever statement Jax comes up with that prevents them from firing me for a moral clause or voiding my contracts at the studio. It's going to be a PR nightmare, and I have better things to do with my time.

Plus, I have no patience for town gossips meddling in my personal life. This isn't the life I expected when I moved back, but I have every right to find happiness in whomever or whatever form I choose. If I want one of the Nip/Tucks' opinions on something, I'll happily beat it out of them.

Letting another tosser fly, I grin maniacally when it nails Amy right in the new nose she got for her Sweet Sixteen. That would teach her —it's a shame I can't give her the same trim off the end in real life. It might force her to eat a serving of humble pie, and maybe she'd back the fuck off for a bit. Hyde mrrps behind me, and I turn, giving her a rueful expression. "No, I will not assault her unless I'm defending myself. It's not my style, and I'd prefer not to add hypocrite to my resume. But it sure as hell feels good to *think* about knocking her down a few pegs."

The animals settle in as I continue to burn off the frustration at my situation and the absence of the people I depend on to manage the wild ebb and flow of my emotions. Once I've warmed up, I move back another five feet, and then another, groaning when I just don't have the arm strength to make the arc at that distance. I didn't MISS the posts on the last round, but I didn't cause a cosmetic emergency for my idiotic bobblehead targets, either.

More's the pity.

I grumble under my breath about the limitations of my muscle development and scoot forward to the first line. The next set of exercises is the hardest, and I'm only accurate about forty percent of the time. With the turbulence in my heart and mind, I can't guarantee I'll even swing that, but I'm not the kind of girl to give into bullshit emotional stuff anymore. Turning, I wave the cats back, and give a piercing whistle so Eury will land. I don't want the darkness and my less than laser focused concentration to result in a tragedy. When everything is quiet and calm, I pull the headband off my head and over my eyes.

The sounds of the night dull to a low roar as I look deep inside of myself, envisioning the placement of the posts, the feel of the light breeze, and the rustle of the grass blades around me. Silence descends in my mind, the only thing in my head a sharp picture of the first target.

The shape of Reese's face, the contrast in the colors, and the circle I want to hit zoom in like the lens on a DSLR. Raising my arm, I hold the blade with enough tension to keep it steady, but not cause it to catch as I release it. I take one slow breath in, feeling the rise of my chest and expansion of my ribs before I let the knife fly on the exhale.

A loud *thwack* is the only noise before I refocus and repeat the same process four more times. As the last blade embeds into a target, I relax my limbs and pull the headband up to peer into the distance, dropping the hand holding the last blade to my side.

"I find myself glad to be on your side rather than theirs, Tilly. That was more than a little terrifying," the husky voice of my ex-bully murmurs as he approaches.

I whip around, glaring at him with all the fear and anger I've been stewing since the trip home from the city practically vibrating from my form. "*You!*" Stalking towards him, I shake the razor-sharp knife without even thinking about it. "You *idiots* left me alone with *no way* to contact you. I wouldn't have *minded* being let off the leash a little, but you disappeared for *hours*, and I was *convinced...*"

Before I realize it, I'm standing with the blade pressed to Edgar's throat, a small bead of blood forming near the tip. My eyes feel like they're burning in the socket, and that weird heat is spreading over me like a wildfire in the dry season. I gnash my teeth as I look at him, all the fury overflowing inside of me at once. A knot of hunger is uncoiling in my gut, and I have no idea what to do with it. The emotions that are flooding me are raw, violent, and outraged in a way I've never experienced before.

"You were convinced of what, drugar?" His response is barely more than a snarl, and that should phase me, but it doesn't.

Instead, it has the exact opposite effect. The low, rumbling growl makes the ball of fire inside spark, and I fling the blade away as I knock him to the ground. My hips bracket his and I pin his shoulders with my hands as I look down at him angrily. The harsh sounds of my breath heaving are the only noise as my body and mind struggle to muddle through what is happening. When he shifts, an answering rumble echoes out and I slam his shoulders down to the ground again.

What in the name of Judas and the eleven traveling hippies is going on *with me?*

"Tell me what you were convinced about," his voice whispers.

I understand the words, but I can't seem to parse a response. All I know is that I want what is *mine* to be *mine*. I need to *know* for certain where I stand, and something deep inside of me is fighting like hell to find a way out to show him that. Nothing is working like it should, and I don't seem to have control of my mouth or my limbs, so I don't know how to express it. There's so much rage and fury, but the fear is behind the wheel as well.

"She can't tell you, Boone. Don't you remember the first time? Think about how it felt to have something pushing its way to the surface when it doesn't know where to go and you can't control it?"

The voice is familiar, but the scent tips the scales. I smell Presley as he approaches and my head whips around to growl from deep in my belly. The ache in my eyes intensifies as I glare at him in warning— he needs to stay away from what's *mine*.

"Holy shit, she's going to—."

"Yes," McSteamy replies, chuckling softly. "Tonight, of all nights, I think the first tether is breaking free. Be ready, Edgar. You'll need to move fast to match her so she doesn't freak out."

Before I can attempt to respond, the tension in my body snaps and I throw my head back, releasing a howl that echoes off the hills like the beginning of a British mystery. Every bone in my body feels like it's stretching and snapping and my skin ripples in a way that isn't possible.

"I can sense emergence, as you know. Control your shift to follow hers so she can see it mirrored back. This is *your* piece of her, Boone. She needs the bond to be completed, and she needs it now."

I wish I knew what he's talking about, but all I can do is continue to scream into the Universe as my vision goes black in the way I've been fighting my entire life. This time, however, I don't see blackness fading into unconsciousness—no, this time my vision flips to red and my fingers dig into his shoulders until the scent of blood permeates the air. It draws me, and I lick my lips, staring at the furrows with a hunger that feels like it's going to rip its way out of me to be sated.

"*Drugar!* You must feed. Bite and drink… make the mark when the fire fills you. It is how we are made. Burn with me." Teddy's voice is dark, rumble and full of the commanding tone that makes my body tremble even in normal circumstances.

My head drops to look into eyes that aren't aquamarine or even human looking. The rings of fiery lava around his pupils are firm as he waits for his order to be followed, and I snap my teeth at him. A brow arches and I give in, yanking his head to the side and burying my mouth there to tear in as instructed. Teeth slide through skin like my blades in butter, and the spill of heat from his wound pulls a whine of excitement out of me.

I feel hands tugging at my clothes, a cool breeze on fiery skin, and a calming softness behind me. Soft murmurs in my ear tell me to adjust until I'm positioned over Teddy's cock, then gentle hands guide me to sink down until I'm full. The sensation of feathers draping over my back as a rhythm starts in our hips is a stark contrast to the hunger and heat consuming me inside.

"That's our girl," Prez murmurs, his fingers tweaking the nipple shields he loves so much. "Edgar, move faster. She has to come before the change is complete."

His response is garbled, I don't understand, but his hips buck up into me, making answering rumbles and snarls escape my lips. A sharp pain right over my clit makes me gasp, and a shudder starts at my toes as the sensations that were building slam into me like a tidal wave. I tear my mouth away from his neck, lapping over the wound as I lift one hand. I don't know why, but oddly shaped fingers trace a flaming symbol midair before repeating it over the bite mark.

Teddy shouts, his cock spilling inside of me as our bodies stutter to a halt. The waves of pleasure make the burning inside of me fade a little and I hear a loud screech like a pterodactyl from the dinosaur movie. The feathers lift from my back as a whoosh of chilly air hits me and I look down at my former bully with a tilted head. A wolfish grin is his only answer before he whispers, "Now, shift!"

That's the last thing I hear before my mind goes completely black again.

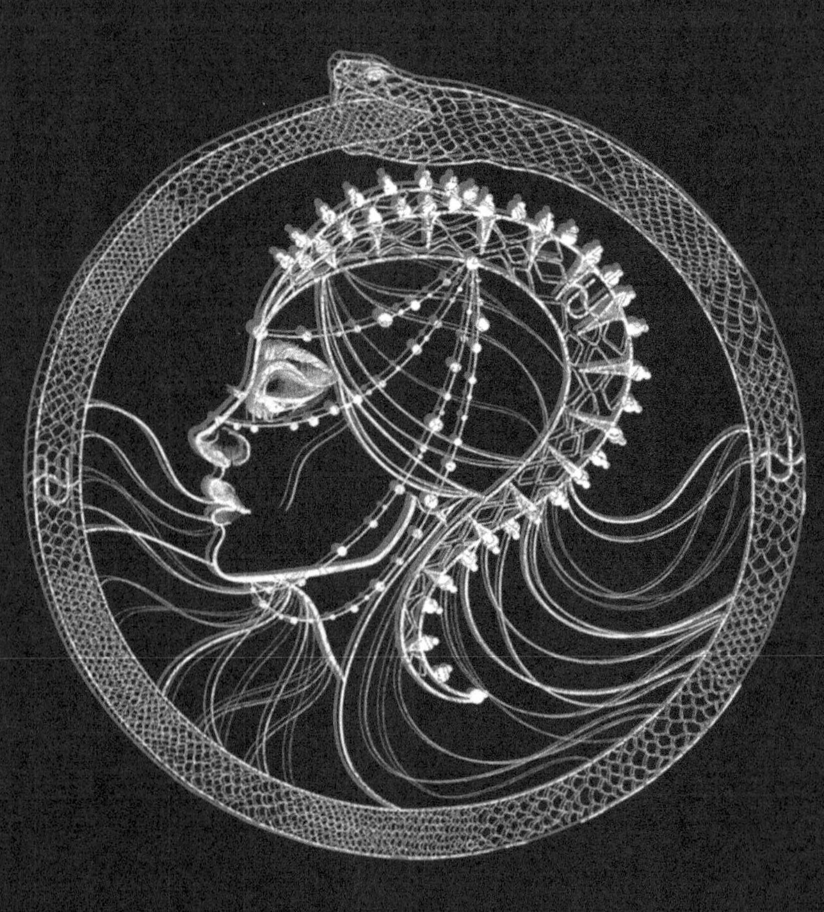

My Songs Know What You Do In The Dark

Running… running… freedom.

The scent of the forest fills my nose—trees, leaves, grass, flowers. Moonlight streams through clouds and when I look up at the light, I feel the wind ruffling over my body. Hair stands on end as a loud mournful howl echoes off the hills. Sniffing the air, I take off, running towards the sound.

Soft flapping distracts me, and I throw my head back as the scent of peonies and snapdragons floats in the air. The sound of fluttering wings followed by heavier, larger ones that carry another familiar scent—vetiver, cedar, and ylang ylang— give me pause, but I howl loudly in response.

Howl?

I lurch forward, the ground soft beneath my feet as I gallop through the brush, eager to find the source of the roiling fire in my gut. I can hear voices, but I can't focus on them as the bone deep drive to hunt my mate.

Mate?

Shaking my head as frustration and confusion fill me, I inhale again, searching for the trail he left. When I pick up the scent of pheromones, dragon's blood, and sandalwood, I bare my teeth in a grin. I have him now—he won't escape me so easily. I pick up my pace, leaping over branches and through the brush like a heat-seeking missile. The clearing is empty when I burst out of the woods, so I sniff the air and a rumble builds inside of me.

There is more than one. Canine and avian I can discern, but two others are human but not. The last is… simian? That is puzzling because the animal has a smell I don't claim as mine—yet. Something about it draws me, but I know the time is not right. Narrowing my eyes as I scan the darkness, I bay into the starry sky, calling to them.

A flash of brilliant light just accompanies the answering howl over the next hill, close to the farm. The overwhelming aroma of horses and manure invade my nose, and I bolt across the field with purpose. I will find them, and I will claim what is mine.

○

The sunlight hurts my eyes when I open them, and I groan as it feels like someone has tried to burn them out of the sockets. I close them to keep from passing out in pain, lolling my head back and forth. Pushing hair off my face, I struggle to sit up, but I'm weighed down by what feels like a metric ton. My hands find warm bare skin and I slide my palms up to broad shoulders.

Teddy.

Movement behind me catches my attention, and a soft kiss on my shoulder makes my lips curve. That's Wolfie for certain. I don't know why the bed feels so hard, but I'm glad that my boys are home. Grumbling to my right makes a brow arch because it's in Gaelic, and the chuckle that answers the muttered sound has to be Prez.

I don't remember everything that happened after they got home, but I can only assume they groveled well. To be honest, I angrier at myself for coming to depend on them so much I lost perspective. I didn't move home to Whistler's Hollow to collect men like a succubus in heat, but now that I have, I don't plan on letting any of them go.

Every inch of my body aches, and when I try to move, I almost burst into tears. I'm so sore; I don't even know if I can do more than breathe. It feels like I've been torn to pieces and reassembled—my joints are aching like I did a 10k with no prep. My skin is stinging from head to toe; did I get into a fight with a wildcat?

"Sugarplum, are you okay?" Wolfie whispers in my ear. His nose brushes the side of my neck and I sigh, a feeling of contentment so enormous that it overwhelms me blossoming in my chest.

I smile, but it hurts, too. "I'm achy as hell, but otherwise, yes."

"You should hurt, drugar," Teddy rumbles as he rubs fresh stubble over my chest. "We were out all night."

"We were? When did we get home?"

A snort, followed by the unmanliest giggle of all time, erupts from the head buried against my right shoulder. His shoulders shake, and before I can ask why he's so tickled, he speaks. "Gentlemen, I believe my Tíogair had one of her trademark blackouts. She doesn't remember our... wild hunt, so to speak."

Frowning, I force my eyes open with a moan of pain. They're dry and burning, especially in the morning's brightness. "I remember coming home, doing target practice, and being angry. After that, I'm not sure."

"You don't remember when Boone and I found you outside?" Prez asks, leaning over my darling to look at me curiously.

"No?" I murmur, not understanding the look of sadness on his face.

"Fuck." Teddy pushes up, finally lifting his weight off me. He runs a hand through his hair, looking conflicted as he shoots looks at all the boys.

My heart thumps and for a moment, I worry they're upset with me. I've never been able to control the weird fits I have, and while I know it's not the easiest issue to deal with, it can't be *that* terrible. "Are you… are you upset? I don't mean to be such a burden. I know you didn't ask to be stuck with my stupid fainting spells."

Wolfie reaches up, cupping my cheek. "Sugarplum, we could never blame you for something you can't control. Before you came back, we would have never imagined finding one person who could not only bring us together, but make us enjoy it as well."

I blink, looking at each of them. I know he's not discounting his obvious love for Presley, but I don't know if I believe all the various personalities surrounding me enjoy being around one another. It's not like I have some magical vagina; I'm just a girl with a wonky memory, dead parents, and a shit ton of pets. "I don't know, Wolfie."

Teddy surprises me by shaking his head. "He's right, Tilly. I was a bit of a hound dog, and I had no intention of settling down, much less moving into a house harem." His lips twist, and he sighs, dropping his forehead to my chest again. "But I find myself less and less eager to go to my place—even when you're not home."

"Aw, Boone! I think you're warming up to Lucy and I," Presley quips, batting his lashes over his love's shoulder. "I enjoy being sister husbands with you, too."

"For the love of curdled Bailey's, you guys are going to make me heave. The lack of self-awareness in you eejits is shocking." Doyle sits up, brushing dirt and leaves off of his chest.

Dirt and leaves? What in the ass nibbling fuck?

"Are we… in the dirt?" I ask, realizing why the light is so bright. The blackout curtains in my room prevent the morning eye strain, though it's a much higher level of irritation than normal. They all laugh, and I glare.

"I think we might be, Sugarplum," Wolfie says. He reaches up and plucks a leaf out of my hair with a soft smile.

"I'm not even going to ask."

"Pup, I think we need to get our girl home and get her cleaned up. What do you think?"

Another snort and a string of Gaelic mutterings make me turn my head. "Would you like to come, Lucky?"

He sighs as if I'm the most trying being on the planet, and rolls his eyes. "Yes, I'll join the four most obtuse polyamorous people on the planet on a journey to the home they should share while they…" Doyle stops, a grin spreading across his face. "The chaos will be lovely. I can't wait."

I sigh, giving what I think is an evil glare. I'm honestly too tired and achy to know if I look threatening or not. "No shenanigans, no chaos —I'm not letting anyone move in if you assholes can't get along or *answer texts.*"

Presley pokes his head over Wolfie's shoulder again. "If we promise to make it up to you, can we go home and shower now?"

His use of the word home makes my chest tighten, and I nod, unable to voice my answer. My assent makes Teddy beam, and he jumps to his feet, bending to scoop me into his arms with a whoop. Holding his hand out to my vet, he tugs him to his feet, and the others follow suit.

My eyes widen as we walk away, and I whisper, "Okay, who wants to tell me why we're all naked?" Their laughter rings through the hills as we head back to the house on a trail I didn't even know existed.

I guess that's a story for another day?

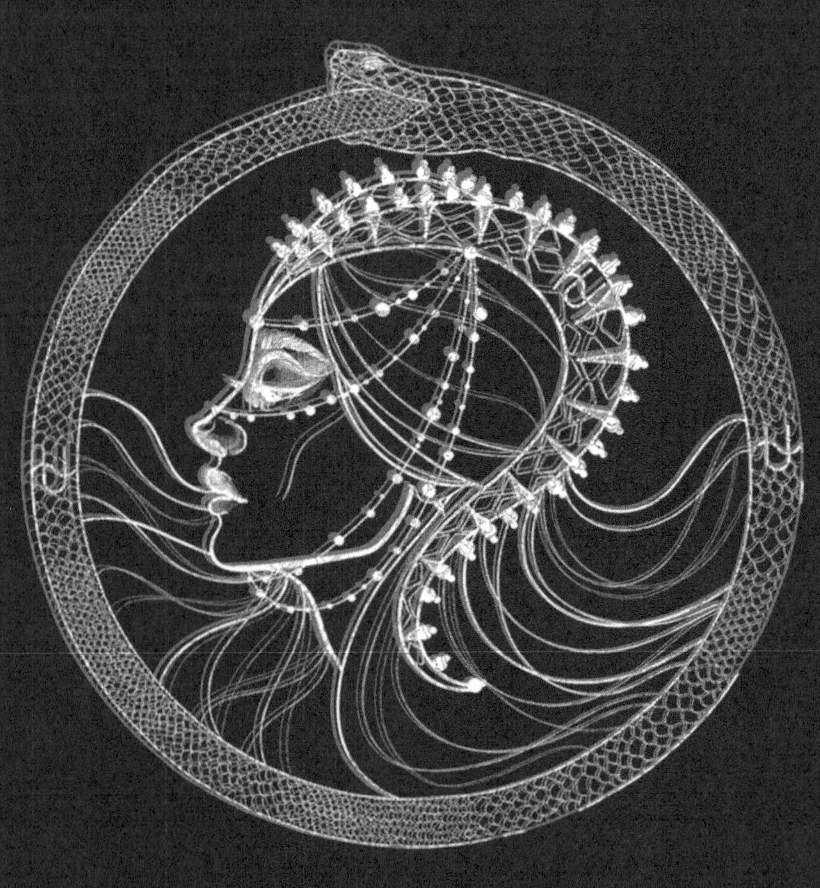

Meant To Be

I was the only one who seemed to understand the panicking animals when we got back to the house. It's not only a gift of my people—at least on my father's side—but my profession. Because of how tightly bonded my sugarplum's companions are, it was normal for them to want to attach to her side the moment we stepped in the back door. Edgar's grumpy brush off as he carried her through the kitchen and up the stairs confused them, and even Prez was too single-minded to give them much thought.

So Doyle is watching me with this amused expression as I treat each one of the six companions to the affection they're looking for. He's not helping, of course, but he didn't head upstairs to get the shower ready, either. His eyes follow me as I fix bowls of food from the cabinets and refrigerator, studying my movements like he has a question he's afraid to ask.

"It'll take a moment for the water to heat, and if I put their breakfast out, they'll all focus on that and not try to pound the door down," I say, hoping to answer his unasked query.

"Aye, it will. My Tíogair has gathered quite the menagerie—both animal and extranormal."

Rolling my eyes, I set the dishes for the dogs and cats down before I check the freezer for frozen bits for Eury and Isis. I could let them out to hunt, but in their current anxious state, I think they'd prefer staying put. "She has, but Jolene is a special woman. You know that as well as I do, Haggerty."

He nods, looking around the kitchen. "Wolfgang, you seem to be the one whose head is shoved least far up his arse, so I'm going to ask you something."

I arch a brow. Where is he going with this? "Okay. But I'm not giving up any secrets unless sugarplum tells us she's ready to let you in the circle."

"I wouldn't dream of putting you in that position," Doyle replies, his eyes alight with mischief. "At least, not yet. The funny little love square is likely to expand if you realize it. I don't mean by adding the likes of me, though I'm not the last who'll appear I'd wager. I mean, have you and your Doctor Feelgood discussed what happens when three becomes four?"

Frowning, I put the plates with the frozen entrees for the eagle and the snake on the counter, knowing they'll hold off until they reach room temp. "There are five of us. You're old enough to know how to count."

His laugh is full of delight as he claps his hands. "Oh, this is *delicious.* You haven't talked about it, and you're all pretending it's not happening. I couldn't have entered stage right at a better time! All the confusion and mishegoss will feed me for *weeks*"

I sigh, turning on my heel to walk into the living room. "I don't know what you're on about, but if you want to be part of the fun, bring your happy ass upstairs."

"Don't start without me!" he calls, following me as he continues to chuckle.

Whatever part of the universe decided my sugarplum should have a mate from a species that always lies and one from a species that can't must have a hell of a sense of humor.

"Hold still, *drugar*. Let him feast."

The growl coming from the bathroom makes me speed up, and my body tightens in anticipation. It doesn't take a genius to figure out what Prez is doing, and I'm eager to join. The laughter behind me continues and if I wasn't so intent on jumping in, I'd do more than raise my hand and flip off the Irish jackass behind me. Last night, my sugarplum ran with us all night long, resplendent in her hellhound form as she embraced what can only be the first side of her to emerge.

She doesn't remember, but she will eventually, and it will be glorious. Until then, we will continue to show her how we feel in the normal way.

"*Ahhhhhhh!*"

Stepping into the bathroom, I grin as our girl hits her first peak of the morning. Her dark hair stands out against the white tile of the huge walk-in shower, and her legs are dangling off the granite bench on the right limply. My angel is kneeling between her thighs, nibbling the insides as she coasts down. As usual, Edgar is taking charge, standing with one hand on Prez's shoulder and the other on his impressive cock. Sliding the door open, I walk in.

"Where would you like me?" I ask, looking up through my lashes in a way I know drives every person in the steamy room crazy. That's another one of our gifts, if you're wondering, and I've never been above using it.

The snort of our new Irish tag-a-long doesn't deter me, and I shrug as he drops onto the bench across from us, steeping his hands as he watches. Edgar ignores him, but I can sense the tension in his frame as he works out what he wants. Prez lifts his head, his eyes flashing icy blue, and I give him a tiny pout. He loves that more than anything, but he doesn't get the chance to respond because my sugarplum opens her eyes.

There's a tiny pulse in the room, so small I think I might imagine it, and I frown. Could something inside of her be trying to push through so soon after the hound? My eyes fly to Boone's, but he's not paying attention to anything as he works out whatever he's got going on in his head.

"Wolfie?" Jolene holds her hand out to me, beckoning me to come closer.

When I bend to kiss her, she turns her head, pressing her lips against my ear. Her whisper is so soft I almost don't catch it, and I have amazing hearing. The words catch me off guard, and I blink, pulling back to look into her eyes to make certain she knows what she's saying. Her lips curve in a lazy, mischievous expression and she nods before blowing a kiss at me.

Son of a pea pickin' Yankee, she means it.

I rise, waiting for her to get settled. She tugs on Prez' arms, pulling him until he joins her on the bench. Every eye is on her as she poises over his inked shaft for a brief second before slamming her hips down with a breathy moan. Sugarplum winks at the rest of us shamelessly, as she leans her back against his chest, and turns her head to nip the cords of his neck. His arms wrap around her, inked fingers making their way to the sparkling nipple shields to pluck lightly.

Holy fuck, they're hot, and they're both watching me. Does he know what our chaotic switch asked me?

My eyes find Presley's again as I pause, watching him lazily thrust as Jolene swirls her hips. Her breathing changes and she reaches up to slide her fingers into his hair. The pheromones in the room are undeniable, and it's making it hard for me to stay still, but I wait.

"Lucy, give the lady what she wants—what we all want," my darling doc grinds out.

She must be doing that thing. We can hardly speak when she does it; I recognize the plea in his tone. Jolene Athena Whitley has some sort of kung-fu voodoo grip when she wants to, and the way her pussy strokes your dick makes it almost impossible not to come on the spot. I can't even *imagine* where in the hell she learned it, nor do I want to. I always give what she wants in the middle of that treat, so I'm guessing Prez is losing his mind.

I turn around, padding over to the abnormally quiet Edgar. He's struggling a little with the addition of the fiery chaos maker, and it's almost like his brain is in overdrive. I know he's not upset about sharing our girl with us or even Doyle. He just doesn't know how to transition from fighting with the idiot to fucking in front of him.

Fluid scene dynamics are hard on the control freak Doms; new possibilities challenge their need to be in charge. My sugarplum has pushed him, and well… Her methods aren't subtle—let's put it that way.

Dropping to my knees, I scoot closer and wrap my arms around his thighs as I bury my face in his stomach. His abs are hard as steel from years of athletics, and my nose brushes his navel as I nuzzle. A hand buries in my hair, fingers sliding through it as I touch and cuddle, working to bring him back to reality. The rumbles in his chest grows as his hand tightens, and I know the submission is helping him calm. He needs to feel like he has the power in the situation—even if the driver at the wheel is riding my partner like a prized stallion behind me.

"More, darling. Help him… ooooh, yes, Presley, right there…" She pauses for a moment, making a gasping sound that makes my dick jump.

Hmm. Not just mine, either.

The twitch of Edgar's cock against my chest makes me swallow hard. I know how to get him back into our normal headspace, and I also know that neither of my loves will be bothered in the slightest. I've certainly noticed how mouthwateringly cut the reigning king of the jocks in our town is, so I'm not adverse. I rub my cheek against his abs slowly, giving him time to adjust or protest if he chooses. When he doesn't, I close my eyes, knowing that this will change the tenor of everything and if it goes badly, I'm the most likely one to get hurt.

I'm definitely not the type to bang people without feelings getting involved, and he's new to this. But my sugarplum and my angel are encouraging me, and they wouldn't steer me in the wrong direction.

Slowly, I slide downward, brushing my lips against warm skin until I reach the dark patch of coarse hair. Inhaling, I have to swallow a moan as the musky scent fills my nostrils. My chin bumps against the head of his cock, and a loud snarl echoes off the tile. His grip on my hair tightens, and Edgar tugs my head back, looking down at me with a wild, confused expression. A smirk is my only response before I pull against his hold, darting forward to wrap my lips around the tip and swirl my tongue over the moisture there.

"Jesus Christ, it's like waiting for glaciers to move," is the mutter from the cheap seats where the Irishman sits.

I lock my eyes on the aquamarine ones staring down at me while I nibble, lick, and suckle. I can feel the trembles in his thighs where I'm holding on, but I continue to tease as he watches. I'm waiting to hear a safe word when I remember HE refused to set one, and that makes me freeze in place. Outside of outright rejecting me, he doesn't have a way out of this if he's uncomfortable.

Motherfucker, that's why everyone in the room should always have...

"Pup..."

His voice is rough and needy, and the tone tells me everything I need to know. My hands leave his thighs to wrap one around the base of his shaft and the other cups his balls. Before he can utter another word, I swallow his cock, taking him as far back as I can. Working my lips and teeth over him as I vary speed and suction, I get a feel of where the sensitive spots are and what he likes. I can hear the voices around me as suck and lick, chasing every twitch and tremor to make him thrust his hips harder in return. Gripping the base of his dick hard, I make sure he can't come faster than I want, because if I'm going to be someone's first male lover, then it should be memorable.

"Lucy, you don't have a goddamned *clue* what magpie is doing to me right now, but you'd better get him off before I fucking die," Prez says before he lets out a strangled sound that almost sounds like he is actually going to keel over any minute.

"Aye, mate. You're a pretty picture, and I'll admit it's been a dog's age since I've watched two lovelies discover something any idiot could see, but I'm just about spent over here."

A voyeur. Of course he is. Fucking Doyle.

"Focus, pup." The soft whisper makes my dick twitch, and I do as instructed, bobbing over his cock faster. "I'm close."

His balls tighten in my palm, and I roll them as I increase the speed of my mouth and decrease the pressure of my hand, stroking him instead. Edgar's hips thrust forward, and his hand guides me as he fucks my mouth harder, and when I feel the stutter of the rhythm, I swallow him down. Hot, salty streams of come slide down my throat as he shouts, and I slow down, licking as his body shivers in pleasure. When I lift my lips, I place a small kiss on the tip as it softens and sit back on my heels to look around.

Doyle is sprawled out on the opposing bench with his eyes closed, his dick in his hand, and a blissed out grin on his face. When I look over my shoulder, my sugarplum is collapsed on Prez, who is running gentle fingers down her arms and murmuring to her softly. Carefully, I look up to find intense black eyes staring down at me, and I duck my head, unsure what to do next.

"Doc? Help Tilly out of the heat, and I'll take our boy. We need to get them dried, tucked in, and cuddled up after a long session in the shower like this. Haggerty, you're the expert because of birth, so you get to go make some chamomile and bring some snacks. No one in this family is going anywhere for several hours. We are caring for one another, and that's all there is to it."

I blink as Edgar holds his hand out, pulling me to my feet. His large hands settle on my shoulders as he walks me out towards the fluffy towels, and while Prez is helping our girl, he leans in and whispers in my ear.

"You can call me daddy, too." The snort that escapes me makes everyone look over and Edgar winks at them. "Just going over the rules if we're going to change how we play."

Oooh. Well, in that case…

Yes, sir.

Troublemaker

"Are you sure this is where Jackson's cookie traced the IP back to?" I chew my lip, keeping my eyes on the road as we drive towards the city. I don't want the boys to know how much I'm dreading this trip because I haven't shared the story of my life prior to my adventures with Seer. It's not that I don't trust them; I simply put this part of my life behind me when I graduated.

The memories of my broken heart live on this campus and nowhere else.

Edgar arches a brow as he looks at me from the driver's seat of the huge SUV. "Of course I am, Tilly. Thorn's family is well known in the legal community, and as soon as he pranced up our walk, I knew who he was. He wouldn't dare lie to me."

"That means he owes him money," Doyle interjects from the back. "I'd put a fifty on it."

I sigh, rubbing my temples. "Is that true, Teddy?"

His lips curve and he shrugs. "I can neither confirm nor deny the accusation, Agent Whitley. I'm a simple football coach."

Presley snorts, reaching up to give him a swat. "Boone, you're insufferable. If there's a person in the entire state who hasn't run numbers through you, I'll be a pickled herring."

"Ew. No thanks," Wolfie grumbles. "Though fish smell might make Jekyll and Hyde like you better."

"Wait. You haven't figured out why the cubs don't—"

Presley turns and smacks Doyle this time. "Mate, you're a bloody landmine waiting to go off every second of the day. Remind me why we let you and your gigantic trap come along?"

"Possibly because you all drive sexy muscle or sports cars, and this is my SUV?" Doyle leans back in the back row, his arms above the dogs and cats buckled in beside him. "Plus, I'm incredibly witty and charming. It's very helpful when trying to subtly interrogate humans."

Humans? Christ, he's weird.

He's not wrong about his capabilities, so I let it go. My hands stroke over Isis thoughtfully, enjoying the feel of her scales. It's the most calming thing in the universe, and I've grown accustomed to having her wrapped around me most of the time. I had to do a little maneuvering at school to get it past Bobbie Jo, but to my surprise, she dropped the subject. "We appreciate you providing the car and helping, Lucky. Don't let their sniping bother you."

Edgar snorts. "It isn't *his* car. This is one of the city SUVs. I could have procured one just like it."

"Ah, and yet you didn't, dog breath! You're not the hero today," Doyle chuckles, winking at me. "Don't be a jealous prat. Just get us there in one piece so Nelia doesn't feed all of us to Zareb."

I giggle. Now *that* I could see. She'd have a hissy fit with a tail on it if we damaged something belonging to the city. "Did Jax mention *where* on campus this computer is when you were having your chat with him, Teddy?" With the aviators and that bomber jacket, he looks like he stepped out of Top Gun, and even though that's never been my *thing*, I'm considering it now.

As if he can read my mind, he lowers his shades for a moment, his aqua eyes dancing with mischief. "He did not. His... friend... couldn't narrow it down that far because..." His brows furrow, and he looks perplexed.

"Because the signal dead-ended at a VPN run through several onion routers bouncing from country to country like a ping-pong ball. At least, that's what Eli said." Wolfie pokes his head between the front seats, smiling at me. "I only understand about thirty percent of that, but it's why he couldn't pinpoint a building to check first."

"Good job, pup," Teddy rumbles, reaching over to ruffle his hair.

He laughs at the glare Wolfie gives him, and I smile despite my melancholy. The relationship between all of my boys has become much more comfortable since the night I blacked out an entire night. They haven't moved in yet—though Teddy insisted on having this weird group of stubbly guys come to inspect the outside of the house to prepare for expansion—but I know it's coming soon. We're coalescing as a family, and while that scares the hell out of me, I enjoy having people to depend on more than I want to admit.

That's probably why our trip to State U to investigate the information Jax gave us is triggering me so much. State U's campus is where one of the worst moments of betrayal in my life happened, and I haven't ever been as low as I was after Trevor dumped me. It took a lot of therapy to realize his abandonment was so impactful because of the distance between my parents and me, but that's never lessened the bone-deep pain I feel when something brushes against the trauma. Taking my guys to the literal scene of my destruction is making my gut knot in fear.

"Sugarplum, you're awfully quiet," Wolfie says, his hand landing on my arm.

I jump a little, and Isis slithers until her head rests on my shoulder, her coils wrapping more firmly around my ribs. She can sense my riotous emotions somehow, and whenever I get upset, the huge snake draws my attention elsewhere by moving and squeezing. It's a pattern that started with the Hollar office and has continued every day since.

"I... I don't have fond memories of my time here. It's why I finished all the upper grad degrees online."

"Have a poor professor, Magpie? A nightmare roomie, perhaps?" Prez asks. I can hear him chewing on a Twizzler and I roll my eyes. He has a sweet tooth like no one else I've ever met.

"No," I answer, turning my head to look out the window so I don't have to meet Wolfie's or Teddy's eyes. "And before you ask, no bullies like high school, either."

Teddy makes a grumpy sound and speeds up, forcing Wolfie back to his seat. "Then we'll get what we need and get out. I don't cotton to the idea of you wandering around alone if this place upsets you. Hell, I don't even remember seeing you while we were here, come to think of it."

The last part is more of a mutter, and I snort. "I worked hard to be invisible after the debacle at home. You nor any of the others who were part of it would have ever seen me. I made certain I was safe by bribing a work-study student in the admission office."

"Oooh, the plot thickens," Doyle calls from the back.

Christ, he adores conflict and chaos. If he weren't so damned hot, I'd smack him on principle.

ONCE WE ARRIVED, THE GUYS REFUSED TO LET ME RUN AROUND alone, but they also acknowledged that given the sprawl of the SU campus, we needed to split up. They sent me with Jekyll, Kali, and Isis while Eury, Hyde, and Hecate went with their favorites. Doyle, as usual, winked and strolled off on his own, whistling like he planned on doing something absolutely unacceptable.

Hopefully, it doesn't involve explosives or any kind of physical fights. I'm well versed in good-looking boys from Belfast and their hidden street skills. I feel Doyle is hiding a fuck ton of things I'd be both fascinated and impressed by—which is why I yelled 'no violence' at his retreating back. That he was heading towards the science building didn't escape my notice; the chem labs are there.

I rub my temples, and Isis adjusts, hissing near my ear. My cadre of animals and I are headed in the building's direction where my parents had offices. Teddy is headed for the main and admin areas, Wolfie is sniffing around the dorms, and Prez decided he'd be best served by nosing around near the graduate and professional degree programs.

We're hoping to find people who knew my parents or get a ping from the app Jax's booty call created. Eli swears he will use the guest Wi-Fi to scan for devices that match some or all of the markers from the signal he found. They need to be within five feet of our phones, so we have cover stories just in case anyone questions our presence.

I'm not sure what finding the computer gives us, but Jax says it connects to some symbols and writing in the mystery trunk and my parents' letters. That has to be connected to his theory about their accident being murder and then… hell, I don't know after that.

If they were into some weird super secret shit and got killed for it, does that mean their activities flagged me somehow for working in law enforcement? I mean, I thought I had clearance to the moon because of all the places I worked or been—including AirForce One —but the rejection that sent me back to the Hollow was shocking.

Could my parents have been on some McCarthy/No Fly type list and it extended to me? I guess it's possible, but it doesn't seem like I would have even gotten a foot in the door to some places I've been over the years, if so. No, this has to be something more sinister and secret to only pop up when I interviewed for the FBI. I'll be damned if I know what it is, though.

The Beauregard Fine Arts building looms in front of me and I stop by the fountain with a sculpture of a Sphinx. The piece is beautiful and created by some famous unknown from France, but even when I tried to research it, I couldn't find any information about the sculptor. I used to sit by this fountain and throw quarters in to make wishes when I was a child, and when I came to SU, it was one of my favorite hangouts. My parents were long since retired, and even though the name on the engraved plaque reminded me of the bad times in high school, the familiarity made me feel comforted.

Of course, given that the great-great something or others of Antigone Lisel Beauregard donated it, I have mixed feelings now. She's long gone, and I'm back here at the beginning of my life again, looking for answers in the same way I was before. The stakes are different, but it's amazing how patterns repeat themselves in our lives.

Sighing, I remind myself that I am not the Catastrophe anymore, nor am I the broken toy that lived on the campus. I'm a successful businesswoman with talent, an excellent education, and enough boyfriends to start a basketball team. I've moved on and up, and memories of the past can't hold me back. With that in my head, I stride to the doors of the building, intent on finding out which current staff members worked here when my parents ruled the English department.

It's Fall Break, so while there aren't many undergrad students milling about, there are troves of graduate students and PhD candidates walking around like zombies. It's easy to ID them because they look like they haven't slept in months, haven't done laundry in a week, and have stains from whatever they shoved in their mouth as they worked. Also, grad students move to messenger bags rather than backpacks, and PhD drones roll their shit around in briefcase luggage.

I don't want any of them to ask where I'm going, so I tuck my sunglasses in my messenger and motion for the animals to be quiet as I creep through the lobby. One girl looks up, sees Isis, and blinks before shaking her head and taking a large gulp from a huge coffee tumbler. She thinks she's hallucinating, and I'd laugh if I didn't prefer her to not think too hard about what she saw. When I get to the elevator, I quietly check the labels for the floors and push the button.

The English department is on the eighth floor, and I hope they still have a listing of offices outside of the elevator doors. In the age of apps, it's possible they've moved to an app-based info system that allows students to locate things through geo-location and that would suck an awful lot. It would keep me from looking like I belong, as well as make it harder to identify the offices. When the doors open, I breathe a sigh of relief. The stubborn refusal of academia and artsy folks to adopt tech saves the day once again.

Pulling out my phone, I hit the school website as I lean against the wall as if I'm texting. I compare the names on the directory to the bios of the professors on the English department page as I cross-reference. There are at least six professors who are high in the department whose information leads me to believe they knew my parents. That's where I will start after I do a quick check for the device we're hunting.

Eli's Snitch app pops up, and I hit the scan button. Jekyll bumps his head against my hand, and I watch him walk over to a sitting area to plop down with Kali. Clearly, they've stood guard at the front, and I suppose that's not a poor plan. A *womp womp* sound lets me know the scan is complete—nothing in the immediate area has earmarks of the trail we're hunting. Waving at my companions, I turn and head down the hall towards the tenured staff offices.

If I'm lucky, these people will be here having midterm office hours or working on papers they need to publish. Otherwise, this is a wasted trip.

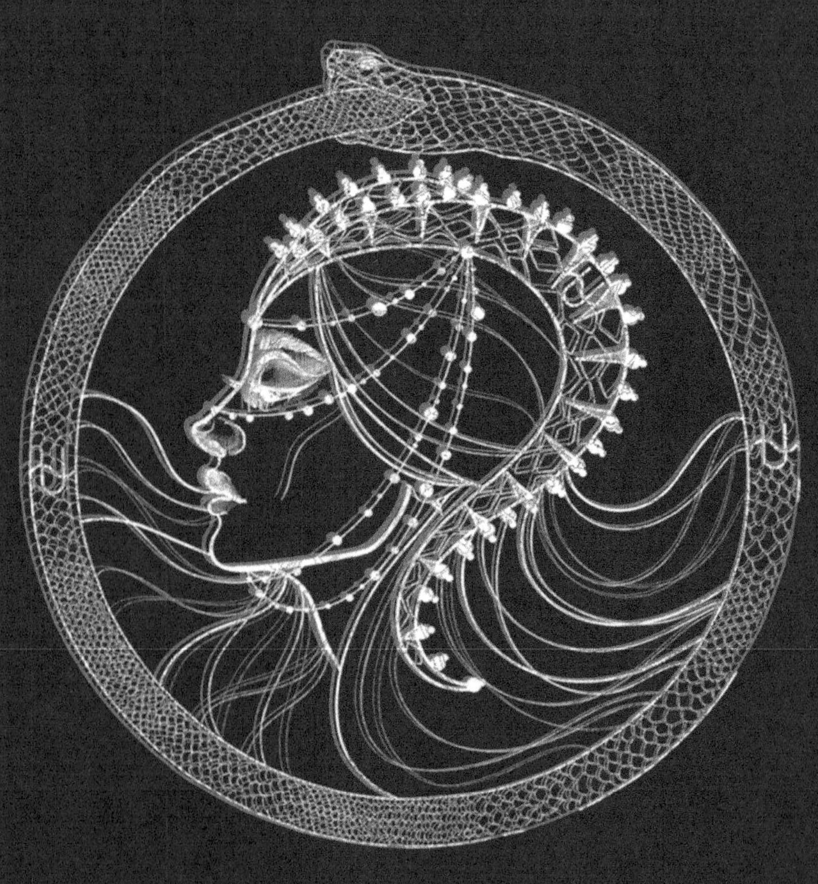

Tonight, Tonight

"So how's life been treating you, Pamela?" I ask, leaning against the counter and giving her a five star smile. I know it will work; Pam was a cougar looking to prey on college boys when I was here, and that was almost ten years ago. She hasn't aged well, and I'll bet she's still pulling her same tricks with any good looking rich male who has to make an appointment in the admissions office.

"Why, Edgar Boone! You haven't aged a whit. You'll have to tell me what's in the water down there in Whistler's Hollow." Her false lashes flutter and I have to work hard to keep the cringe from showing as she leans in to give me a good view down her blouse.

"Just good, clean living, sugar. My Pop always says the secret to eternal youth is loving your job, and I love the hell out of mine."

Yeah, I'm laying it on thick.

Mentioning the Senator is dirty pool, but I'm not above it by any means. Living at the foot of a scheming local politician who fought his way to Senator taught more before I was out of grade school than most people learn in a lifetime. Power is power and even more so when money backs it up. The key is to always keep the mask in place when dealing with those who respond to it.

As if she heard my thoughts, Pamela flutters her hand over her tanning bed chic décolletage and damn near simpers. Yes, simpers. It's a trick Southern women have down to a science and I've never seen a woman anywhere else even accomplish mimicking with a modicum of authenticity. "You always were a charmer. Give your daddy my best, won't you?"

It takes a lot not to laugh in her face. Pop couldn't care less about her 'best' if it's not an election year, and that's being kind. He doesn't even care about MY best, for fuck's sake. "Of course I will. The Senator adores his constituents."

Her giggle grates on my nerves, and she leans over more, placing a hand on my arm. "Well, I suppose it's about time you tell me how I can serve you today, you silver-tongued devil."

I wasn't an angel when I attended State U—in fact; I spent a lot of my time here trying to blitzkrieg my way through sorority row. Minor scandals to rebel against my parents' expectations that I find a suitable wife and start setting the stage for my career in politics were the goal. Mother wanted to Manchurian Candidate me into Pop's seat to 'continue the legacy' of Boone men in service to our country. Codewords for controlling my life so they could continue to control the state while my father golfed and slept his way through the waitstaff at the club, if you ask me.

So I made enough trouble to prevent a campaign, but not get thrown in jail.

Of course, given today's standards, I could probably still make a run for the Supreme Court, even with the keggers and trail of bimbos.

"I'm glad you asked, Pam. I'm doing a project for the PR department in town. We have an understanding, so to speak, so he recruited me to help research at my alma mater." The brilliant grin I give only encourages her creepy focus on me, and I feel my balls shrivel up.

It's official—Edgar Olivier Boone III is completely off the market, and it's all because of one annoying brat and her little dog. Younger me would stab me with a switchblade in shame.

"Ooooh! Very secretive and SO civic minded. Your daddy will be so proud. Of course I can help you, sweetie," Pamela coos.

Must. Not. Let. Her. Keep. Saying. Daddy.

Before she can ruin my sex life for a week, I shake my head. "No, he's not involved. Very busy going back and forth between here and D.C. This is strictly on a local level. I'd be much obliged if you could tiptoe your fingers through some files and make me copies of alumnae from the Hollow. A list of names of students and maybe some staff files?"

Her expression changes, and she looks unsure. "Those files would be confidential, Eddie. I'm not sure——"

"I'm sure I could swing back after I've talked to my colleague and maybe find time for a drink? When do they let you off the chain?" I smirk, feeling like an ass internally, but knowing my reputation precedes me.

Pamela's demeanor flips right back at my words, and she tilts her head. "Well, in that case, how could a girl say no?"

I don't have the slightest notion of coming back here after I find the guys and Tilly, but this twit doesn't know that. I simply turn the charm up, crossing over to the chairs across from her desk and sit down. "That would be right neighborly of you, Pam. I'll wait here while you put that together and think about where we should go."

She giggles again, but finally sits back down at her desk, tapping away at the keyboard with her long acrylics. I pull my phone out, hoping the others are also having success.

Bully Asshole: I feel dirty AF, but I've got my part handled. Check in.
Doctor Asshole: The med school didn't turn up much, but I picked up some more info on the drug sample. The new guy here has seen it before. He transferred from Hopkins and he's kind of a trip.
Sugarplum: Wolfie, you've been on everyone's phone again!
Cute Asshole: I plead the Fifth. Also, the dorms are pretty dead. The few RAs and students have little to offer except the occasional bad pickup line.

Bully Asshole: *snarl*

Irish Asshole: If that wasn't the most adorable thing I've seen—I could sodding puke.

Sugarplum: Play nice, boys. I'm working my way through the tenured staff in my parents' department. No joy yet.

Doctor Asshole: Magpie, you're turning him into a brat. The icons on this chat alone…

Bully Asshole: Well, it's downright flattering now that you mention it, Doc. Maybe this Sex and the City wannabe here would like to see.

Sugarplum: That's not funny. Stop wasting time texting and get this shit done.

Uh-oh.

Tilly might fight me for control and make herself an alpha brat, but that tone is not good. She's not playing. What the hell did I do? I switch over to the guys' chat, frowning at the screen as I tap a new message.

BigDog: Anyone know what just happened?

Pup: You stepped in shit, that's what.

BigBird: That was sincere, Boone. She's pissed.

Jackass: Methinks someone hit a nerve. Didn't you notice she's been off since we left the house?

BigDog: She was awfully quiet on the road.

Pup: There's something about this place bothering her and whatever it is, you triggered it.

BigBird: We should just ask her.

Jackass: Clearly, she wants to tell us. After all, hiding it is the best way to accomplish that.

BigBird: See if your cougar knows anything about her time here. If something terrible happened, it will have gotten around campus on a report.

Pup: I don't know…

BigDog: If I don't find out, I'll call Thorn. He knows her from her time here—he made that very clear on his visit. Don't forget to do the scans wherever you are.

Jackass: Aye, aye, Captain Dumbass!

Rolling my eyes, I close the chat and open the app Thorn's bottom made. Snitch comes up and I push the green icon, holding my phone still as the bar creeps across the screen. When it comes up negative, I frown. There are a lot of computers here, and quite a few have easy access if you're good at distracting the staff like me. Pamela left while I was texting to make copies in the file room, and I could do anything I wanted at seven different PCs if I had a reason and the skill.

There will be a lot in the dorms, and definitely in the Science building. We'll have to split up after we finish these places to hit the business complex and the library as well. Where else would they have a lot of computers? It feels like just about anywhere these days—even the art department will have them for digital shit. It will not be easy to narrow the search parameters if we can't find a building to point Thorn toward.

At least they figured out the fucking trail didn't point to a phone operating system, or we'd be truly fucked.

I consider entering the group chat again and dismiss the idea. Whatever has my drugar in a snit isn't going to get resolved over text. Like most shifters, she prefers touch and scent to help her calm, and I don't want to trigger a random shift on campus. It would require a lot of cleanup on the Society's part, and since most extranormals attending State U have long since emerged, they don't have the resources here to deal with a newbie.

I'm going to wait and I *hate* waiting.

"Eddie, don't you fret! I'm about halfway done. You won't be tied up too long."

Vomit. Pamela's insinuation makes me gag, and calling me 'Eddie' only makes it worse.

The only person to *ever* call me that was Amy Matilda Behle herself during the five painful weeks we dated our junior year. Our parents damn near insisted on throwing us together until we gave in, and it was some of the most miserable weeks of my life. She fretted and fawned like I was a trophy, and even the douche I was in high school couldn't deal with her. I told my mother a few choice lies about her character and not long after, I could break up with her.

Margaret Emily Boone is *not* the woman you want to trifle with, and Amy's parents knew it. They backed her off faster than green grass through a goose. That was the last time they tried to wrangle me into a relationship until college, and I think my mother realized there was a severe shortage of girls in town she'd approve of.

Christ, I haven't seen her since that phone call.

She'll have heard about the trial. I'm surprised I haven't gotten a phone call about my behavior or consorting with Satan's mistress or some other colorful colloquialism. She'll never understand our living situation, and I'm going to book an appointment with her before I move in.

I'd rather stick my dick in a blender, but if I don't clear this up, I'm concerned about what she'll do. The girls who attacked Jolene through the newspaper have nothing on my mother. She could piss off the pope and then convince him to serve tea.

Pamela interrupts my thoughts as her high heels click across the tile. She has an enormous stack of printouts and folders, and when she slams it on the desk, my eyes widen. What happened in that file room?

"I just cannot *believe* that girl is here!"

This doesn't sound good. "Uh, Pam? What's eating you? I don't enjoy seeing a pretty lady so upset."

"Well, I shouldn't tell you… it's office gossip."

I arch a brow. That's Southern woman for 'ask me again,' and even I know it. "Pam, I am a vault of secrets. You can trust me—I am a judge, after all."

"Just between you and me and the fence post, there's a former student on campus and well, I'm surprised she had the guts to show her face after pitching such a hissy while she was here," Pamela says, shaking her head. "Bless her heart. That girl wasn't right in the head."

Eyeing her, I work to calm the sudden attention my sides are paying to her words. Something smells wrong, and I'm sure I'm not going to like this conversation. "What happened?"

"I'm surprised you don't remember, Eddie. It was while you were here. Jolene Whitley had a bad turn with that fiancé of hers, and we damn near had to send her to the looney bin. You know he ended up marrying that girl he dumped her for, so I'd say good riddance to bad rubbish, but she was hysterical for almost an entire semester."

I blink. Fiancé? Looney bin? What in the actual *fuck* went on that I missed partying myself into oblivion?

"How did you… work it out?" I ask quietly.

"Jackson Thorn was her RA, and you know *his* history, so he dug her out and they got thick as thieves." Her nose wrinkles and she sniffs as she hands me the stack of papers she compiled while she ran her mouth. "It doesn't surprise me. *His* kind is always good with the crazies."

Fury sparks in my veins and I yank my prize to my chest to keep from doing something I'd regret. My voice is low and dark as I glare at the nasty woman in front of me. "Pamela, you're giving a sermon from the confessional. I'd think long and hard about how being ugly on the inside might inform the outside. Thanks for the files."

Her mouth drops open in a perfect 'o' as I turn to walk away and I ignore her frantic shouts about coming back to set our date. If brains were leather, she wouldn't have enough to saddle a June bug.

Pamela just spilled the beans on why Tilly was having an episode, and we need to figure out how to get her to tell us the story. I need to find the guys and put together a plan to help her find peace before it drives a wedge into our little family.

Sit Still, Look Pretty

Jolene

After we left campus, the boys tried like hell to pry into the past. I could hold them off by reading from the thick stack of files Teddy found, but that won't last forever. Eventually, I'm going to explain what happened with Trevor and why it broke me so thoroughly. It's not anything that doesn't happen all the time, but I'll have to delve into my psyche more than I'm comfortable with yet.

They won't see me the same way, and I'm not ready to see heat replaced with pity.

When we finally got back to the Hollow, Doyle headed off to return the SUV to city hall. Prez and Wolfie head back to their offices to check in with patients, and they left me with the animals and Teddy in front of the school. He's been quiet compared to the others, and I'm not sure what's going on in his head. The chick in the office skeeved him out—that much he told us—but he hasn't tried to push me like the others. It makes me wonder what happened in that admissions office, and why he seems so subdued.

"Saoirse texted me. She said the weird contractors were back while we were gone. After they left, she and Julia's little group went on a trip to… Salem? I have no idea why they would need to travel there, but something required her attention. Who knew they had fashion emergencies in witch trial land?" I shake my head and shrug. "But she said they'll be back before Halloween. Something about costumes and what she has planned."

"Tilly, that's downright terrifying. Who gave her permission to design Halloween costumes for the spooky season event?" Teddy turns to look at me, his expression aghast.

"I don't think anyone gave her permission, dear. Seer has never been a 'permission' sort of gal. She just does things. It should be interesting at least. There's a shit ton of us, and she only has about two weeks to finish them," I muse, tapping my fingernail on my teeth.

Edgar blanches again and grumbles under his breath. "We'll see about that. I'm going to have a conversation with that sparkling pixie before I end up as Barney or some such travesty."

I cover my mouth with my hand, trying not to giggle at the image. It's hysterical and within Seer's wheelhouse to do. She and Teddy have a fond, yet contentious, relationship, and her sense of humor dictates messing with him at every turn. He *should* be a little worried. "Should we load the kiddos up and pick up some dinner from *Derby Pies* before it gets busy? It is Saturday and they'll be slammed once it gets dark."

His lips curve. "If you have pizza tonight, does that mean we're going to run in the morning? I don't mind chasing you, but I can't see the other leprechaun sprinting after us for five miles. Maybe pup and the doc, but not him."

My eyes narrow as I usher the dogs, cats, and snake into the car. "Don't be rude."

"Never, Tilly. You misunderstand—I love the chase, even if it is at the crack of dawn."

Making a sour face, I slide into my Impala, adjusting my sunglasses as I wait for him to join me. I don't know if he meant it or not, but after revisiting my trauma today, I'm not in the mood for anyone to question my workout routine. I'm doing a pretty good job of controlling how out of sorts the whole adventure has made me, but I can't guarantee something small won't tip the scales. I'd prefer not to lose my shit in public again so soon after the debacle at the Hollar.

"Good. I don't like to lose daylight when I've got so much to do. You know it's midterm projects time at school—or you would if you taught something outside of the gym—and the private students are prepping for the Holiday Exhibition. I'll have to spend a lot of time in both studios, and I'm afraid it'll make me resort to terrible food too often."

Once he's belted in, I peel out, heading to *Derby Pies* in uncomfortable silence. I don't know if he's trying to read my mood better or if he's ruminating on the same thing as before, but my arrogant asshole keeps his yap shut for the ten minutes it takes to arrive and find somewhere to park. He doesn't even comment on the Starsky and Hutch slide I do into the parking space, and normally, he'd grunt and grumble about unnecessarily showing off being dangerous.

Of course, it's dangerous; that's why it's fun. He's such a fuddy duddy sometimes.

"Stay," I say to the small pack in the back seat. "We'll be right back." They give me dirty looks, but with Isis wrapped around me, the animals have been more forgiving of me taking off without them. I guess they figure a big ass snake is a pretty good warning to anyone who wants to mess with me.

"Me too?" Teddy smirks.

"As if you'd listen," I mutter, shooting him a look that says I know he wouldn't.

"You seem grumpy, drugar. What can I do to help? Want me to read you dirty books in the bath again?" His grin is rakish, and I almost unfreeze a little when I see it.

"Just come running with me in the morning. I can't eat like this so often if I don't keep up with my regimen. I won't be as charming when I blow up like a balloon," I grumble. "You remember, Edgar. Don't tell me you don't."

He frowns, grabbing my hand and stopping me before I enter the pizza joint. "Stop right there, Tilly. That's loser talk and I won't have it."

"Edgar, I am *not* one of your team members. I'll talk like a loser if I damn well please. I spent all of my school years as one, and I'm okay with not being some rabid attention seeking bint with bleached hair and fake boobs."

I think I broke him because he looks truly stunned. His mouth opens, then shuts, then opens again as he struggles to find words. That's fine; I don't need his pity or his comfort. I lived through the torture his friends put me through, and through Trevor's betrayal—I don't need anyone to make me feel better about my life. Glaring, I yank my hand away, striding inside with a snarl of irritation. Why can't people just leave well enough alone?

"One extra large California Chrome Veggie Lovers, an extra large Animal Kingdom Meat Lovers, one Exterminator Mouth Burner, a Venetian Way Fettucine Italian, and three orders of garlic cheese bread," I rattle off, making sure I get everyone's favorites. Shit. "Oh, and a dozen meatballs, please."

"Feeling hungry, Jolene? I'd say I'm surprised, but given how long I've known you, I'm not," the snide voice behind the counter replies.

Blinking as anger floods my system, I look up to see Sherilynn Foster Grant giving me murder eyes. Well, that sentiment is shared, and my fists ball at my side as I look into her spiteful face. Isis shifts, but it doesn't help like usual. I'm poised on the knife's edge today, and some asshole pushing my past in my face isn't helping. "Sherilynn, how unpleasant to see you. I'm ordering for the crowd at my place, and I don't have time to dick around with you. Are you putting in my pizza order, or is that too much math for you?"

Her head tilts as she gives me a vicious smile. "I don't know. It seems like you've found a guy for each hole, so I'm sure you need all the sustenance you can get. It'd be a shame if..."

The nasal whine of her voice cuts off and I arch a brow, assuming Teddy is giving her his enraged big D look. When I turn, it's both

Teddy and Benjy, and they look fit to be tied. Before Teddy can open his mouth, Benjy waves his hand.

"Don't worry, E. I've got this. Take your girl outside, and I'll bring the pies when they're done," he booms, his enormous frame menacing as his eyes rake over the woman he's divorcing.

Teddy nods at him, a look passing between them I don't quite understand. "Thanks, big guy." He takes my hand, prying my fist open to tug me out the door. When we cross the threshold and the door closes, he looks at me in concern. "Don't let her get to you, Tilly. Some people never grow up."

"I am not in the mood for stupid bitches, Teddy!" I shout. My entire body is shaking with rage, and nothing Isis is doing is helping. I don't feel like I'm going to black out, but the heat is spreading from head to toe. It's like the anger is raising my body temp, and I have no idea why.

"Well, isn't this quaint?"

A delicate sniff draws my attention, and I whirl around, ready to blast the next stuck up tramp who wants to come at me. My jaw drops when I see the perfectly coiffed, elegantly dressed maven of Whistler's Hollow society herself staring at me like I'm a dog that shit on the Berber. My eyes close and frustration washes over me like rainfall as I realize what's just happened. I will not be able to walk this back without a lot of groveling, and I don't know if I can get there at the moment.

Margaret Emily Boone witnessed me losing my shit on the sidewalk in front of *Derby Pies*, and I've committed a cardinal sin in her eyes. Edgar's mom was bound to have issues with me, our situation, and my past, but now I've shown her I'm unsuitable, regardless.

Just. Fucking. Great. This is the day that keeps on giving, I swear to Mars.

"Hello, Mother. What are you doing downtown at this time of night? Shouldn't you be at the club holding court with an Old Fashioned by now?" Teddy's voice is calm, but I can *feel* the apprehension vibrating from him.

Her laugh is like glass breaking, though I'm sure she believes it to be charming. The matriarch of the Boone family ignores her son's question, turning on her heel to walk towards a SUV parked a little way down the street. Teddy follows her without a word, and I do the same, marveling at the level of power she holds that even my dick swinging boyfriend simply follows her without even being told to. She stops in front of—I shit you not—a raspberry colored Porsche SUV, clicks the remote in her hand and holds the small bag in her hand out. I blink, watching Teddy walk over, take it, and place it on the passenger side.

Holy shit, is this bitch serious? A Yorkie could have carried that tiny bookstore bag in its teeth; she didn't need him to 'load' it in the car for her.

"Edgar, be a dear and run inside to get your food. I haven't seen Jolene Whitley in a dog's age. I'd like to talk to your friend."

My eyes narrow and the heat that started filling my veins during the confrontation suddenly bubbles hotter. If this woman thinks I'm going to stand here and let her give me some speech about how I'm not good enough for her son's pedigree, she has another thing coming. I said I wasn't in the mood for Sherilynn and I'm even less inclined to listen to some old bat's judgy horseshit.

"Mother…"

Margaret waves her hand to dismiss him, and he glares. Then turns to me with a questioning expression. I hold back the sigh threatening to escape and nod at him, knowing I'll only make things worse if I don't stand up for myself now. Her smile is almost feral, and the burning in my gut increases, spreading to my eyes as well.

This may not go well—the last time I felt like this, I had to be carried out by the boys. I wait for Teddy to step inside before I deign to face the Witch of Whistler's Hollow with a bored look.

"Margaret, it's nice to see you. I haven't seen you since… the night of the Cotillion, I believe." I don't add she was part of the crowd of adults snickering in the background and I know it. She's well aware of her behavior and I have no intention of rehashing *that* night with anyone.

"Oh, yes. Such an unfortunate incident. I remember your parents had to keep you home for the rest of the year. Children can be so cruel."

Especially when they're coached by adults, you bloody cunt muscle.

But I don't say that. I simply force a smile to my lips and nod, ignoring the tightness of my skin and the urge to tear her to pieces on the spot. "Yes, they can. One would think their behavior wouldn't reflect so poorly on their upbringing, but teenagers are so easily influenced by group dynamics and the urge to please authority figures."

Her eyes widen and she gives me a look that would freeze the balls off a walrus. "Yes, well, at any age, it's hard to keep your progeny from making mistakes by falling in with the wrong crowd."

Oh, it's on now, you plastic filled trophy wife.

"Indeed. Luckily, I've noticed some of the worst offenders have moved past their insecurities and ingrained biases to be more accepting and lovely to be around. Others…" I let the sentence trail for effect, enjoying the rage filling her eyes. "Let's just say breeding can't fix some defects."

She's about to retort when Teddy comes out with the stack of pizzas, and her expression changes to one of placid disdain. "Edgar Olivier Boone III, your father didn't raise you to treat people to garbage for dinner. What are you thinking?"

He rolls his eyes. "Mother, we chose this meal together, and I'm sure all the residents of our house will be happy as pigs in shit when we bring it in."

Margaret gives him a scathing once over before pulling open her car door with a vicious yank. "Fine. But don't come whining to me when you're too slow to coach the team or you stop getting invitations to the society events. I won't intercede if you let yourself go to pot, son."

I snort rudely, shaking my head. "Trust me, Margaret, Teddy is getting a full workout daily—sometimes even multiple times a day. His tight little buns aren't in danger a whit."

Edgar's laugh is smothered in the boxes as he hides and his mother huffs before sliding into her car and slamming the door hard enough to rattle the windows. She makes a fast u-turn when she pulls out, not even waving goodbye before she burns rubber down the street like she's been lit on fire.

"Hmmm. Guess Miss Raspberry Por-shay doesn't like me coming from a secondhand store," I quip, shrugging my shoulders. "Oopsie."

Teddy groans at my terrible joke, clicking the lock on the Impala. "That was bad enough to earn you at *least* three swats, Tilly."

I grin. Maybe it wasn't such a waste of time after all. Wait till he hears the rest of what I said to his bitchy mother—that should get me strung up by the ceiling hooks for a bit.

Goody.

Boys

Jolene

We still haven't talked about the day at State U, but that's mostly because I've been running around hell's half acre. Midterm projects have been kicking my ass, and the time I've spent explaining to parents that students' grades in art are absolutely part of their GPA is horrifying. Some kids are there because they want to learn or love to create, but there are almost as many who chose this as an arts elective expecting the same 'pass if I see you in class' attitude my predecessor must have had. I don't work that way, and the demands of the small town elite won't cow me.

Don't want to fail? Do your work and show up.

I won't penalize someone for not being gifted in visual arts; everyone learns differently and I measure success not in perfection, but in the joy of creation. However, sitting in class and acting like a 90s cartoon with the clay or snickering during figure drawing is not the path to my good graces. Teddy offered to intervene with some of the football parents, but I refused. Students and parents alike need to recognize my authority in the classroom and respect my judgment. Otherwise, I'd be stuck bowing and scraping to some mercurial shitheads whenever they feel like tossing a barb my way.

I had similar problems with my private lessons. Britannia isn't as snarky; in fact, she's been damned near silent for the past couple of weeks. She comes in, works on her projects, cleans up, and leaves without saying much of anything. I'm not sure what happened— maybe she grew the hell up. I thought the change in behavior would mitigate the stress of running the studio and teaching while hunting for clues for the mysterious shit we research in my garage.

Unfortunately, that wasn't the case.

Once Britannia was off her bullshit, other students started acting like their shit smelled like roses. The Barrington twins and their friend, Ariel Nancy Behle, have been torturing me with snide questions, muttered remarks, and ass-sucking attitude. I've spent weeks hearing the perennial junior high school taunt—the 'whore' cough.

Luckily, I know very junior high girls don't know their asses from their elbows, and expecting them to understand the complexities of polyamorous relationships would be ridiculous.

Besides, they're repeating what their mothers are saying. I can't blame them for being jerks; you can't make excellent decisions when you're only provided half of the information.

The stress from managing their bullshit for two weeks is weighing on me, so when I pull up to my house to find a crew of short, gruff people carting building materials up my front lawn, my jaw drops. Edgar is sitting on the porch with a bourbon, watching them in the waning light of the evening like a feudal lord. The imagery is giggle-worthy, but the activity is not. I have zero interest in putting up with a bunch of builders whacking away at my place while I try to relax and decompress.

What the actual fuck was he thinking? It's a school night, and while he doesn't have to be up early, the rest of us do. I'm going to murder him.

"Teddy!" I call as I stomp onto the porch. "What in the name of Colonel Sanders is going on here?"

His grin spreads as he stands, walking to the edge of the verandah with his glass in hand. "Tilly, thank hell you're home. The pup and doc are in the backyard, and the Irish git is playing Halo on the Xbox. He's a sore loser, and I had to come out here before we had a tussle."

Rolling my eyes, I cross my arms over my chest and tap my foot. "That does *not* explain why there's a small contingent of dwarf-like people hauling two-by-fours across my lawn at six pm!"

Edgar arches a brow, taking the steps one at a time to move towards me. At first, I don't realize why he's moving so slowly, but then I take in his appearance. He's clad in a tight white compression shirt and his loose grey 'coach pants'. The athlete's muscles he works so hard on are on full display, and my eyes widen as I watch him come down the stairs so slowly I can see everything—and I mean *everything*—move. Licking my lips, I open my mouth to chastise him again, but nothing comes out.

"Something wrong, drugar?" he asks, his face a picture of faux innocence.

That motherfucker.

He planned this to the tee, knowing I wouldn't be able to yell at him when he looks like a fucking football god. I mean, I could give a red randy shit about sports, but watching Teddy play shirts and skins with his buddies is on the shower playlist. It's lady porn, and the scent alone is enough to make you lose your underwear.

"Uh… no. I would like to know… why…" I mutter, blinking my eyes and shaking my head to clear the lust fog that seems to filter through my system. "Why… house."

His laugh is deep and masculine, and if I could glare, I would. "Why house, huh? Mostly because we don't sleep outside in the weather, Tilly. Everyone needs shelter," he chuckles, stepping in front of me and running his fingertips over my flushed cheek.

Taking a deep breath, I close my eyes and fight the animal part of my brain so I can focus. I don't know what this man does to me, but every cell screams for him the second he comes into view. I feel like there's an invisible tether between us that draws me, and when it tugs, I have no choice but to obey. "The supplies."

"Oh! *That*," Teddy says, lifting my chin and waiting for me to look him in the eyes. "Well, we need to expand the house before everyone moves in. Your parents had more land than I realized, and the boys and I are working on adapting the place to accommodate our pack."

My eyes narrow. "Expand how?"

He drops a kiss on my lips and pulls back, holding out his hand. "Come see. It's pretty amazing, if I say so myself."

Isn't he being charming? That's not suspicious at all.

But I take his hand, letting him lead me down the front walk to the driveway. He stops, looking up at the second floor, and I blanch. We can't add another floor to a house this old. What the hell were they smoking? I mean, I don't know when it was built because I remember a little of my childhood, but I'm over thirty and…

"Stop thinking so hard, Tilly. I can practically hear it." Ignoring my frown, he gestures at the facade. "We considered going up, but it's not new enough. Plus, I think it would ruin the look. So we decided we're going to go out and back."

"Uh-huh."

"Like I said, I didn't realize how much land your parents had, but it butts up against Jamie's. I figured it out the other night when—uh, when we were out all night. The pup reminded us that if we all move in here, we're going to have our own places to contend with. None of us were keen to sell, so he and the doc decided they'll convert their place into a full-fledged clinic—human and animals. It'll free up some space on Main for more small businesses—which Doyle talked to Nelia about. She loves the idea."

I squint up at him. "How long have you been planning this?"

"Since the morning after our little all nighter," he winks, tugging my hand. "We've had plans in the works for a couple of weeks now.

We're going to add all the amenities we need to function—you're gonna love it."

"Who in the hell is paying for all of this and where are we going to live while this goes on?" I ask, following him as he pulls me around the side of the house.

Teddy snorts. "Uh, gambling kingpin of the state. You remember that, right?"

"I'm not a charity case, Edgar Olivier Boone III!"

"Of course you're not, Sugarplum." Wolfie jogs up, clad in similar loungewear to Teddy, his face all smiles. "We're paying for what we want to add. That's only fair."

Damnit. He's got me there, even if it is only semantics. "I don't know. It sounds like a lot, and how are we going to live here with people banging around?"

"My crew only works when we're not here or when scheduled, Tilly. They're the same company that helped build your annoying bestie's house down yonder." Edgar smirks at the last part because he knows I marveled every day at how fast they erected that place and how amazing it looked when they finished.

"Fuck," I mutter. I'm running out of protests fast, and I don't know if I'm fighting him out of pride, stubbornness, or brattiness now.

"Soon enough, sugarplum. Come see what Prez and I are doing," Wolfie grins, taking my other hand to pull me away from Teddy.

I don't miss the look that passes between them for a second, and my lips curve. He stops, tilting his head, and Edgar chuckles, following our excited lover as he heads for a space filled with planks and rolls of wire. Prez is standing over it, holding a large blueprint. McSteamy scratches his head, turning the diagram once before studying the space again.

"What's going on here?" I ask, looking at the piles of materials curiously.

"Prez is gonna build his aviary back here," Wolfie says, his eyes lighting up. "And even better, we get to have *chickens*!"

"What."

"Yep. Chickens. It's gonna be great for cooking, and I can't wait. I mean, fresh eggs all the time…" Wolfie stops when I don't respond and pouts. "Sugarplum, you don't look happy."

Shit. Now I've harshed his cheerful buzz. I can do that to anyone but him, and Teddy crosses his arms over his chest, giving me a judgmental glare. "I mean, it sounds cool, baby, but we have a house full of predators. Snakes, cats, and eagles EAT chickens."

Prez comes over and waves the rolled up design at me. "They do, but the plans for the aviary and the hutch are very sophisticated. I promise, I've never once lost a bird to predators at my place. We won't be losing any here, either."

My expression is uncertain, and I let go of Wolfie to place my hands on his chest. "I believe you, but if you let me name an animal that another one of my animals eats, I'm going to be very upset. I… I don't deal well with loss."

His smile is gentle as he pushes a hair off my face. "You may think that's a big secret, magpie, but it's not. We're more intuitive than you realize. We would do nothing to hurt you. You can trust us."

Wolfie leans in between us with an excited grin and whispers, "Did she just call me baby?"

Oh, fuck me.

These idiots and their laundry list of pet names, and I've barely done more than call them silly names in my head. Of course, I'm a hopeless twit who's withheld that kind of affection. Raising my hand, I pinch the bridge of my nose when I realize the last person I had a real nickname for was Trevor, and he did *not* turn out to be my white knight. I haven't named anyone since; it's some sort of trauma reaction.

If these guys knew what a goddamned mess I am inside, they'd run for the hills, not build us a fucking nest.

"Sugarplum? What's wrong? You look upset suddenly," Wolfie says, pulling back from Prez and I.

"No, no. I'm not." I look at each of them, smiling at the trio of matching outfits and worried expressions. "I'm not upset at all. I'm a little overwhelmed at what you've got planned, and maybe apprehensive because…"

"Because what, drugar?" Teddy asks as he moves to wrap his arms around me from behind.

Confession time. Great. "Apprehensive because I've never lived with anyone besides my parents as a kid and Seer when we toured the world. I don't know what it's like to have… roommates."

"Pssh, magpie. That doesn't matter. We're not roommates," Prez scoffs.

"You're not?"

"No, sugarplum. We're not roommates—we're yours," Wolfie whispers in my ear.

A tight feeling swells in my chest, and I cough when I try to speak. My eyes burn, and a little ball of fear ices in my gut, but I ignore it as I lean into the three of them. We're quiet for a while, just standing in the middle of the yard, wrapped around one another.

"Oi! When were you assholes going to tell me our girl was home?"

I turn my head, seeing Doyle in identical—yet all black—duds, stalking across the lawn as if he's going to beat the hell out of the guys for leaving him out.

Maybe the expansion isn't such a poor plan. Maybe this time, it's different.

Confident

Jolene

"**I**s she fucking *serious*? I'm going to *kill* that Jameson drinking rave fairy!"

The growl from the bedroom makes me giggle. I knew the minute the garment bags arrived via messenger this morning that we were in trouble. Seer and her crew haven't made it home yet, but the note included said they would be back in time for the ball. Their costumes are part of a group costume with my crew and I left the discovery of what mischief she was up to until the last minute on purpose.

This is one of the biggest events of the social season. It will feature all the freshly announced debutantes and alumnae—meaning both in-town and out-of-town attendees. In the Hollow, the 'season' comprises the presentation ball in the late summer—which I missed—and several other large-scale events throughout the year. They spent most of the year on charity events, community projects, and various public appearances that are used to network with the elite. At the end of the 'season', the *Black and White Ball* closes the year and completes the presentation of both the girls and their escorts in society.

It's an antiquated tradition, but it's part of the fabric of our town as surely as horses and bourbon. As a prominent community member—try not to laugh when you say that—and business owner, I'm expected to attend as are all of my guys. Unfortunately for them, the Halloween Masquerade is costume required, even for alumnae.

Thusly, Seer took it upon herself to design a group themed outfit for our band of merry misfits that has Edgar losing his mind. I haven't opened my bag yet because the instructions pinned to it are very specific. Seer's crazy loopy handwriting on the tag says I should don certain undergarments and fix my hair and make up a certain way. I'm not sure what she's got cooking, but since the makeup part is simple so far, I think I can handle it.

That might have been part of her selection process, or she may have chosen the theme to aggravate my grumpy ass in the bedroom, but either way, I have a feeling this is going to be… special. Hell, I'm not even sure it'll be acceptable for polite society, but since they're already calling me a whore, I don't rightly give a shit.

"Sugarplum, you're going to want to see this," Wolfie says with a grin. "I need some of your supplies in here to finish the growly hound and I. Do you mind?"

I blink as he gathers up shadows, powders, brushes, and liners in a small basket. I'm not sure where the basket came from, but his grin makes me suspicious. "Why would you need both smoky and autumn tones, and where did you learn to do makeup?"

He laughs, leaning in to kiss my temple. "There are lots of things you don't know about me, love. You'll have to unravel them one by one when the house is done."

My eyes widen at the moniker, and he chuckles, sashaying a little as he heads out the door. Wolfie is downright adorable when he gets saucy and, like Prez said, he's developing a mischievous streak a mile long. I find it cute, and Teddy seems to enjoy it, so I figure I'm a beneficial influence. At least, that's my story and I'm sticking to it.

Humming under my breath, I look at Seer's list, frowning when I see lashes. *Christ, she has faith in me, doesn't she?* This is more paint than I've ever put on without her. Hopefully, I don't look like I got ready in the dark. Maybe Wolfie can help me with this part? I'm not sure I'm ready to attempt false lashes and whatever the hell she means by '*uwu fat curl 'fro*'. I finish up the eyebrows, drawing the lines like her diagram and filling them in quickly. Amazingly, they don't look stupid as fuck. Now, to call reinforcements.

"Wolfie?" I call, putting a base coat of mascara on my eyes per the paper. "I'm going to need you."

"Oi! Just because I drew the short straw and got the easy costume doesn't mean I can't help!" Doyle shouts from the other room. A low dark growl that can only be Teddy is the response, and I cover my mouth as I giggle.

"Unless you can help me put on false eyelashes, then I don't need you at this moment," I yell back, adding another layer of liner around my lids as I read through the list.

"Feck. Not my area of expertise, Tíogair. I'm free for a zip up, though, when you get there."

"Make yourself useful, Haggerty. Go refill the glasses since you're the only one fully covered and not trussed up like a turkey," Prez shoots back.

Ooh. That sounds quite interesting, and I'm kind of excited now.

If the guys are all in various states of undress, I'll have a lot of roaming eyes to fend off, but that's a small price to pay to watch them move all night. The distraction might keep me from having a panic attack about being back in the Whistler's Hollow Junior Ladies Society headquarters. I haven't been near that building since the night of the catastrophe, and I'm not looking forward to it one bit.

"I'm coming, sugarplum." Wolfie pops in, chest bare and covered in some sort of golden, glittery body shit and… oil? What in the name of Hillbilly Buck from Heehaw is he dressed as? He looks like he's ready for a shoot in Maxim. His eyes light up when he sees my face, and he claps his hands. "You did a right fine job so far. Hop up on the edge of the tub, and I'll get your peepers fancied up real quick so I can get back to Grumpy Bear out there. He's way worse off than you."

I arch a brow. "I'm following Seer's rules because it's always fun, but should I be worried? You look like a foxy boxing wrestler and you don't seem perturbed in the slightest. Teddy sounds like he's going to go alphahole any second."

"Oh, sugarplum. Not that bad. He's not used to… needing to be masculine enough not to be masculine in public. Once he wraps his cute head around it, he'll enjoy pissing off the normies—particularly his parents. He's not there yet, though, so you have to let him settle." He picks up a weird scissor thing that looks like something out of Torquemada's go bag, then opens the box containing the lashes. His hands are nimble as he applies glue, picks them up with the shiny device and moves towards me. "Now, close your eyes, and keep them that way until I say."

"Isn't this a switch?" I mutter, doing as he asks.

"No, love, *you're* a switch. Well, okay, you and Prez, though I'm uncertain about Doyle. He seems to listen to you better than I've ever seen him listen to anyone before. I can't get a read on him, anyhow."

I sigh, smiling to myself as he continues to babble on about our little crew fondly. Wolfie is the sunshine spirit in a pool full of sarcastic assholes, and I can't imagine not having his bright smile around. Even though he's a worse morning person than Teddy—which I've never understood—and a slob of the first degree, I'm looking forward to tripping over his shit all the time. I don't know exactly what 'amenities' they have planned because I've been told outside of the damned chickens, it's a surprise. Whatever it is, I don't care—I want them here all the time, and I'm tired of fighting myself on it.

"Wolfie?"

"Yes?" he replies as he repeats the weird sticky process on the other eye.

Trying to make sure I stay still so he can do this right, I murmur softly. "I'm really glad you guys are moving in. I mean, I'm trying to say…"

His fingertips rest on my cheeks as he uses some rubbery thing to press along my lids slowly. "We know, sugarplum. That's why Teddy booked the el—er, the contractors. Once they finish here, they'll work on turning our old house into a wellness complex, and his place into a team gathering spot. He's converting it into some kind of club-house and guy cave type place."

Frowning, I have to work not to move again as I whisper, "Isn't that what the locker rooms and the coach's office are for?"

"Well, yes, but I think he means for the staff, more often than not, and maybe the team when he wants to have bonding shit. Prez might be better at defining it than me… his years on the soccer teams make him more qualified. As you can tell, I've never been a rough and tumble guy. You can open 'cause I need to see if they're good."

My eyes open, and I give him a soft smile, reaching out to grab the back of his neck and pull him closer. Once I kiss him thoroughly, I rest my forehead on his. "I like you the way you are." I pause and smirk. "Clearly, Teddy does, too, because I'm the one person on earth allowed to use that name. I started calling him that in elementary school—before all the lines were so distinctly drawn. Even when he was with the girls who were mean, he never made me stop and he wouldn't let anyone else use it."

"And you didn't realize that had to mean something, sugarplum?" Wolfie asks, pulling back a little. "I know you were hurt badly at the end, but consider you have always been something special to him. I think if he'd known what they were going to do, he would have stopped them, parents be damned."

Blinking, I think about that. I've never thought about what would have happened if the girls hadn't gone rogue and switched their evil plans to me when I helped Allegra Constance Holmes on that fateful night. She was a late transfer—moving here in our senior year—and besides the Nip/Tucks torturing her; she spent a *lot* of time in Andromeda's office.

That wasn't necessarily suspicious because quite a few of us took more time with her than others, but Allegra eclipsed the rest of us by far. She had a class period in counseling every day, and the elites loved to rub that in. They were convinced she belonged in a loony bin because of her daily appointments and appearance.

I didn't know her well; no one did. The only reason she wasn't the recipient of their wrath that evening was because I was walking by the room where Amy Matilda and the others were discussing the plans. I scurried back to the dressing rooms, filling Antigone and Allegra in as quickly as I could. Antigone came up with the plan for me to switch places in the lineup with Allegra and rushed off to let the escorts know.

The boys—Edgar, Benjy, Billy, Sander, and Dylan—were nowhere to be found, according to Antigone. I remember assuming they were out smoking weed and it wouldn't have been unusual for that to be the case. Once all the athletic scholarships were locked, the boys went a little crazy with rebellion. WHFS' janitor quit over some pranks they played in the last three months of school. So the three of us worked to execute our plan to prevent them from making Allegra the butt of the jokes for the next decade.

Unfortunately, I claimed that title. How is another story, but perhaps I need to forgive Teddy for not being able to control the girls when he wasn't even around? It's always been possible that the boys didn't even know about the original plan to hurt Allegra, and his behavior afterward was a stupid kid doing stupid things because his parents encouraged him.

Well, shit. I may have some apologizing to do.

"Hold that thought, sugarplum. You haven't seen what we're all wearing yet, and we haven't opened your bag. Reserve some of that fire for the big reveal," Wolfie says as he holds his hand out.

My eyes narrow. "Why would you say that?"

"I've guessed what the theme is, and based on everyone else, I can't WAIT to see what your crazy bestie did with your costume. You're going to need to walk in with the confidence of Beyonce, love."

Oh, fuck me.

Couldn't things be simple just this once?

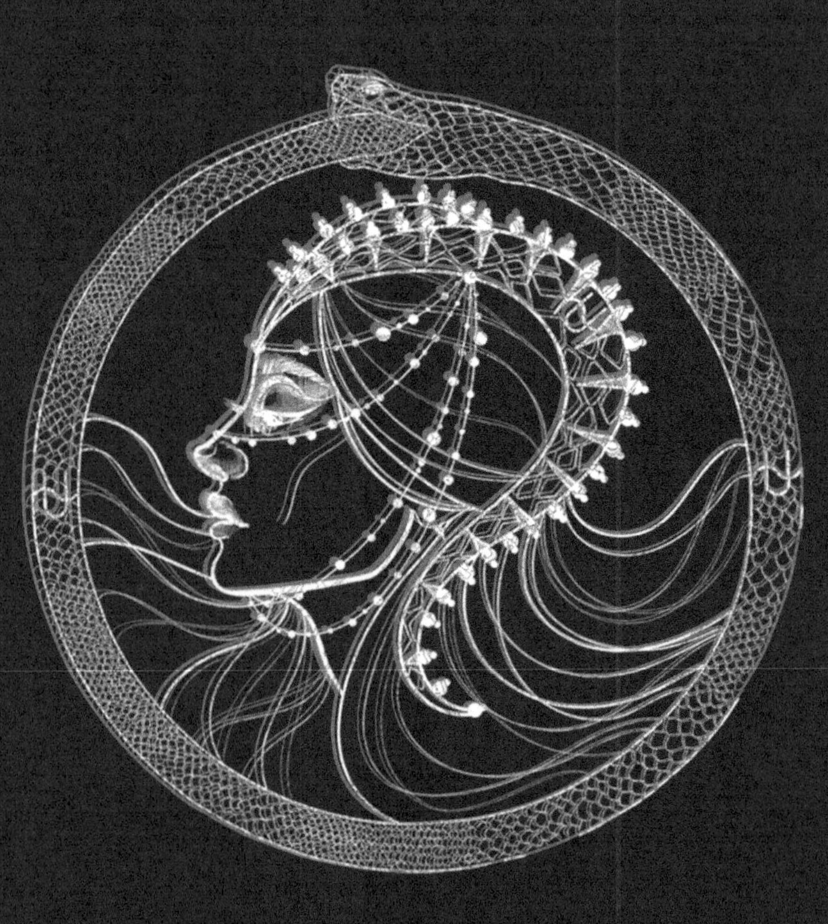

Wreck Havoc

Saoirse

We can't let this take too long. Peanut will wonder where the feck we've been, and I can only make so many excuses for our absence. She doesn't believe that we got called away as it is."

Julia looks at me, pushing her silvery hair out of her eyes. She knows that even if I've rejoined her polycule, my first allegiance always has to be to my charge. Guardians frequently have to make choices they aren't fond of when their charges need them, but it's what they have trained us to do since birth. "Flash, you know we need to deal with this. There's no way the coven hasn't made their way here. We thwarted their activities in Salem until we're ready, but…"

"I know, J. But we won't be able to help protect them and keep her in the dark until she's fully emerged if we don't get there to ward off any issues." I tap my foot, gazing into the distance, waiting for Bane to appear. She called us to fight off the 'tiny problem,' two weeks ago, but what we found was a major uprising.

Tharin shifts his bulk. "The increase in activity from non-Society malcontents is troubling."

"Fuck yeah, it is. They've had to recall loads of retirees to assist the current Guardians. People who haven't been active in decades or longer are now trying to catch up with both tech and magick. It's a goddamn shit show," Zasha grumbles. "Meanwhile, we just got settled for the first time in easily as long, and we have to zip around."

A flash of light announces the elder Guardian, and we all wait until she stalks up to our group. Andromeda Bane has been molding pre-emerged hybrids for longer than any of us have been alive, and that's saying something when you count Zasha. Her dark obsidian eyes glitter with impatience as she runs them over us, silent until her enormous ghostly gumiho approaches. The phantom fox shakes its massive tails, sparkling magick separating over us as it takes an aggressive stance.

"There's no need for theatrics, Andromeda. Call Kumiko off before Zasha and Seer lose control. You know we can't have an event outside of Whistler's Hollow," Julia says as she rolls her eyes.

"I do not take orders from you, Ricci. The Society and the Council are my only masters and even they do not give me sarcasm when they hand down missives. Know your place." Andromeda retorts.

"Lasses, we dinna have time to swing dicks. Our little group needs to get to our house to change and head for the ball. Bane, you need to find Mayor Nelia and fill her in on the mission. She needs to prepare her resources to create a search party—the witches and mages cannot find the entire town in one small building. It would be disastrous in more than one way." I sigh, looking at the watch on my wrist. We've wasted enough time waiting for her to get here; there's none left for disagreements.

"Aye, the pixie is correct. We all have roles to fill this evening, and our ability to stop the impending doom is waning as we waste time," Zasha adds, yawning as if he's bored out of his mind.

He's beautiful to look at, but he's such an asshat when he isn't being entertained.

"Fine. I will make haste to the home of the Mayor, and you will take care of your end of town. Make certain you warn any of her mates or potentials when you arrive—they will have to keep their cool in order to maintain the illusion until she's fully emerged." Bane turns on her heel, an ear-piercing scream echoing through the hills as she calls Kimiko to follow.

Her form goes from corporeal to mist as she transforms into her supe side, and the gumiho follows suit. They fly, puffs of mist trailing behind them as they travel across the sky.

"Always with the dramatics," Julia mutters.

I sigh. If the surrounding people could get along, it would make my job infinitely easier. Unfortunately, given the personalities of my friends, lovers, and colleagues, that's a dream I may never achieve.

Regardless, it's time to party, and we have costumes to don.

"Shhh…" I murmur, waving at Julia and the guys. "They're calling the debs in, one by one. After that, they'll call the alumnae in, in order of graduation. The town elders will be escorted down the steps into the ballroom first, and if we're lucky, they'll call our girl near or at the end. Once she and her men are in the ballroom, we can join them."

Tharin grumbles, shifting in the biker outfit that makes him look like the Prez of the baddest MC in the universe. Of course, he's much older than the invention of the motorcycle. His kind doesn't even need vehicles for transportation. Zasha claps him on the shoulder, his creepy butler outfit and long twisted locks out of character for him. Neither of them complained about their costumes, and I'll bet Peanut had a much worse time with her crew.

I did that on purpose. I wanted her to wheedle them into wearing the most revealing costumes—she needs to get her mates settled so she can emerge. The growly ass Coach texted me while I was gone to let me know her hound made an appearance, and I could hear the excitement in his voice until he added the little caveat. She doesn't remember the run and the shifting, and I'm not sure if that's because she's not fully emerged or not. Even Bane had no idea why she blacks out all the time or why she loses time so often.

Holding up my hand, I tiptoe inside and slip behind the curtains so I can watch the girls as they descend the stairs. They all look like glittering Southern Princesses—a theme that could only have been chosen by the organizing committee. Their escorts are in matching princely attire, cleanly shaven and shining like Charming himself. A semi-circle forms at the base of the stairs as they all stand perfectly still and coiffed, waiting for the emcee to announce them. Once he does, they break off pair by pair, heading into the crowd to greet the honored guests.

Now it gets interesting: the old geezers, silicone housewives, Council members, and alumnae come next. Usually, the Mayor would lead this, but since she's absent, that little rat assistant and his cunt daughter command the crowd with their Alice and White Rabbit outfits. He waves magnanimously, looking for all the world as if he owns the town. What a feckin' joke that wee runt is.

Following that act are a slew of people dressed as everything from the Duke of Bridgerton to the evil queen Cersei—all making their way down the staircase after they're announced with the pomp and circumstance of a royal ceremony.

Oh, for the love of Guinness stew, I'm dying to see what happens when Jolene and her boys hit the top step!

I adjust my top hat, creeping closer so the tap shoes don't click on the tile. Julia and her men are inching closer, curious to see what I've done. I don't blame them—they don't get the reference even though Julia is in a slip dress. That's okay with me, but I know Peanut figured it out as soon as she saw the alpha dickface's costume. Oh, to have been a fly on that wall…

"Miss Jolene Athena Whitley, class of 2007. She is escorted by…" The announcer's pause is heavy before he continues, and I growl under my breath. That's another name to add to my revenge list for later. "… she is escorted by Mr. Edgar Olivier Boone III, Mr. Wolfgang Lucien Fletcher, Mr. Presley Hemingway Hamilton, and Mr. Doyle Aloysius Haggerty."

Covering my mouth so my giggles don't alert anyone to my presence, I watch Peanut step up in the sexy maid outfit with the teased hair. She's got Edgar on one arm in his leather and fishnets, his lips bright red and eyes rimmed in kohl, and on the other, a glittery, oiled up Wolfie in his gold briefs. Presley looks so much like his character in the glasses, boxers and Oxford that I almost want to shake my hand, and Doyle is smug as fuck in the tweed suit. I knew giving him the clothes that cover the most would spark a fight, and I can't say I'm not loving it.

The gasps fill the room, and I clap from my little hiding place as they descend the stairs with their heads held high. Edgar surprised me—I figured he'd refuse and in the end, Peanut would have to cajole him into something close enough to match them all. I'll be damned if he's not wearing every piece from corset to three-inch heels, giving evil glares to anyone who looks at them speculatively.

"*Edgar Olivier Boone III*! What in the name of Zeus are you wearing?!!"

Uh-oh.

Margaret Emily Boone and her husband, the Senator, step out of the crowd in not-very-subtle Jackie O and Kennedy get-up that makes me want to puke. Her face is a mask of horror, and for that alone, I feel like I've won. I know he couldn't have had a simple life with parents like that, and after spending time with him at Peanut's, I understand why he was such an ass as a kid.

"I'm Dr Frankenfurter, Mother. Don't be ridiculous," he replies, waving his gloved hand airily.

Her face gets even redder and Julia whispers, "We should get in there before someone slips. Your girl's eyes look like they are getting heated."

I nod, motioning to Zasha and Tharin to follow us into the crowd. We sidle up to Peanut and the prodigal son, making a visual show of our support. His parents can't be so ignorant as to not recognize that the four of us are Guardians, and even their status as elders in the town won't save them if they cross us.

"You are *humiliating us*," Margaret hisses at him.

I wait for Peanut to snap, but before she can, the cutie vet moves forward. Blinking, I watch our Rocky, clad only in his hot abs and tiny shiny undies, step up to the most powerful family in town. He glared at the two idiots, his chest puffing, and I'll bet he's struggling not to release his wings. His eyes go frosty as he stares them down, refusing to speak first.

"Fletcher, this is none of your concern, but your mother would have fits if she saw this nonsense." The Senator fiddles with his suit, trying to make himself appear larger.

"My mother has fits regardless of what I'm wearing; she's in an asylum, Senator. Thank you for drawing attention to that," he shoots back. The temperature drops a few degrees in the room and I look at Julia, hoping we won't have to intervene. "However, she'd never treat me the way you're treating your son in public. The tone and words you just used would horrify her, and your intolerance should horrify everyone else."

"Pup…"

Peanut holds her hand up to her ex-bully, joining Fletcher as he stands firm with the arrogant elders. "He's right. Edgar is ten times the man today than he was when we were younger, and he's infinitely more of a man than you, Senator."

The jowly politician makes a strangled sound, but his wife stops him. "You don't want to make this choice, son."

"Mother, the choice has already been made," Edgar replies, cutting his eyes to the blackened teeth shaped burn on Jolene's neck. "More than once."

A shriek of recognition escapes her as she follows his gaze to the shiny, half-naked doctor sporting a matching mark on his shoulder.

The vet in question bats his lashes, smirking as she realizes he has a cascade of feathered marks on his other shoulder. It must belong to the other doc, but clearly, young Wolfgang is a mated man.

Peanut frowns, not understanding why old Maggie's having an episode, so I push through the crowd to shield the lot of them. My eyes flash with the power of my people as I stare her down. I can call upon immense strength if I need to, and the powers from the other side aren't anything to shake your head at. She may be a harpy, but I am much more powerful, and I can take her down without revealing what I am.

"Perhaps ye might reconsider your position, Missus. Insulting my mates innit the best plan, ye see. I won't hesitate to defend my girl and her men. I doubt the higher ups would forgive us if this devolves into something… less friendly."

The old bird's eyes widen, and the Senator stiffens.

"Mother, this is my family. I have plenty of money and influence, even if you threaten to cut me off. You don't have a card to play. Back off and let the debutantes have their stage back. We're supposed to be the adults in the room," Edgar calls from behind me.

His words make Peanut flush and she edges closer to him, holding onto his arm. The doc comes to the left side, and the vet steps back to be welcomed into the arms of all three. Doyle moves to flank her from behind, his eyes dark as he watches the self-righteous couple huff. He's older and more powerful than me, Andromeda, or any of Julia's boys, and boy, does he look pissed.

I wouldn't want to be the Boones in a few days. That shifty little arsehole will make their lives a misery for some time. He doesn't appreciate humans or lesser beings judging his antics—I can't imagine how he feels about them criticizing people he's taken as his own.

"Peanut, if we're done taking out the trash, I've got a mind to find some alcohol. How about you?"

She grins, her lashes fluttering as tosses a sarcastic smirk at the stodgy old buzzards. "Bourbon is the balm for all wounds, Seer. Welcome home, bestie."

I don't know if I agree with the bourbon, but I am glad to be home. I missed my girl, and I can't wait to hear what she's been up to.

Bad Guy

Looking around the room, I tilt my head. We're several levels below the Society meeting place in the same room they held the trial in. The Mayor asked me to be present as security, though my skills aren't made for aggression. She's aware I can't warn her of impending doom even if I see it, but she insisted I attend this secret consultation. The chamber is quiet, and the lamps flicker on the walls as I sit as far back as possible without being outside of the room. Nelia asked for an observer, and I can do that.

The Mayor enters from the back of the room with Zareb, a hooded figure following her. I can't see the face, as it's shadowed by the large opera cloak, and the voluminous size of it conceals everything but their height. The person's presence piques my senses, but I haven't had a vision yet. That's strange, but the room hums with a power level I rarely experience outside of my homeland.

"I have asked Hugo to observe only because I am hoping you will trigger something in him. As you know, he cannot relay any information that could alter the course of events. However, if he gathers new information to report back to his source, they may decide to impart some of his findings. We are at an impasse," Nelia says, glancing at me.

Zareb raises his head, sniffing the air as he senses something, and I feel the air in the room grow tense. He stalks back the way they entered, shaking his mane in aggravation. I arch a brow and the hood moves as a low, throaty laugh echoes in the room. Nelia watches her companion exit, her braids clicking at her waist as she joins the stranger in chuckling.

"Your companion is quite agreeable, Cornelia. He is watching the others while you give me updates on your progress." Her guest crosses the room, stopping in front of the enormous relief artwork in the wall. The silence settles over us as we wait for the mysterious visitor to study the figures and symbols on the artwork.

"It's beautiful," Nelia murmurs. "Perhaps not accurate to the letter, but…"

Another laugh makes the cloak tremble. It's raspy this time, and I feel a familiar zing as my eyes cloud. I don't know why that sound is setting off my powers, but I lean back in the chair to allow the flow of the universe to run through me. This is the reason she wanted me here and I'm curious what will come of it.

"Ah. Your friend is having his moment." Boots click on the floor as they approach. "I've never seen one of his kind that isn't female. Everything has changed so much over the years. We rarely come out of hiding unless the Society requires our presence for a vote. When all of this began, we had to stay hidden and now we have grown quite accustomed to staying under the radar."

Nelia sighs, leaning against the rostrum. "It was a different world. What you've helped build made our town possible—it made all of our lives possible. The supe world is better for what you've sacrificed."

"Yes. Our intent was to make a more tolerant world for our children —for all the children. I fear the foundation we worked so hard to put in place may be in danger. The key may lie with your undertaking, Cornelia."

Sucking in a breath, I see colors and shapes and scenes that I can't place. Usually my visions are more coherent than this, but like everything about this evening, my power seems to be shadowed in darkness. I don't think it is the Mayor's visitor, but it may have to do with whatever this 'undertaking' is.

"You were successful, old friend. But the darkness never rests. Many prominent individuals opposed the changes and have continued to vocalize their opposition. Is it possible they may be responsible for the fog?" Nelia gestures at me, and I know she realizes that I'm not receiving the same signals I normally do.

The shadowy figure steps away from the artwork, walking towards me. Raising a hand within the robe, it points at me, murmuring, "*Eleftheróste to myaló tous. Sikóste tin omíchli*[1]."

Power tugs at my skin, crawling over me like bugs. I've felt nothing like it and I spent most of my life at the feet of the most powerful beings in existence, but this is different. Mayor Cornelia's strange guest is wielding a mix of energies so potent that it knocks me back into my seat. I close my eyes as visions flood my consciousness, playing at hyper-speed.

"Holy fuck," I cry out, struggling to control my form as the magick she's drawing on strips me of all of my carefully constructed barriers.

"Be careful. You cannot harm him," Nelia warns. "The wrath of his brethren would be severe, and it will displease me. They have not forced me to show my true self outside of my home in decades."

"Nelia, it is not good for shifters—especially ones with your gifts— to stay in human form for too long. Your mates do you a disservice," the shadow replies. "I will not harm your seer. I need to see if imbuing my unique powers will break the block placed around her."

Placed around whom? What is this meeting about?

The Mayor didn't ask me here to observe, that much is obvious. She wanted me to be this person's guinea pig. Nelia has a plan, and she needed someone with my strength to experiment with. I wouldn't have been opposed to it if she'd asked, but I'm a tad insulted she felt she had to deceive me.

"She has completed a mate bond, but the fog persists. The others believe it may continue to lift as her other sides emerge and she completes the bonds with them. I'm unsure if that is accurate, but I'd like to find out before our enemies find their way here. She's not ready."

Oh, now I understand.

Cornelia Sykes is playing the long game—she's hoping that she can shake the suppression spell from Jolene by calling upon this ally. I don't know yet why that's important nor who these enemies they're speaking of are, but it's possible this is all part of the cloudiness in my mind surrounding our lovely art teacher.

"Only one so far." The laugh is deep from behind the hood. "Times change and misogyny remain the same. In a world where the buffet is limitless, we continue to allow society to put us on a diet. I have not been restricted in centuries and much like you, I've found life has only been sweeter."

"Agreed." Nelia looks over at me, tilting her head. "Hugo, how do you feel?"

Like a Mack truck hit me and offended, they chose me as a science experiment, but I don't say that. Before I respond, I take a moment to inventory my body, mind, and power center. "I feel as if something may have freed up inside of me, but I can't tell you what. I don't know if what you were attempting was successful yet."

"You're upset with your Mayor. Don't be; she wasn't a fan of my plan but I insisted. I didn't believe it would work as well if you prepared yourself. We need to understand this suppression spell placed on your friend—it wasn't the doing of the Society and we haven't been able to identify the magick."

I blink. The Society doctor did not do Jolene's suppression before she was adopted. Who outside of the snakes even knows that's how the lost children are managed until adulthood? Why would anyone want to interfere with one specific hybrid?

"She's not the only one, Hugo. Jolene is the one we have access to. She may also be the only one to inherit multiple sides, but we don't know that, either. One of our own has to be involved in targeting specific individuals and use our own practices to hide their devious ways." Our mayor sighs, looking tired under the Ramonda costume. The Queen of Wakanda suits her, but the obvious staring does not.

"Nelia, is she in danger? Is that why we are here tonight… of all nights? The veil is thinnest, and we gathered the entire town in one specific place—while we are across town with a hooded guest with the powers of multiple species running through them?"

The stranger claps in delight. "He is clever! I shall report that to his patron. The females of his kind are quite dim. That's how the golden boy has always preferred them. But your seer is special, Cornelia. Keep this one close. Oh, I cannot wait to tell Leo about him. He'll never believe it."

Who the fuck is Leo?

"Give him and the others my best. It has been so long since we've all gotten together. You barely leave your compound anymore, and my mates hate international travel. It makes it so difficult to keep in touch," Nelia sighs.

"I will. My *polykoúlas* prefer to stay where it's safe ever since… well, you know. Masaru took the loss the hardest, and he has never reconciled the choice we had to make. Leonidas and Kedar try to draw him out, but it never bears fruit. I occasionally venture out like tonight, but I have Shade, Ariell, and Dax with me. They have the companions back in the castle we rented out for the weekend."

Castle? Sweet merciful Artemis, who is this person and how does Nelia know them?

Anyone who can rent out the only castle in the entire state for a quick trip is more wealthy than most rock stars. Maybe that's the reason for all the secrecy—this is a shifter celebrity still in the closet. If so, they're hiding a cadre of people and a compound overseas.

"I hate to interrupt the catch up session, but is anyone going to answer the question? What is happening tonight that made this meeting necessary?" I ask, feeling irritated that they seem more concerned with gossiping than providing information.

Nelia gives me a sad smile. "We're not sure, Hugo. Andromeda and the other Guardians have returned with less than fortunate news from Salem. There may be a rogue faction headed here and we are uncertain it doesn't connect to this situation. The bad guys are multiplying and they have far too much power to ignore."

Sitting quietly, I absorb their words. I haven't been able to get as close to Jolene as I've wanted to, but she's been so consumed with her students and the townspeople bothering her. I felt bad for trying. I don't want her to be harmed, nor do I want anyone to whisk her away to protect her before I get the chance to rectify my error.

"I'll help Bane search for the witches. I'm not needed at the ball, and your absence will be noticed soon."

The cloaked one chuckles again. "Ah, the valiance of youth. Come, MacAuley. We will locate Andromeda and assist her. It has been even longer since I have seen her." The pause is heavy as the stranger sighs. "She may not be as eager to see me. Best be cautious."

Cannon fodder for a centuries old rivalry—sounds like a Saturday night at home. I'm not sure I want to be the monkey in the middle for that, but since I volunteered, I have little choice. Nelia winks at me, and I roll my eyes. She knew and didn't warn me. Yet another demerit for her in my book; she'll be in the negative soon.

"If Andromeda Bane will be displeased to see you, I'd prefer to follow you in rather than lead. I don't know you well enough to take a shriek from her as my punishment for arriving with you in tow."

"It will be more than a shriek, I guarantee."

Marvelous. I can't wait.

---

1. Free their minds. Lift the fog.

Discipline

Despite her brave face in front of Teddy's parents, our girl is as jumpy as a long tail cat in a room full of rocking chairs. Her eyes keep darting around, watching the people as they stare at us. Saoirse's choice of costume was brilliant, but the dissonance between our getup and everyone else's only underlines that we are different.

Supes in the Hollow live a very heteronormative existence—probably because of the towns deal to place the kids. No one ever made a big deal about Prez and me, nor did they say anything about the Mayor, but that wasn't thrust in their face all the time. Even though shifters have multiple mates in other conclaves, the Hollow's conservative atmosphere makes us seem out of the ordinary. The infamy surrounding Jolene and Teddy's family connections doesn't help, either.

I know my sugarplum doesn't care what they think, but she also doesn't like them treating her like shit because of their opinions. It makes her angry because she believes they will treat us poorly. She isn't ready to admit how she feels, and I know that has to stem from a past trauma. The four of us talked after the visit to State U and we agreed to let her lead the discussion until she's comfortable.

She's tapping her foot, her arms crossed over her chest as the elites and debutantes mingle on the floor. They'll start dancing soon, and I know the formal part of this will be hard for her. I look over at Teddy, catching his eye as he sips his bourbon. His lips curve and I flush, tilting my head towards the hallway to the back rooms. He elbows Prez before leaning in to whisper in his ear. The two of them converse for a moment and then my darling doc turns to Doyle.

While they converse, I walk up behind our girl, whispering in her ear. "Follow me, sugarplum. I have something to show you."

"You do?" she asks curiously.

Excellent. Distraction was my aim and I think I hit my target. "I do. Come with me."

I hold my hand out, grasping hers as I lead her through the crowd. People stare at me, but I'm not shy about my body. Nudity isn't a big deal to my people and I don't care what anyone but my family thinks. Sugarplum glares at the women and it makes me grin. She's getting closer to admitting her feelings every day.

When we reach the back hallway, I turn to look at her. "They don't show you these rooms when you come through here to school. This area is only accessible once you come back as an adult."

I let go of her hand, pressing my fingers to the biometric pad. Her eyes widen as the lock clicks and the door swings open. She follows me past the row of closed doors until we reach the one at the very end. Pausing, I wink at her as I show her into the library. Jolene's gasp is reward enough when she sees the interior.

Whistler's Hollow Junior Society headquarters houses the town's most valuable times in a two story room that makes most libraries look small. Ladders climb to the ceiling on shiny golden rails in front of shelves full of first editions and historical texts from around the world.

Of course, the level below the building contains a vast collection of Society volumes, but that is only accessible through the tunnels under the town. Those have to be entered through the meeting place, and she hasn't been inducted yet. But that doesn't matter, because the majesty of this level is enough to make her squeal in excitement.

"Wolfie, this is amazing!" she cries, throwing her arms around my neck.

"I know. They have built it over hundreds of years." I watch her explore, listening closely to the change in music in the main ballroom we just left. The presentation music is starting and I want to keep her occupied through the debs' dances. I know that was the scene of her humiliation all those years ago, and she doesn't need to relive it.

"Ahem."

Sugarplum turns to look at Teddy with a beam of excitement. "Teddy, look at this place! Books two stories high, ladders, thick carpet, big chairs… it's gorgeous."

He chuckles, stepping into the room and closing the door behind him. "It's something, that's for sure. Looks like the Pup had the right idea bringing you back here."

"This is every girl's Beauty & the Beast dream, Teddy. Of *course* it was a good idea!" She skips into the middle of the room, the fluffy skirt of her short maid dress bouncing. Even with the crazy ratted hair and thick overdone makeup, she's beautiful when she's not weighed down by all the bullshit in her life. "I could break into song; that's how good this is!"

I wince. "Don't get carried away, sugarplum. We don't want people knowing we're back here." Also, her singing is like someone is strangling a cat, and I have the most sensitive ears of all of us.

Eyes narrowing, she stomps over to one of the tall ladders, climbing up and swinging her arms until it slides along the wall. "I'll pretend you didn't say that, darling boy."

Teddy gives me a bemused look, his heels clicking on the parquet floor as he heads over to her. "Tilly, you shouldn't start something you don't intend to finish."

She climbs a little higher on the ladder and wraps one leg around it. Her back arches as she hangs off it like a pole dancer and pouts. "Maybe I intend to finish it. Are these rooms soundproof? Can you even get out of that getup, Teddy Bear?"

Oooh, now she's pushing. She's crazy if she thinks Edgar is going to back down from a challenge like that. His scent changes, and he smirks at me. We know what these rooms in the back are like—we have used them for function and form for many years. Sugarplum has no idea how they're equipped and we do. Business upfront and playtime hidden beneath is almost the motto of the supes in the Society.

"Pup, our girl wants to play. I think I'd like to accommodate her—this time. I'll get the party favors and you go warm her up." His eyes flash black and my cock hardens so fast it hurts.

Since he and Prez marked me, I'm instantly ready when they use the 'tone'. I don't know if that's because I've been claimed three times or if it's a function of the mate bond. It's different with my sugarplum because her supe sides haven't emerged enough to complete our bond. The small dusting of stars that formed along my Adonis belt is faint and you'd never see them amongst the tattoos if you didn't know to look.

"Wolllllfffieeeee," Jolene coos, bending impossibly far back until the ends of her hair touch the ground. "I'm waaaaiiiting…"

Holy fuck buckets. The crimson of her lips and her tits almost spilling out of the low cut costume is entrancing. I walk closer, licking my lips when I hear the dark growl from the other side of the room. Grinning to myself, I give my walk a little shake as I approach her, feeling his gaze on me as I go. A wall of lust fills the air and the temperature rises, telling me at least two parts of our lover are taking notice.

My hands land on her breasts, tugging them free of the neckline to flick my fingers over her nipples. She's got new jewelry on them—shields with fangs and blood drop gems piercing through the center. It makes my gut tighten, and I lean down to nip at them. A moan of pleasure makes me grin, so I continue playing with them the way Prez showed me.

"*Drugar*, you look stunning upside down and flushed. Give our pup some love as well. I want you both ready for me."

I can hear him rooting through drawers, and I'm about to respond when I feel teeth pulling the tiny gold briefs down. Sucking in a breath, I use one hand to hold myself up and the other to run up her thigh. Before I can reach her pussy, she's wrapping those cherry red lips around my cock and swallowing me down. I don't know what the fuck she did in the past, but a Cirque du Soleil-style upside-down blowjob is pretty impressive.

My hips thrust involuntarily as her tongue plays with my piercings, and I sink two fingers into the dripping wetness between her legs. Another moan vibrates over me as I circle her clit and bite down on her nipple hard. I have no idea how long we can do this, but the fog settling over me is making it hard to care. All I want to do is make her come while I fuck her mouth.

"Beautiful," Teddy whispers, appearing behind me like a ninja.

The heat emanating from him mixes with desire and I roll my hips to move between my sugarplum's mouth and the planes of his body behind me. The bite mark on my shoulder burns, and I struggle to keep my true nature contained. I know my ears have slipped—that's always the first—and a tiny nip at one tip makes my cock kick. The swarthy man at my back has figured out it's an unignorable turn-on for me, and he's using it to push the level of ferocity in the room.

"She's getting closer, Pup. You might lose control. What should I do about that?" he whispers, nipping again and chuckling when I shudder from head to toe.

Fuck if I know.

He's claimed me, he's touched me, and I've tasted him more times than I can count. Prez enjoys watching and my sugarplum likes to join in. I've been letting him lead since this is new to him. So I whimper softly, turning my head to look at him as I add a finger to make her moan around me again. "Please."

"Oooh. I like when you beg me, Pup. Maybe you deserve a treat," Teddy says before leaning in to kiss me hard. When he lifts his head, his hands slide down to squeeze my ass.

Sweet baby Hercules, I'm getting fucked and I have zero intention of stopping it.

Popping her lips free for a moment, Jolene pants against my skin. "I'm the one with the blood gushing into my brain, assholes. If you don't flip the skirt up and make me scream, no one's getting fucked."

There's a lot of rustling behind me, but I'm more entranced by our girl lifting her hands to grip my waist. Once she holds on tight, her left leg stretches up to wrap around the outside of the ladder, spreading her legs wider in front of my face. How in the *fuck* did she—

Her breath is warm against my dick as she laughs. "I suppose you idiots could have asked if I'm a better dancer than I am a singer, but that's your loss."

"Not today it isn't," Teddy growls, his cock magically freed and rubbing against me in a way that makes my teeth sharpen. He knows he's doing this and she can't see, which makes it even more dangerous and hotter than fuck. His teeth nibble on the mark and I tremble. "Feast on our girl while I get you ready, Pup. We'll punish her later for the omission."

There's so much sensory stimulation happening I can't do much more than whimper, so I let him kick my legs apart further while I dive under her skirt. The crotchless panties I exploited earlier make it easy to lap up the juices flowing from her and just as she suckles again, two fingers coated in warm lube slide inside of me. I can't stop myself, so I nip her clit firmly, knowing it'll break the skin. She cries out around my dick and I know this is going to be loud and hard.

"That's a good boy, Pup. Make her scream for us. She can't see but she can feel and you know what to do. You're aching to do your part, and I'll make you howl for me."

Jesus fucking Christ on bicycle, I'm not gonna survive this.

Teddy adds another finger and my sugarplum swallows me down so far that I wonder if she can breathe, but the humming vibration making my cock sing says she can. I know he says she can't see, but I'm fairly certain she's going to notice if my skin changes colors, but I don't know if I can control it. My teeth scrape over her as I tease and suckle my way around her drenched sex, grinning when I feel the shivers.

Our girl is going to have fun once we can show her what each of us can *really* do when we're not hiding behind the human guises. She likes a little rough in her stuff.

"Are you both ready to fly?" Teddy whispers in my ear. The gravelly tone lets me know he's going to unleash a bit of his hound, and I almost lose my balance. I press my hips back into his hand and then rock into the hot warmth of my sugarplum's mouth eagerly. His hands join Jolene's at my waist and I feel the head of a hot, broad cock pushing against me.

Fuck yes, I am.

Sugarplum starts a deep, teeth scraping rhythm and I bury my face in her dripping pussy, lashing tongue and teeth over her. I almost scream when Teddy pushes his dick in because not only is he bigger than Prez, but the heat from his hound makes my eyes cross. Just when I think I'm going to explode before everyone else like a fucking teenager, the stretch starts and my eyes fly wide open.

"Teddy! What in everything unholy—"

This time, he doesn't laugh; he damn near roars. "*Drugar*, hold on tight with those pretty thighs. This is gonna be rough."

For once, she does as she's told without a fight, squeezing my head as Teddy takes control of the rhythm, rocking us so hard and fast that the ladder creaks. It occurs to me it could break, but my eyes lose focus as the heat, fog, and a sprinkling of my magic fill the air with so much sensation that my thoughts scatter to the wind.

The orgasm that rockets through us makes the world melt and I can hear the sounds of pleasure, but I'm too far gone to make sense of it all. Teddy is the one howling like he's calling a pack, and I think the trilling is me… but the shriek that shatters the barware set isn't either of us.

When his hips finally slow and I lift my head, the muscled man who's laid claim to both of us literally lifts us from the ladder, carrying the both of us to the wide flat couch. He lets sugarplum slither onto the cushions first before crashing us down and curling around us with a grunt that passes for a command.

There should be words here and I should make sure we say them, but we need a few to come back to Earth.

Also, I'm gonna need the wings to go back to where they belong. If I can figure out how with my brains scrambled.

They're gonna kill us for letting them miss this shit; I know it.

Toxic

Teddy, Wolfie, and I sneak out of the library with as much dignity as we can. The boys have assured me they fixed my hair, so I don't look like a troll doll that's been fucked six ways from Sunday. I don't have much I can do about the lipstick. I'll be damned if Wolfie didn't apply Teddy's makeup with some sort of magical glue because he looks fresh as a daisy.

"Don't worry, sugarplum," he murmurs as we follow Teddy into the ballroom. "No one but our folks will have noticed."

I snort. "I should be so lucky."

"They'd better not bother any of us or I'll be far less kind than I was to my mother," Teddy growls, grabbing my hand to tug me into the crowd of dancing people.

Smiling to myself, I pull Wolfie along as well, following him as he seeks the rest of our motley crew. "Careful, Edgar Olivier Boone III. People might think you're off the market."

"I am."

Wolfie chuckles, pointing to where Prez and Doyle have been cornered by the Behles. They aren't yelling, but the energy radiating from my Irish lover is intense. I highly doubt that asshole is going to lie off—if he didn't realize this isn't the venue for the discussion before, my arrival won't change his behavior. I look for Seer, seeing her in the corner with someone I don't know.

I'm going to have to employ the 'loud club, but we need a distraction to escape' protocol from Germany. Turning to Teddy, I tap his shoulder so he'll stop. "I need you to lift me up high. The guys need a distraction, and I know how to get one."

He gives me a doubtful look, but leans down, cupping his hands for me to step on. Grasping his shoulders, I step up, letting him lift far above the crowd like a goddamned ESPN cheerleader. Seer sees me and her eyes widen. I grin, moving my hands and arms in a series of motion a little like baseball signs so she knows what I need. Once I finish, she nods, winking at me as she excuses herself from the chatty person to do as I ask.

If this works, I'll keel over. It's not something Seer and I haven't done before, but this is Whistler's Hollow, not Europe. I don't know if starting an impromptu flash mob will work, but I'm willing to try. Hell, these idiots couldn't think worse of me if they tried, so it's not like I'll ruin my sterling reputation.

My bestie comes running up, her eyes dancing as she whispers in my ear. A chuckle falls from my lips as I hear what she chose—this should be pretty interesting when played by a small orchestra with the smoky chanteuse they have singing. I'm surprised they agreed, but I guess everyone needs a little amusement at a stiff-necked party like this, right?

We take our places in the middle of the dance floor, waiting for the first chord from the strings section to draw attention. When the sharp sounds of the bows being drawn hard across them echoes in the room, everything stops. All the whispers and noise of the crowd goes silent as we dance along with the beat, and when the singer finally chimes in, a roar of applause starts.

As we move through the first verse of Queen B's song, girls come running up, joining in despite their ballgowns and heels. Before the end of the bridge, there are almost thirty students and alumnae slinking through the most famous performance of this song as if we practiced for weeks. The beat drops for a second, and I look down, feeling the touch of something at my feet.

Isn't that a kick in the ass?

Bending for one of the low squats in the chorus, I lift the waiting Isis to my neck, letting her coil around my arms and shoulders. The added weight makes the dance harder, but luckily, I'm not a wilting Southern flower. The group tightens in the middle of the song, and a chair appears out of nowhere. Sitting down, I push and pull at the surrounding girls, laughing as I watch the huge dresses fan around me like giant set pieces when the girls kneel. Seer hops up, jogging over to grab Doyle and Prez for the next part and I groan. This is going to end up on the front page of the fucking paper, for sure.

However, it freed them from Mr. Behle's clutches and that was the plan, right?

Surprisingly, Doyle steps up quickly, playing his part as he lets me grab his shirt and dance with him during the bridge. He moves fluidly, following along as I lead him around the writhing mass of girls. Prez comes up behind me, holding onto my hips as we move. The other girls break into the crowd, pulling tuxedoed guys into the middle to dance with them, and I wiggle my way to back to let them take my stage.

After all, it's their ball, and I've got the attention of the guys I want.

The song changes to another up beat dance number, and I hold on to Doyle's neck. I may have started something that can't be stopped— there's a line forming by the conductor's stand. Boys are waving bills at them, presumably to request songs their dates will want to dance to. I may have completely ruined the dance floor for the rest of the night. As my eyes coast over the crowd, I see women of all ages bumping and grinding and having a ball.

Maybe that's not such a bad thing. All they needed was a little encouragement, and this became about having fun instead of showing off like a bunch of rich assholes.

Wonder what price I'll pay for that?

WHEN WE FINALLY TAKE A SEAT AT THE TABLE RINGING THE DANCE floor, I'm beat. Starting a dance mob is hard work—props to people who do this shit for a living. I fan myself with my hand, leaning back on my chair. Isis slithers onto the table, coiling near my arm and I sigh in relief. "Thank you, friend. I need a brief break."

Wolfie appears with two Manhattans and Prez in tow, grinning broadly. "The line at the bar is insane. Half the people are using—" Teddy narrows his eyes at him and he pauses before continuing. "Using their *influence* to cut the line and it's chaos."

"How did you get our drinks, then?" I ask, grabbing mine as if it'll disappear if I wait too long.

Doyle appears behind him, smirking as he flips a quarter over his knuckles. "Charm, love. I'm infinitely useful in a crowd."

"Oh, yes. He's *very* charming," Prez snorts. "He charmed the *entire* line, so they got out of the way. Lucy could order right away."

Teddy pinches the bridge of his nose, taking the drink Wolfie hands him. "Fucking hell, Haggerty. Are you *trying*—"

I glare at all of them. "Why are you fighting suddenly?"

Wolfie drops onto my lap, looking delectably mussed from all the strenuous activities. "Sugarplum, you were amazing out there. I know you told us you could dance, but…"

"You can do more than just 'dance', Tilly," Edgar says, egging a finger at me. "You've had some sort of training. That's not the girl from the society balls in high school."

I shrug, twisting my lips and bobbing my brows. "For me to know, boys."

Seer pops out of the crowd, tugging Zasha and Julia along behind her. Tharin lumbers along behind him, looking comically cheerful for a guy the size of an orc. "Peanut! Why'd you leave?"

"I'm exhausted, Seer. It was time to cool off." I pat the seat next to me, sitting with my chin on Wolfie's shoulder. He beams at her and I laugh softly. I've known no one so comfortable being loved on than him.

"Now she's taking my seat! Make room, Boone. Your lap will have to do," Doyle complains, sidling up to Teddy while batting his lashes.

Teddy glares at him. "Get fucked, leprechaun." His lips curve and he jerks his chin at Prez. "You can sit if you like Hamilton."

I blink, turning to look at him as Wolfie and Seer snort behind their hands. "Did we all get drugged again?"

"I'm being friendly! You said to stop arguing," Teddy smirks, patting his lap. "You didn't say *who* I had to be friendly with."

"For feck's sake, Peanut. I have trouble with three; how in the bloody Hades do you put up with four of them?" Seer makes a face at me as Tharin sits in the chair and makes room for her and Zasha. Julia stands by his shoulder, but she gives the two sitting on her enormous consort a fond smile.

Same girl, same.

"I have no idea, Seer. Every day I wake up and wonder if today is the day I become a mass murderer. I mean, like you said…four." I yell when either Prez or Teddy pinch my ass hard in retaliation.

Before she can respond, Mayor Nelia approaches with Zareb in tow. "If it isn't the infamous Miss Whitley and her motley crew! I see you're making waves yet again."

My cheeks flush bright red as I look at the elegant woman dressed in what must be a bespoke Queen of Wakanda costume. "Yes, ma'am. I felt the party needed a little levity."

"What does the song say? You said 'this looks like a job for me'?" Nelia gives me a mischievous grin.

Teddy raises his glass at her. "If chaos is present, either this Irish asshole or our girl are present."

"Sometimes both," Doyle chimes in, looking proud. "She's a brilliant student."

"Where have you been, Nelia? We missed you when we came in," Prez asks, looking up at her curiously. "It's not like you to be tardy."

Her eyes widen and there's a slight shake to her hand as she waves him off. "We're all getting older, Mr. Hamilton. It took me longer to get ready this evening."

I frown, a weird sensation prickling over my body. She lied; that was a complete falsehood, and it's making me itch from head to toe. What in the hell? Squirming, I rub my cheek on Wolfie's shoulder to keep from scratching my face.

"What's wrong, sugarplum?" he asks, looking down at me in concern.

"I don't know," I mutter, wiggling in my chair again as the feeling continues to spread through my limbs. I have no idea why every time I turn around, I have some sort of physical ailment. This town is making me paranoid; I swear.

"Psst." Teddy crooks his finger at Wolfie, and Prez rolls his eyes as he hops off to switch places with my McDreamy vet.

I wrap my arms around him, smiling up at his handsome face. His glasses worked perfectly with the costume and I haven't gotten to see him enough today to tell him how adorable he looks. His fingertips brush my jaw, but he watches Teddy whisper in Wolfie's ear. A frown forms and I tug his face back to me. "Jealous, baby?"

He snorts. "Not even a little. Just curious about what they're planning, magpie. Boone loves to cause trouble, and Lucy loves to please people. There's a little praise kink in our boy, you know."

"Duh," I mutter, reaching up to tiptoe my fingers over his chest. "I was only making sure. You're all so... important to me. I don't want there to be secrets."

His eyes widen, and his expression is panicked. "Who said anything about secrets?"

Arching a brow, I shrug. His response is unsettling and paired with that weird feeling I'm getting from Nelia as she chats with Doyle. It's not good. "No one."

"Good. Because there aren't any. Secrets, I mean," he adds hastily.

That doesn't feel suspicious at all.

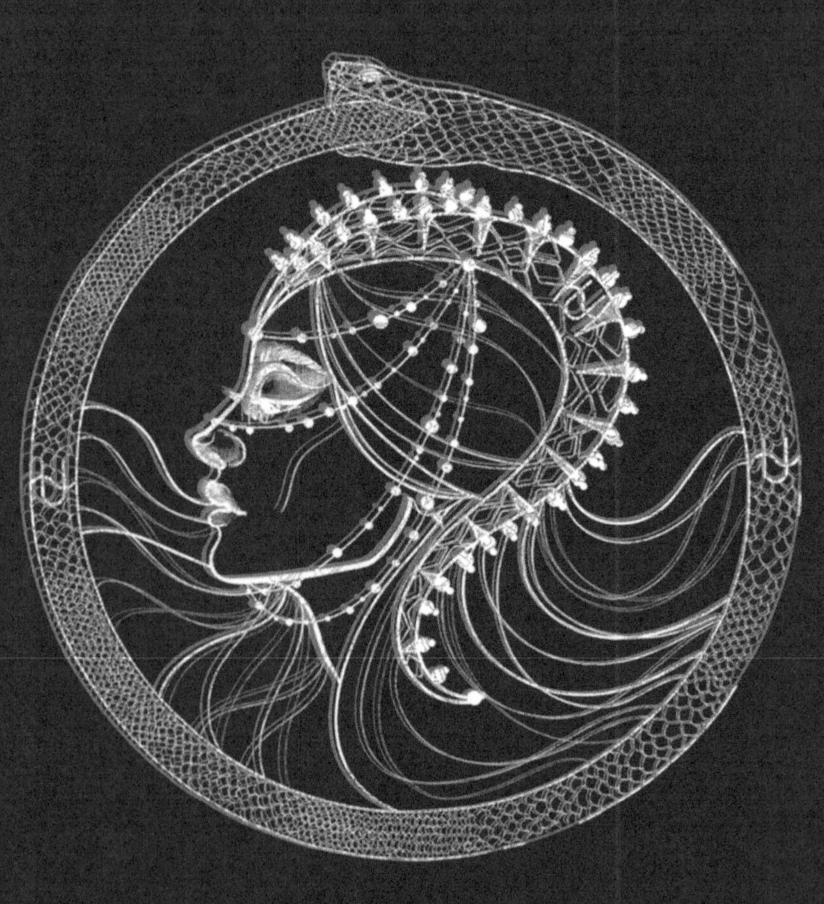

WITCHES BURN

ANDROMEDA

Nelia sent her pet seer along for the ride. His powers are not useful for battle or capture, but I can understand her desire to trigger his gifts. Even if he is forbidden from directly impacting the timeline, he will report to his patrons and if they feel the Society needs certain details, they will share them.

Of course, that's assuming the whims of the most powerful extranormals on the planet benefit us. Human myths speak of their volatile tempers and capricious emotions—they're not wrong. The tales of triumph and failure because of their kind, regardless of affinity, are littered with subtle warnings about their lack of compassion for beings other than themselves.

The Society has an alliance with every major group of deities for hundreds of years, but that does not make them trustworthy. They exist for their own amusement and nothing more. Their glory days of being worshipped by humans and supes alike are long over and they no longer seek to protect or guide us. However, good relations with the pantheons are needed for us to function.

There's also the minor matter of the Society taking the results of their 'faux pas' in enclaves around the world. It would be quite embarrassing if the many illegitimate hybrids were allowed to come into their powers without guidance. Our enclaves raise them, train them, and assign them to strategic positions all over the world without revealing their parentage unless specifically instructed.

There's one such individual living and working in the Hollow as we speak.

"I see nothing," Hugo says, emerging from the copse of trees to the south.

Kumiko swoops out of the forest to the east, materializing in front of me and fluffing his tail. Closing my eyes, I bond with him, absorbing what he saw on his flight. He did not find them, nor did he see any signs that the coven had been in that area. Unfortunately for us, we still have much ground to cover and not much time to do it. We could use Julia and her band of merry men to help find our targets before they can do any damage.

There are far too many extranormals in this town to allow them to set off the equivalent of a paranormal bomb. Unemerged supes, exiled demigods, and unstable magick users plus a building full of powerful alumnae make tonight the worst possible time for an attack from a rogue faction.

"Do you have a cell phone number for someone at the party who could pass a message to Julia?" I ask him as I stare at the vast fields and forest around us. "We need her people to assist us with locating the coven. We cannot do this alone."

Hugo pauses, watching me for a moment. "I could call Boone and ask him to send them. They should be together at the ball."

"Do it. Get Julia's team here while I do a flyover. You'll want to cover your ears until I'm out of range." I whistle at Kumiko, letting the mist consume me as I take to the air with a wail that echoes off the hills.

Once he has the team in place, I can return and strategize. Until then, I will scan the landscape as I sing, hoping either my song or my eyes bring us the information we need.

"Where is Bane? If Peanut figures out we're gone, it's going to be pretty feckin' suspicious. I don't understand why the bloody h—"

Swooping overhead with a screech that silences the bitching below, I land in front of the crowd dressed in Rocky Horror garb with a glare. Younger Guardians are always so feisty when they're called to action when it's inconvenient—dealing with beings younger than a century is tiresome. I feel like I'm herding cats, and I get enough of that in my day job.

"Silence, you twittering fools. Being conscripted to service is part of your purpose in this world and we have no time for whining. None of you missed the last party in Pompeii to serve your charge, nor did you miss visiting Atlantis before the great submersion. THOSE are events to be angry about missing out on—you are missing a ball full of teenagers and supes that occurs every year."

Julia blinks. "Fucking hell, Bane, just how goddamned old ARE you?"

I snort, corporealizing inches from her face. "Old enough to tell you I have not always been in this form and you don't want to know the story of how I joined the Shee. Now, focus!" I flick her nose with my fingers, making my point.

Tharin lumbers forward, always the peacemaker, despite the fiery legacy of his people. "Forgive us, Andromeda. We are in your service, as always."

Hugo steps forward, rubbing the back of his neck as he looks around. "I feel something. I cannot say what… but you were right to call for reinforcements."

"Well, let's get this party started!" The Irish firebrand grins as her teeth lengthen and her body glows a bright golden color tempered with sea green.

Smirking, I nod at the others, pointing a finger at them as I shriek. "Change!"

I watch as Tharin's bulk grows larger, scales covering his body until he shifts into the ten foot tall wyvern hiding beneath the guise of the gentle giant. His partner Zasha is next, glowing green and blue, until his half-shifted merman form appears clad in the armor of the royal Petrov family of the Bering Sea.

His trident shimmers in a brilliant silver that matches the color of his hair as he turns to watch Julia's short locks turn into a mass of writhing snakes. Her scales are emerald green and the end of her tail rattles as she slithers backward towards her mates. The last to emerge is Saoirse, her wings bursting free as the gilded armor and sword common to her mother's side appear like magic.

They are not an enormous army, but between the five of us, there are over two thousand years of experience. We have seen most of human history, and much of supe history. Our powers are formidable alone, but together, we harness the sea, the air, fire, and the earth. If this coven believes, they can defeat all of us, they are gravely mistaken.

"Kumiko!" I cry, raising my hand to my companion. He is a soul-eater, and he, too, will rise to the occasion. "Call their companions whence they hid them!"

I smirk as they give me surprised looks. As if I was not aware that Guardians *always* have companions and theirs must be hidden to keep their status relatively secret from the Irish lass' charge. Kumiko raises his head and lets out a mournful wail that echoes over the hills like a soul screaming for mercy.

Good. I hope it scares the Hot Topic panties off those piddling witches.

The air is calm as we wait, tension filling the silence. Before long, a huge black winged horse with fire in its eyes swoops out of the sky. It lands like an earthquake, tossing its mane angrily. On its back is a small, chubby blue dragon and a large blue-ringed octopus with a bubble over its head. I turn to ask Zasha what in Zeus' beard he's done to his deadly friend when a roar announces the last of the companions. A large Nemean lioness comes rushing out of the trees, skidding to a stop in front of her mistress with a look of arrogant disapproval.

"I would ask why a dragon has a smaller drake as a companion or what magick allows an octopus to roam the skies, but the Nemean and the Aethon overshadow them somewhat," I quip, arching a brow at the astonishing brood.

"We don't have time for an old-fashioned story time, so I'll cut to the chase: Zasha is bloody marvelous at poker. The Greeks… less so. We each were granted a boon to receive a companion, and we chose." Saoirse lifts a shoulder carelessly as she hands the bubbled cephalopod to her mate and hops onto her horse as if it isn't several feet taller than her.

"I'll bet Ares, Poseidon, Hephaestus, and Hera never invited a Guardian to a poker game again." My muttered response makes Zasha throw his head back and howl. No wonder most of them have been assigned to wander the planet, filling in after their charges have long since emerged. They pissed off powerful people.

"Indeed, Andromeda. We have paid for our hubris many times over. But our friends were worth the pain. Oliver is one of the most clever companions I've ever seen, and his bubble allows him to travel with me unaffected by lack of water."

Sighing, I pinch the bridge of my nose. I may well regret involving this band of merry fools in this mission, but for the moment, I need them. I'll deal with the political fallout later.

I fucking hate Olympus and it seems like I'll be making a visit.

My brow arches when I realize the seer has been quiet, and no companion appeared to aid him when Kumiko called. How strange.

"I have not yet been blessed with the comfort of a companion. Most of my kind find theirs when their powers emerge, but sadly, I have not," Hugo says, his eyes turning eerily white. "But that may change…"

Save me from the mysterious ramblings of soothsayers, I swear to Hecate.

"Fine. I will take Kumiko and scour the north. Tharin and Zasha head west. O'Flanagan, take Hugo on Aethon to the south. Julia, cover the ground to the east again. This time, you will use your powers to feel for magick. Each of you can make use of the tattoos to draw the lower tier extranormals hiding out of the dark to aid the search. Send the signal up when you find where they have set up their circle, but do not engage until we have arrived."

"These bitches must have put on some big girl panties after Salem," Julia hisses. "We almost wiped them out on their home turf. If the lost ones had emerged, it would have——"

"Yes," I cut her off. "It would have stopped this before it started. But those girls were not ready and nothing we could have done would force them to emerge until their time, Ricci. We must shut down this Samhain spell and find out who is pulling their strings. That is our mission for this evening. Now, go!"

The group splits, heading in different directions by land and sky. Kumiko and I fade to mist, soaring on the winds to the north.

The night is dark and foggy, so we blend as we fly over horse pastures, dirt roads, and farmland. I watch for telltale signs like smoke from a fire, sounds of voices, or the scent of herbs, but find nothing. I chose north because it has more open land with less population and I believed I would locate their secret spot before the others. My form is easier to hide and I might learn their plans before they realize I'm present.

It has baffled me from the beginning that a small group of unknown witches garnered enough power to threaten a historical stronghold. Magick users of all species have inhabited Salem since long before the human 'witch trials' and all of them survived that purge with help from shapeshifters. This coven has some sort of powerful ally and they are invested in destroying what the Society has spent hundreds of years building.

Their last attempt to remove the binding spells from all the magickal youth in Salem may have failed, but we never learned why they sought to release the veil. There is a much bigger plot at hand, and though the Society is not convinced, I feel a mutiny is underway. Only members with centuries of service are aware of how the spell is placed on the hybrids and how to remove it when they come of age.

Whoever is directing this coven has inside information, and they seek to make the untrained young hybrids look dangerous.

At least, that's the only conclusion I've been able to garner from these gambits. Deduction and riddles are gifts of my species and long before I joined the Shee, I was solving problems with others of my kind in Society salons. Half of the things humans think they invented were dreamt up by my people and whispered in their ears to allow progress to move them forward.

My inability to piece together their motives and endgame disturbs me. I only know that if we do not find out what the big picture is, it endangers all extranormals. Our treaties with the humans are as fragile as those with the pantheons, and breaching them will be bad for everyone.

It may be dramatic, but my gut tells me that avoiding a multi-species war may become our main objective if we don't find out what these people are up to.

What does that human in the movies say?

Oh, yes. I'm too old for this shit.

Something Bad's About To Happen

After the dance marathon, my guys and I chilled at the table we claimed. Drinks are flowing, laughs are echoing, and it feels like we're all gelling as a family. It makes me smile, and I wish the rest of my companions were here.

I miss the kitties, dogs, and even Euryale. Isis' arriving has helped the anxiety buried deep within me at being at the site of one of my deepest traumas calm, but having the full complement would be even better. I can't help but look around the room and feel the bottom drop out of my stomach when memories flash through my mind.

"Sugarplum, you're frowning again. Are you sure you don't want to escape while people are distracted?" Wolfie leans over from his perch on Teddy's lap, looking into my eyes in concern.

I shake my head. "No, it's okay. We're expected to stay until the last dance, and with all of you close by, I'm doing okay. I promise; I will not lose my shit."

Edgar sits up suddenly, tilting his head in a manner that is very reminiscent of Kali and Hecate. "I'm not sure I agree. Perhaps we should go."

"Teddy, it's fine. Don't get all alpha on us. I'll let you know if I need a change of scenery." I reach around Wolfie and Prez, squeezing his hand.

"No, Tíogair. I don't think he's wrong. There's something odd in the air; even I can feel it." Doyle's brow furrow and he scoots his chair closer to our group. "I should dispatch Odie to fetch the other animals."

"Who or what in the fuck is an Odie?" I ask, punching his shoulder. "I thought you said there are no secrets!"

Doyle grins and shrugs carelessly. "Odie's not a secret, Tíogair. He's my raven, and I haven't brought him around yet because your house is turning into a veritable wildlife preserve."

Giving him an annoyed look, I punch him again. "As if one more bird is going to matter when Prez is building a fucking aviary! What were you going to do when you all moved in?"

"I live by the seat of my britches. I figured it'd come up, eventually."

Rolling my eyes into the back of my head, I sigh and rest my forehead on Wolfie's shoulder. Doyle loves to cause trouble, even a little shit like this, and I know he's enjoying himself. Giving him the reaction he wants will only make him enjoy it more. I lift my head and shrug. "So call this Odie and get the others if you feel it's the right thing to do."

Wolfie flat out snorts at the pout on Doyle's face when he realizes I will not fight with him. "Oh, sugar, you clipped his wings, but good. He was spoiling for a fight."

"Good girl, Tilly. Make him work for it," Teddy rumbles, his eyes dancing with mirth. "Can't have him thinking he's in charge."

Doyle rises, walking past me and ruffling my hair. "Ah, Tíogair. You make life interesting. I'll be back to continue our dance once I've contacted Odie."

As he walks away, I look at the others with a frown. "Did you know?"

They shake their heads, and I wrinkle my nose. "He's such a goddamned mystery. None of you were this hard to get close to."

"Honestly, *drugar*, you're closer to him than anyone in town outside Mayor Nelia. That jackass has lived here for years and he hasn't batted a lash at anyone. You're the first woman he's paid attention to since he showed up. Hell, I don't even know where he lives." Teddy looks at the others and they nod in agreement.

"Does that strike you as odd?" I ask, tilting my head. "I know he's on our side—I don't believe he'd do anything to hurt me—but I want to get to know him better. I want… I want us all to fit together."

Prez leans over, making Teddy growl as he shifts on his lap. He and Wolfie switched places after they got a fresh round of drinks, forcing Edgar to give in and let him sit on his lap. "Magpie, he'll come around. He strikes me as a lone wolf and he has to learn to play on a team. Give him time. He asked you if you wanted him to call his raven—in his own way. That's progress."

"I didn't think about it that way. I suppose it is better than doing whatever the hell he wants without telling us." I ponder for a moment, then smile at my McSteamy doc. "Thank you for saying that, Prez. It helps."

"Uh, guys?"

All four of us look up at the lumbering giant in front of us. Benjamin Louis Foster, the jovial proprietor of the Speakeasy, is wearing a Beast at the ball costume. It couldn't be more appropriate for his hulking frame or mane of wild dreds. His chestnut colored skin is perfectly suited to the golds and royal blues of his formal waistcoat and my jaw drops as I take him in. Scrawny Benjy was decent looking at the door of the bar, but *this* Benjy is straight up on fire.

"Hey, man. What's up?" Teddy grins, holding his fist up to bump.

"I… I have a bad feeling, E. Something is going down, and soon. Sherilynn and all of her friends are MIA. They literally disappeared —one by one—and I didn't notice because I was trying so hard to avoid her." He shuffles his feet, looking uncomfortable. "She hasn't taken the separation well. I hope she isn't acting out because of—"

"Dude, Sherilynn was a viper in high school, and she made you miserable from the moment you married her. Whatever she has cooking isn't about you—it's because she and the other girls follow Amy Matilda like lemmings off a cliff," Teddy chides, shaking his head.

"She knows we didn't separate solely because of her behavior. I didn't tell her, but she's not stupid, man. I'm worried they have something ugly planned—again." His gaze cuts to me and my entire body freezes in place.

Oh, no. No. No. No.

They can't have some elaborate bullshit planned in this place, at this event… I can't. I don't think I can go through this again—not a repeat of the past. I've been healing, but the wound is not closed and I don't know what I'll do if I have to relive it.

"Sugarplum, I'm gonna need you to breathe," Wolfie whispers, leaning in to put his forehead on mine. "I can feel your pain. I wasn't here when it happened, and I've only heard stories. But I know you were a kid and you're a beautiful, accomplished woman now. They can't hurt you like they did before."

The golden sheen of glitter on his skin intensifies, and I can feel his warmth surrounding me. It helps, as does the tightening of Isis around my ribs. A tear slips from my eye as I whisper, "Wolfie, you don't understand. It wasn't just them. There was more to it—more than people know."

"Jolene, I know you don't have any reason to trust me, but I came to help you guys slip out before whatever happens goes down. I saw Haggerty outside. He's waiting for your companions, but he knows to be on alert just in case something is coming from outside of the building." Benjy shifts uncomfortably, holding his hand out.

I look at the boys, surprised when Wolfie stands and they all nod at me. "If you think we should follow him, I trust you."

"Benjy tried to stop what happened in high school, Tilly. He's the one who came out to find us when he overheard the girls giggling in the back. We were all too stupid, high, and full of our parents' toxic bullshit to understand what was going on," Teddy says quietly. "We didn't listen and by the time we got inside, the damage was done."

I blink, looking at the enormous man holding his hand out. "Is that true, Benjy?"

He nods, flushing red under his copper hued skin. "It is. Teddy convinced me that there was a secret room upstairs, and I saw her approach them. I heard what they offered and how it came about. I ran to tell the guys, but they were… hell. They were stupid kids; we all were. I never got to tell you how sorry we were."

Fucking hell. That makes me madder than a cat being baptized. For years, I thought everyone in this town took part or took pleasure in my humiliation, and I was wrong. Benjy tried to prevent it and the guys might have helped if they weren't stoned out of their gourds. I had allies; they were just fuck-ups.

"Thank you for telling me that," I whisper, taking his hand. I'm not a small girl, but his size dwarfs me a bit and I've never had that happen before. At least, not up this close. Tharin is easily this size, but I've never been this close in proximity.

"We should get moving, guys. If Benjy's feeling is right, whatever those bitches have planned could happen any minute." Prez tugs Teddy up after he stands, looking around the room suspiciously.

"He's right, Tilly. We need to get gone before it all goes to hell. Benjy has a good sense of impending doom. It's eerie." Edgar peers across the room, his gaze piercing as he takes in the scene.

"Okay. Let's figure out how to get five people in outrageous costumes out the back before anyone notices," I concede.

"I think we should part ways. Magpie, you stay with Benjy. Pretend to dance and we will all split up. Once we're clear, he can pretend to walk you out to the garden. No one will suspect anything because we're not along for the ride," Prez murmurs.

"Agreed," Wolfie says. "Once we're all outside, Teddy can bring the car around. I'll go with you, and Benjy can round up Doyle. He's got a truck, so the rest will fit in the back."

Benjy gives me a shy smile, and I follow him out to the dance floor. He holds my hands carefully, starting the waltz as the music plays. I follow him easily, trying not to let the emotions running through me show in my face. It's not his job to clean up a messy, weepy Jolene and I hate letting people I don't know well see me vulnerable. But the tears slide down my cheeks unbidden and when I sniff, he stops for a moment.

"Jolene, don't cry. I'm a big , burly dude and people will think I'm scaring you," he jokes, reaching up to wipe a tear off my cheek. "Guys like me already have a bad rap with women."

I snort, the tears making the sound gurgly. "Benjy, your giant Hulkness is not making me cry. If anyone thinks that, they can get the fuck right off. I've kicked asses as big as yours in the ring."

That's not exactly true, but it made him smile, and his shoulders loosen up. I hoped he'd relax a little with a joke because I can't control the waterworks at the moment and I don't want people to figure out that we're a diversion. He winks at me, then twirls me in a circle before tugging me back into the two-step frame.

"Well, you are kicking my ass at dancing. I took the ballroom classes for the wedding, but we didn't end up using it. I think it was because Sherilynn never could find a foot that wasn't her left one."

Laughter bursts free before I can stop it, and I smile up at the Disney prince in front of me. "That is the second best thing I've learned all night. Thank you again, Benjy."

He grins and leans in. "I think Prez is the last one out. We should start making our way to the——"

"Ladies and gentleman, if we can have your attention please!"

I look up at the orchestra with an icy ball of fear in my stomach. At the microphone, Amy Matilda Behle and her four sycophants stand tall in their five versions of Harley Quinn costumes. Not one of them has the depth to understand that character's inner turmoil, madness, or redemption arc, but there they are, tarted up and sashaying across the stage.

"We have an amazing surprise for you. Are you ready, Whistler's Hollow?"

Squeezing Benjy's hand hard, I wait for the shoe to drop. Something bad is about to happen, and I'm going to need all the support I can get.

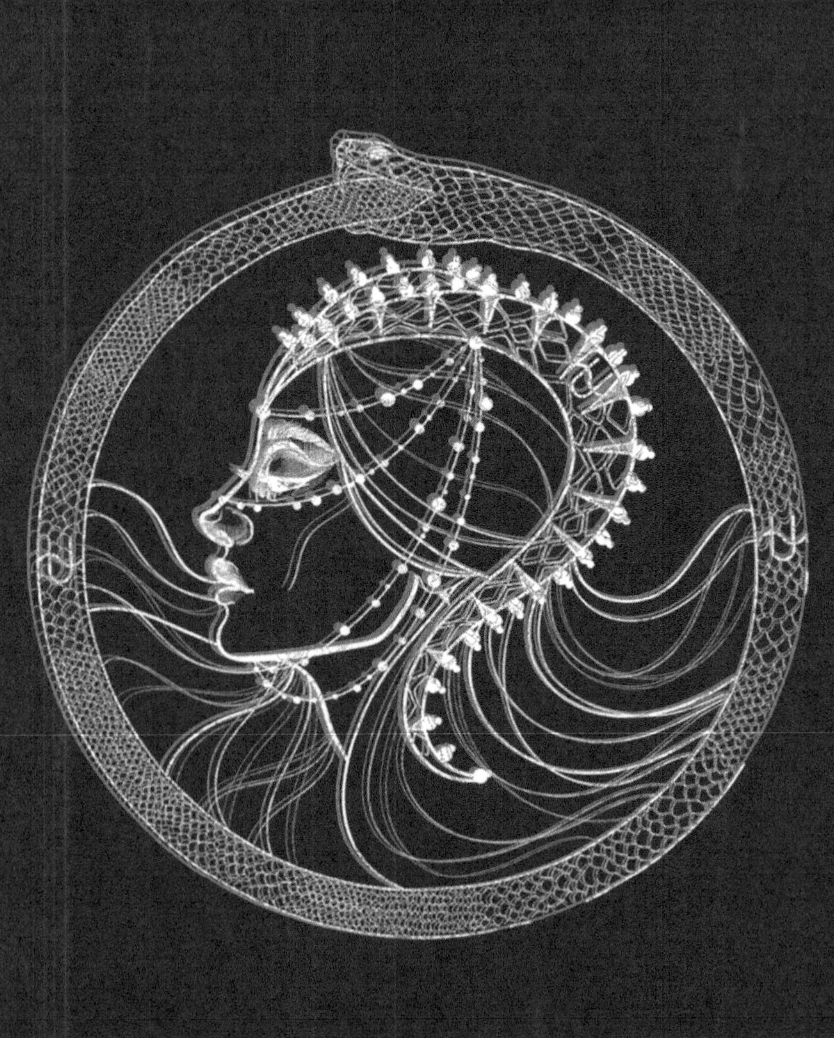

This Is Why We Can't Have Nice Things

I don't know why Benjy and Tilly aren't out here yet. It's making the hound pace, and the other two are pushing against my control as well. I'm practiced in ensuring that all three of my sides don't unleash at the same time—it's how I kept it a secret for so long. However, anything to do with Jolene strains the tethers I hold them with back so tightly that I often fight for a grip like I did when I was a new shifter.

"Where is she?" Wolfie murmurs, squeezing my shoulder hard. "They should be back by now."

Prez tugs him away, his eyes full of understanding. Wolfie needs reassurance, and I don't have enough spoons to give it to him. "It's okay, Lucy. We all know Benjy won't allow anyone to harm her. The moment she walked up to him at the bar, the pull started, and he dealt with it far better than any of us have."

Our submissive fae nods, his eyes full of worry. He believes us, but he also can't control his reaction to his mate anymore than I can. The marks we've left bind us to her, and although she isn't able to complete the rituals yet, our souls gravitate to her because of our supe sides.

He's only made one mark, but I can tell by the cool temperature of his touch that his mother's influence is rearing its head as well. I have no idea how that will work; that piece of him has been locked up for so long that even Prez doesn't know how it will react to any of us.

Or if it letting it free will call a being none of us are prepared to deal with. His birth mother makes my adoptive mother look simple, and that's saying something.

Doyle comes striding up with Jekyll, Hyde, Euryale, and my hounds as I ponder. There's an enormous black raven on his shoulder and I'd swear it's not a normal bird. It's not as big as Eurayle, but you don't have to be a bird expert like the doc to know it's unusual. "Where's my Tiogar? I've got her animals."

"Doyle, what the fuck is that thing on your shoulder? It's not a goddamned Raven?" Prez asks as he walks closer.

"Aye, Odie is special. That's a story I'm not inclined to tell you just yet, Hamilton. In time, when we're all much cozier, I'll regale you with the tale of how I won him."

Jesus Christ in a pumpkin carriage. He's determined to be an ass since he thinks he's saved the day.

"Haggerty, we don't know where Benjy and my drugar are. They haven't come out yet and we were about to discuss whether we should wait or go in for them," I reply. "There are pros and cons either way and—"

I stop short when the air grows cold and before I can warn the others, a large group of supes converges upon us by air and sky. My skin tingles as fur ripples over me, a loud howl echoes as my hound goes into protective mode. Inside, I frantically try to soothe him, but his pack is in danger and nothing I'm saying is pulling the cranky asshole back in. Before I know it, I'm half-shifted, staring at my pack and a bunch of somewhat familiar scents.

"Jaysus feckin' Christ on a Triscuit, Boone. It's us," the armored woman says as she lands a giant fiery looking flying horse in front of me. She's got MacAuley with her, and both of them look worse for wear.

I've not seen Saoirse shifted—I scented her sides, but never got confirmation. Guardians are so damned tight lipped you'd think they had fucking NDAs half the time. The cold air whooshes over me and when I turn my head, there's Andromeda and Kumiko. A huge lioness bounds of the trees with a goddamned gorgon riding it, and I'll be damned if a fucking wyvern with passengers doesn't land next. What the hell is going on? This is a battle contingent of Guardians, and every one of them seems to be grimed up like they've been to war.

"Uh, not to be the doctor in the house, but all of you seem to be injured in various ways. Why the *fuck* is everyone injured?"

Every single person slowly turns to look at Presley. He's the most chill of us all, having a temper that's almost impossible to set off. He looks like he's about to murder someone, and the silence hangs in the air as we all try to work out what we're seeing.

"I asked a question, *people*! Why do you all look as if you've been to a war?!"

Andromeda snaps out of it first, walking over to him with a fond smile. "Dr. Hamilton, there is no cause for worry. My fellow Guardians and I have neutralized the threat—for the moment—but we came here because of something our foes said while we were banishing them. As you know, there has been a rise in attacks on extranormals—particularly hybrids and lost ones or those connected with them—and the Guardians have been stretched thin between fighting these battles and protecting our charges."

Wolfie nods. "The meeting after the trial was virtual, but some of the other enclaves expressed concern that their people were being hunted. No one has proved it was more than a theory. Most of the incidents appear to be accidents or job related mishaps."

"That is a carefully constructed lie, Dr. Fletcher. The Society fears we have a leak or leaks and all general communications with members are crafted to keep those persons from reporting that we are aware they exist. The coven we banished this evening was more powerful than their training or age would normally allow, and they followed us home after an unsuccessful attempt to erase four unemerged lost ones." Bane shakes her head, looking at the group assembled before pointing at us. "*Human!*"

Even my hound runs for hills, and my body shifts back into its normal form—well, except for the naked part.

Doyle rolls his eyes at all of us standing there bare as they day we were born, tsking under his breath. "Shifters are so high maintenance."

With a snap of his fingers, a pile of clothes lands at the feet of every one of us save Andromeda and Hugo. Her banshee form doesn't strip her, and MacAuley's supe side doesn't change him in form at all. Though, after tonight, I'm uncertain I know anything about any of them because I'll be fucked if I knew Haggerty could do that.

Wolfie chuckles, tilting his head. "You even made sure Prez and I could change. I knew you liked us."

The red-haired supe waves his hand as if dismissing a fly. "Par for the course, Fletcher. I was tiring of watching people eyeball your arse." Prez and I whip our heads around at the same time and the jackass collapses in a fit of laughter, clutching his waist. "Ah, *there's* my thanks. Oh, that was beautiful boys; we'll have to do it again sometime."

Prez is too agitated to deal with him, so I pick up his clothes and toss them at him. It's odd for me to be the cool head, but considering we're standing here naked with what used to be a wyvern, a merman, a gorgon, and a banshee, it's not the weirdest thing that's happened. Picking up the set in front of me, I nod at the others to indicate we should follow along.

"Not to be a negative Nelly, but I still haven't heard a reason you're here or what this has to do with us." Prez tugs on his jeans and then the tee shirt, glancing at Andromeda.

"Were you not listening, hound? We overhead something concerning while we fought the witches off. Despite the wounds your doctor noticed, we came to warn you," Julia says with a glare.

After I dress, I turn to the makeshift battalion. "What was this information you heard?"

"They mentioned an event happening on the other side of town that would distract all of those who could defend against their attacks. I doubt the ball is big enough to overshadow a large magickal pulse," Hugo says quietly. "I believe them."

My eyes widen, and I look at our guys. "Holy shit. Benjy and Tilly are still MIA."

"If Jolene is in there with no protection, I fear we're wasting time out here." Zasha tosses his long hair over his shoulder, giving the entire crew a serious look. "The witches came here. They could have gone anywhere to regroup, but attacked in this place on this night."

Motherfucker. Can our girl catch a break just once?

With a jerk of my head, I head for the door flanked by the companions. There's a lot of muttering, but they all follow as I jog up the steps and stride into the hall. The crowd is thick—packed tightly all the way to the entrance to the ballroom. I have no idea what is going on, but it's quiet as a pin. I'm not quite tall enough to see over the crowd at this distance, but I nod at Seer.

She climbs up Tharin like he's a tree, settling on his shoulders to peer over the milling people. "Holy fuck."

"What the hell is going on, O'Flanagan?" I growl.

"Edgar, we have a problem. Our girl is in the thick of it and I'm not sure she's got a grip. We need to get in there fast."

The tone of her voice worries me, so I turn to the group. "Who had the best chance of parting this crowd without making a bigger scene?"

"Turning them to stone or setting them on fire won't help," Julia snarks.

"If Boone lets his second out, it'll start an orgy. Bane will make people run and trample one another. MacAuley isn't offensive," Doyle muses. "I could help, but I'd prefer to keep my power under wraps."

Sighing, I clap Wolfie on the shoulder. "Feel like spreading a little happy dust? It should make the people in the back malleable enough for us to get to her before something bad happens."

"I knew you just wanted me naked again," he quips, winking at me. Tugging his shirt over his head, he hands it to Prez and closes his eyes. The change is almost instantaneous, and his colorful wings shine in the low light. Fluttering them gently, he lifts off the ground before the glitter floats across the room.

It won't be long now. Fae dust is one of the most powerful coercive substances on the planet and our darling pup has the strength of the Royal court in his veins.

"If we didn't have to tiptoe around the humans or unemerged teens, this would be so much easier," Zasha grumbles. "This is why I hate children."

I bark a laugh, shaking my head. "I can't believe you three were ever Guardians for anyone. You're all prickly as fuck."

"We never had children, Boone. We all had lost ones—adults who may or may not emerge. Most of them did, and we met at various Society events," Julia says observing the surrounding people.

"I think they're ready." Prez says. "Let's push through. I don't enjoy waiting."

I lead the way, using Kali and Hecate to growl off anyone who isn't compliant enough to get out of our way. When we reach the front, I stop short, sucking in a breath when I see what the commotion is about.

Standing at the front of the orchestra are the former mean girls of WHFS dressed as multiple Harley Quinns. That's not surprising. What is shocking is the woman standing toe to toe with Tilly dressed in the modern version of the Cruella de Vil outfit. She's smirking like the cat that ate the canary and clinging to the arm of a scrawny asshole dressed as the idiot from that zombie show.

Tilly is white as a ghost and she looks like she's going to pass out at any second. Isis and Benjy are probably the only reasons she's not on the ground in one of her blackouts.

I don't know who the guy is, but no one who went to school with us could ever forget Antigone Lisel Beauregard. She's the reason Jolene is traumatized; she created the catastrophe with her betrayal.

My *drugar* is facing down her nemesis—alone, in the place she was destroyed as a teen.

No one said life in a small town was boring.

Not Your Barbie Girl

Jolene

I sense the guys arriving, but it's like I'm encased in a bubble of fury. The rage within me is flowing through my veins as if it's replaced the blood, and my entire body is sparking with energy. My ears are ringing and the dull throb of my speeding up heartbeat pounds along with the shrill sound. It's as if time has stopped around me, and I'm merely existing as a physical representation of the emotions swirling within me like a wildfire of pain and vengeance.

Antigone Lisel Beauregard is the last person on this *planet* I ever wanted to cross paths with again.

Of course, Amy Matilda and her cronies know that. They're the ones who convinced her to commit her first betrayal. That they brought *him* along means they know what bullshit she pulled at State U. For all I know, they helped orchestrate it.

People can grow and change, but mean girls like Amy Matilda derive their power from controlling others. Their entire identity is based in the reality where they are the top of the food chain at all times. It was a culture shock, I'm sure, for Amy to arrive at Brown and not be the Queen Bee she would have been if she'd stayed at State U. Meddling with the lives of her ex-peons back home would have satisfied her desire to destroy anyone who dared to pick themselves up after she squashed them.

Hell, I wouldn't even be surprised if those bitches had a bet going about how long it would take to make me crumble. Bored rich kids are like that everywhere—selfish, self-centered, and cruel.

"Oh, Jolene. What a turn on the old song… it was me who took *your* man," Antigone crows, shaking her long wavy red tresses off of her shoulder. "I've been waiting to say that for *years*! I even spoiled my costume theme so I could have flowing red locks to make it even more ironic."

I blink, still not able to speak because of the amount of absolute murder coursing through my mind and heart. Isis tightens on my waist, and I feel the rest of my companions step into the bubble I'm trapped in. Soft snarls and growls escape the servals and hounds, followed by a screech and a caw from the birds above me. The connection between me and the animals intensifies as they move closer, and it's like my brain is ping-ponging from them to the guys.

Why do I feel so weird? Why can't I speak?

I want to scream at the woman who almost destroyed my psyche twice, but I can't get anything to come out.

"No witty retort? Nothing to say from the great savior of losers every-where?" The man next to Antigone cringes, and I look at him with curiosity.

Trevor hasn't aged well in the past decade—likely a product of being married to a shrew like her. His clothes are designer, but he's gained weight and his skin is sickly pale. The goatee on his chin looks ridicu-lous; he never could wear facial hair well. His expression is defeated, like he has no choice but to stand here and watch her try to destroy me one more time.

He was a coward then, and he's a coward now.

What surprises me most is the lack of emotion I feel looking at him. When he walked out on stage with her, descending the small steps like the King and Queen of prom, I thought my heart would try to rip itself out of my chest. But all I feel now is a dull ache where love once was and pity for the man who died when he made his choice all those years ago. I'm not even angry with him—only her—and that's puzzling.

"Sugarplum, we're here!"

Wolfie's cry snaps me out of the trance. The violence within me channels itself from my feet to my head, and tears form in my eyes. They aren't tears of sorrow, though; they are tears of fury. All the emotions dancing over my skin like sparks converge in a shield over my skin, pushing words out of my stomach into my mouth like a fist.

"Who do you think you are?!"

My voice booms in the room like I'm using a megaphone, and my body feels weightless as I lift my hand to point at the woman in front of me with a sneer gracing my lips. I turn my head, hoping to give a panicked look to my boys. It feels like I'm not in the driver's seat in my skin and I have no idea what is happening. Am I getting ready to black out again? Fuck, I hope not.

"Tiogair, you need to breathe and let it happen." Doyle's words echo in my mind as his hand rests on my shoulder. "Don't fight it. I can sense your fear, but what is inside of you will protect you. Let go, and I promise, you will be okay."

Closing my eyes, I do as he says, letting go of the tenuous grip I keep on my emotions in public. I vowed never to let people who sought to harm me see how I felt again, but with the boys forming a half-circle around me, I feel stronger. I can handle the pain if it's coming.

"Well, isn't this sweet! The Catastrophe has a stable of men she services. It doesn't surprise me to find out you've become the town whore, Jolene. You were always running after men like you had an itch to scratch when we were younger," Antigone laughs, waving her hand carelessly.

Her friends watch from a distance, and I wonder why they aren't stepping up like my guys. I knew Amy and her crew were vicious, but I didn't realize they were cruel enough to weaponize someone and leave them stranded to take the blame. More's the pity for her, though, because I'm not the lonely girl I was the first time a scene like this occurred.

I'm stronger, smarter, and I have a cadre of people behind me. My ex-best friend and ex-fiancé no longer hold the power over me they did when Trevor broke our engagement to be with Antigone. The years of therapy and work on my self-esteem will not be destroyed simply because this bitch exists in my stratosphere again.

"I asked who the *fuck* you think you are, Antigone. Have you gone deaf or is the space between your ears echoing?" I growl, stepping forward to get in her face.

"Uh, Teddy? Do you see…?" Wolfie's question cuts off, but I ignore him as I continue to glare at my nemesis from school.

"You've been nothing but trash, Whitley, and I haven't regretted ratting you out once in thirteen years. You *deserved* your punishment."

It feels like I'm floating in space; that's how infuriated I am. The indignation is like needles poking through my flesh, and I lift my chin as a strange sensation burns its way up my spine into my shoulders. I raise my hands in the air as my vision darkens and the tears continue to run down my face. "*Den eísai áxios tou chrónou mou, adýnami. Tha érthei i óra sas kai tha eínai éndoxi. Xekiniménos kléftis!*[1]"

A giant burst of energy escapes, the sound like a thunderclap inside, and panic sets in when I realize I'm definitely blacking out this time.

What in the hell *just happened?*

"Andrew, she still hasn't emerged yet. They promised she was special, and she's useless! We'll never advance our standing in this godforsaken town if she's a dud!"

"Have patience, Eloise. Andromeda said some children emerge late—even after college. Those children are usually the strongest and most powerful because they tend to be ones left by higher tier extranormals. She could even be multi-sided. We

have to wait it out. Besides, it's not like we're going to disown her if she turns out to be without a supe strain, right?"

The silence is heavy as they look at one another. Neither of them heard me creeping down the stairs to find out what their latest fight was about. Unfortunately, like always, it's about me. Every time I spy on them, all they're ever arguing about is why I'm not good enough. Or at least, that's what my mom seems to think. Something I haven't learned or developed is making her want to send me away, and I have no idea what it is. I'd fix it if I knew. Many things come naturally to me as I learn quickly. I'm sure I could do it if I knew what to focus on.

"We took her in on the condition she would help us further our careers, Andrew. You weren't supposed to get attached to a mutt. If she can't help us by the time she turns eighteen, we'll see her off to college and that will be that. It's not as if adult children want to spend a lot of time with their parents, anyway."

Her heels click on the parquet as she walks into the kitchen. My dad follows her, whispering his response in a harsh tone. I'm sure they're being quieter in the kitchen because it's below my room, but they don't know I'm not up there. I guess it's comforting to know they're trying not to be cruel to my face, but somehow, it doesn't keep the tears from falling. I wipe one off of my cheek, frowning when it comes back a brilliant red.

That's odd. Did I cut myself and I haven't realized it?

If I'm bleeding, I'll have to head upstairs and clean up. Mom will be furious if I dirty her floors and blood is impossible to get out. She nearly lost her mind the first time I had my period and stained an expensive set of Egyptian cotton sheets. As if I could have predicted that, right?

Closing my eyes, I smile to myself as I make a dash for the stairs, moving fast enough that it feels like I'm flying. If only I could fly away from here, I'd never come back—not in a million years. Between the mean girls and the elite boys., I hate school and now that I know my mom wants to get rid of me, I hate her, too.

Maybe someday I'll find a place I belong, but I know in my heart it's not

Whistler's Hollow. I'm going to travel the world and when I've lived the best life I can, then maybe I'll come back to show them how wrong they were about me.

Someday...

I WAKE UP, SUCKING IN A DEEP BREATH AND LOOKING AROUND IN A panic. The room is all white, and everything looks sterile and clinical. I try to raise my arms, but I can't because something is tying them down, and it's *not* for happy fun time. This is tight and meant to keep me in place.

Where in the actual *fuck* am I?

"Hey! Hey, assholes! I'm awake and I am not happy!"

My shouts echo off the walls of the room, and I flop back with a huff of irritation. A red light blinks on a camera on the wall and I glare at it before flipping the lens off. If someone thinks I'll be an easy victim, they've got another thing coming. I'm confused, angry, and worried, so these fuckers are going to be very sorry once I get my limbs free.

Where are my animals? Where are the guys? Who in the hell let some Frankenlab kidnap me?

The door swings open, and I level myself up, preparing for a fight even if I don't know how I'll manage it yet.

Jolene Athena Whitley isn't going down without a fight.

PRE-ORDER REJECTED IN THE HOLLOW (BOOK TWO) NOW!

---

1. You are not worthy of my time, weakling. Your time will come and it will be glorious. Be gone thief!

REVIEWS, PRINT, AND MERCHANDISE

If you have enjoyed this book, please leave reviews! It helps other
readers find my work,
which helps me as an indie author.

Thank you!

Reviews are appreciated on the following platforms:

Amazon
Goodreads
Bookbub
StoryGraph
TikTok
Instagram
Facebook

To purchase print copies or merchandise, go to The Worlds of
Cassandra Featherstone

Sneak Peek: Home to the Hollow

Chapter 1- Road to the Hollow

Jolene

"I'm sorry; could you repeat that?"

Looking at the agent in front of me in disbelief, I lean forward as if changing my position will alter the words that came out of his mouth. He grimaces, clearly unused to relaying this news to prospective trainees. After a moment of silence that feels oppressive, he clears his throat. I wait, unwilling to make his job easier.

"Miss… Whitley," he begins, pulling at the knot on his tie as he stands. He walks around the mahogany desk, coming to lean against the corner diagonal to me.

The crisp navy suit is standard government official, and the Harvard stripe on his tie tells me all I need to know about his upbringing. This guy grew up with a silver spoon in his mouth and rose up the ranks in the F.B.I. by playing politics. Handling a situation like mine is probably not his typical task, and I wonder why they chose him for this duty. I meet his gaze steadily, having learned the tricks of his trade from years of dealing with CEOs and officials with significantly more status than him.

He sighs, clearly disappointed that I'm not a blubbering mess. His wife—I can see the ring on his hand—is probably a sorority belle from UV that lets him run roughshod over her to secure her position as trophy wife. This man has aims much higher than his current position in the DOJ, and he's less than thrilled to be here speaking with me.

"Miss Whitley. As I said, I cannot release the information used to make hiring decisions. You can make a FOIA request, if you so choose, but I was told that because of the circumstances of your childhood, that request is likely to remain classified."

"Circumstances of my… I grew up in a small town in the Midwest, not Beirut! My parents were teachers, for the love of God. They have awarded me three degrees, and I developed a career consulting with governments and CEOs of multi-national corporations! I have *never* failed a background check, Agent Grant. This is outrageous."

Crossing his arms over his chest, he sighs again, running a hand over his slicked back hair. "I cannot speak to that. I can only relay the information that we have denied your application, and that re-applying during another session will not change the results. You simply cannot work for the F.B.I. or any other agency under the Department of Justice."

I stand, infuriated beyond all reason. My eyes flash with anger as I stare him down. "This is *not* over, Agent Grant. I am *more* than qualified. There is not one blemish on my record. I deserve to be here. I will fight this decision tooth and nail—I have aimed all of my education and training at working within the behavioral unit of this agency."

Shaking his head, he pushes off the desk and drops back into the luxurious chair. "You can do what you wish, Miss Whitley, but the answer will remain the same. I suggest you focus your considerable talents and effort on finding another career path—one that is actually open to you."

My face is a mask of shock, but I quickly school it, picking up my purse and turning on my heel to stalk out of his office. I wasn't lying; I intend to fight this to the fucking Supreme Court if necessary. I've been working towards being a member of the profiling team since I left teaching, and I have every confidence that I can prove that I'm not only qualified, but in no way a security risk.

How *dare* they turn down my application and refuse to give me a reason? That can't be legal! It's a government position; they have to release the records if I request them. But the agent seemed to believe that I'd run into a brick wall with such a request, so there's something going on. Did I piss off some diplomat while I was in Europe and not realize it? Is someone pulling the strings to destroy my career?

I look around and realize that I've exited the building and I'm standing in the elevator to the parking structure. I was so angry that I made my way back to my car completely on autopilot. I check my pocket and realize that I even signed out and returned the visitors' badge. Taking a deep breath, I close my eyes.

It's been a long time since I was so angry that I had a functioning black out. The last time was when my parents got killed and because of my assignment, I couldn't come home for their funeral. The time before that was the last day I worked in a school. Both times, I lost time like this—I was functioning like a regular person to everyone around me, but when I came to, I had no idea what I'd done during that period. It usually lasts for weeks, but this time, it was only about fifteen minutes.

Clicking the remote to my car, I climb in and rest my forehead on the steering wheel. Each time this happened in the past, I spent months piecing together what happened while I was out. Through careful interrogation and immaculate people skills, I could recreate every minute of the lost time and record it in the journal I've been keeping since childhood. The school therapist always made me show her the journals to prove that I recovered my memories from the episodes.

Andromeda Bane was *not* a woman to be trifled with and even the kids and teens at the schools knew it.

I sigh. I haven't thought of her for a long time. The image of her powerful features and kind eyes fills my mind, and I reach up to wipe a tear from the corner of my eye. She clearly brooked no shit, but she was always available when I needed her. Her name was a threat and a prayer at Whistler's Hollow Formative and Finishing Schools. Those of us who grew up under her care defended her to the others —the ones who landed in her office because of intentional misbehavior rather than diagnoses.

My head lifts, and I sniffle, my heart crushed at what may be the end of my dreams. Perhaps it is time that I go home and face the place where my parents died. I haven't been there since I moved back to the States because I can't bear to see my childhood home without my parents in it. When they died, I used a state-side attorney to settle their affairs and hired a service to come in and air the house out every couple of months. I couldn't bear to sell it, although I never intended to return to the Hollow. It took my parents, and I never wanted to see it again.

But without the F.B.I. training, there's nothing for me in Richmond. I moved here when I came home from Europe so that I'd be in proximity to my dream, and if that truly is impossible, there's no reason for me to stay. Most of my belongings are still in storage despite living here for two years. I needed little creature comforts to work at the college while I finished my doctorate in Clinical Psychology online. I've been a nomad for so long that I haven't taken the time to develop relationships or put down roots here—even my lease is month-to-month.

It occurs to me I've been sitting in my car in the lot for a long time. If anyone walked by, they'd think that I've lost my marbles. I need to get home, make myself a drink, and think about this.

I never thought I'd be considering moving back to Whistler's Hollow.

Unfortunately, the past is no longer in the past.

Get the mini-omnibus of Road, Return & Roused here!

SNEAK PEEK OF HOIST THE FLAG

Under My Skin

Jack

Of all the things humans invented to destroy one another—from torture imple-ments to weapons of mass destruction—social media is by far the most insidious.

Sighing, I flick through my feeds on the bird app, then the influencer gram, and finally land on the clock app. I don't care if my volume is on high and the trending sounds echo throughout the room while I check up on my stats. A shudder runs through me when an icy tongue curls around my clit exactly how I like it. "Good girl, Quee-nie," I murmur distractedly when my body reacts to her efforts.

I know. Hashtag rude, right?

I shouldn't be so callous, but we both know the score here. My hand drops to her hair to pet the platinum strands gently and she damn near purrs. If only the royal court knew our secret, it'd be a scandal to end all scandals. Every muscle in my body clenches when she uses her magic to assist her fingers with filling me in every possible way. It's a ploy to get me to put down my phone and pay attention to her as she services me. I can scent her desire from here, but she won't come until I permit it.

By the aroma in the room, she desperately wants to be given permission, and that's why I won't.

When I arrived in their kingdom centuries ago, her fresh faced sister had recently gotten coronated and her reign as Queen ended. While my girl swore this was entirely the best move for the kingdom, the wild magic she'd never been able to control rebelled. It didn't appre-ciate the demotion from Queen to keeper of the Enchanted Forest. The new queen and her consort were at their wits' end trying to figure out how they wanted to rule the kingdom, but since darling Queenie here kept making monsters accidentally, they couldn't get anything rolling.

I was tired of my latest gig—and to be honest, after that bitch Jill pushed me down a fucking mountain, I needed out of that toxic mess of a relationship—so I answered their ad on the supernatural slayer of LinkedIn. The royal couple advertised a position for a court advi-sor, but I soon found out they wanted a magical babysitter for their erstwhile relative. For decades, I struggled to clean up after her tantrums, listening to her sing that annoying ass song every time she fucked up, and then one day, it happened.

I yelled at her.

Not the brightest thing to do, I'll admit, but my career has been plagued by ill-advised actions that lead to nursery rhymes, songs, and now, TikTok videos of all my spectacularly poor decisions. I'm the most infamous Jack of all time and I hate it with the fire of the thousand suns that never shine in this arctic wonderland. Usually, my fuck-ups have to do with affairs of the heart, so despite what Queenie is currently working like a champ to do, I didn't get involved this time.

But I did figure out that putting the headstrong ex-ruler of the land into sub space—frequently—and fucking the shit out of her fixed the problem. Unusual problems often need out-of-the-box solutions, my friends. Since this one also meant I wouldn't have to go find outlets for my needs, I hopped on board—with stringent boundaries and rules. The last thing I needed was to turn the ex-Queen into a stage five clinger and get my ass shit canned when I broke her heart.

Part of my disastrous love life issues is my magnetic draw—the hint of succubi way back in my lineage is a gift that never stops giving.

"Jackieeeee," the icy queen whines with perfect timing. "I want to make you happy. Let me make you feel good without all of that silly work you're doing."

The clinger theory didn't work, by the way.

Sitting my phone aside, I peer down at her fondly. I care about her, even if I don't love her. Her supposedly 'kind, gentle' sister got a taste of power after her first year of ruling and now she's become a narcissistic monster that feeds on being cruel to others. Her princely consort is long gone and no one else will have her because the poison seeping from every word and deed is so toxic. Poor Queenie here spends most of her time avoiding the court because it makes her cry crystalline tears of sorrow when she talks about how it used to be before her sister went into full villain mode.

I'm her only ally and they pay me to be here—is there anything so sad?

"Queenie, I'm sorry I've been distant. I know you're worried about the party at the castle tonight. You're being such a good girl and I'm a bad Madame."

Her head lifts and her eyes widen with horror. "Merciful Odin, no! You are the one bright spot in the kingdom since she... burned down... my forest."

I forgot to mention that, right?

Earlier this year, my Queenie was at one of the bi-weekly 'attendance mandatory' parties her bratty sister throws for herself and she saw an old friend. Unfortunately, the *akhlut* wasn't attending the party as a guest; the Royal hunters tracked it down and captured it for the new queen's amusement. The poor creature was being forced to remain in its terrestrial form so it could hunt down enemies of the crown for sport.

To say she lost her shit would be an understatement.

It took weeks to thaw out the court, rebuild the castle to specifications, and confirm that the queen's 'pet' had escaped to the sea. While I was busy overseeing those efforts, Her Royal Bitchiness sent her army to burn down the Enchanted Forest and melt every single ice sculpture her sister made. It damn near destroyed my charge—I couldn't get her to do anything, even in subspace, except weep.

My punishment was also severe, but I wear the scars with pride. I refused to bind Queenie's magic, and I used connections all over the world to prevent her sister from getting another supernatural to do it. I even involved the Society, and they put her back in her place. After all, even the immortals of fairy tales and lore must bend to their will when they are unanimous.

That cost me, too, but I'm almost at the end of that sentence.

Four more weeks and I'm free to abandon my duties as keeper of this miserable prison of ice, snow, and cruelty. At the end of December, the agreed upon term expires and I'm taking off for sunny climes and complete retirement. No social media, no assholes teasing me about breaking my crown or being nimble and best of all, no more wielding frost magic for the nastiest royal narcissist I've ever encountered.

I haven't told Queenie that my time here is limited. The plan was to ease her into the idea of my absence while finding her a suitable Domme to meet her needs. I'd started looking for one via the *Obedience* app for supes, but after the forest fire… She's been far too fragile and I don't know how to broach it without an extinction level event.

It's not my job, really, but I've been here so long and she's come so far. I'm terrified her sister will hire a flunky with questionable morals to bind and imprison her when I go. The thought bothers the hell out of me on so many levels, but I can't put my finger on why. It has to be the top in me wanting to ensure my sub is safe and protected even when I'm no longer in charge of her.

Bollocks. Everything is a mess and it would be easier to find someone to take her beehive wearing ass out, so I'm certain Queenie is safe.

"Darling girl, why don't we curl up until it's time to get ready? I can feel your unease and I've not been doing a very good job of making sure you feel safe."

All traces of her magic leave my body, forcing a growl to escape my lips as the impending orgasm recedes.

Blast my soft heart. I gave myself blue ovaries—willingly.

"Really?"

I sigh again, flipping my head back on the pillows as I hold my arms out. No matter how fucking detached I try to be, I always do this shit. All my jobs end the same—a romantic disaster that could have been avoided if I hadn't let my pussy do the thinking. I'm hopeless… absolutely hopeless.

"Yes, love. Grab your Marshmallow and come here," I whisper.

"Can we call Trixie?"

My lips curve up and I give her a nod, watching as she puts her fingers to her lips and whistles. Within seconds, my thieving capuchin comes swinging into the room via the rope nets on the ceiling. Trixie drops onto the bed, dancing around for a moment before handing Queenie a pile of sparkling jewelry with a proud expression.

"Trix!" I admonish. I'm sure my monkey has pilfered her loot from many people around the summer castle and I'll be hearing about it from the guards any minute.

Queenie gasps when she opens up her hand, showing me the snowflake necklace. "My mother gave me this when they left for their trip. I… haven't had it in possession since long before your arrival."

Her whisper is full of awe and I narrow my eyes as I consider how carefully my girl spoke. "Why haven't you had a family heirloom that belongs to you for so long?"

"My sister confiscated it when we were little. She said she believed it was making my powers go crazy and had the guards lock it away."

Motherfucker. That bitch was always a sociopath; she scared everyone less because she wasn't freezing people to death by accident.

"Let me help you put it on." I take the fragile platinum chain and wrap it around her neck, settling the sparkling diamond and aquamarine encrusted charm between her breasts. "It looks lovely."

Queenie beams and snuggles into my side as she yawns. "Never more lovely than you."

Trixie chitters, giving me a reproachful look as I hold the now sleepy woman in my grasp. I roll my eyes back and stare up at the ceiling, wondering how I'm going to tell her I'm leaving without breaking her heart.

And maybe mine.

Get Hoist the Flag now!

Sneak Peek: Bloodthirsty

Queen Bee

Remy

The lights are dimmed in the club, and the spots click on as the curtain starts to slide open.

It's a full house tonight in the little burlesque club off the Rue Pierre Montaine. *Chez Arc En Ciel* is not well known in comparison to the *Moulin Rouge* or *Le Lido*, but the wealthy from both sides of the Seine gather here for shows four nights a week. If you pass the various layers of security checks to even be permitted to book a reservation, you also have to be able to afford the two thousand euro per guest cover charge. That's if you don't eat or drink anything the entire time, and that behavior would get you blacklisted before you even hit the doors to get escorted out.

Intro music starts to pump through the speakers and I stand on my mark in the opening position. My cane is resting on the wooden boards of the stage by my front foot as I pretend to lean on it. Roars of applause echo through the room as our troupe of dancers catch the lights, sequins sparkling like diamonds when the stage lights rise. We're dressed in pinstriped black pant suits and fedoras to match the big band style opening to the song. As soon as the horn-filled intro finishes, the dance begins.

I follow the routine with precision, snapping and popping my hips to the beat as we spread out across the stage. My eyes are scanning the crowd, but you'd never know by the huge fake smile on my face. Two fan kicks later, I've rotated past the proscenium, and I think I've found my mark. Twirling, I stop exactly in the place I need to be for the bridge, singing along with the pop song as if my life depends on it. It might, to be honest, because I need to sell my cover tonight so no one notices me.

The Guillotine moves in the shadows, but tonight, she's in the spotlight.

My ass shakes as I dance my way through the song, swinging the prop cane I'd replaced with one of my own design. You'd never know the difference by looking at it, but it's not the painted balsa wood the other dancers have for a very specific reason. I need it to complete the mission that forced me to spend two months in Paris working my way into this job at *Chez Arc En Ciel*. If I can't strike tonight, the surveillance, counter intelligence, and time spent building this cover will be wasted because my mark is leaving for Asia tomorrow.

Tonight, the Cobra dies for his sins.

As the break of the song slows the music, all of the dancers pour into the crowd to wiggle around the rich assholes. It's choreographed, but it's also to advertise each girl for private dances in the lounges upstairs. We're not strippers—not that there's a damned thing wrong with a woman using her body to support herself—but we do bare more skin in the closed rooms. The typical *laissez-faire* attitude of the owners is that as long as we kick thirty percent of the fees customers pay for those dances, they don't care what any of the girls do in the rooms. I'd find it sleazy, but the girls who work here are highly skilled performers who choose to make thousands of dollars a night rather than peanuts in some ballet troupe or chorus line.

By the time I've flirted and schmoozed my way to the VIP tables, the Cobra is staring intently at all of us. Spotlights pin each one of us on the floor at the bass hits, and I swivel my hips as my free hand slides down to the secret spot on my jacket. In unison, we tear the jackets off to reveal rhinestone studded bras with straps crisscrossing our waists like shibari ropes. A lift of the fedora and pop of my hip along with the beat draws the fierce looking brawler's eyes directly to me. I pout prettily and stalk towards his table with the swagger of a tiny dicked asshole that owns a monster truck.

His thin lips pull back over the famed curving fangs he had implanted. Dark glittering eyes follow every move I make as I approach, and I pretend to whip my hair side to side as I check for his guards. They're here somewhere, but I need for them to be far enough away that I can beat my escape before they notice. When I get within inches, I tap his leg with my cane and spin around to shake my ass in his face. The grunt of approval makes me want to heave, but I turn, holding onto the prop with both hands. My feet click on the floor in a softshoe step as I make 'fuck me' eyes at the dirty bastard. He leans back, his pants tented as he gestures towards his lap.

Fucking gross.

I don't necessarily care about his weapons trade or what happens when people get the shit he moves. My job is to take him out, and I haven't the slightest clue why. The reason he's been sentenced to death isn't part of my contract, and I'm nothing if not a dispassionate observer of the darkest parts of human desires. Twelve years at *l'Academie* ensured I care very little about anything that isn't directly related to my ability to complete my jobs.

Sighing, I dance closer and drop onto his rather unimpressive erection and wiggle. There's plenty of cloth between us to prevent him from doing anything I'd make a scene over, so I focus on the task at hand. I slip the cane behind his head, resting the wood against his neck as I tug him forward. The move reads as playfully bringing his face to my breasts, but at the last second, I click the release built into the custom weapon. One end slides open to reveal the razor sharp garotte and before he can say a word, I yank it through.

Faint gurgling is the only noise besides the end of the song, and I carefully slide the sides of the cane together. Climbing off the nasty fucker, I put my hands on his cheeks so I can pretend to flirt with him while I arrange the head so it looks as if he's leaning back in the booth. It has to look realistic enough to allow me to get back on stage with the others and the next number to begin. When I have it settled, I back away from the booth blowing fake kisses as I walk backwards through the crowd. I almost collide with a dark haired guy with his collar pulled high as I head for the stage, and I roll my eyes. Whatever celeb that is trying to keep their face away from the paps is doing a shitty job of it.

My heels click on the wood as the entire troupe takes a few bows and shuffles off stage left to the wings. The next group enters on the opposite side, and I let out a slow breath of relief. I haven't heard shouting yet, so I don't think the Cobra's men realize he's down. All I have to do now is take this emetic pill, have an episode in the dressing room, and I'll be sent home without another thought.

That's when Arabella Montaigne the burlesque dancer will cease to exist, and Remy Arsine Benoit will re-emerge.

I smile to myself as I chew on the tablet that will have me wretching my guts out in a few moments. This is a more complex extermination than I usually prefer, and I can't leave my normal calling card behind. The Cobra's head had to remain in the booth to provide cover rather than be delivered to his home in a basket.

Such a shame, that. I quite enjoy the reactions my little gifts engender when they're discovered.

Walking into the dressing room, I carefully begin to strip my costume off, putting all the pieces in my bag. Every item in the locker room that belongs to gets placed in the duffel carefully as I wait for the effects to hit me. It won't do to leave loose ends even if my prints have never touched a single surface in this place. My gut starts to roil and I turn, facing one of the other dancers as the vomit finally comes. Gracelia screams like she's being skinned when I hurl on her and it's everything I can do NOT to smirk through the chunks.

"C'est la merde!" she shouts, running for the showers as if she's on fire.

It takes less than a minute for the owner to come in and send me home for the night with a concerned look. I walk out the back door of the building with everything in my bag just as the sirens start to scream in the distance.

Perfect timing, as always.

I jump into the first cab I can hail, directing him to the *Hotel de Crillion*. Their suites are the ritziest in Paris, and it's my go-to hideout when I'm here. I used to exclusively stay in the Bernstein Suite, but some rich fuckwad purchased it six months ago. If I could track them down and beat the hell out of them, I would, but my schedule is booked until late 2025. Assassins with my skill set and accuracy are getting harder to find. The digital age has forced many of the old guard into retirement because they refuse to adapt. Too many cameras, crime labs, and hackers running about to be able to do everything Cold War style.

The future of murder for hire is millenial, people. We're old enough to be stable but young enough to be agile with new technology and methodologies. Plus most of them are broke AF from crooked ass student loans.

It's not an issue I have, obviously, but I've been in the business since I hit double digits. You don't survive *l'Academie des Invisibles* if you haven't killed someone before the end of primary school. It's unheard of.

I was eight the first time I used the weapon that would become my signature.

Shivering, I tap on the window of the cab and bitch the driver out. He's taking a longer route than necessary to raise my fare, and I'll have his guts for garters if he doesn't knock it the fuck off. A string of curses in French erupt from him when I voice the accusation, and I slam my palm on the window with enough force to crack the plexiglass barrier. He almost drives into another car, but when he regains control, he makes the requested adjustments to our route.

After a few more arguments and a traffic jam around the *Champs*, we finally arrive at the front entrance to the *Crillion*. I throw the euros at him in disgust, memorizing the medallion number for later. He's not worth my time in terms of a mark, but I have quite a few contacts who might be interested in blackmailing a cabbie in town. Getaway cars are cliche in the crime world now. Most ne'er do-wells like myself find greater comfort in anonymous taxis or ride-share accounts hacked through the deep web accessed on burner phones.

If your ride doesn't know you're a villain, there's no one to flip if law enforcement comes looking.

Of course, it helps that I never look the same for any job—not ever.

Arabella Montaigne will not be used as a cover in the future, and once I move to the location of my next job, I'll ensure that she meets with a terrible fate. It's a lot more work to slowly kill off my alters once I've used them, but it's also why I've never even come close to being caught. The dancer with long wavy red hair, freckles, and big green eyes will never grace the streets of Paris again after I hop a plane. She will, however, get a small story in the paper and an obituary when I decide how she tragically dies.

And like a phoenix, The Guillotine will rise from her ashes to be born again.

Get Bloodthirsty now!

About Cassandra Featherstone

Cassandra Featherstone has channeled her lifelong passion for writing into a flourishing career, a journey that started when she first grasped a pencil as a gifted child with ADHD.

Her debut novel, born during the solitude of COVID lockdown in March 2020, draws on a tapestry of personal encounters and insights that resonate deeply with her readers.

An international bestseller, Cassandra has topped Amazon charts in categories such as LGBT Anthologies, LGBTQ+ Mystery, and Bisexual Romance, among others. Her works navigate the complexities of bullying, PTSD, body dysmorphia, mental health struggles, personal reinvention, and the empowerment of claiming one's own space. Importantly, Cassandra offers a thoughtful and respectful portrayal of LGBTQIA+ relationships, subtly reflecting her own connection with the community through her narratives.

Her literary repertoire spans sci-fi fantasy, urban fantasy, paranormal, and comedic genres in academy whychoose settings, with a strong commitment to portraying consensual, safe, and accurately depicted BDSM and kink lifestyles. Her books are an invitation to explore transformative stories that are both inclusive and engaging.

Often affectionately called 'The Muppet' for her wacky theater kid personality, she resides in the Midwest with her tech-savvy husband, their creatively inclined college student, a literary-minded dog, and four scheming cats.

READ MORE AT CASSANDRA'S WEBSITE OR HER FACE-BOOK PAGE. SIGN UP FOR EXCLUSIVE CONTENT AND UPDATES HERE.

Join her Master List for promo and ARC opportunities by scanning the QR below:

ALSO BY CASSANDRA FEATHERSTONE

THE MISFIT PROTECTION PROGRAM SERIES

Road to the Hollow

Return to the Hollow

Home to the Hollow

Rejected in the Hollow

Revealed in the Hollow

Healing in the Hollow

Revenge in the Hollow

AUDIO OF THE MISFIT PROTECTION PROGRAM SERIES

Road to the Hollow

APEX ACADEMY CAPERS

Come Out and Prey

Let Us Prey

In Prey We Trust

Oh Holy Spite (3.5 novella)

Eat. Prey. Love.

Prey It By Ear

AUDIO OF THE APEX ACADEMY CAPERS SERIES

Come Out & Prey

Let Us Prey

In Prey We Trust

TRANSLATIONS OF THE APEX ACADEMY CAPERS SERIES

Come Out & Prey (German)

Let Us Prey (German)

In Prey Trust (German)

DISCORDIA UNIVERSITY

Veiled Flame (Book One)

Quiet Burn (Book Two)

Zero Spark (Book Three)

SECRETS OF STATE U

Blood on the Ice (Book One)

Suspicions on the Stage (Book Two)

Ç

Hell on Wheels (Book One)

Jammer in the Box (Book Two)

F.E.A.R. ACADEMY

Failed State (Book One)

Title TBA (Book Two)

VILLAINS & VIXENS

Bloodthirsty (Book One)

Ruthless (Book Two)

Wicked (Book Three)

AUDIO OF THE VILLAINS & VIXENS SERIES

ANTHOLOGIES

Unwritten

Shifters Unleashed

Jingle My Balls

Love is in the Air

Silent Night

Snowed In

All Hallows Eve